THE ENCHANTED LIES OF CÉLESTE ARTOIS

THE ENCHANTED LIES OF CÉLESTE ARTOIS

RYAN GRAUDIN

REDHOOK

Redhook Books/Orbit
Hachette Book Group
1290 Avenue of the Americas
New York, NY 10104
hachettebookgroup.com

First Edition: August 2024

Redhook is an imprint of Orbit, a division of Hachette Book Group.
The Redhook name and logo are registered trademarks of Hachette Book Group, Inc.

Library of Congress Cataloging-in-Publication Data
Names: Graudin, Ryan, author.
Title: The enchanted lies of Céleste Artois / Ryan Graudin.
Description: First edition. | New York, NY : Redhook, 2024.
Identifiers: LCCN 2024007823 | ISBN 9780316418690 (hardcover) |
ISBN 9780316419062 (ebook)
Subjects: LCGFT: Fantasy fiction. | Novels.
Classification: LCC PS3607.R3815 E53 2024 | DDC 813/.6—dc23/eng/20240226
LC record available at https://lccn.loc.gov/2024007823

ISBNs: 9780316418690 (hardcover), 9780316419062 (ebook)

Printed in the United States of America

LSC-C

Printing 1, 2024

To the daydreamers and midnight wakers,
myself among them

Abracadabra—an exclamation for magicians originating from ancient Aramaic, meaning "I will create as I speak."

"Du cœur de l'homme, de toutes les voix de la nature jaillit la divine symphonie."

—quote above the boxes of
le Théâtre des Champs-Élysées

1913

Paris past midnight is a magnificent creature, conjured from curving iron and café lamps. Its gardens swallow every color of spring. Electric lights pave the boulevards. Doors open to cabarets and salons, where sugar drips through absinthe spoons and pianos fall into familiar songs. Every corner is en fête, each shop window resplendent.

There is even more than this, for imaginers like yourself: people who entertain dreams beyond sleep. Men and women who compose stanzas as they stroll by the Seine often find themselves stopping, overcome with a strange *want* to turn toward the river's Left Bank. It feels as if someone is calling, crooning the meter that has eluded them, the rhyme they've so long hunted. It makes them step past every regular haunt, until Notre-Dame de Paris cuts shapes out of the night. Here, in the cathedral's shadow, the path turns, tugging toward the Fontaine Saint-Michel, where an angel and a devil clash in bronze. Many of your fellow imaginers will halt to study the sculptor's work.

They do not know the statues study them in return.

Some never will, their minds deemed too empty of wonders. No angled alliteration, no winged tigers, no flames of ice. These people stare at the fountain water, which is made milky with starlight, and blink themselves back to sensibility. How late it is! What are they doing in the fifth arrondissement? Best to walk back now.

But you...

You pass the test. The sound of steps on stone causes you to turn, and only then do you notice that one of the fountain dragons has *come to life*. Lion head, serpent tail, feathers, and scales all moving seamlessly into an alley across the street. You decide to follow. How could you not? Down the street you go—the world changing at its edges—beneath lamps whose flames burn every color.

The door to the salon opens of its own accord. When you step inside, it becomes clear you aren't the only one who's been lured by the dragon.

"Welcome, welcome!"

"Come, friend! Dream and have a drink!"

The place is full of life: Painters, philosophers, poets. Ladies with loose hair and coal-struck eyes. Men whose cigarettes smell not of tar but cinnamon. Exhales leave their mouths in the shapes of zeppelins and dragonflies. Real birds cut through these clouds. One or two land on the loungers' heads, rummaging amid hairs to pluck out a string of golden light before flying off again. No one seems bothered by this. They wave at each newcomer between their laughter and grab one of the many flutes filled with glowing drinks of all shades: green, violet, rose, sky.

A glass is pushed into your hand.

What is this place? The question never quite parts your lips, for the aperitif smells like a favorite childhood memory and tastes even better. Each tongue takes it differently: smoked butterscotch, fog on a valley floor—never something as straightforward as chocolate. By the time the beverage washes down, it doesn't matter that the wallpaper's flowers are blooming, or that the woman by the bar has gold skin around her eyes—bright as a saint's halo—or that her gown of sheathed emerald feathers unfolds into wings.

Your hostess.

Your harvester.

No, no. It does not matter at all…

This is a place where the mind can play, a place any imagination would want to be.

There are other places for those who have eyes to see: The daydreamers and midnight wakers. The hungry-hearted. People who cannot help but try twisting knobs on locked doors, just to see if one will open.

They do, on occasion.

They open to boulangeries whose bread never goes stale, to cabarets where women grow wings and shed them just as quickly, to churches where the ceilings echo with gargoyles' whispers, to the table of a fortune teller who claims she can change the stars themselves—though her price is far too steep for most. There is also rumor of a book—bound in leather and tucked in a shop in the ninth arrondissement—where you can read your ending in the final chapter.

But it is just as easy to ignore the future, to get lost in the enchanted mirrors of Versailles—which play their memories of lavish balls over and over again—or to find yourself wandering through Saint-Ouen's flea market to the stall of the Fisherman of the Moon. Most of what he sells seems worthless: yellowed opera programs, chipped tea sets, broken watches, tattered maps, rusted keys, carnival tickets—all the usual bric-a-brac plucked from Paris's finer garbage heaps. But if you open the pocket watch, you might find that its hands spin straight to a fateful hour—*your* fateful hour—then stop again. If you stare carefully enough, you might see phoenixes flying through the china teapot's pattern, stirring the weeping blue willows and warming the spout's porcelain with gold flames. "They keep any tea piping hot," claims the Fisherman of the Moon. "This was Marie Antoinette's favorite set!"

And who knows what other doors that rusted key might open?

It would be very, very tempting to try...

A word of warning, before you venture too much farther. Magic is not all wonder. Sometimes the shadows in an alley have settled for a reason—there are certain hidden corners that should stay hidden. There are some secrets that should remain entombed, locked inside the jaws of the catacomb walls, in skull after skull after skull after skull.

Every city is built upon its dead, after all.

Even the glittering ones.

PART I

THE FORGER

Once upon a time, there was a girl who told lies to make things true.

Her tongue was made of silver—or so her parents said—and she learned at a very young age that words could be used like currency. She drew money too, with a steady pen and a crooked heart. She handed men pieces of paper, and in turn they gave her silk gowns and jewels. The transaction felt almost like casting a spell... so much so that she began to call herself an Enchantress. It was the closest she'd ever come to magic.

Until now...

Chapter 1

The Enchantresses

Père Lachaise was home to some very unusual ghosts.

The cemetery sat in Paris's twentieth arrondissement and had been swallowing the bones of its citizens for over a century. Politicians and paupers and priests... Their graves had been built with the same care as houses, fitted with doors and stained glass windows. It was prime real estate. Peaceful too. At six o' clock, when mourners were ushered out, you could find the edge of silence.

You could also find Céleste Artois wandering through ivy-throttled graves, saying the strangest of prayers.

She'd grown up with a crucifix hanging over her bed—the hallmark of a good Catholic girl—and even though that cross had gotten left behind when she'd run away to the City of Light, she was still in the habit of confession. Well, confessing. She supposed it didn't count when there wasn't a priest to listen to the list of sins. It also probably didn't count when you weren't *really* sorry for the crimes you committed. Céleste was no longer good. Nor was she Catholic. She wasn't even a girl anymore... It had been nearly seven years since she'd started her new life in Paris. A life built with brushstrokes and white lies.

"I sold one of my paintings this afternoon!" The cemetery had plenty of crosses for this ritual, but Céleste paused by a stone saint instead. "I told the buyer I was cleaning out my dead uncle's estate. I also led him to believe it was a genuine Eugène Delacroix, so I'm getting better..."

At lying? At painting? Or both?

Both was the hope. It was more than hope, really. In order to pull off a good confidence scheme, you had to *believe* the fantasy you were selling. Céleste had needed to become the artist. She'd immersed herself in the palette of the Romantic master—Eugène's stark lights and dramatic darks. His revolutionary reds. The paint had gotten trapped beneath her fingernails, but this didn't pose much of a problem, since Céleste had pulled on black gloves to turn herself into a bereaved niece.

Leftover tears still clung to her lashes as she stared up at the statue. "Is it truly stealing if someone hands their money to you?"

A priest would have said yes.

The marble saint said nothing.

Céleste smiled as she knelt by the base of the grave he guarded. Her coin purse jingled. It was a good take. The mark had been willing to spend five hundred francs on her canvas—and he'd been smiling too, when he'd paid the sum. Mostly because he was under the impression that he could turn around and sell the painting for ten times as much.

"You'd think rich men wouldn't be so greedy..." She peeled off her gloves and began digging through moss. "But there's always more to be taken. It doesn't matter if you're six feet under or on top of the goddamn world. Corpses can be stripped, and kings can be beheaded. There is always more to be taken, so it's best to be the taker."

The saint still did not look convinced.

Céleste dug deeper. The hole wouldn't be fitting any coffins, but it was enough for her to wedge the francs inside and cover with a cluster of ivy.

More leaves rustled on the far side of the grave.

"Hello?" she called out.

Nearby tombs yawned. Vines continued their slow crawl over names and dates and epitaphs. The hairs on the back of Céleste's neck whispered that someone was there... someone who should not be. The cemetery gates had been locked for over an hour now, and Père Lachaise's guards didn't dare walk the lanes this close to dusk. Ghosts came out in the gloaming, they claimed, spirits of the underworld rising closer and closer to the surface.

Céleste Artois did not believe this, mostly because she was the one who haunted the grounds. She was the pale woman who wandered through the graves every evening. She lit the candles that flickered through the windows of division sixty-two's largest mausoleum. She slept over dead men's bones. She brought new legends to life—stories of plague victims and noblewomen caught up in the Revolution's guillotine—never mind that it was Napoleon who'd opened this cemetery, well after the heads had finished rolling. The central figure in each of the guards' tales was a young lady with shock-white hair. *If you see her strolling the roads of Père Lachaise, beware...*

Also, if you see her rummaging through the conservation office for toiletries and bathwater, ignore that too. On pain of termination.

The senior groundskeeper was the real reason Céleste could squat there. Her campsite remained undisturbed because he ordered his underlings to look the other way. He did this because after Céleste had bribed some keys off him, she used the incident as blackmail.

It was cheaper than rent. Safer than most houses too, thanks to the gates and the guards and various traps set up by the other members of her gang. Céleste wasn't the only "ghost" in Père Lachaise. She wasn't the only Enchantress either. It was a shared title—divvied up into three equal parts, just like these buried francs would be.

"Hello?" Céleste called again. "Sylvie? Is that you, *ma rêveuse*? Honoré? I'm not in the mood for an ambush—"

Leaves parted for a flash of fur. It was just a cat, one of the many who prowled this place. They were always slipping in and out of crypts, too busy with their own secrets to bother with Céleste's...

She coughed and patted the saint statue's foot. "I'll be back for this, so don't go anywhere."

The marble felt cold. Her joke, clumsy.

It had been a long day, made even longer by her button-up heels, so Céleste shucked them off and wandered barefoot down one of the cemetery's windier lanes. This corner of Père Lachaise was more overgrown than the rest, left to its own devices by junior groundskeepers. Ghosts weren't the sole reason. There were other hazards there: pits filled with broken glass and trip wires tied to stumps. Céleste was usually good about avoiding those, but that night her toes snagged an alarm strung with bells.

"BEGONE, OR I SHALL HAUNT THEE UNTIL THE END OF THY DAYS!" Honoré Côte leapt out of a tomb inscribed with the exact same name, brandishing a cheese knife. It was Camembert—not blood—stuck to the edges.

"Céleste!" The young woman blinked, looking vaguely disappointed that there was no one to stab. "You didn't say the watchword."

"*Ab Aeterno.*"

"That was yesterday's password." Her friend scowled.

"Cocorico?"

Honoré crossed her arms.

"'I'm exhausted and all I want is to eat cheese'?" Céleste snatched the knife, which was dull enough to make the Camembert taste sharp when she licked it. "What were you going to do with this anyhow?"

"If you don't know how to serve death with a cheese knife, then our *défense dans la rue* lessons have been in vain."

Céleste couldn't tell if the other Enchantress was joking or not. Honoré's humor went well past the gallows, but self-defense was a serious matter for a gangster's daughter. *Défense dans la rue* was nothing to laugh at either. It was street fighting. It was boxing. It was jiu-jitsu. It was using every dirty trick you could to keep your opponent from slitting your throat.

It was something Honoré Côte was very, very good at.

One swipe, and the knife was hers again. "No more cheese until you tell me today's watchword!"

"What if I told you we made five hundred francs today instead?" Céleste asked.

"Really?" The other Enchantress's blade lowered. Her face brightened—enough to highlight the angry welt where a moustache had been pasted to Honoré's upper lip. "Five hundred?"

"Our mark was practically salivating when I walked back into the restaurant. Your disguise worked wonders!"

Céleste couldn't take sole credit for this sin. Truthfully, it had been Honoré who'd led their mark to believe that the painting was a Delacroix. Even less truthfully, it was "Monsieur Alexandre Dumont, purveyor of fine art" who'd stopped by the man's table and commented on the quality of the canvas the "bereaved niece" had left him to guard.

"I wasn't sure..." Honoré tugged at her shirt's high collar, the one that hid her distinct lack of an Adam's apple. "My voice slipped a few times, but I suppose he paid more attention to the words than the tone. I told him he could sell the piece for six thousand at my shop."

Somewhere in the other Enchantress's tailored suit was a case of calling cards, inked with Céleste's oh-so-sharp fountain pen. The address for Monsieur Dumont's store would lead their eager mark to an empty street corner. The painting he'd purchased wouldn't take him much further...Any other purveyor would be quick to point out that it was not, in fact, fine art.

It was a fine forgery.

"Well, you were man enough to fool him," Céleste said.

The other Enchantress nodded at Céleste's bare feet. "I'm sure you did your share of ankle flashing to get him up to five hundred francs!"

This *was* a joke, Céleste knew. Long-standing between them. Almost as old as their friendship. In the five years they'd known each other, the other woman had worn more names than gowns. Being a young lady in Paris meant navigating a number of social obstacles—corsets and curtseys and a whole host of things Honoré didn't have patience for. This was the reason she sported trousers and shortened her hair with the sharpest of knives. Céleste saw little need to carry weapons up her sleeve the way the other Enchantress did. Men, as a species, were easily distracted. Often, all she had to do was show a sliver of skin, and most marks became paraffin wax in her palm.

You'd rather stab someone than seduce them? she'd asked Honoré.

To keep my ankles to myself? Absolutely.

"There was no ankle flashing this time. Merely a few tears." Céleste smiled. "Like I said, your disguise worked wonders. Though it appears 'Monsieur Dumont's' moustache was reticent to depart your person."

"Is it bad? I tried a new adhesive, and it was a little too… adhesive."

"It's not… not bad."

"I don't understand why moustaches are fashionable." Honoré's nose wrinkled. "They itch like hell."

"Most men don't use glue."

"Well, it's better than wearing a corset. Ribs already *are* cages! Why must you lace another one on?"

Céleste did not disagree. Her own bodice was digging into her skin, and she knew that if she didn't interrupt her friend's speech, it would grow into a ten-minute diatribe about the flammability of crinoline. *Do you* know *how many women go up in flames every year? Dresses are death traps! Death traps that hardly ever have pockets!!!*

She fished her empty coin purse from her belt and showed it to Honoré. "I already deposited today's take."

"At la Banque d'Ossements?"

Pasted moustaches had taken the gang's confidence schemes a good ways—men almost always trusted other men—but fake facial hair didn't quite cut it when it came to Paris's banks. Women weren't allowed to open checking accounts, so the Enchantresses were forced to store their spoils with the dead instead. *The Bank of Bones*, they called it. Fifty francs with the mortal remains of J. M. N. Leroux de Prinssay in division twenty-five. Two hundred with Susan Durant in division fifty-six. Seventy-five by the lair of the feral orange tomcat, money none of them would ever touch again if they wanted to keep their fingers.

"Five hundred in division eighty-six."

"Whose grave?" Honoré pressed.

Ah… Céleste tried to remember, but her thoughts crawled with ivy. Had she really not stopped to read the name? "I got distracted. There was a cat." The other Enchantress made a stony face; not unlike the statue Céleste had tasked to guard their new treasure. "There was a saint too?"

"There are thousands of saint statues in this cemetery," Honoré retorted. "This is precisely why we have systems in place, *mon amie*! If we don't record names, we'll forget where we've stored our fortune! If we don't use the watchwords, I might mistake you for an attacker!"

"If I were a wheel of Brie, that would be terrifying—"

Another rustle came from the underbrush. Honoré's face hardened even more as she raised her cheese knife, and Céleste felt her own laughter die in her throat.

"Hello! I mean—*allons-y*! Please don't stab me!"

Honoré sighed and lowered her knife as the youngest Enchantress leapt out of the bushes.

Sylvie was small for her eleven years. Fae-sized. Her dark hair grew as wild as a thicket. Her eyes were brown too, but they were always wide, reflecting the sky, so Céleste sometimes painted them blue in her memory.

There was a baguette in the girl's arms this evening; the loaf of bread was almost taller than she was. "I found dinner!"

"Did you find it, or did you steal it?" Céleste had a sneaking suspicion.

It was confirmed with a slight shrug. "We steal stuff all the time."

"We acquire francs from those stupid enough to part with them," Céleste corrected. "We do not raid neighborhood boulangeries, especially if we want them to sell you *pain au chocolat* every morning."

Sylvie bit her lip—the girl did like her sweets. She was forever distracted by pâtisserie displays, and at any given moment, she had at least two macarons on her person. Honoré joked that if Sylvie ever got cut, she'd bleed sugar. Céleste just hoped the girl would make it to adulthood with all her teeth.

And no arrest record.

"What if a police officer had seen you, hm? Bread isn't worth getting locked back in the orphanage, is it?"

Sylvie suddenly looked very small. Almost as small as the day Céleste and Honoré had caught the girl trying to pick their pockets. She'd been starving then. Beyond desperate.

"I didn't mean— Please don't cry, Sylvie!"

Too late. Dark eyes shone darker with tears.

"*Ce n'est pas grave!*" Honoré to the rescue. "We'll leave extra change at the boulangerie tomorrow. Right now, this bread belongs in our bellies. I've got cheese to go with it. And some *tarte au chocolat.*"

At the mention of dessert, Sylvie grinned, her tears miraculously vanished. *Pretending.* Of course! Céleste couldn't decide if she was incensed or impressed.

The girl clasped her hands together. "You remembered my birthday?"

"How could I forget something that happens every two months?" Honoré replied dryly.

At least that. Sylvie didn't know her actual date of birth, which meant the Enchantresses ate cake whenever the girl wanted to make a birthday wish. If all these festivities were true, she'd be closer to forty than eleven.

"I'll go get a candle!" she said brightly.

There was no sign of tears whatsoever on Sylvie's face as she dashed into the mausoleum.

Céleste followed. The original Honoré Côte must have loved astronomy, for no expense had been spared on his tomb's glass roof. It was fashioned like an observatory, salted with constellation etchings. As a result, the place was far brighter and far warmer than one might expect. Each Enchantress had staked out a side. Honoré's held a collection of non-cheese knives and fake moustaches, while Sylvie's had to be scoured for stale pastries every night before the rats got to them.

Céleste's corner could hardly be called a corner.

Silk gowns were draped like curtains. Diamond necklaces dangled in place of chandeliers. And among all this sat the strangest studio any artist in Paris could claim. Canvases lined the wall next to a variety of wigs. Paintbrushes lay out to dry on the central tombstone. Flecks of color splashed the stone next to wax candle drippings—late-morning light was best here, but Céleste often painted by flame as the other girls slept.

Sylvie had set her baguette on top of the central stone's faded epitaph: HONORÉ CÔTE, WHO STARED AT STARS UNTIL THEY HAD NAMES.

Monsieur Côte's name had been stolen by the Enchantresses, like everything else here. Was the dead man turning, just a few feet below, knowing these young women had converted his sacred resting place into a space for their criminal activities? If he had been anything like his namesake, he'd be proud.

And perhaps a little exasperated by the crumbs.

Sylvie kept pulling croissants out of her pockets. It was truly impressive that she'd managed to snatch such a lot of fresh bread without the baker noticing. Then again, the youngest Enchantress had fingers lighter than feathers, so light that she'd even managed to slip a ring right off Honoré's own hand, back when they'd first met...

"What did you do for your birthday, *ma rêveuse*?" Céleste asked, as she began sorting through dresses. Some were lavish and others were dirty, but they all had stories sewn into their hems. The bereaved niece was only one of many aliases. "Besides pilfer pastries?"

"Oh, this and that."

Céleste chose a silk dressing gown and turned to face her ward. There were only thirteen years between them, but she knew she was the closest thing Sylvie would get to a *maman*. It was one of the few roles Céleste could not unbutton or step out of.

"What exactly?"

"I woke up." The girl began counting with her fingers. "I peed in the bushes. I thought I was done, but then I had to go back and—"

"You don't have to be that exact!"

Sylvie flashed an impish grin. It looked like it belonged to one of the goblins illustrated in the stack of Andrew Lang fairy-tale books by her bed. The ones she'd flipped through so many times that their spines had tattered. The books were beautiful, arranged in a veritable rainbow of colors, their covers gilded with portraits of fairies. But the stories inside were written in English, a language none of the Enchantresses had mastered. This didn't stop Sylvie from reading them over and over. She'd come up with her own versions over the years.

Her imagination was . . . vivid.

"I explored a secret tunnel down by the Seine that led to a chamber full of spiders and bones. Then, when a gentleman stopped to ask where my parents were, I pretended to be a long-lost princess. Then I tried taming a tiger."

Céleste strongly suspected this had been a stray cat.

The feast was their usual fare: bread, cheese, *tarte au chocolat*, and a bottle of drinking water they'd filled in the closest Wallace Fountain. Honoré spread out a picnic blanket—which also served as the tarp beneath Céleste's easel and was covered in colors upon colors—on the front steps of the mausoleum. Crystal goblets were filled to the brim as Sylvie started describing the "tiger" she'd tried to tame. It had indeed been a cat. And not just any cat but the feral orange tomcat who'd commandeered a good number of their francs. "I tried luring him with some pâté, but he just turned around and lifted his tail stub. That means 'no, thank you' in cat-speak."

"As if a cat would ever say 'thank you.'" Honoré snorted.

"They do," Sylvie insisted. "They talk all the time. We just don't listen well enough."

"Could you imagine? I bet they'd sound like crotchety old men and shunted prima donnas, cursing things just because they can."

"Or perhaps they could tell us whose grave I buried today's francs in," Céleste offered.

Honoré rolled her eyes. "You'll have to dig that up for yourself, *mon amie*. And, Sylvie, you *do* know that if cats *were* as big as tigers, they'd probably kill you. Right? Next time you have good pâté, don't waste it on moggies. Put it on some bread instead." She ripped off a piece of baguette with her teeth.

"This is why I don't take you to parties," Céleste said.

"The bread or the cynicism?"

"What's cynicism?" Sylvie snatched the loaf from Honoré, ready to take a bite of her own.

"Cynicism is the needless interruption of fairy tales." Céleste grabbed the bread before the girl could really sink her teeth into it. "Knives aren't just for cutting people, you know."

When she returned the baguette to Sylvie, along with the appropriate piece of cutlery, the girl began sawing. Bits of crust flecked the ground, but the blade was too dull to slice all the way through.

"That knife is meant for cheese," Honoré told Sylvie. "There's a sharper one under my pillow you can use."

As Sylvie slipped back into the tomb to find it, Céleste studied her other friend. The same gothic cheekbones that suited Honoré to suits made her expressions more nuanced than most. Her blonde hair was rumpled from "Monsieur Dumont's" top hat, but her eyes were flat, like the surface of a dark lake at dusk. Anyone else might mistake this for calmness, but Céleste knew better.

"What's wrong?" she prodded. "Is it the francs?"

"It's not the francs."

"What, then?"

"There's a difference between cynicism and realism," growled Honoré. "Between tigers and talking cats and moggies."

"She's only making up a story."

"Stories are like sugar. If you consume too much, things start to rot." Insects sang to the evening light. The other Enchantress held her knees close to her chest, and early shadows settled into her face. "You shouldn't let Sylvie think we can just make believe our way out of mistakes."

"Isn't that what we do for a living?"

"We lie, yes, but not to each other. Not to ourselves."

Céleste looked down at the *tarte au chocolat*. The silky chocolate at its center had been cracked by a small candle, ready for Sylvie to blow out. Was it so wrong to let the girl keep eating cake?

Céleste didn't believe so.

She didn't *want* to believe so.

"I just..." Honoré glanced back into her namesake's tomb. "I don't want Sylvie to get lost."

Too late. Céleste could see that their ward was unsheathing a blade from some bedding. *Très Arthurian.* Their lives were closer to a fairy tale than not, and it was better to be a lost child than unwanted. And better unwanted than...whatever Honoré once was. Céleste knew the young woman's father had been a gangster, because of the ring she sported on her right middle finger. Distinctly designed for violence—the top was forged as a dragon's head, and the bottom was thick enough to touch a curled fist. Any punch it delivered would leave a nasty bruise. The fact that Honoré wore the ring led Céleste to believe that the young woman's father was dead, but the subject had never been broached.

Best let sleeping beasts lie and orphans dream.

"The kid just wants a cat."

"Well, I don't," Honoré grumbled. "They have fleas."

Céleste knew her friend, knew to stay silent as church bells joined the crickets around them.

After the first few tolls, Honoré raked fingers through her hair and sighed. "Sylvie has to grow up sometime. She can't keep just running around Paris pretending she's some secret American heiress. Real life is hard. Real life is shit. We've got to start preparing her for it."

Céleste looked down at their collection of cheese knives. "I suppose you'll teach her how to be fatal with cutlery?"

"She shouldn't be scampering around the streets without *défense dans la rue* lessons. I was already proficient at her age."

It was hard to imagine Honoré as an eleven-year-old. Or a little girl, for that matter. Obviously, she'd been nothing like Sylvie, who was now skipping out of the tomb, her knife stabbing straight up, oblivious to the fact that she'd impale herself if she slipped.

"Keep the pointy end down!" Céleste urged, shooting Honoré a look. "Do you really think it's a good idea to teach Sylvie to stab things?"

"Oh, I don't need to learn that! Stabbing is easy!"

Honoré let out a sigh.

"See?" Their ward plunged the blade into the *tarte au chocolat*. "I hereby declare it time for dessert."

Chapter 2

Fiddle Game

Céleste Artois was always hungry. This was the reason she both loved and hated fiddle games—the con could be pulled in an afternoon. In the span of an hour, even. The venue was, by necessity, a fancy restaurant. Her job was to eat there alone, to order every elegant thing on the menu, to chew, to swallow, then to dab the corners of her mouth with a napkin and pretend she was satisfied.

This was the hardest lie to tell.

How could she be satisfied at an establishment like Foyot's? This restaurant was made for hunger. It catered to imperialistic palates; sitting across from the Luxembourg Palace made it a convenient haunt for senators. There were even deeper pockets at other tables. Some of this wealth was older—men with titles and ties that went all the way back to a time when France had a crown. Others had made their money with railways and streamliners—*nouveaux riches* was what they'd been called in her father's circles. Arnaud Artois had always said this term with a slight sniff, as if his family's crumbling château could make up for the fact he himself was an exceedingly bad businessman.

If only it had...

Céleste wondered what term best suited her. *Nouveau pauvre*, perhaps? Did that accurately describe an heiress who'd lost a fortune, then spent the rest of her life trying to steal it back? Never mind that she'd nearly succeeded. Never mind that she *could* afford to buy every item on the menu, including the béarnaise sauce that was rich enough to be its own meal.

She was still starving.

She knew that everyone felt this way, to some extent. It was the reason the Enchantresses' confidence schemes were so successful: Every person was born with a hole inside them. Shapes varied—love, power, fame, revenge, fortune, life itself—but the emptiness was universal. Promise to fill someone, and they would follow you anywhere.

They'd pay any price.

"More wine, mademoiselle?" A waiter approached the table, holding a bottle of Pontet-Canet that might as well have been squeezed from garnets for how much it cost.

Personally, Céleste thought it was a crime to answer *no*.

Professionally, she had to. "A coffee will do."

Coffee would afford her more time to scout for a mark.

This was probably what foxes felt like when they slipped into henhouses, Céleste mused as she scanned the rest of the restaurant. Fiddle games were quick-pick affairs, limited to whoever happened to be sitting nearby. Such as the gentleman with his mistress two tables over—her without a ring and him covering his with a napkin. No target there. He was too taken with the promise of sex to bother with greed. Céleste skated her gaze over several tables with politicians and paused to study a portly fellow reading *Le Petit Journal* through his monocle. He might do. Though on second glance, Céleste realized he'd fallen asleep. This confidence trick required someone conscious. Someone who fancied themselves an entrepreneur. Someone callous and careless and tipsy enough to employ both traits.

Someone like the young man at the corner table, crowing to his companion about the previous evening's exploits over a plate of foie gras and his fifth flute of champagne. "They have an elephant in the garden of Moulin Rouge! Not a real one, of course. There's a staircase in its leg that leads to an opium den. The women up there… Have you ever encountered a belly dancer, Baptiste? I met several on my tour of the Balkans with Father last summer. They were bendier than the Montmartre variety."

Yes, he'll do. Céleste sipped her coffee down to the dregs. *Typical cock: too busy preening to notice there are teeth nearby.*

Or to notice his tablemate's discomfort. Baptiste flushed to the already-flaming roots of his hair, slipping down his chair until he was more tablecloth than not. He'd probably request the check soon, which meant Céleste needed hers to come first.

She flagged down the waiter, listening in as her mark kept rambling.

"Have you ever been to the Balkans, Baptiste? It's beautiful, but a bit backward—did you know they believe in vampires there? Actual vampires? With fangs and everything! One of the dancers, she started telling me stories. Says they don't take just your blood but your soul too so that you don't even go to heaven when you die. Not that I've been a paragon of virtue, but still! You'd like to think Saint Peter would open the pearly gates when you shed this mortal coil, no?"

"I don't think you have to be worried about vampires, Henri," Baptiste told his friend dryly.

"They *did* discover a body by the hotel." The mark took yet another swig of his champagne. "That's what sparked the entire conversation. Some poor soul was entirely exsanguinated! Well, I say 'soul.' Ha! The police were never able to identify him—the dancer told me it was a sign. 'Always keep one eye on your shadow,' she said. 'Keeps the devil away.'"

Henri squinted down at the floor, and Céleste wondered if maybe the young man was a little too tipsy to play this fiddle game. Then again, he was clear-headed enough to allude to Shakespeare. And if he really did believe in vampires, then he'd have no trouble believing Céleste. Besides, the waiter was already returning with her bill.

She smiled graciously.

Out came her coin purse.

Let the show commence.

"Oh dear..." Céleste smoothed her gown, knees tilting toward the corner table. The mark's eyes cut away from his own shadow to the soft edges of her skirts. Easy enough. "I'm afraid I left my money at the flat. It's been a tumultuous morning—you see, my uncle passed away and I've been helping my brother clear out the estate and I needed to step outside for some air and I must have forgotten to check my purse..."

"Are you saying you have no way to pay?" asked her waiter.

The gentleman reading *Le Petit Journal* awoke with a snort. The lovers whispered secrets across their table. Baptiste looked slightly less mortified now that his companion was no longer Foyot's most scandalous guest.

"The flat is only a few blocks away. I can be there and back in ten minutes. If you want, I'll even leave my uncle's painting as collateral." Céleste lifted a parcel from underneath the table and unwrapped it. The cloth dropped back to reveal another Delacroix replica. "It's worth the meal at least."

"I'm afraid that's against our policy, mademoiselle."

"Please..."

She didn't even need to use the next line: *What would you have me do?* Henri puffed out his chest and strutted to her table.

"I'll settle the lady's bill," he said.

A fifty-franc note passed hands, simple as that.

"Thank you, monsieur!" Céleste thrust the painting into her "rescuer's" arms before any debt could be cited. "My uncle's flat is three streets over. I'll be back with your money before you finish your champagne!"

"Oh, I doubt it." This mutter from Baptiste gave her pause. If he suspected a trick, it might be better to cut and run.

"I'll return," she said firmly. "My brother asked me to get this painting appraised."

Baptiste shook his head. "That wasn't— Let's just say Henri has never left a glass wet. We'd be happy to watch your artwork for you."

So the man wasn't suspicious. He was *honorable*.

Maybe too honorable for this game...

But they'd reached the point of no return. Henri set the unwrapped painting on their table and refilled his flute with a sixth bubbling serving, raising it to her in a toast. "Hurry back!"

It was a May day with a feathery sky: suited to strolling. Céleste bustled down the street for the benefit of any diners who might be peering through the window, slowing only when she rounded the corner. Running would spell trouble to the police who patrolled the streets around Luxembourg Palace. This was one of Paris's more well-kempt districts—more cars than carriages meant that less horse shit ripened the curbs. There was less soot too. Most of the gas streetlamps had been swapped out for electric lights. People walked here without fear, even at night. They wandered through blooming gardens and stopped to smell the roses and took all their beautiful surroundings for granted.

Céleste wasn't a particular fan of the flowers, herself, these days. Every time she coughed, she cursed them: *Damn hay fever!*

She had been cursing a lot lately.

Spring air thickened in her throat. She paused to catch her breath before turning into an alleyway. It was as posh as the rest of the sixth arrondissement—not lined with trash but ivy. *A secret garden*, Sylvie might have called it, if she weren't busy swinging a small loaf of bread at Honoré's walking cane. The two Enchantresses were standing at odds with each other. Céleste recognized the stance. She'd been made to practice it over and over again, during her first *défense dans la rue* lesson.

Now it was Sylvie's turn.

"The cheese knives were too sharp, then?" Céleste nodded at the *ficelle* in the girl's hands.

"For Sylvie? Yes," Honoré grumbled.

"Anything can be a weapon!" The youngest Enchantress sounded like one of the parrots at the free menagerie of the Jardin des Plantes, echoing back a phrase it didn't quite understand. "A scarf can be used as a garrote! A hat can be thrown at your opponent to blind them!"

"And what will you do with breadcrumbs?" Céleste wondered. "Summon a flock of vengeful pigeons?"

"That *would* be more fun than footwork," Sylvie said.

"Fighting isn't supposed to be fun," Honoré replied. "And footwork can be the difference between life and death. If you aren't standing right, you'll find yourself on your back, and once you're on your back, your attacker has the advantage. He's probably going to be a man, and he's probably going to weigh more than you—"

"Ha!" Sylvie reached out with the loaf, poking Honoré on the center of her tightly bound chest. "I win! You're supposed to say 'touché,' right?"

"Only if you're fencing," Céleste said.

"Fencing!" Honoré's nose wrinkled as she brushed crumbs from her three-piece suit. "Fencing is for rich people with nothing better to do. When you're in a street fight, there's no time to say 'en garde' or any of that other honorable bullshit. If you wait around for your opponent to talk, you'll find their blade slicing your throat—"

"That's not always true," Céleste broke in, before the diatribe could get too grim. "It wasn't true when *we* first met."

It had been in an alleyway much like this—perhaps it *had* been this alley. Her memory of that evening was fuzzy with falling snow and the cold shock of leaving Twenty-Seven rue de Fleurus. Gertrude Stein's famed salon wasn't far from there, so it was entirely possible that this was the side street where Céleste had found herself held up at knifepoint.

"You mean when Honoré tried to rob you and all you had was an art portfolio?" Sylvie piped up.

Honoré hadn't been Honoré then. Céleste hadn't known who she herself was either. The name at the bottom of the sketches had belonged to a girl who still had a father. A fortune. A future.

She'd had nothing to lose when she handed the drawings over to the thief.

"Yes, well, Céleste wields words just as well as any blade," Honoré recounted. "She was quick to disarm me."

"As I recall, *you* were the one who convinced me to take up a life of crime."

A dimple appeared next to Honoré's pasted moustache. "Speaking of robberies, did you find a good mark?"

"At the corner table, by the window. They should be easy enough to fool. The one who covered my bill keeps going on about vampires."

Honoré laughed then and twirled her cane. "This will be entertaining. Keep practicing your footwork, Sylvie! I'll be back soon." The Enchantress strolled off to do her part, not stopping to smell the roses.

Céleste clenched her teeth and coughed again, into her bare wrist. The wine had been a poor choice. It must've stained her lips, close enough to the color of rouge to go uncommented.

"What did your mark say, about the vampires?"

Céleste pulled her gown's sleeve over the smear of wine and looked back at Sylvie. It probably wasn't prudent to explain to an eleven-year-old what *exsanguinated* meant. "All sorts of nonsense. He's quite drunk…"

"Did he see one?" The girl's grip tightened on the bread. "Here?"

"In the Balkans." Céleste caught herself. If she fed Sylvie's imagination any further, Céleste would be up all night for the next week, telling the girl that the shadows that streaked across their mausoleum's glass ceiling were cats. *Only* cats. "He heard stories about them from a belly dancer. She was entertaining him—trying to get a good tip, I'm sure."

Sylvie frowned. "Where are the Balkans?"

"Turkey. Serbia. Very far away," Céleste assured her. "You'd do better to focus on Honoré's imaginary enemies."

Sylvie gave a hopeless sort of sigh and finally bit into her bread. Her dark curls quivered as she chewed. "I'd rather play the fiddle game."

"You do play!"

This was loosely true. About as loose as the change in any failed mark's pockets. If Céleste wasn't able to secure a sale, Sylvie bumped into the man on his way out of the restaurant and relieved him of his banknotes anyway. The girl tried to grab the business card that "Monsieur Dumont" had left there too. They were painstaking to draw, and Céleste preferred to use them twice, if possible.

"I know, I know. 'Always have a backup plan.'" Sylvie was using her parrot voice again, repeating the phrase Céleste said so often herself. "But I don't want to be a contingency! I want to eat in the fancy restaurant with you!"

"I'll teach you the role when you're older."

"I *am* older. I just had a birthday."

It was hard not to laugh at this. Even harder not to cough. "You need to work on making your lies more believable," Céleste said. "Maybe we can practice telling tragic backstories to strangers at the Théâtre des Champs-Élysées tonight."

Sylvie's wish—for her *thirty-ninth* birthday—was for the three Enchantresses to attend a ballet together. Céleste suspected this was the result of the Ballets Russes posters that had recently gone up all over the city: drawings of a dancing man wearing nothing but damn roses. She also suspected that the only reason Honoré had agreed to go see such a sight was because this Delacroix forgery was the last of their paintings. The Enchantresses needed a longer con to tide them over while Céleste worked on more masterpieces.

The thought wearied her.

She'd been sleeping more at night, instead of painting. It was hard to stay inspired with an endless string of battlefields and maidens floating in lily pads—poor Ophelia. So many painters had tried to capture her demise. Delacroix himself had done so, not once but twice! Céleste's own versions sold well. No doubt the young men who bought them went home to hang them on their walls next to *L'Inconnue de la Seine*. The plaster death mask of the nameless girl who'd been fished from the river was—eerily enough—very much in vogue. Copies decorated a fair number of Paris's drawing rooms.

Everyone loved a drowning woman.

A good sob story.

"The best lies are rooted in truth," she told Sylvie. "And you might as well turn your pain into profit. Try to talk about the fact your parents died—"

"But they might not be dead," the girl said.

Before Sylvie had found her way to the other Enchantresses, she'd been trapped in an orphanage on the outskirts of the city. It was a careless place, where sawdust was substituted for flour and children's pasts got lost with the rest of the paperwork. Sylvie tended to write her own versions, same as she did for the English fairy tales. Most of them involved missing royalty, in some fashion. Each one ended with a happily ever after.

The only person she'd be fooling with that sort of story was herself.

"Maybe not." Céleste tugged carefully at the sleeve of her own mourning gown. "Your mark doesn't need to know that though. They just need to feel sorry for you. They need to feel like they have the upper hand."

Sylvie's own hands fluttered at her sides as they continued their liar's lesson—as if she were a fledgling, eager to fly. But there wasn't much time to come up with a good script for the ballet attendees. Honoré had finished reciting her own lines. There was an extra swagger in the young woman's step as she returned to their alley.

"That *was* entertaining! Excellent selection, *mon amie*. Though you should hurry back before Henri gets too inebriated. He just ordered another bottle of champagne to celebrate his financial windfall. Sylvie! Did you *eat* your sword?"

"Only half," chirped the youngest Enchantress. "Now it's a dagger!"

Céleste fought back a smile. Of all the people she'd ever met, Sylvie had the most literal hunger. The kid's stomach was a bottomless pit. It was no wonder she wanted to go back to the restaurant, where the scents of butter and cream ribboned the air, and the waiter was bringing a plate of cakes to Henri's table. Along with a fresh bottle. The mark was trying to hide a grin of his own. He hid Dumont's calling card too when he spotted Céleste, covering it with a linen napkin as she approached the table.

Good.

"Oh, thank you, messieurs! I returned with your francs as fast as I could!" The sum had been in her skirts all along, but Céleste made sure to pant as she deposited the money on their table. It was too easy to act out of breath. "My brother asked where the painting was, and I told him it was already with the appraiser. I don't know what I'd do if I lost it..."

Henri didn't even glance at her francs. "It was no trouble at all. In fact, Baptiste and I were discussing how nice this would look on his wall. Why don't we save you an errand?"

"You—you wish to buy it?" A quick frown.

Tensions played out beneath her mark's face too: excitement, agitation, don't-let-the-chance-of-a-lifetime-slip-away. "How does four hundred francs sound?"

Delicious. Céleste savored every new bill that was placed onto the tabletop. "Monsieur, it's too much! This painting may not even be worth half that. Let me get the appraisal first—"

"No!" Sweat jeweled Henri's hairline. "Four hundred and fifty francs."

She eyed the painting and then the money, pretending to look torn. "I don't know..."

"Trust me, your brother will be overjoyed when you return with this sum," Henri said. "So will Baptiste's wife, when he gifts her this painting. Right, Baptiste?"

His friend grunted—then had a foot-to-shin flinch. "Er, yes."

Men were rarely as honorable as Céleste hoped. Not that she was in any position to judge, stuffing so many francs into her coin purse. She took an éclair too, when Baptiste offered the plate of pastries—ostensibly out of guilt. He felt *sorry* for her. Sorry that she was being cheated out of a small fortune. The feeling wouldn't last, of course, when he realized it was Henri who'd been hoodwinked. But the Enchantresses would be attending a ballet by then, with different clothes, names, and faces, shaking coins from some other rich young man's pockets.

The éclair would be long gone too.

Sylvie was waiting outside the restaurant, feeding pigeons with the last crumbs of her *ficelle*. Her face fell when she saw the purse Céleste was carrying, heavy with money Sylvie wouldn't be able to steal herself.

"But I wanted to be the backup plan!" She scowled. "I was going to ask him more about vampires."

"You'll have plenty more chances to steal tonight. For now, I've brought you a new blade." Céleste grinned as she handed over the éclair. "You should eat it before Honoré tries to teach you more footwork."

Chapter 3

The Rite of Spring

The ballet that night began on a bright note. The Champs-Élysées was one of Paris's best-lit neighborhoods, with electric streetlamps along all its major avenues, and when Céleste stepped out of the cab onto Avenue Montaigne, her crème de menthe–colored gown turned into something truly liquid. Drinkable. Several gentlemen stopped to stare as the young woman made her way to the theatre entrance, so mesmerized that they didn't see that they, in turn, were being sized up, measured by the fabric of their waistcoats and the contents of their pockets.

By Honoré and Sylvie, respectively.

It had been a long time since the Enchantresses had performed a long con, but Céleste fell back into her role with ease. *Be the shiny thing. Be as gold as the doors of the Théâtre des Champs-Élysées, which are brilliant enough to break a bird's neck.* Brilliant enough too to bounce Céleste's reflection back at her. Her wig was black, and her smile was perfectly painted on. Only her eyes felt familiar, as gray as Père Lachaise's gravestones. And just as haunted.

There was a wealth of potential marks in the theatre, though the audience was a strange mix. This ballet had brought out the bohemian crowd. Men who tied their hair back with twine and had pencils tucked behind their ears in case inspiration struck. They were frowned upon by the wealthier patrons—the ones who wore tails and tulle, diamonds and ospreys. By the stage was a woman dressed in a boa made of peacock feathers. Deep teal, velveteen purple, a green as drunk as Céleste's gown... it was unlike anything she'd ever seen, which meant it had to be worth some money. The woman wore gold too. Her wrists shimmered with bracelets, and when the orchestra began tuning, she waved her arms as if she herself were the conductor. Strange... too strange to make a target of, certainly.

Their next victim was more likely among the gentlemen who milled at the edges of the theatre, talking business. Honoré's moustache and suit blended seamlessly as she eavesdropped for opportunities. From this distance it was easy to lose her in the crowd.

Sylvie, on the other hand, was starting to stand out.

The youngest Enchantress was in the middle of the aisle, holding a pocket watch—twenty-four karats and ripe for stealing. Or it would have been, if the man who owned the timepiece hadn't secured it to his vest. Twice. His first fob chain dangled loosely. The second linked Sylvie—undeniably—to the crime.

She'd gotten herself caught.

Céleste made a quick study of Sylvie's would-be victim. He was quick too. He'd already snagged the girl by the wrist, and the fact he chained his valuables twice over meant that he was familiar with thieves. Aside from the watch, he didn't seem to have much worth stealing. Whereas most men in this theatre sported top hats and dapper suits, this one wore a looser version of the outfit: no jacket, only a vest to keep his rolled sleeves in place. His hair was as dark as calligraphy ink, but colors splashed his fingertips—so Céleste could place the man as a fellow painter.

She found herself wanting to paint *him*.

The sensation surprised her. It had been years since she'd worked with live models—or had any desire to—but there was an edge to this young man that drew Céleste in, a sharpness that had nothing to do with his jawline or his forearms. Both were so defined that she'd need to whittle a pencil to its finest point to mark his likeness onto paper. She'd have to press harder for the brows, except at the part where a scar nicked through the right arc. This, along with the small blue mark that had been tattooed beneath his left eye, only made Céleste aware of how symmetrical the rest of his face was. What beautiful bone structure! There was a divot on his chin that sparked an irrational desire to place her own thumb there.

She reached for Sylvie's hand instead, her heart racing. "Pardon me, monsieur! And pardon my sister, please. I asked her to find out the time, but she hates speaking to strangers, so she must have tried to peek at your watch. She meant no harm."

This was where Céleste would normally swish her skirts to show a sliver of ankle, but something told her this man would see past that. She couldn't decide what color his eyes were. Brown, technically. But it was the kind of brown that broke into different colors, depending on where he stared. Hints of amber. Flecks of mica. They flashed when he watched Céleste. Not quite gold, but not quite angry either.

"Your *sister*?" He danced delicately around the word. His scarred eyebrow lifted in a broken arc, no doubt trying to bridge the differences between Céleste's pale features and Sylvie's shading. "I suppose you both do share the ability to stop a room."

The theatre *had* paused, Céleste realized, when she dared to break away from his gaze. Other ballet patrons were watching the taut gold watch chain, waiting to see what this handsome stranger would do.

He continued speaking, low enough for only Céleste and Sylvie to hear. "I'm afraid your sister has made a poor choice."

It's certainly worse than stealing a few stale loaves of bread.

If the artist filed a police report, Sylvie could get locked away… Céleste gripped the girl's opposite wrist and started counting out the exits in her head; they were already starting to shrink—an usher was making his way down the aisle. On the other side of the theatre, Honoré had unbuttoned her cuff links and was all but leaping over seats in an effort to reach them. Businessmen forgot about potential investments. Ladies gasped behind their fans, scandalized.

How much of a mess would it be if Honoré pulled a knife from her suit? And she would, if she thought the other Enchantresses were in danger.

Céleste wasn't sure they were just yet.

There was still room to talk her way out of this... she could see it in the artist's eyes, the way they lit from Sylvie to his watch. The extra chain's gold links winked like a fuse beneath the theatre lighting, but his grip on the girl's other wrist wasn't as tight as it could have been. Again, Céleste noticed the paint splashing his fingertips, the rough crack of a callus beneath.

They had more common ground than not.

"Monsieur, please. The only scenes I enjoy creating are still lifes with fruit and flowers and the occasional lobster."

A smile. It was crooked, yes, but a smile nonetheless. "I bet you have a damn hard time getting lobsters to sit still."

"Not really," Céleste quipped back. "Sisters are much more of a challenge." She nodded at Sylvie. "I'm sorry for the trouble mine has caused you. Would you happen to have the time, monsieur?"

The artist shook his head and turned toward the usher.

Shit.

Honoré was still several rows away. Sylvie squirmed. Céleste wondered if she should wrench the girl free and run—if she'd even be fast enough in these skirts. But before she could try anything, Sylvie's victim released her himself, waving the usher away with paint-streaked fingers.

"No. As I said, your *sister* made a poor choice." The artist tugged on his double fob chains. His smile looked just as taut. "My watch doesn't tell time."

Tick tock. It took Céleste another second to realize what had happened.

He was letting them off the hook.

Sylvie, however, still wasn't releasing the watch. The girl's fist tightened over the timepiece. "It's not broken! I can feel it ticking!" the youngest Enchantress insisted.

"That would be impossible." The artist pulled his fob chains even harder, reeling the pocket watch from her palm. There was an hourglass with wings engraved in its filigree—a symbol that meant *time is fleeting* in the language of tombstones—but when he opened the watch, it was clear that the hands were frozen. Stuck at 8:45. "See?"

Sylvie stared and stared, as if she could make the gears move by sheer force of will. "Why would you wear a broken watch?"

"Why would you try to steal one?" he asked, not unkindly.

"It's shiny."

"Ma rêveuse!" Céleste scowled.

After so many homespun fairy tales, Sylvie chose *now* to tell the truth? Admitting a crime was the worst crime of all. "Oh... that's right. I'm supposed to tell you that I'm an orphan. And you should feel sorry for me."

"Is that so?"

"It is!" Sylvie chirped. "Do you feel sorry for me?"

"Not particularly," the artist told her. "But I understand, seeing as I too am part magpie," he said with a wink.

Sylvie cocked her head. "You're a bird?"

Not a bird but a fellow thief, Céleste realized. That would explain the second fob chain. It would also explain why he hadn't raised more of a fuss with the theatre staff, why his lips were still set with that slightly crooked smile. She didn't realize how hard she was staring at them until his eyes found hers again.

"I find it difficult to resist shiny things," he said.

Crème brûlée. That was their shade, she decided, just as Honoré arrived, ready to speak in a proper baritone and sweep the other two Enchantresses away. But as soon as she saw the artist's face, she froze, as rigid as the ring on her middle finger. Céleste knew for a fact that this wasn't because of how handsome the man looked. No, there was some different chemistry between them.

Something that caused Honoré to break character—when she spoke, her voice was high and cracking. "Rafael?"

It was the artist's turn to straighten. His eyes widened. "Gabriel?"

Honoré had stolen plenty of identities over the years, but as far as Céleste knew, she'd never named herself after an archangel.

"No..." The artist was staring at the dragon ring, his face pale. "*Mon Dieu!* You look just like him..."

Honoré looked as if she'd been stabbed. Her own knife stayed tucked up her sleeve, glinting just past that unbuttoned cuff.

"Wait!" Sylvie chirped. "You know Honoré?"

"Honoré?" The artist's eyebrows rose as his hand wandered to the back of his neck. "That wasn't her name when—"

"Rafael and I grew up together." The other Enchantress shoved her fists into her pockets. She was no longer frozen but shifting back and forth, matching the uneasy sounds of the orchestra.

"My name's changed too. I go by 'Rafe' these days."

This got a snort from Honoré. "Rafe?"

"It fits better on the bottom of a canvas," he answered.

"Still painting, huh?"

"Céleste paints!" Sylvie volunteered gaily.

Rafe's eyebrows arched even higher. "Oh? So that part was true?"

It was. And suddenly, this made Céleste feel as wriggly as Honoré or that lobster she'd dropped into a boiling pot of water. That still life had been relatively painless. Well, not for the lobster. She'd split its shell for dinner that night, and somehow, now, she could feel that too: seen at the seams, then cracked open.

Was Céleste becoming a worse liar?

Or was this man an even better one?

Judging by Honoré's reaction, it was the latter. "What the hell are you doing here? Shouldn't you be in Constantinople by now? Or stowing away on some luxury streamliner?" There was a bitterness to the other Enchantress's voice that Céleste had never noted before. "Eating some shit like caviar?"

"Caviar are eggs, I believe," Rafe said, with a voice that did not match the way his hand gripped the nape of his neck. "Though I can't say with any certainty. I never did manage to make my way to first class—and it turns out that Paris is the best place in the world to be a penniless painter. *Me voilà!*"

"You aren't penniless! You have a gold watch." Sylvie reached for his timepiece again, tapping its glass face with her finger.

Just like that, the watch started to work.

Céleste inhaled sharply when she saw the hands move. They weren't ticking but *spinning*, gliding over minutes and hours, until they came to a halt at half past twelve. The theatre suddenly felt as if it had fallen out of time itself. The stained glass ceiling—which had been pieced together to look like sunrays bursting through storm clouds—went dim. Violins sharpened their tune. Dust swirled in the stage lights, and Céleste started to sway.

Sylvie reached out to steady her.

Rafe did too. "Is everything all right, mademoiselle?" His hairline somehow looked even darker as his brow furrowed. "Are you well?"

Honestly? No. Céleste was seeing things that weren't there. The open watch spun from his waistcoat. *8:45.* Gold backing. *8:45.* Gold backing. *8:45.* Behind her, the instruments ceased tuning, and there was the rainlike patter of ballerinas' slippers behind the curtain. She thought she'd had more time than this...

"*Mon amie?*" Honoré whispered.

"I'm fine," Céleste said. Everyone else in the theatre was taking their seats, and a hush had sunk into the venue, making its velvet richer, its shadows bolder. "We should sit."

Rafe closed his watch. An odd look passed over Sylvie's face as the artist returned the timepiece to his waistcoat, securing the loose fob chain for good measure. This was probably the first time the youngest Enchantress had failed to pick a pocket. It wasn't an easy thing, to discover you were not invincible.

Céleste's steps wobbled as she started down the aisle, and when Honoré offered a steadying arm, she did so with her left. The hand with the dragon ring stayed stuffed in her pocket.

"Good thinking on the fake faint," her friend murmured as they found their seats.

Céleste still felt lightheaded, but she did not say so. She didn't ask about Rafe either.

"Did you overhear any investment opportunities?" she wondered instead.

Honoré shook her head. "All anyone was talking about was this ballet…" She pointed to the second title in the program: *The Rite of Spring.* "It's about a Russian virgin who dances herself to death as a pagan sacrifice. Most avant-garde."

"Was it written by a man?"

"Obviously."

The stage curtains lifted, and ballerinas in long white tutus began fluttering to the music of Chopin. Sylvie watched, rapt, the dancers turning like stars in her eyes. Even Honoré got caught up in the fluent movement of the performers' limbs. Crescent-moon Cs and serpentine Ss. Across the aisle, Céleste could see Rafe sitting on the edge of his seat, running his thumb over the face of his pocket watch. The rest of him was still, so still, and the stage lights brought out the most dramatic shading around his face. Again, she felt her fingers itching for a pen.

His gaze met hers, suddenly, as if he hadn't really been watching the dancers after all.

Céleste's pulse quickened.

The edge of Rafe's mouth sharpened—another smile?

She found herself matching it, even as she looked away to join the polite smattering of applause when the first dance ended. The lady sitting in front of the Enchantresses did not clap. It was the same woman wearing the peacock boa—her pale shoulders peeked through its feathers. The bones beneath were sharp, the muscles tense. She was no longer watching the orchestra but the side stage, where the dancers were disappearing. The shadows there struck Céleste as strange. She studied them for a moment and realized they were stretching in a way that didn't agree with the spotlights. They looked almost *sticky*.

Her grin slipped from her face.

Was she seeing things again?

Suddenly, the other woman stood. Feathers fell in an iridescent trail down her back—not a boa at all but a cape. It swirled around her heels as she leapt toward the stage: up and over. She disappeared behind falling curtains.

"Is she allowed to do that?" Sylvie wondered.

Honoré looked up from the program she'd been poring over. "Do what?"

"The woman sitting in front of us just jumped backstage," Céleste informed her.

"Oh..." Honoré stared at the empty chair for an extra beat. Her brow crinkled. "Maybe it's part of the performance. I'll admit I'm curious to see what the fuss is about. Virgin sacrifices aside, a ballet can't be *that* scandalous, can it?"

Céleste wasn't sure. She looked back to the shadows onstage, but they had settled. The audience had done the opposite. They lit up the back of her neck with their whispers. She heard someone *hiss*, and again she was reminded of a fuse...

Rafe was no longer in his seat when she glanced across the aisle, but for some reason, her pulse kept on thundering. Her heart felt like cannon fire in her chest as the musicians lifted their horns to their lips. There was a furious rush of spring pipes, the exact sound you'd hear if you stepped on a hornets' nest. Curtains drew back. The dancers behind them bore no resemblance to the ballerinas from before. Their homespun dresses shuddered as they stomped across the stage; their braids swung in unwieldy arcs. With each press of their feet, the shadows by their slippers stirred, around and around and around.

The darkness did not merely stretch this time. It swarmed.

Céleste watched in horror as the shadows broke apart and grew dozens of tiny wings, whipping up into a cloud strong enough to make the painted background flutter. The spin of Rafe's watch, she could pass off as dizziness, but the dark fog onstage only grew worse as she gripped her seat. Her chest tightened too. This couldn't be happening. This shouldn't be happening. Was she hallucinating? She'd heard of people doing that, calling out to long-dead parents or seeing angels at their bedsides, but that was usually right before their final breaths.

She couldn't breathe now. Panic gripped her throat, forcing her to cough into her opera gloves. Rouge smeared across their creamy fabric. No...not rouge. Céleste stared at the color. It was wrong, wrong, wrong. Too dark. Like the floor by her feet, where the shadows seemed to rush around her ankles, tugging like some inevitable tide…

There was a scream.

It might have been hers. That would explain how Céleste heard it above the cacophony that called itself an orchestra. But when she heard the piercing sound again, when she looked up, there were no shadows on the stage at all—the dancers were stomping on a floor filled with feathers. Swirls of teal. Pliés of purple. The last gasps of green as they were pulverized.

There was no starry light left in Sylvie's eyes when she caught a crushed feather in her cupped hands.

On the other side of Céleste, Honoré flinched. A crumpled program had hit her between the shoulders, thrown by some upset audience member. It was impossible to tell who. When Céleste turned around, all she saw were hostile faces. It was as if the pagan pulse of the drums had slithered into everyone's veins. Beautiful women in beautiful gowns snarled like tigers. The gentlemen next to them rolled up their sleeves.

And their shadows. Their shadows were pulling away just as the dancers' had, smudging the outskirts of the Théâtre des Champs-Élysées like a charcoal drawing. Céleste could no longer see the gilded quote above the wealthy men's boxes. She couldn't even see the shine of the exits.

"We need to leave!" Céleste screamed over the orchestra. The musicians kept on playing, despite the fact that more projectiles were being launched at the stage: Programs. Fruit. A champagne glass. This shattered a bit too close to Honoré's top hat as she wedged it back on her head.

"Immediately," she agreed.

Sylvie was already in the aisle. Céleste tried to follow, but two men lurched in front of her, their fists flying. Smashed spectacles and black eyes. It was exactly the kind of brawl you'd expect in a back alley.

The kind of fight Honoré trained so relentlessly for.

The other Enchantress threw herself in front of Céleste, clearing a path with a few well-placed jabs. Her eyes lit up as she began to undo her cuff links. "Go, *mon amie*! I'll meet you and Sylvie back at the cemetery!"

Céleste pushed toward the rear of the theatre, trying to catch up with the youngest Enchantress. Shoulders, elbows, feathers, shadows, screams—everyone was screaming, and somehow this made her feel better.

Someone stepped on her dress.

Then her toes.

The floor felt mired, as if she were sludging through mud instead of carpet. Céleste managed to pull herself up the aisle and through the lobby, then finally into the night. Here she stood. Out of breath. Scanning the sidewalks frantically for Sylvie. There was no sign of the youngest Enchantress in the steady pools of light cast by electric streetlamps.

Other ballet attendees had begun gathering beneath them. Women sobbed about their torn gowns, while men with bruised knuckles tried to comfort them. Someone was calling for the police. Accusations were flying: "Those damned bohemians were the ones who started it! Throwing fruit as if they were jungle apes!" followed by, "Better fruit than a bottle of Veuve Clicquot!"

No one was talking about the way the dancers' shadows had swarmed like hornets.

Céleste stared back at the theatre. She did not spot Honoré. She almost didn't recognize Rafe either, when the artist stumbled out. His hair had come untied, falling in front of his face. Through black tangles, she could tell his lip was split. Bleeding. He didn't seem to see Céleste until she was close enough to take a second swipe at his pocket watch.

She resisted the urge.

Barely.

"Have you seen Sylvie?" she asked instead.

Rafe wasn't smiling when he swept his hair from his face. His jawline looked sharper than ever. "Who?"

"The magpie girl—"

Something about his stare caused Céleste to falter. She'd lost her wig, she realized. It had gotten ripped off in the chaos, and now her roots were showing—hair that had gone as silver as starlight despite her youth. It was her most striking feature, in more ways than one. She gritted her teeth whenever fellow painters compared her to an Alphonse Mucha drawing and suggested that she wear a lily behind her ear, like some budding spring goddess. *How lucky you are to be born with such beauty!*

They had no idea how wrong they were.

But Rafe made no mention of flowers or the unnatural shade of her hair. "Ah, yes. I saw your sister helping herself to more sparkly accoutrements in the lobby. She seemed to be enjoying the crime immensely. But you, mademoiselle..." His gaze landed on her gloves. "You're bleeding."

There was no denying it, but her tongue searched for a lie out of habit. Out of sheer self-preservation. *It's makeup. It's red wine.* But none of these excuses were convincing enough.

It was blood.

It was hers.

Céleste was not all right. Up until now she'd been able to ignore it, to dismiss it, to tell herself—and the other Enchantresses—that her hay fever was simply worse this spring.

But roses couldn't do this.

Not even damned ones.

"You're bleeding too," she told Rafe.

"Eh." The artist dabbed his lip. The skin around his right eye had an extra shine—the beginnings of a bruise. "I've been in worse brawls. This isn't even my first fight at a ballet, if you can believe it. Did our mutual acquaintance start this one too?"

Honoré. There was still no sign of her, but Céleste did spot Sylvie exiting the theatre, wearing a sapphire necklace. Obviously stolen. It was bound to attract the attention of the police officers who'd started to canvas the crowd.

Sylvie's eyes lit up when she caught sight of Rafe and Céleste, and as the girl began to make her way toward them, Céleste felt her own red panic rising again. She wanted more time. She wanted her stained gloves to be a costume, something she could peel off or pretend away. She wanted the youngest Enchantress to stay out of jail, out of sight of the policeman who was now interviewing witnesses by their lamppost.

"Excuse me!" Céleste grabbed the man's uniform sleeve, tugged all his attention toward her. "Monsieur! What on earth is going on? I demand an explanation!"

The officer paused when he saw Céleste, and she felt the loss of her wig more keenly. She could see Sylvie from the corner of her eye—the pause of silver and sapphires. This became a shooting star streak as the girl made her way across the street, fading into the evening. Céleste exhaled and released the policeman's sleeve.

"I'd like an explanation as well." The officer produced a notepad and a pen. "No one seems to be able to tell me why this riot broke out. Did you see anything of note, mademoiselle?"

I saw a broken watch tick. I saw shadows spin their own dancers. I saw an entire theatre of people possessed by some strange darkness.

Céleste knew how these things sounded. "There were feathers," she said instead.

Rafe looked at her sharply.

"Feathers?" the policeman asked.

"The woman seated in front of me was wearing a feathered cape. She jumped backstage before the music began, and then there was a scream, and then . . . feathers. Floating everywhere."

The policeman nodded, but it was clear he wasn't taking her seriously. He wasn't even taking her statement. His pen tapped idly against his notepad. He glanced back at Rafe. "And you, monsieur? Did you see this woman with the cape?"

"I—I can't recall," he said slowly.

"And the feathers?"

Rafe pinched his lips. "All I saw was an ostrich headdress getting plucked like a Christmas quail. To be fair, it was difficult to see much of anything. That theatre was chaos incarnate."

"Clearly," the officer said. "The ladies seem hysterical."

Céleste's fist tightened around her bloody gloves. Hysteria—always the convenient excuse, always targeted at women.

But was it the truth this time? Was the consumption inside her so hungry that it had climbed from her lungs into her brain? Had her panic somehow set off the rest of the audience?

"The gentlemen were even worse," Rafe told the police officer, who was taking down *his* statement word for word. "The wealthy crowd and the bohemians have always been at each other's throats about the meaning of art. My guess is that tonight was the ballet that broke the camel's back."

Men and women kept fluttering like moths around the brightly lit theatre doors—but if you looked high enough, you could forget the chaos. Céleste stared up at the stone edifice—where a carving of Apollo played his harp for the nine muses. The woman standing behind the naked god had a massive pair of outstretched wings.

That was the sort of statue she'd want guarding her own grave.

She hated that this thought came to her so quickly. Hated that she'd have to walk back to the cemetery—with all its buried bones and unspent gold—and tell the other Enchantresses that they needed to plan for a future without her.

She didn't want to go.

Not yet.

But what choice did she have?

Rafe's watch chains winked at Céleste beneath the lamplight. "I think I could use a drink after that rampant display of chauvinism," he said, once the policeman wandered off.

"What, you didn't have enough champagne bottles flung at you during the riot?" Céleste asked with a smile.

A small smirk grew on Rafe's face too. "I *did* get hit by a tin of caviar, if you can believe it."

She didn't believe him, but it was a nice excuse to laugh. For just a moment, Céleste Artois could forget about the terrible fate that lay ahead. She found herself wanting to hold on to the feeling a little longer.

"What do you say, mademoiselle? Shall we bid adieu to this unruly scene and start another? I know of a charming place on the Left Bank that serves no fish eggs whatsoever."

Chapter 4

Absinthe Makes the Heart Grow Fonder

Absinthe had never been Céleste's preferred drink. It wasn't that she disliked the flavor—the sharp sweet tang of anise that caused the tongue to feel slightly numb after a few sips—or the ritual of slotted silver spoons and sugar cubes. It wasn't the stories of a fairy as green as the alcohol itself or even the darker tales of insanity that the drink's opponents liked to tout. Her avoidance had always been personal, a grudge against the smoky salons where emerald fountains flowed. Places where all she'd heard was no, no, no. Where her sketches weren't afforded a second glance. *Good, but not good enough*, one particularly drunk artist had said. *Let me show you how it's done.*

He'd pulled out a pencil and tried to sketch her.

Then he tried to kiss her.

It had put a terrible taste in Céleste's mouth, but it had also given her a fresh conviction. If she couldn't be good enough, she would be awful. If no patron was willing to pay the tuition she needed to attend Académie de La Palette, she'd draw the damn banknotes herself.

Rafe's history with absinthe had clearly been different. "I'll have *une correspondance*."

The bartender understood—Parisians had been ordering absinthe this way for decades, by asking for "a ticket" to the Charenton asylum. It was tongue-in-cheek, obviously, but when the man asked for Céleste's order, she wanted to laugh. Hysterically. She already felt she was losing her mind, so why not go ahead and summon a fairy or two?

"I'll take one as well," she told him.

The bartender appeared unbothered by the state of Céleste's torn dress and the bruises on Rafe's face. This could have been because they'd wandered out of the eighth arrondissement, across the river, and down the Left Bank, in search of a café more affordable for penniless pockets. They'd ended up in the Latin Quarter, where university students drank cheap wine and *The Rite of Spring* was far enough away to feel like a fever dream.

Céleste shivered, despite the fact their table was by a set of doors open to the warm night air. The lamps were hot too. She tried not to focus on how their flames cast her profile against the wall, where a poster advertised Eau de Récollets mineral water. A winged woman bottled water from a geyser, and the yellow words above her claimed this was a cure for arthritis. Céleste felt herself sneering as she read them. Miracles! Magic! *Snake oil.* She used to wonder at the sort of people who fell for such ruses. How could you be so gullible, to believe that a few extra francs spent would take away pain?

She knew now it had nothing to do with gullibility. It was a distinct choice to fool yourself. To celebrate birthdays you'd never see. To go to a ballet and leave with a stranger. To toss your bloody opera gloves in the Seine and watch them drift downriver. To lift your goblet of absinthe before the sugar cube dissolved. To swallow it all down before you could cough it back up—sludge and sweet rot.

Rafe raised his eyebrows as she set her empty glass on the table. "I was going to propose a toast to my second ballet brawl. *Tant pis!*"

Céleste ordered another drink. "I'm more curious about the first fight," she told him.

"It wasn't nearly as dramatic as tonight's." His burnt-sugar eyes caught the candlelight. "There was no Veuve Clicquot artillery involved. Théâtre de Belleville has always been more of a working-class establishment, cheap enough for the masses to enjoy. I tried to be even cheaper and snuck into a show without paying. When the ticket holder found me in his seat, he raised a ruckus. Anne—sorry, I mean, Honoré—kicked him in the crotch."

"That sounds like Honoré." The crotch kicking, Céleste meant. Not the other name; her friend had never uttered it before. She'd never said anything about Belleville either, which was strange, considering the neighborhood was only a few blocks from their cemetery camp.

The watchword system made more sense now.

As did the pits of broken glass.

"I take it she hasn't changed much?" Rafe said.

"Well, she *has* grown a moustache," Céleste replied slyly.

"That was unexpected," the other artist admitted. "She pulls it off well. A little *too* well. I hope I didn't upset her by commenting on the family resemblance."

Honoré is always upset, Céleste wanted to say, but the bartender had come back with a second glass of green liquor, another sugar cube. He seemed determined to prepare it properly, pouring the water through the spoon himself. It was a slow process. Drip, drip. Long enough for her to think about what Rafe had said.

"Who is Gabriel?" she asked, once the bartender left them alone again.

Rafe pinched his lips. "You and Honoré... you're close, yes?"

"Like sisters."

The other artist stayed silent for a moment.

Somewhere up the cobblestone lane, a violin started playing. When Rafe spoke, it was clear he'd chosen his words with care. "If she hasn't told you about Gabriel, there's a reason. She was always trying to protect him too. But I shouldn't say anything more. It's not my story to tell."

Céleste considered this. She considered the man sitting across from her as well. Tangled black hair, scars, and such an easy smile—too easy, perhaps. "She never told me about you either."

The tattoo below Rafe's left eye flinched as his smile disappeared. "Yes, well, there's not much *to* tell. We were kids together. Kids who ran around with knives and tried not to fall on them."

This made Céleste think of Sylvie rushing from their tomb, so eager to cut her birthday dessert. It had been hard to imagine Honoré as a young girl then. Just as hard as it was to imagine why the other Enchantress was so unsettled by this man, yet *not* threatening to stab him.

"There's got to be more to your story than that," Céleste said delicately.

Perhaps she hadn't been delicate enough. Rafe's tattoo wrinkled again. He glanced at his drink with a look that suggested he wanted to quaff it. "Honestly, I'm surprised Honoré remembers me. I—I was—" He cleared his throat. "Well, I was the black sheep of Belleville. Never quite fit in there, no matter how many red scarves or shiny boots I wore. My parents were from Spain, but they moved to the neighborhood shortly after I was born, so I don't think that's the reason it never felt like home."

"Could it have been all the stabbings?" Céleste reasoned. Belleville was one of the more dangerous parts of Paris, thanks to a gang known as the Apaches.

His scarred eyebrow twitched. "Did my fair share of that," he said. "Stealing too. *Mamá* always hated that I was getting into trouble. My father was different. As long as I brought home money to help with the rent, he didn't care where it came from."

Céleste arched a brow. "But now you're penniless."

"Practically." The artist's hand went once more to his watch, covering the chains protectively. "I needed to get the hell out of Belleville. I needed more."

"More than money?"

"So much more." Rafe leaned forward in his chair, his eyes catching the glimmer of the lantern, his voice going as deep as the shadows. "I needed magic."

The fiddle song up the lane went sharp. It was Céleste's turn to stare down at her absinthe. Perhaps she shouldn't have guzzled that first round so fast. She'd hoped the hallucinations would stop once she'd started drinking or that she might at least be able to blame the alcohol, but Rafe kept on speaking in his low, smoky way, sending sparks from Céleste's neck down to the base of her spine.

"Magic exists. You might not believe it yet, but you see it, don't you? You saw the feathers at the Théâtre des Champs-Élysées, and I'm guessing you glimpsed the shadows too." His hands gave a small flourish in front of the lantern, casting the shape of a fox on the wall beside them. The creature pulled away from Rafe's silhouette—trotting several steps before disappearing into Céleste's shadow.

She could *feel* it.

An unspoken whisper against her skin. A breeze on a windless night. "That..." Her throat was dry. She swallowed. "That was you?"

"The fox? Yes. The shadows during *The Rite of Spring*?" He shook his head. "I was merely a spectator."

Céleste waved her own hand in front of the lantern. Her shadow stayed hand shaped. "How?"

"Magic is a law of the universe," Rafe said, "the same way water is wet or the sky is blue."

"Yes, but I can *see* the sky." She nodded at the night just past his shoulder, where the moon would soon unpeel over zinc rooftops. "I've been able to see the sky since I was born."

"You probably saw magic then too," Rafe said. "Most children do, as I understand it. But we grow up and grow blind. If you're lucky enough to find yourself Enlightened again, you have to make the most of it." He looked back at Céleste's profile cast over the mineral water poster. "You strike me as an opportunist. Can I see your hand?"

Her shadow reached out to his. "Are you going to predict my future?"

"That's beyond me," Rafe said. "If you want your fate spelled out, you should go to the Seine. There's a woman there who reads palms like novels. But she takes a piece of every fortune she tells. You leave every reading with one less crease."

"I take it you've never been?" His own hand was warm, calloused in the exact same places as hers.

"It's easy to lose yourself in magic, if you aren't careful." Rafe ran his fingers over her own, drawing new lines over Céleste's palm. It was just a whisper of a touch, but a whisper was enough. Her shadow shivered. The sparks at the base of her spine flared enough to make her lean forward in her chair.

The lantern flickered on the table between them.

Heat prickled Céleste's cheeks. It flushed down her chest when she swallowed, but she didn't pull back.

Rafe didn't either. Instead, he looked more closely at her palm, where crimson paint from her Delacroix forgery was starting to peel. "I see you're an artist after all," he said warmly.

"I dabble."

"I'd say it's more than that."

There was something hypnotizing about the way his gaze reflected the lamp's flame. Magnetic, even.

"It could have been." Céleste forced herself to glance back at her absinthe glass. Its contents matched the green of her dress, the green of the lily pads she'd planned to paint around her next version of Ophelia. A project that would never be finished. She didn't want to spend the rest of her life drawing drowning women. "Once. I had big dreams when I first came to Paris, but Paris had no dreams for me. I gave up painting for myself, and I'm good at pretending I don't regret it."

At least, she *had been*.

It took a concentrated effort *not* to meet Rafe's eyes. Not to think about the tones she'd mix onto a palette to bring out their brown—fox fur and amber and fire. Even then, it would probably be impossible to capture the way they glimmered. Did it have something to do with magic?

"I understand," he said. "I used to play fiddle games with Honoré too. We were trying to save money for train tickets, but—well, it was never enough. Even when it was." He fell quiet for a moment. "You're wrong about the dreams though. Paris has more to offer than you'd think... if you know exactly where to look."

"I'm guessing you do."

His smile curled the edges of his lips. Easy again. "I've never met another Enlightened forger before. I may have an... opportunity for you, if you're interested."

Normally, her answer would be no. Céleste only ever worked with the other Enchantresses, and she already felt bad enough for abandoning them—Honoré would be waiting up for her. Sylvie too was probably awake, counting cats as they padded over the mausoleum dome, smudging stars with their paws.

She should return to them.

She should say no.

The fox leapt back to Rafe's shadow when he released her hand, streaking over the Eau de Récollets poster in a way that made its yellow letters stand out even more... If this man was bullshitting her, she couldn't see how, and if he was telling the truth...

It meant Céleste *wasn't* going mad. It meant miracles did, in fact, exist.

"What does the job pay?" she asked.

"More than money," he said.

"Shadow puppets?" She tried to keep her voice light, dancing on strings, lest it betray the hope she tasted.

Rafe's shadow nodded, while his gaze stayed still. "Or wings. Or paintings hung on the walls of the Louvre. Or rubies that make your lips just as bright when you wear them. You can ask my employer for anything in his power if you bring him enough dreams."

"You steal... dreams...?" Her thoughts spun, trying to wrap around what he was saying. "From sleeping people?"

"The dreamers aren't asleep. They've been awoken to magic—'Enlightened' is the technical term. They spend their evenings imagining all sorts of things in La Fée Verte's salon."

La Fée Verte. Immediately Céleste thought of absinthe advertisements, each featuring a beautiful, eerie woman dressed in green. "The green fairy?"

"It's what the imaginers call her. Very few magicians have real names," Rafe told her. "La Fée Verte is the hostess of an enchanted establishment on the Left Bank. It's an incredible place! Ideas have power there. Real power. They can be converted into spells that bring statues to life or change the river's currents or shift the very stars themselves... It's why La Fée Verte invites the city's most creative minds to her salon every night. It's why she collects their thoughts."

"And why do *you* take them?" she wondered.

"For the same reason you will, I expect."

"What's that?"

"A future."

Céleste looked back at her hands, at their shadows cast over the promise of the winged woman's poster. She turned them into fists. "Why come to me with this?" she asked.

"I need help," Rafe told her. "The job is big, and my employer is getting impatient. A second forger would take some of the pressure off."

"You haven't even seen my work," Céleste pointed out.

"There's no need. If Honoré vouches for you, that's enough for me."

"Honoré would call you mad."

"She's called me worse." Rafe laughed. "But magic *is* madness to those who can't see it, so act with care. Don't go telling police officers you see feathers everywhere when they don't... That's a surefire way to get yourself an actual ticket to Charenton." He drained his goblet's absinthe down to its sugary dregs and stood. "There are far better destinations. Cursed pyramids, mystical monasteries, mountain caves inhabited by hermits who live forever, bazaars where starlight is bottled and sold... The horizons are endless! Even in La Fée Verte's salon, there's a room where you can paint landscapes and *walk through them*."

"Really?" Céleste stood too, breathless, trying to ignore the iron taste on her tongue as she placed some francs on the table.

"I painted a city underneath an ocean once and almost drowned trying to explore it, before I thought to give myself gills—"

"There are men who live forever?"

"Ah." Rafe hesitated, then shook his head. "Not men."

"Hermits."

"Myths, more like. Even if there were truth to them, it's not the kind of magic you or I could steal. We are but mere mortals."

As if Céleste needed reminding.

She stuffed a cloth napkin into her purse, just in case.

Rafe ducked out of the café and began walking. His shadow rippled—and not just because of the lane's cobblestones or the gas lamps that lit their way. He was beckoning her. "Follow my lead. From here on out, we're proper painters, with heads full of stardust. I trust you can act the part?"

"That depends on whether the stardust is a metaphor," Céleste said, still breathless. It was hard to keep up, especially now that magic was in the mix.

"The stardust *can* be poetry," he said, as he stepped out onto Boulevard Saint-Michel. "Or songs. Or sketches. La Fée Verte is able to pull such things from people's minds. You'll see when we reach the salon, but first you have to think lots of whimsical thoughts: glass snowflakes, swords in lakes—those sorts of things. It will make her more likely to invite you inside."

Céleste had walked this street many times, following its tram tracks to the river, but Rafe didn't venture that far. They stopped short of the bridge, by the Fontaine Saint-Michel. She was familiar with this landmark too—how could she not be? The fountain was striking. A heavenly battle played out in its bronze: the archangel's sword always pointed down, the devil forever crouched under his heels, and a pair of dragons spouted water for generations of pigeons. There was no winner, no loser, no change.

Tonight, however, one of the sculptures started moving.

The dragon on the left-most pedestal winged down to the plaza, where Rafe and Céleste stood.

"Holy hell!" She gasped.

Rafe laughed. He didn't seem to mind that the statue had fangs the size of steak knives or that these were looming just over the couple's heads. "It's all right!" he promised.

"It's a goddamn dragon!" she hissed.

"Not damned by God at all." Rafe placed a hand between the

beast's curled horns. "And I believe it's technically a chimera, from ancient Greek mythology, but that's neither here nor there."

The statue itself was most definitely *here*. And alive. It seemed to be nudging against Rafe's fingers, the way a cat might demand to be scratched. "How is it doing that?"

"Magic," her companion replied, his tone teasing.

"No shit."

"That's right! No shit! It's stardust, like I said." Rafe started rubbing the statue behind its lionlike ears. At this point, Céleste wouldn't have been surprised if the bronze beast started purring. "This magnificent creature was sculpted in 1860 by A. Jacquemart, who left small sparks of himself in his statues. All the best artists do that, you know...lose slivers of their soul to whatever they're working on. La Fée Verte figured out a way to harness that energy. This statue is her gatekeeper now. He weighs your thoughts to see if they're worth entertaining. Why don't you go ahead and give him a show?"

Céleste studied the statue more closely. In Greek mythology, chimeras were cobbled together using random animal parts, but the way A. Jacquemart had sculpted this piece felt far more flowing: lion jaw into ram's horns into bat wings into a scaled tail. *Dragon* was a better-fitting term.

And more whimsical, to boot.

She thought of the stack of fairy books by Sylvie's bed, flipping through their illustrations of buried treasure and looming kings. These had to be fanciful enough. Right? Or could the statue sense that she was using someone else's story? A. Jacquemart hadn't given the dragon pupils, but she knew, somehow, that it was staring, searching her mind for bright thoughts.

After a long moment, the statue turned and stepped into the street.

A dragon, Céleste thought faintly. *A dragon is walking across Boulevard Saint-Michel.*

The sculpture gleamed against the headlamps of passing automobiles; slashes of light brought out the bronze scales of its tail. This was an astonishing sight, but none of the drivers braked for it. Someone *did* honk at Céleste and Rafe when they followed the beast.

On the opposite sidewalk sat an alley she didn't recognize. This street wasn't rue de la Huchette or rue Saint-Séverin. It shouldn't have been there at all—the cast-iron flower lights of the nearby MÉTROPOLITAIN sign usually bloomed over storefronts, but tonight their orange rays illuminated a gap in the buildings.

The dragon's scales gleamed as it slipped through.

A few of Rafe's hairs were glowing too—impossibly silver—as if they'd just walked for years instead of minutes. He did not look old. More like a knife's edge under a midnight moon or a wish waiting at the bottom of a fountain.

Céleste wasn't sure which metaphor suited him more.

"Are you ready?" Silver hairs glinted as Rafe tilted his head after the dragon.

She followed the artist's gaze through the alleyway's shadows. A few steps in, and the buildings took on a *grown* quality, as if their architects had simply planted drawings in the earth, then let water and sunlight do the rest. Columns climbed like vines. The balconies' wrought iron wrapped around itself, blooming at the ends. Lamps with iridescent flames lined the lane, lighting doors with jeweled knobs. Things kept sprouting in the corner of her vision. A turret. A staircase. More doors.

The dragon of the Fontaine Saint-Michel trundled past these, its tail slithering down the leaf-covered lane, then curling around taloned paws as the statue halted by a green door. It had no emerald knob. The only decor was golden script written over the mantel: IN SOMNIS VERITAS.

The statue crouched beneath these words, waiting for Céleste and Rafe.

Was she ready?

She wanted to say yes, but how could anyone be ready for this?

"I—I have no idea."

"Well, the statue didn't eat you, so clearly that's not true." Rafe leaned in then. There was no lantern between them, but Céleste's cheeks still warmed. She felt him pick a bobby pin from her hair so that a long ribbon of it fell to her shoulder. "There! You see? Stardust."

She blinked, breathless again. A few of the strands tickling her collarbone were no longer white but opal, shining in the same way as Rafe's. The artist hadn't moved. The heat of his closeness had become glittering.

"What—what is happening?" Céleste reached up to grab a shining hair. Her heart trembled like an overstrung fiddle, and a rosy flush bloomed across her décolletage. "Don't you dare just say 'magic.'"

Rafe laughed and took a step backward into the alley. "Words cannot compare to what awaits us behind that door, mademoiselle. I'd much rather show you."

Céleste let him go a few steps farther before she decided to follow. She didn't want to appear too eager. She also wanted to make sure Rafe approached the dragon first. She was fairly certain he'd been joking about the statue eating people. Then again, she'd thought he'd been bullshitting about magic too. But the truth of it changed everything. How could you read someone else if you couldn't even predict the shape of their shadow? When their very edges kept shifting?

Currently, Rafe's silhouette seemed to be on its best behavior. There was no sign of a fox when he approached the dragon by the green door, and when he bowed, his shadow followed suit. The sculpture nodded back. The entrance to the salon swung open.

Laughter poured out onto the cobblestones, along with light, so much light. Most of this emanated from the salon's ceiling. Céleste's breath caught—again—when she saw its stained glass pattern. It was nothing like the dome in the Théâtre des Champs-Élysées. Instead of storm clouds, there were leafy patterns that kept on growing: green, green, gold, matching the feathers of the songbirds that soared just beneath the glass. There were dozens of these creatures, perched on candelabra that looked like twigs and hopping between plates of cakes covered in crystallized violets and flutes of purple, blue, pink drinks.

This was the sort of magic Sylvie wove through her stories, the kind you always hoped to spy in the corner of your eye or under the folded shadows of circus tents. To see it in the heart of Paris was... overwhelming.

Céleste paused on the threshold, trying to swallow her shock, but it was impossible. It was *all* impossible! The chandelier of butterflies fluttering over revelers' heads. The way the wallpaper's flowers grew and unfurled. How smokers puffed out rings shaped like Spanish galleons or Pegasus. How these floated past bubbles filled with swimming goldfish. Or the fact that a woman by the bar was wearing a gown of petals that bloomed and shed and bloomed again. There were more decadent dresses on the dancers who pushed through the velvet drapes in the far corner, exiting a room filled with a song Céleste had never heard before, yet had always known.

Everything here had the dizzying flavor of déjà vu.

Even the colors Céleste had no name for, those hues no paint knife could mix. The drink Rafe placed into her hand was one such shade.

"Here," he offered. "This helps make everything a little easier to swallow. My first night here, I was practically petrified on that settee over there until I had my first sip of sunset."

She studied the slender glass. The fizzing liquid began to settle into a nominal lavender, then a violent violet, then a purple so rich, it could pass as black. "Sunset?"

"That's what mine tastes like." There was a glass in Rafe's hand too. Its contents glowed orange, much like the fur of the luminescent tiger that was prowling around the room. "Everyone's welcome aperitif is different. Your flavor might be sugared plums or a sonata or a horseback ride through a frosty field. There's no telling until you try."

"Sylvie tells me you should never accept food or drink in the other world, lest it trap you. She's an expert on fairies."

"Still young enough to see them, I'd wager." Rafe tapped his flute against hers, then tipped his glass to his lips. "This drink won't trap you though. It's meant to do the opposite."

"Rafe García! There you are! All dressed in bruises!" A line of winged horses, composed of cinnamon smoke, blew over Céleste's head and trotted in a circle. The man who'd made them was walking toward the couple, his silk robes swishing. The way he sashayed made Céleste think of Honoré—because it was so different and yet so similar to the way her friend moved through the world. Defying its every expectation. "And who is this magnificent creature at your side? Are you sure she isn't a figment of someone's imagination?"

He would have kept on speaking forever, perhaps, if Rafe hadn't interrupted. "Good evening to you too, Jean."

"Jean Maurice Eugène Clément Cocteau." The bracelets on the new man's wrists and ankles matched his singsong voice. His lips—which looked to have some rouge on them—pursed as he took another drag of his cigarette. Soon a second herd of pegasi circled the trio's heads like a merry-go-round. "But what in heaven's name happened to your dress, *ma chère*? Did you stumble across a herd of ravenous goats?"

"Worse," Rafe interjected. "We went to a ballet."

"Ah—*The Rite of Spring*! I was commissioned to draw the poster for that show, you know. What a riot! Have you caught wind of the rumors, dear Rafe? They're saying there was a duel between Sancts backstage!"

The back of Céleste's neck prickled—with shadows and feathers and whispers of magic. "Sancts?"

"He means the magicians," Rafe clarified.

"What a dull term! You make it sound as if they simply pull rabbits from hats!" Jean scoffed, then turned to Céleste. "Magicians are mere men. Sancts are so much more than that, *ma chère*. They are wings on holy buildings and black-cat fears. Hieroglyphs and wives' tales! They are... transcendent. At least, La Fée Verte is. Behold! Our muse!"

He gestured toward the bar, where flutes had been stacked in a pyramid, overflowing with the color-changing drink. Just behind that, Céleste saw a figure wrapped in a dress of emerald feathers. *Woman* was the wrong word for her. *Angel* would have been a slur too, even though her face seemed to be filigreed with gold. She was a very bright thing indeed. The skin around her eyes was shining, and her arms were sheathed in bracelets, and her laughter belonged in a champagne glass. Everyone around the Sanct seemed inebriated. Even Rafe was staring wistfully. Céleste herself felt a strange *twist* in her chest when she saw the green gown wasn't a gown at all but a pair of massive wings. When La Fée Verte unfolded these, songbirds came to roost, slipping into the Sanct's larger feathers, *becoming* them.

"Ah!" Rafe jumped, and Céleste did too, when she saw the fiery tiger had joined their group. Its tail twitched over the rug, spilling harmless sparks as it watched the trotting pegasi. "I see someone has been quoting Blake again!"

"Is . . . that the tiger's name?" she asked, uncertain.

More flying horses spilled from Jean's lips when he laughed. "Oh, *ma chère*! He's referring to William Blake. The English poet. You know the line, 'tyger, tyger burning bright'?" One of his hairs began to sear. Stunningly gold. All the nearby songbirds turned their heads toward it. "Here, if you say something with enough conviction, you can bring it to life." Jean plucked the shining strand with practiced fingers, then threw it to the floor. Quick as a *FLASH*! A real blinding light.

When Céleste managed to blink away her tears, she saw a second jungle cat with flaming white fur.

More than just a metaphor.

"Voilà!" Jean bowed, and the green birds that had gathered around them flew off. "A tyger!"

"I wouldn't recommend plagiarism though," Rafe added in a low voice. "La Fée Verte has little patience for the practice. There's no power in it."

Bracelets chimed as Jean waved his hand. "She'll forgive me! I'm one of her most prodigious imaginers! But back to the real problem—you cannot wear such a drab gown, *ma chère*! We must dress you in something divine! What do you say? Silk? Glitter? Embroidery that twists into a tattoo? Don't be shy! We're all Cinderellas here!"

"My name is Céleste," she finally managed.

"Celestial! It suits you! Should we conjure you a gown of stars, perhaps?" Another one of Jean's brown hairs began to glimmer. "The fabric would be dark taffeta, and opals would form the constellations—and—*and* every few minutes, they'd ignite!"

A songbird swooped down from the chandelier, snatching the bright hair in its beak and tugging, out, out, so Céleste could see glimpses of Jean's dream dress burning through the gold. She could only imagine what Honoré would say if the other Enchantress saw her wearing it. "I'm not sure fire and taffeta are the best combination, Monsieur Cocteau..."

"Fire?" Jean shook his head, and the bird flew off—gold streaming from its beak. "What fire? Forgive me, I lost my train of thought. Well, really, I lost the thought." His sharp chin turned back toward the bar, where La Fée Verte's wings were fanned out wide. She had her hand out too, welcoming the songbird as it dropped Jean's dream into her palm. "It must have been beautiful..."

The green bird slipped back into the Sanct's feathers as she held the idea up to the ceiling's stained glass light, the way a jeweler at Mellerio dits Meller might examine a diamond.

Céleste was watching closely too. Close enough to see that the bracelets on her arms weren't bracelets at all. They were ideas. When La Fée Verte turned, they shimmered with dozens of dreamlike scenes. Jean's flaming dress soon joined them.

"What kind of muse *takes* ideas?" Céleste wondered.

"Our kind," Rafe said softly.

"C'est la vie!" Jean let out a sigh. "Such is the price of an evening here. All gods require sacrifices. Better lighting up her wrists than locked inside our skulls, no?"

Céleste wasn't so sure. Magic was real. She knew this now, beyond a doubt, and she also knew that any real thing could be stolen. The true question was *how*. Did Rafe mean for them to walk up to La Fée Verte and twist the thoughts from her arms?

If so, he'd chosen the wrong Enchantress.

But the other thief made no move toward the bar.

He strolled, instead, toward a wall of velvet curtains and pulled them back, revealing a ballroom where the floor had been enchanted to look like a night sky, where dancers created their own constellations with each bright step. "Come, mademoiselle. Let us dream the night away."

The Seer of the Seine

Beneath the arches of the Saint-Michel Bridge, you will find a sight that raises the hair on your arms. According to the older stories, this would be where trolls lived, asking for tolls of blood and bones.

Not so, in Paris.

If you go down the algae-lined stairs to the edge of the river, you will find a boat that should not float, with rotten boards and a rusted roof, where purple smoke plumes through a pipe, turning just like the strings of beads hanging over the cabin door. These twist even harder when the Seer of the Seine exits. The skin around her eyes is scaly and silver—much like a fish belly. The rest is covered in wrinkles, but the lines sit strangely. They do not match her smile as she invites you on board. They do not agree with the way her eyes narrow when she studies your palm, when she places a finger on your life line and lifts it like a string. She takes a small pair of scissors, *snips* off the end, and adds that future to her own flesh. Such is the price of a platitude: A few days here, a few months there. A firstborn. A second. Can you really miss what will never be? Do you want to know your future badly enough to hand it over to someone else?

The Seer of the Seine knows that you do.

She knows a lot of things.

She knows stars and cards and crystal balls. She knows the river too, understands shit can be read much like tea leaves. This is why she casts her net out into the brown waters every day, pulling in bottles and boots and twisting eels. These make slapping sounds on her splintering deck as she picks through the other offerings: coins, clay pipes, a bloated bird carcass.

The Seer pauses when she sees the opera glove.

There is a red stain on the palm.

She holds it to her nose and sniffs.

She brings it to her mouth and licks.

"Interesting," she mumbles to herself. "Very interesting." Most of the eels start to fall still, but one manages to splash back into the Seine, disappearing into the muddy water. The Seer watches her river with careful eyes. She knows an omen when she sees one.

She understands that the currents are shifting.

Chapter 5

The Vault of Dreams

It's easy to lose yourself in magic.

Céleste could see why, as she walked across the midnight dance floor, slipping into a designers' tent, where moving wooden mannequins showed off outfits made of mist and rainbows. Jean got left behind here—but not before he'd dressed everyone, choosing a pair of curled ram's horns for himself. Rafe refused his own set of towering antlers—"I'd rather *not* get snagged in a chandelier, thank you very much"—but he did accept a purple velvet suit. Céleste ended up wearing a gown that looked like an oil spill. The fabric was dark but fluid, shedding iridescent droplets while she explored. Such a trail might be useful for finding her way back out of the salon. Its halls were labyrinthine. Tangled, sometimes with ivy, other times with lines of verse, and still other times with ribbons. It was easy to get turned around when architects kept conjuring new rooms and rearranging doors. Easy too, when poets asked jasmine to bloom like stars from the ceiling, where acrobats swung from vines and artists painted wings to help other revelers reach them. The deeper they ventured into the salon, the wilder it felt, like a midsummer forest, complete with bacchanal clearings and birds, birds everywhere, as green as leaves. Their beaks and talons wriggled with gold. The imaginers below seemed too immersed in their thoughts to care that their sentences faded or that their heads were a few hairs lighter.

The songbirds streaked like small comets overhead.

Rafe followed their shining trail.

Céleste followed him through a garden where ice sculptures sparkled beside fires. Past a library where writers talked in plush chairs, watching their stories take shape in the overhead smoke. Over a desert with dunes made of diamond dust. She finally stopped to empty her shoes, spilling jewels on the floor and gasping, not at their splendor, but with how weary she was. There was no room in her lungs for air anymore. There was a faint metallic taste on her tongue that had nothing to do with the gold-dusted cakes everyone else was eating.

"How much farther?" she asked Rafe.

"You'll drive yourself mad, asking that question here," he told her.

"As if I don't already feel that way," Céleste muttered. "Following a strange man into a maze of poems..."

"Touché." Rafe scuffed some of the diamonds with his boot. "I only meant that the salon shapes itself around whoever attends, so the maze is different every evening. I usually just follow the birds until they start circling... That's how I know I'm close."

Céleste didn't ask him to elaborate. She'd seen enough to know where they were going. Just that one glimpse of La Fée Verte laughing behind the bar had shown her how similar the two of them were. Not the magic part, of course, but the show. The custom cocktails, the flaming wildcats, the dewdrop dresses, the (probably) fake diamonds... these were all diversions. Something to distract the Sanct's marks while she took them for all they were worth. What did the green fairy *do* with the ideas she seized? Besides turn them into jewelry?

If the Sanct was anything like Céleste, she'd have a stash...

And if Céleste was going to steal from that stash, she'd have to stop her gown from leaking everywhere. The skirt's slick fabric pulled apart without much fuss as she knotted the ends around her ankles. Voilà! *Pants!* She could make pockets too; all the better for hiding her spoils.

Several songbirds passed as Rafe helped Céleste to her feet, their emerald feathers soaring over the field of sunflowers that lay ahead. Whoever had imagined the flowers made their petals shine like their namesake, and they flared even brighter when La Fée Verte's flock started to swirl, around and around, then down.

"Ah..." Rafe pointed at them. "That's it. We should cloak ourselves."

"Cloak ourselves?" Céleste asked. "With what?"

The other thief looked down at the diamonds he'd scuffed. "You'll have to share my shadow this evening."

His silhouette began to stretch over the jewels. There was no fox this time as it joined Céleste, as it rose, up her legs, up her arms, over her head like a mourner's veil. She could still see the field around them, but its flowers had become a few shades dimmer, the air a few degrees cooler. There was something warmer as well—the fizz of a just-struck match.

Rafe's eyes remained as bright as embers when they met hers.

"Stay close," he whispered.

As if she had any other option. "So this trick makes us invisible?"

"Invisible enough," Rafe said, as he started pushing into the field of flowers. "The shadow itself is still there, so we have to walk through other shadows to stay hidden. That part can be incredibly irksome, but it works. The birds have never noticed my presence."

Céleste couldn't say the same. This man's shadow felt like silk—smooth but also shocking, if you touched it the wrong way. She stayed less than a step behind him as they crept through the field, zigzagging over silhouettes cast by hundreds of floral suns.

The birds left shadows too.

There was an entire cloud of them swirling around a staircase, darting down its spiral steps one by one. Céleste and Rafe followed them deep into the earth—deeper than the sunflower roots, deeper than the Seine or the Métropolitain. There was a cave at the bottom, but its stash was nothing at all like the Enchantresses' Bank of Bones. Chimes dripped from the ceiling like stalactites—swaying gently into each other as the birds flew beneath. No, Céleste realized as she studied the layers upon layers of gold.

Not chimes.

This was a Vault of Dreams.

The birds had brought their guests' ideas here...where they'd been strung up from the ceiling like drying herbs. Scenes shimmered from the closest ones. Storybook slivers: A foraging reindeer sprouted lanterns from its antlers. Snakes turned into swords before becoming snakes again. There were cities that grew taller in moonlight and ships that could carry a man into the stars themselves. On and on these wonders stretched, impossible and achingly beautiful. There had to be thousands of them.

Ripe for the taking.

"Shiny, no?" Rafe plucked an idea from the ceiling. "It's enough to make a magpie out of anyone."

It was. She felt that strange *twist*—again like wings—in her chest when Rafe handed her the chime. She studied the scene inside more closely. A reindeer with brassy fur grazed in a meadow of fiery flowers, and every time it swallowed one of the flaming blossoms, the teardrop lamps hanging from its antlers flickered brighter. Beauty for beauty's sake.

But it had to be for something else too...

Why else would La Fée Verte go to so much trouble to collect them?

"How do you turn an idea's power into magic?" Céleste wondered.

Monsieur Cocteau had broken his hair to conjure the tyger, but she didn't need a whimsical reindeer. She needed to heal herself. Should she wave the dream as if it were a wand? *Abracadabra?* Should she swallow it like some flaming sword? Those were acts she'd seen magicians do...

But Sancts weren't magicians.

According to Jean, they weren't even human.

"Alas, I cannot," Rafe told her. "That's what makes a Sanct a Sanct. That and the masque of light around their temples—it flashes whenever they cast larger spells. Mostly. My employer is a little less luminous."

"He's a Sanct too?"

Rafe nodded and tugged down a second dream: snowflakes swirling across a blue-glass beach. "He doesn't host a salon, but he still wants ideas. My task is to forge as many of these dreams as possible and take the originals to rue des Ombres."

Céleste knew the best jobs were pulled when you placed something substantial in your mark's hands—a deed for imaginary land or a just-dried canvas. That way they wouldn't realize they'd been left with nothing.

She stared down at the flaming reindeer.

She was used to holding a brush or a pen, but this…

"How the hell do you forge a dream?"

"Well, first you have to stop swearing so much," he said, lifting the snowstorm between them.

Céleste raised her eyebrows. "It sounds as if Monsieur Cocteau should have given you some pearls to clutch."

"Pearls would be tame, compared to most of Jean's accessories." A look of amusement crossed Rafe's face, made even cooler by the snowy blue shine of the imagining. "Personally, mademoiselle, I don't give a damn about your vocabulary, but copying dreams is just like tracing a signature—you place yourself in the signer's shoes and imagine what that person was thinking. I find that curses rarely conjure dreams."

She supposed that made sense. "So how do you conjure yourself a copy?"

"I think of what the original imaginer must have been imagining, and then I say it out loud: *blue beach, blue sky, blue blizzard, blue forever and ever, a moment frozen in time…*"

One of Rafe's hairs began to glow, filling their joined shadow tent with new light.

Sapphire sand.

Ice in the waves.

Snow howling.

He pulled this from his head and strung it from the ceiling. The original went into his velvet suit pocket. He nodded at the dream in Céleste's hands. "You try."

"There was once a reindeer with lamps on its head." She paused to check the ends of her own hair, but none seemed to be glowing.

"You have to believe what you're saying," Rafe told her. "Believe it in your bones."

Céleste shut her eyes and let her thoughts carry her back to her grave, to her easel and her canvas, to those evenings when she got carried away in colors while Honoré sharpened her knives and Sylvie made up stories for her fairy books. This reindeer would fit well in those tattered pages...

"The beast stood in a field of fire"—or so Sylvie would say—"with flowers in its teeth and lights in its horns. It grazed there every evening to keep the darkness at bay."

"There!" Rafe's voice lit up the space between them.

A hair did too, searing over Céleste's shoulder.

She tugged it free. The scene inside wasn't a perfect match—her reindeer had darker fur and was more aggressive about ripping flowers from their roots—but the forgery was passable enough to make Rafe smile.

"You *are* good," he said.

She slipped the original idea into her pocket and looked back through Rafe's shadow, at how the cave stretched out, out, probably all the way to the stone quarries of Montparnasse in the south of the city. Maybe it went even farther than that, all the way to Versailles...

"Your employer wants *all* these ideas?"

"He doesn't know *what* he wants," Rafe said. "Every night he sends me here, and every night I forge as many ideas as I can, and every morning... well, he's insatiable." He moved on to the next set of chimes: A lion with a mane of flames. A sky with more than two moons. "I've been doing this for five years now."

"How do you still have hair?"

"It grows back by dawn, if you drink the digestif before you leave. Otherwise, Paris's wigmakers would be incredibly wealthy."

They do well enough by me, Céleste mused, before she thought up a story for the second moon in that strange sky. It was the same color as her star-kissed hair, but the shape reminded her of an eye, as if the night itself had been startled awake.

They worked for a long time in the cavern, replacing dreams with glimmers from their own heads. Despite Rafe's assurances, Céleste still feared she'd be bald by the end. So much of her hair was strung from the ceiling, showing floating mountains and underwater cities. The actual imaginings dragged down her pockets, so when she ascended the spiral staircase, her pants tolled like bells. Hopefully anyone listening would think this was a part of the original design.

Rafe halted when they reached the top step. "Shit," he said.

Her heart hammered, expecting an onslaught of green wings, but when she looked around, she realized La Fée Verte's flock had thinned. No more ideas were being brought to the Vault of Dreams. There was no more sunflower field either. A thick fog settled where the stalks had been.

"What is it?"

"I lost track of time."

"That must happen a lot when you wear a broken watch," Céleste pointed out.

"I never said my watch was broken. Merely that it doesn't tell time." Both fob chains rattled as he pulled out the timepiece and started to wind it. Hands spun. Gears clicked. And then Rafe García disappeared.

His shadow vanished too.

Céleste gasped as the fog around her brightened and swirled. "Rafe?"

She waited for one moment and then another, but he did not return, so she walked to where the clouds were thinnest. There were some imaginers lounging on settees, their limbs as limp as rags, but the rooms were no longer bursting. Dancers were busy unlacing their slippers, and the cake platters were down to crumbs. More mist was growing from the edges of the walls and creeping over the carpet, so that she couldn't follow the oily trail of her gown. It would've met a dead end anyway. There was only one hallway remaining, siphoning guests to the front room. Its wallpaper flowers had furled, and the butterfly chandelier was no longer fluttering.

She still did not see Rafe.

Jean was there, standing by a mannequin from the designers' tent. All the wooden figures were lined up by the front door, wearing the revelers' discarded clothes. The young man was in the process of changing—a challenge considering his ram horns. "*Ma chère!* There you are! You vanished before I could fashion you a crown of flowers! Black lilies to go with—oh—" He put a hand to his chest in mock horror. "What on earth did you do to *this* dress?"

"I turned the skirts into trousers," she told him.

"Why?"

"Why not?"

"Nothing breathes in pants." Jean grunted as he buttoned his opera outfit back on. "I would wear dresses every day of the week if I could!"

"Don't you?" Céleste nodded at the robes he'd discarded over the mannequin's stiff shoulder.

"I said '*day*'—" The young man paused, staring just over Céleste's shoulder.

"I think women's trousers are a wonderful idea."

She didn't have to turn to know who spoke.

There was a glow that grew brighter as La Fée Verte stepped around to study Céleste's outfit. "I've been trying to plant the concept for years. You wouldn't think the idea of pants for women would be so difficult to grow, but Paul Poiret is the only one of my designers who's done anything about it in the waking world."

La Fée Verte was not wearing trousers. She wasn't even wearing a dress—her body was covered in a thin shift of mist. Clouds wisped along her curves, and she didn't seem to care that the rosy pink of her areolas was easily visible. What could have been lewd was, in fact, the exact opposite. This woman knew how to wear power, even if she wasn't clad in much else.

Between the two of them, Céleste felt like the naked one, especially as the Sanct kept staring. "I like the flow of the bottom into the top—all one piece. It's clever. Are you a couturier?"

"A painter," Céleste answered.

"Is that so?" The bracelets on La Fée Verte's arms flashed when she crossed them. A songbird landed on her shoulder, then slipped into her wing. "I'm not sure I saw any of your work tonight."

You might if you go down to your vault. Céleste tried not to think this, tried not to move, tried not to search every shadow she could for signs of Rafe. "I went looking for the landscape room, but I never found it. Or maybe I did, and I just didn't know I was walking through someone else's painting..."

"You'd know if it was Picasso's," Jean offered. "Cubes everywhere! But no one could blame you for wandering instead of wondering on your inaugural evening. My first night was a whirlwind. Quite literally. Top hats and tutus flew everywhere. I feared La Fée Verte would never invite me back, but now she cannot live without me."

A smile tugged the Sanct's lips. "You exaggerate."

"And that is why you love me!" said Jean.

"I do," La Fée Verte told him.

This mark was nothing like the others Céleste stole from: men flushed with Veuve Clicquot and their own importance. She wasn't sure what to do with the softness in the Sanct's voice.

Even Jean hesitated. The corners of his eyes glimmered, but his voice held too much hope for this to be tears. "Enough to let me see past sunrise?"

La Fée Verte's own gaze hardened, then flashed. Two glasses of silvery liquid appeared in her hands. Jean's face fell when she handed him the digestif, but he lifted it to his lips without complaint.

Céleste did too. The drink tasted like the final page of a book falling shut or that last slant of sun escaping through drawn curtains.

The actual fog around them was growing thicker, filling empty plates and misting over furniture. It started to envelop La Fée Verte as well—so that she looked as if she belonged on the ceiling of the Sistine Chapel. "Come back another midnight, and I'll show you the way to the painters' wing," she promised. "Perhaps you could draw up another skirtless dress. For now, I must say au revoir to you and that beautiful ensemble."

She stepped back into the cloud.

Jean sighed.

Céleste sighed too, only hers held relief. She could still escape with everyone else's dreams and try to find Rafe in the alleyway—

"Wait!" Jean caught her by the wrist and waved at the mannequin that wore Céleste's old dress, which now resembled a wilted piece of lettuce. "As much as it pains me to say, you should change back into your old outfit."

"Here?"

"There's no time for modesty, and no need, really."

Céleste might as well have been another mannequin where this man was concerned. It wasn't modesty that made her hesitate, but it was a good excuse. "I couldn't possibly!"

"Suit yourself." Jean gathered up the green dress. "We must take the goat gown with us, at least."

She saw the flaw in her plan as soon as they stepped into the alley. The fog was rolling through here too, threading alongside vines and snuffing out the opal flames of the lanterns. There was little need for their light—the sky overhead was going through the shades of Céleste's first drink in reverse.

Jean stayed a few steps ahead, and Céleste did not think it wise to linger. She didn't want to stop on the main boulevard either, even though the Fontaine Saint-Michel's statues were back on their pedestals—as stiff as bronze should be. Jean's horns matched the dragon's. The rest of his features were tauter than an acrobat's tightrope. It was the look of a man bracing himself for a fall.

"Here." He tossed her gown back to her. "I like to make it to the bridge if I can. It is the most terribly beautiful view in all the world..."

Again, Jean seemed to be exaggerating.

When Céleste joined him on the Pont Saint-Michel, facing east, she found a fine-enough scene. The kind she might have tried to paint when she was younger. *Paris, on the Edge of Waking.* Where the bready fumes of boulangeries mixed with lavender clouds, while booksellers opened their sage-colored booths along the banks of the

Seine. The edges of the river were turning molten, and soon the bells of Notre-Dame would sing along its length—five strikes for the break of day.

Even with his ram's horns, Jean did not look out of place as he leaned over the balustrade. Another few shades of gray, and he could've passed for one of the city's statues.

"You know," he told Céleste as she joined him, "you really should change—"

That was when the sun struck.

It hit Jean's horns first. Their tips began to burn—sparks, becoming ash in the golden light. This floated from the bridge, drifting over the boats moored at the quai, over the unconcerned heads of the booksellers, over zinc rooftops.

The oil-spill outfit was next.

Céleste swore as dreams spilled from her vanished pockets. The sunlight did not seem to burn these, and they didn't break on the sidewalk either, only rolled toward Jean's shoes. The man made no move to help gather them. Smoke drifted from his head—in the shape of phantom horns—as he stared out over the Seine. There was no fog on the river, but it had settled in Jean Cocteau's eyes. Their light had been snuffed out.

It reminded her of the way Honoré slept sometimes.

Lids open. Seeing nothing but nightmares.

This certainly felt like a bad dream, standing on one of Paris's busiest bridges in her underwear. Céleste swore again, tugging the green dress over her head. "You could have warned me with a little more detail, Monsieur Cocteau!"

He blinked at the sound of his name. A frown twisted his lips. "I'm sorry, who are you? And more importantly, *ma chère*, what happened to your dress?"

"We went to a salon—"

"Did we?" Jean shook his head, as if he'd tried to reach for the memory and found only cobwebs instead. "It must have been wonderful fun."

You have no idea, Céleste thought, watching ash float over balconies full of fluttering laundry, moved by the same wind. Her companion did not seem to see the glowing motes. He didn't notice the stolen dreams she'd gathered either.

So why did Céleste know to hold on to them? Why hadn't the sun struck her in the same way? She recognized others from La Fée Verte's salon—clothes rumpled, eyes dulled—but they did not recognize her. They moved through the dawn like sleepwalkers. There was still no sign of Rafe. Had he forgotten about their evening together too? Or had he abandoned her on purpose?

Either way, she was stuck holding magic she could not use, could not take back, could not—

"Would you like to borrow my jacket?" Jean was already slipping out of it, handing her his tailored overcoat. It had not one, not two, but *three* pockets. He raised an eyebrow as Céleste stuffed the dreams into them—motions that came across as rifling. "There should be enough francs in there for a taxi fare too, if you need it."

Now *that* was a thought. Rafe had mentioned a street, where he took the stolen imaginings every morning: rue des Ombres. Céleste had never heard of it before, but perhaps if she tried to take a taxi, she could find the Sanct who'd pay her for these dreams. It wasn't rubies she'd ask for, not when her lips were already so red without rouge...

She still had a chance to heal herself.

Céleste thanked Jean, then made her way to the opposite end of the bridge, where a Renault AG was waiting at the corner. Its driver seemed used to strange customers. Especially at this hour. He didn't bat an eyelid at Céleste's jacket, only took a longer drag of his cigarette and let out a stream of ordinary smoke.

"Where to?"

"Rue des Ombres." Céleste slurred her voice just enough to make the man believe she was drunk, because what other person would ask to be driven to the *Street of Shadows*?

She knew the request was foolish.

She thought she knew what his answer would be too.

"Sorry, mademoiselle." Sparks scattered as the cab driver stubbed out his cigarette, but he kept speaking. "That's a trap street. Mapmakers put them on their maps to catch copycats. Can't take you to a made-up place."

Her heart pounded beneath a pocket full of dreams. "But you know where rue des Ombres is?" She tried to bite back her excitement. "Where it... would be?"

The driver shrugged. "It shows up on the maps next to Place de la Concorde, and that's real enough. I can take you there. S'long as you can pay."

She was too tired to negotiate, and at this point, she did not care what the fare was.

Céleste nodded.

Chapter 6

Deal with a Devil

The ride was short—downriver to the eighth arrondissement—but it was also bumpy, and by the time Céleste stepped out of the narrow cab onto Place de la Concorde, she felt rattled. The square was one of the widest-open spaces in the city. It had no steeples or trees. Only a lonely obelisk rose into the morning sky, absolutely out of place. She saw plenty of wings carved into its hieroglyphs, but that power belonged to a different land, to the cursed pyramids Rafe had so casually mentioned...

There was no sign of a street in the obelisk's shadow.

No sign of a magical street anywhere.

"Excuse me, but do you know where on the maps rue des Ombres was drawn?" she asked, as she paid the cab driver.

He took her money with the tilt of an eyebrow, then looked to the north, where two identical buildings bookended the square. "It cuts straight through the Hôtel de Crillon over there. I'm afraid it's a dead end."

Céleste felt afraid too as she made her way toward the hotel, trying not to dwell on driver's last words: *Dead end. Dead end. Dead end.*

She halted in front of the Hôtel de Crillon. The building had once been a palace, and it had regal bones—Corinthian columns and stone garlands. There were arches all along the ground floor, where inset windows offered glimpses of the lobby's plush rugs and potted plants. One arch drew Céleste's eye... not because the sight inside was splendorous, but because there was no view at all. It sat—black—at the center of the building. She was only sure that the archway had a way through because she saw a stray cat slip out.

No.

Not a cat.

A fox made of shadows...

At the café, it had been flat, shade on a wall, but there was more form to the fox now as it wrapped around Céleste's ankles and circled back toward the arch.

"You bastard!" she hissed as she followed.

Rafe was waiting in the arch, leaning by a placard that read RUE DES [redacted]. The last part was a scorch mark—smudged with the same soot that darkened the rest of the place. "Technically no. My mother and father were married—"

"You abandoned me!"

"Again, technically no. I lost you, and by the time I realized you weren't in my shadow, it was too late to go back inside the salon."

Most of that was a lie, judging by the fact he'd had time to change. Rafe was no longer wearing the velvet suit Jean Cocteau had conjured for him, but he wasn't wearing his opera outfit either. "You couldn't have waited for me by the fountain?"

"No." His glance darted back toward the bald morning light of Place de la Concorde, as he sank even deeper into the darkness of the arch. "The sunlight burns away everyone's memories..." His eyes narrowed back on her, so different from Jean's lost expression. "How did you manage to get here?"

"I took a taxi."

"A *taxi*?" Rafe's laughter rang around the arch.

"Yes. How did you get here?"

"I flew."

She laughed back, until Rafe pushed off the wall and his shadow leapt onto his shoulders—flaring from its fox shape into two whispering wings.

The joke's on me, then.

There were no feathers that turned into songbirds, but Rafe's wings were still breathtaking. They shimmered—not with light but the way her oil-spill dress had. Shadows swirled down the other thief's back, in every single shade of gray, before washing out into the surrounding darkness. There was plenty of it. Rue des Ombres seemed to be more of a tunnel than a proper street, stretching into what should have been Hôtel de Crillon. Céleste couldn't see what was there instead. Her eyes were still adjusting from the daylight she'd stood in just moments before.

Rafe seemed to be taking extra pains to avoid the sun. His boots stayed firmly in the shade. Only the tip of a wing reached out to where Céleste was standing, unraveling like a stream of smoke. It was different from the burn of Jean's ram horns.

"I was with Monsieur Cocteau when the sun rose. Everything between us burned away."

Rafe nodded. "It's that way every morning."

"So why didn't I forget?"

"Because you aren't Enlightened. I thought you might be, before I studied your hand, but all I saw there was paint . . . no cut . . ." Rafe's mouth tightened. "Jean Cocteau could see magic last night because he had La Fée Verte's blessing. That never lasts past dawn, but there are others who see beyond the sunrise."

"Children."

"Most people glimpse magic before they grow up, and most see magic in their final days too."

This was no shocking revelation. Rafe was telling Céleste what she already knew, but his saying so out loud made the tunnel's darkness shift. When she coughed, the sound collapsed in on her. She pushed aside several dreams to retrieve Jean's pocket square, which looked as if it had never been used for a sniffle, much less to sop up blood.

There was more than before.

Much more.

"Consumption?" Rafe asked.

"Your guess is as good as mine." She failed to say this dryly. "I haven't been to a doctor. I didn't even start coughing up blood until yesterday."

The other thief's face darkened then. "Doctors won't help you," he said.

She'd figured as much.

"La Fée Verte won't either." Rafe's hand wandered past his split lip, to the gleaming skin of his punched eye. "But my employer has the means to keep you alive, if that's what you want."

"Who *wouldn't* want that?" Céleste wondered.

There was a shivering silence, and Rafe's wings started to drip off his back, down to his boots. His shadow began slithering into the tunnel. His shoulders tensed. Céleste sensed a deeper change too—something that suddenly made it hard to recall the artist's smile. Never mind all the moments she'd mentally sketched it.

"My employer can be . . . difficult," he said haltingly. "You're in a unique position, coming to him like this. Don't accept the first terms he offers—"

"I almost sold the Eiffel Tower for scrap metal, once," she told him. "I know how to negotiate."

"You know nothing here." Rafe's shadow kept stretching down the tunnel. His lips pulled thin as he turned to follow it. "We should hurry. He's growing impatient. I'd advise you to put that pocket square away," he said over his shoulder. "And whatever you do, don't ask his name."

Céleste folded the bloodied handkerchief and tucked it back into Jean's jacket with care. She hurried along the tunnel's scorched stones, catching Rafe before he reached the door at the sunless end. There were no golden words inscribed on this mantel. Its wood looked unpainted, and there was a keyhole that kept changing shapes, letting out strange slants of light in various colors and shades.

Rafe did not knock.

His shadow slipped through the keyhole instead, and its shapes stopped rotating—pausing to let out an amber shiver of candles.

The lock turned.

The door opened.

Céleste did not think she was inside the Hôtel de Crillon when she stepped over the threshold. The place was ornate, but a good deal of the furniture was covered with white sheets, which were in turn covered with drips of wax. Candles all over the room had burned to their stubs, and most of the light was now coming from the fireplace. A figure sat in a wing-back chair by the dying flames. Hidden from view. There was a decanter of wine on the adjoining side table, paired with a mostly drained glass.

Their employer had been drinking red. Expensive, by the looks of it. Legs of wine stuck to the sides of the glass, dripping back down into emptiness. Instead of pouring himself another serving, the man in the chair was spinning a globe. Lazily. With a single glove-covered hand. This sight set Céleste on edge, and she couldn't say why until the sphere drifted to a stop...

The lines were all wrong.

This world looked nothing like the one her childhood tutors had been hired to show her: France, Britain, Germany, Austria-Hungary, the Russian Empire, the Ottoman one. Yes, the continents were the same, but they'd been divvied into shapes no atlas would display. Into colors that went well beyond grassy green or parched brown. Blue, orange, red, purple, black. There were splashes of gold as well—one of the largest haloed the City of Light.

She found herself searching for the Balkans then.

These countries were covered in darkness as deep as Rafe's shadow, which now slithered across the Turkish rug. The artist himself acted almost as if he were being pulled by it, coming to a stop only when he reached the wing-back chair.

"You are late." His employer spoke French, but the words sounded archaic. As dusty as the rest of the room. "You should consider yourself fortunate that I'm in such a convivial mood. I haven't enjoyed a theatre performance like that since Madame Lavigne's last opera."

Rafe's gaze flickered—oh so briefly—toward the decanter.

Céleste felt another cough claw up her throat. She tried not to reach for the pocket square. She choked. She swallowed.

Even the fire felt cold in the silence that followed.

"You are not alone," said the figure in the chair.

"No," Rafe answered. "I found another forger to help with our search. She's good. Even better than me, I'd wager."

"Oh? What *would* you wager, Monsieur García? The remainder of your name? That silly watch? I'm afraid the stakes are much higher than that." A finger landed on the globe, exactly where Paris should be, and started the world spinning again. "Come, mademoiselle, let me look at you."

The globe kept swiveling, its borders blurring when Céleste approached the chair.

People did not look this perfect. They didn't have eyes like just-cut sapphires or hair as bright as turning wheat or skin pale enough to be gypsum. Perhaps that was what made Rafe's employer seem sculpted? Or was it the stoniness of his face, a total lack of emotion that made him look even more like a statue than the Fontaine Saint-Michel's dragon?

He had pupils, at least.

There were other markings around his eyes—much like La Fée Verte's—but where hers burned gold, his appeared charred. So black, it would look like a mask, if Céleste squinted. She didn't dare break her gaze with this man though.

Her stare kept wanting to slip.

Her fingers did not itch for charcoal—this time—but the pocket square.

"I see." The Sanct in the chair steepled his own fingers together. "Beware your bleeding heart, Monsieur García. You won't last long if you listen to its every whim."

"I am not a whim," growled Céleste, who was so very tired of men talking around her. "I'm not a figment of anyone's imagination either, but I'm damn good at stealing them." She pulled a dream from her pocket—the reindeer again—and offered it to Rafe's employer.

He seemed . . . wary . . . as he took the imagining. The beast in the clearing stiffened too; its lanterns dimmed, and the flowers by its hooves sputtered. When the Sanct held the scene to his face, his masque looked more like a void, like that space between stars no one stares at too closely.

Céleste could hardly bear to watch either when he carelessly tossed the dream into the fire. "This is not what I'm looking for," he said.

"I have more." She knew better than to pull them from her coat pockets. "I can go back to the salon and steal as many ideas as you'd like—"

"A bit difficult to do if you're dead." The Sanct cut her off, his voice as sharp as a guillotine. "But I suppose that's what you're wishing to avoid. Your desperation does you credit, Mademoiselle Artois, and you do come so highly recommended."

Céleste bristled at this.

How did he know her name?

And...was that her opera glove he was wearing? There was a stain at the center, in the same shape as that first cough, though most of its color had been washed out. The fabric dripped with river water when the Sanct held out his hand. "Perhaps you and I can strike a deal? Dreams for days?"

She stared at her lost glove.

Rafe was looking at it too, the slightest trace of a frown on his face.

"How many days?" Céleste asked.

"How many dreams can you forge?"

This wasn't an answer, not really. It was a loophole. The kind of question Céleste so often tossed out to her own marks when they got too eager for whatever prize she was offering.

"None," she told him. "Until you prove that you can heal me."

The Sanct clenched his fist. When he opened it again, Céleste's bloodstain was gone, the glove's fabric as crisp as the day she'd bought the set at Galeries Lafayette. He held his hand back out.

She did not dare shake it.

"That's not proof," she said.

This got her a smile. "The Seer said you would be sharp. Then again, she says many things that don't always turn out to be true—told me you were born in a castle with hair as black as midnight."

Céleste stayed very still when the Sanct stood and stepped around her, pausing to examine her shock-white hair. She did not flinch when he picked one. She didn't even feel the pinch, but she could see the strand clearly between his gloved fingers.

It *was* black.

Black and writhing.

This hair wasn't an imagining, but a much darker memory. Céleste saw herself inside, her mourning dress as black as her hair, standing outside a pair of locked gates. There was an *A* wrought in their iron, but they would not open for her, no matter how fast she talked or how loud she screamed. They wouldn't open for any Artois again. She had nothing to her name but an envelope from Académie de La Palette, inviting her to come learn the finer points of art in Paris.

That had gotten taken away too, in the end.

"That's mine!" Céleste tried to snatch her worst moment from the Sanct's fingers, but the memory dissolved as soon as she touched it.

"Powerlessness does not sit well with you, does it?" He was still smiling when he said this.

Céleste pulled her hands back to her sides to clench the wilted green skirts of her dress. Had she overreached? This Sanct was even harder to read than Rafe—who was standing still by the dream-fed fire. His shadow was back to normal. No foxes, wings, nor stretching strings. The only discrepancy was its head shaking ever so slightly.

The Sanct was too busy circling Céleste to notice.

"I understand," he said. "I know how it feels to be thrown out of your own home. I know what it is to have nothing to your name—not even the name itself." The Sanct passed the globe without spinning it, pausing instead by the decanter. He grabbed it by the neck. "I know how bitter such things taste. How hollow they leave you."

Firelight danced strangely off the container's glass, flames pirouetting like ballerinas. Céleste could even swear she saw a tutu as the Sanct held the decanter out to her.

"Proof, mademoiselle. Take a sip."

She did.

This wine was far richer than the vintage she'd enjoyed at Foyot's yesterday. Yet it washed down smoothly—like silk in her throat. As soon as Céleste swallowed, it felt like someone had taken a knife to her corset and sliced the laces free. She could *breathe*.

The Sanct took the decanter from her hands, watching her with those cold jewel eyes. "Better, no?"

Céleste kept waiting for the catch, the cough, but it didn't come. She nodded.

"That should last you several hours," he told her. "Maybe even days, depending on the stage of your consumption."

Céleste tried not to lick her lips as the Sanct placed the wine back on the table.

She would need more than that, then.

Much more.

"If I keep bringing you dreams, will you pour me a glass?"

"Of this?" His dark masque seemed to blur as he shook his head. "No, Mademoiselle Artois. This power would be wasted on you, but if you bring me more ideas from that wretched salon tomorrow, I'll introduce you to another one of my disciples. The Mad Monk. He's made quite a name for himself as a mystical healer. Perhaps you've heard of him?"

The title was familiar, but only in the same way La Fée Verte's had been. She'd read about the Mad Monk in the papers. He was a caricature of a person—a priest who held court with some royal family...in...Russia, was it?

She looked for Saint Petersburg on the globe.

It was just as black as the Balkans.

"So you have." The Sanct smiled and spun the globe again. "Rest assured, mademoiselle, distance is not an issue. I have the whole world at my fingertips." He grabbed his vest. There was no double-chained pocket watch hanging there, but a ring of keys. Scores and scores of keys. A few gleamed as gold as the halo around Paris, which the Sanct seemed to be tracking. "Well, almost. I need more dreams. Will you steal them for me, Mademoiselle Artois? Do we have ourselves a deal?"

It would have been hard to breathe, if it weren't so easy.

She glanced back at Rafe.

His shadow gave nothing away, but she remembered his warning: *Don't accept his first terms.*

"I want more than days," she said.

"Keep bringing me ideas, and I'll have the Mad Monk heal you on a weekly basis."

Better. But Céleste wasn't sure she should accept the second set of terms either. "I'd like to think on it."

She thought she saw Rafe flinch, from the corner of her eye, but again she didn't dare look away from the Sanct. He did not appear disappointed. His face was stone again as he began to peel off her opera glove.

"Very well, but I wouldn't take long to deliberate, if I were you." The Sanct held up the piece of Céleste's costume—his meaning as clear as its fabric—before tossing it into the fire. "Your days are numbered."

The Mad Monk

You may know this Sanct by another name, if you turn your ear to the gossip of Saint Petersburg, to the rumors that swirl there—heavy as January snow. *There are dark powers behind the throne. Rasputin has the empress herself under his spell! I've heard she's taken to his* bed *as well.* It would be wise for you not to believe everything that you hear.

The fact of the matter is only two of these statements are true.

Grigori Yefimovich Rasputin is well-known for his miracles. He haunts a gilded palace that brings winter to every season. The Romanov family is even older than its house. And their royal blood? Over the years it has thinned: child to child to child, so that the young Tsarevich Alexei can barely hold his own. One prick from a needle means doctors, nosebleeds need towels, and something as simple as a fall can lead to a hematoma or even—heaven forbid—a last sacrament. Thus, the young prince finds himself caged, palm to frosty panes, while his four sisters tie on their skates. Every once in a while, Alexei manages to give his sailor nannies the slip, abandoning pillow forts and tin soldiers for adventures in the wider world. These do not always end well, but the threat of death can't stop a ten-year-old boy from wanting life.

It is, however, enough to bring a queen to her knees.

Tsarina Alexandra has begged God in all her languages: English, German, Russian. She is desperate in the way only a mother could be. She blew the doors of her palace wide open, and when Russia's finest physicians could not slow the crimson tide, she turned to more mystic solutions.

She turned to *him*.

Starets, she calls Rasputin—a holy man. And who can blame her? Tsarina Alexandra has watched him pray over the broken body of her son, has watched Alexei's bruises fade and his blood recede. Rasputin plays the part well. He fed on faith once. It's why he knows the Psalms by heart, why he can recite verses about lambs and pastures and the Lord's cup without flinching.

He fed on faith once.

But then he met a different god.

Chapter 7

Tigers Don't Change Their Stripes

By the time Céleste returned to Père Lachaise, its gates had opened to welcome the cemetery's earliest mourners. She did not have to dig her key out of her coin purse, which was now so light, she'd nearly forgotten it in the cab of the second taxi. She'd spent the remainder of her francs on the ride home from Place de la Concorde. There was nothing left for her to bury.

It was amazing how much better her body felt as she walked down the lane, drinking up the smell of dewdrops. The morning was fresh and glittering.

"Where the hell have you been?"

A statue rose from the roof of a nearby tomb, and Céleste flinched before she realized it was Honoré. Dark circles were cemented under her friend's eyes—her evening had been just as sleepless. Without the wonders.

Céleste had already composed her confession for the statues: *I abandoned my friends and wore Rafe's shadow and stole magic from a fairy and took a taxi to a street that should not exist. Then I fenced imaginings to a shady sorcerer who divined my past and offered me a future.*

I must keep forging dreams—night after night after night—if I want to stay alive.

She no longer tasted rust, but something else weighted her tongue. Rafe's warning: *Magic is madness to those who can't see it, so act with care.*

Honoré wouldn't send her to an asylum, but she wouldn't believe Céleste either. The thought of how her friend might react brought a laugh.

The other Enchantress jumped from the tomb, scowling. "It's not funny, *mon amie*! I've been worried sick! I thought you might have gotten trampled in the mob, and I was all set to go back to the theatre when Sylvie told me she saw you with Rafe."

"He helped me distract a policeman so the officer wouldn't notice Sylvie. We went out for a drink afterward, and the night got away from us."

Honoré's eyes narrowed. "It looks as if your dress did too."

There was an edge to the other Enchantress's voice as they wound down the path toward their grave. It would've been easy to mistake for jealousy—envy as green as her ragged gown—but Céleste had told Rafe the truth. She and Honoré were like sisters. Nothing less. Nothing more. This was a more protective gesture.

"There were some . . . costume changes . . ." Céleste said delicately. "But Rafe was a gentleman—"

"Rafael García is trouble," Honoré said flatly.

"No more trouble than you or me," Céleste reasoned. "Or Sylvie."

The youngest Enchantress was asleep in her corner of the tomb, wearing the necklace she'd nicked the night before. Diamonds and sapphires reflected the sunlight every time she snored.

The remains of the *tarte au chocolat* sat on the central tombstone. Two days old. Mostly melted. Céleste helped herself.

"Both of you are going to turn my hair gray," Honoré groaned. "Where did Rafael take you last night?"

"A salon."

"Where?"

"Why does it matter?" Céleste paused to lick chocolate from her fingers.

Honoré's lips went thin.

"Somewhere on the Left Bank. The place was full of painters." Neither of these things was a lie. "Rafe showed me some of his work."

"No shit?"

"No shit."

Just stardust.

The other Enchantress sighed. "He was always full of it, when we were younger, always making these grand plans. Starting an artists' colony in the Americas or escaping on the Orient Express and painting his way around Europe. All three of us were going to go to Constantinople, when my brother got old enough, but—" Honoré caught herself then. Her fist ground into her palm—the one that had gone smooth at the center, not because she knew her future but because the horns of her dragon ring had rubbed it raw.

Any other time, Céleste would have let this silence stretch, let sleeping beasts lie and orphans dream. "But what?" she whispered.

A stricken look settled on Honoré's face. "It all turned to shit. He ran away, and...well, I was wrong to trust him." She looked like she was about to say something more, when Sylvie started to stir. A whole stack of books slid off the youngest Enchantress's mattress. "Just be careful with Rafael, *mon amie.* Don't get too charmed by him. Tigers don't change their stripes."

The flaming ones do, Céleste thought. If anything could transform a person, it was magic. The boy Honoré had grown up with in Belleville wasn't the man who'd swept Céleste up in his very own shadow, though she could not help but pause at her friend's phrasing: *He ran away.* Had Rafe abandoned her in the salon on purpose? Had he had second thoughts about sharing his employer's spoils?

The covers of the fairy books gleamed gold when Céleste started gathering the volumes from the mausoleum floor. Their illustrations struck her differently now. So did the painting of Ophelia waiting on her easel, still in its sketched stages. The drowned woman's lines looked ghostlike—more haunting now that she knew the truth about her own health.

"You're supposed to stack them in a rainbow!" Sylvie sat up and started rearranging the fairy books to her liking. "Crimson, red, orange, yellow—"

"I know how rainbows work." Céleste smiled at the memory of a salon guest wearing one as a cape. She wished the youngest Enchantress could have seen it. Along with all the other dreams she'd walked through last night.

There were still a few imaginings in her jacket, but she couldn't pull them out without unfolding the bloodstained pocket square first. She probably should've tossed the kerchief away, before Sylvie went rifling through her pockets, but Céleste wasn't sure how long she had until she'd need it again.

Sylvie placed the crimson fairy book at the top of the pile. There was a gilded knight on its cover—his sword held out over a headless dragon. Fairies, flowers, and stars swirled around what would otherwise be a violent scene, but what drew Céleste's gaze the most was the winged woman hovering like a teardrop over everything.

"Does Rafe paint rainbows?" the youngest Enchantress wondered. "He seems like he would, with all those colors on his fingers."

That had been Céleste's first impression too.

"I'm not sure," she answered.

"What does he paint these days?" Honoré asked.

"He showed me a fox."

This made Honoré snort. "Is that a metaphor?"

Maybe. She still wasn't sure how Rafe was able to shape his shadow or what he earned with the ideas he stole. His employer hadn't uttered a word when he tossed those dreams into the fire. He didn't pour Rafe a glass of wine, nor did the artist seem eager to linger for one—his silhouette leapt for the door as soon as the flames ceased sparkling. He only stopped at the end of rue des Ombres, at the border of sunlight. Seeing him standing there, with such rigid shoulders, reminded Céleste of a painting she'd finished some months ago. The subject had not been Ophelia but Orpheus, the man who'd gone to hell and back to rescue his wife's soul. All he'd had to do to escape death was keep his eyes down and keep walking...

Rafe did glance over at Céleste as she stepped into the morning sun.

"Well?" she asked. "Should I accept his offer to meet the Mad Monk? Or should I wait until he's actually in a convivial mood?"

"That *was* convivial, for him." Rafe exhaled. "Practically a bouquet of sunshine and roses compared to my first meeting."

"I've seen corpses with friendlier smiles," Céleste said dryly.

For some reason, this got her a laugh. "Yes, well, as I told you before, my employer is difficult, but you managed to get some decent terms. The Mad Monk will keep you from an early grave—"

It was Céleste's turn to laugh. She said nothing of Père Lachaise.

Rafe's chin dimple deepened as he frowned. "If you don't believe me, read the papers. He's been tending to Russia's crown prince for years."

She looked at the yawning darkness over Rafe's shoulder, where the door's keyholes were back to their endless rotation. "What's the catch?"

"For you? Nothing. Like I said, your terms were decent. If you'd like to join me tomorrow evening, let's meet on the Pont Saint-Michel at midnight. If not..." Black hair swept into Rafe's face as he gave a quick bow. "Well, it was nice knowing you, Céleste Artois."

He stepped into the sun then, turning into just as much of a sleepwalker as Jean had. Céleste held back to watch; the doorman at Hôtel de Crillon flagged down a cab for him before reciting some address in Montparnasse: "Two Passage de Dantzig." That street seemed real enough. Rafe's amnesia had too...

He hadn't been completely truthful though.

There was a catch.

Céleste stared at the other two Enchantresses, wondering how she'd be able to explain her nocturnal absences. She might be able to sneak away for a night or two. But ten? Twenty? More? Honoré was too sharp not to notice.

"The fox was a fox," Céleste answered, trying to make her voice sly. "This time."

"What else would it be?" Sylvie blinked.

Honoré rolled her eyes. "He did like doodling them, if I remember correctly. A fox chasing its own tail—he called it his sigil."

"I like foxes," the youngest Enchantress declared. "I like Rafe too."

"He's asked me back to the salon, this evening," Céleste said lightly. "I think I should go."

Sylvie grinned at this.

Honoré did the opposite.

None of what Céleste had said was a lie, but this didn't stop her stomach from turning. Neither did another bite of the birthday tart. What was the alternative though? Letting everything rot? Painting absinthe-colored lily pads until a stray cough spattered them red?

No.

If she played this new arrangement just right, she could survive.

She could handle a charming thief and a shadowy sorcerer.

She could have her cake and eat it too.

Magic was everywhere, it seemed.

As Céleste wandered through the city that evening, making the walk from the cemetery to the Seine, she found herself pausing every few blocks. Had that alleyway always been there? What about that strangely fruiting tree by the Bastille? Or the poster for a venue called Cabaret d'Ailes—which boasted women with songbirds swirling from their wings? When Céleste did a double take at this advertisement, she could have sworn the drawing's subjects had moved. The stained glass windows of Sainte-Chapelle were moving as well, shining from the inside out and spinning like a kaleidoscope, as she walked toward the Pont Saint-Michel. Despite the late hour, the bridge was almost as busy as it had been that morning, when she'd watched Jean Cocteau's horns dissolve.

Rafe was perched close to this spot, his legs dangling over the balustrade. He was all tense lines, hunched over a notebook and furiously scribbling with a pencil. Was it a sketch or a sentence? Céleste couldn't tell. He snapped its pages shut and tucked the book into his vest as soon as he saw her approach.

"You're early," he said, by way of greeting.

She joined him at the balustrade, listening to the hush of the river beneath them. Rafe's hair was not tied back tonight. It wasn't shining yet either. The strands were nearly as dark as the waters below. So was the stubble on his chin—which did nothing to soften his jaw, only brought its edges into sharper relief. *7B.* That would be the pencil she'd choose to capture Rafe. Perhaps 8B for his black eye. The injury looked worse than before, but when his gaze landed on Céleste, she felt something bright.

"How would you know?" She hitched up her skirts and swung her legs over the ledge to sit next to him. It wasn't very ladylike, but Rafe grinned, offering an elbow to steady her. "Did you manage to fix that watch of yours?"

"I wouldn't dare!" he said, then nodded back toward the cathedral, where two towers rose downriver. "Not when I've got some perfectly tuned church bells to tell me when it strikes twelve."

"They don't chime this late," Céleste said.

The thief kept smiling. There was a strange scent on him, she realized, now that she sat so close. Smoke, but not the ruinous kind. It was more like the incense priests sometimes burned at mass—only spicier.

"Au contraire." He waved over the water. "They ring when the Quartier Secret opens, but only if you have ears to hear such things. La Fée Verte doesn't start Enlightening her guests until midnight."

"So who woke you up this evening?" Céleste wondered.

His smile vanished then. "Who do you think?"

"He really doesn't have a name?" Throughout the day, she'd taken to imagining it as a smear of soot, just like the sign of his hidden street or the absolute black of his masque: [redacted].

"No. And even if he did, I wouldn't speak it here. There are too many ears." Rafe glanced back to the foot of the bridge, where the Fontaine Saint-Michel split the street in two. Its statues stayed still. Almost as rigid as the thief's own arm. Céleste could feel the sculpt of his muscles under his shirt—she could see a scar too, streaking his forearm, all the way to the rolled sleeve.

These were more than just the marks of a painter.

They were *trouble.*

She wondered, again, if there was any merit to Honoré's warning. If she'd been wrong to trust Rafe...But what would happen if she pushed away from the thief now? She needed his shadow to slip into the Vault of Dreams undetected. Even more immediately, Rafe's arm was the only thing between her and the Seine. While the waters were beautiful—carrying the reflections of the quai lamps—they were also deadly for someone wearing so many petticoats.

So Céleste kept her elbow entwined with Rafe's, linked almost as closely as the fob chains of his pocket watch. "Let's talk about your timepiece, then. If it doesn't tell time, then what the hell do you use it for? Abandoning innocent maidens at sunrise?"

His grin returned at the word *innocent.* "That's not its primary function, no. I found this watch at Saint-Ouen's flea market, at a stall with knickknacks of the more magical variety. The Sanct who sold me the timepiece said *he* found it at Fifty-One rue de Montmorency—the oldest house in Paris. It belonged to the alchemist Nicolas Flamel."

"The house or the watch?"

"The house certainly did," he answered. "I'm not so sure about the watch, but alchemists work with gold, no?"

The timepiece flashed as Rafe fished it from his pocket and placed the open face on Céleste's palm. Gears began to grind—*tick, tock, tick.* Hands twitched. Forward first, then backward, stopping exactly where they'd started: at eight forty-five.

Rafe's brow furrowed. His voice dipped low. "That's interesting."

"What?"

"We have the same time." He looked up from the clock—quick enough to make his eyes flint. "This watch is enchanted to tell you your fateful hour."

"You want to know when you'll die?"

The thief shook his head. "It doesn't always mean death. The time marks something life altering. At least, that's what the Fisherman of the Moon told me when I bought the piece."

"Death *is* life altering," she pointed out wryly.

"So are many other things. Fame, fortune, love, power, freedom..."

Rafe's words drifted out over the river. Céleste couldn't help but compare them to her own list: Every one of these was the perfect piece of bait for a confidence scheme. "And what is it you want your fateful hour to mark?"

Rafe looked back at the watch in her hands, hesitant. "I used to dream of establishing an artists' colony, where you could paint whatever the hell you wanted without worrying about Terreur looking over your shoulder."

"In the Americas."

"Ah—I take it you've been talking to Honoré."

"Not about the magic. I needed an excuse to get away this evening, so I told her you were taking me to a salon." Céleste watched the other thief's expression closely. "It turns out she remembers quite a lot about you."

Something strange happened to Rafe's face then. It softened. He looked almost eager—the way Sylvie did when she was waiting for a bedtime story. "Like what?"

"You liked doodling forest creatures," Céleste replied lightly.

"What else?"

"She said you made plans to paint your way across Europe, but it all turned to shit." Céleste could tell this was true by the way Rafe flinched. His jaw worked back and forth, while the muscles in his scarred arm seized. "You ditched Honoré, apparently. She warned me not to trust you, and I have to say, after that little mishap in the mist last night, I can't help but wonder if she's right."

The Seine rushed on beneath them, all the louder for Rafe's silence.

"Not a day goes by where I don't wish that story had ended differently," he said, finally. "If I could use this watch to turn back time, I'd do it in a heartbeat. As for our arrangement..." Rafe's voice crackled as he looked up from the timepiece. His gaze had caramelized. "I don't believe your hour has anything to do with your death, Céleste Artois. My guess is that it's the opposite. I think you'll help me complete this job, and then we'll both get what we want."

"An artists' colony?" Céleste said testily.

"My priorities have shifted since Honoré last knew me," he told her. "Magic has a way of changing everything, for better or worse. It cracks the world open like an egg and can do the same to you if you aren't careful—"

"I'm not too worried about becoming an omelette," Céleste broke in sharply. "What *does* make me wary is a man who expects me to believe my future is inextricably tangled with his. It's a pretty weak line, all things considered."

"Not everything is a script, you know." Rafe's answer was nearly as tight as his hand when he reached to take back the watch. That spiel about fateful hours might've been bullshit, but Rafe wasn't faking the tension in his wrist.

The watch was worth more than gold to him.

Céleste kept holding on to the timepiece, just to see how hard he would pull. "What's the real reason you recruited me, hm?"

"Because I don't want you to drown in lungfuls of your own blood." The chain between them went taut. Rafe raised his eyebrows. "Is that an acceptable motive?"

"Better," she ceded, doubling down her grip on the watch. "But, given the fact that we only met yesterday, you need more backstory to make it believable. Add in a moving monologue...something about how you once had a sister who wasted away from consumption and saving me would be a way to heal your grief. That sort of thing."

Rafe glanced at the strained gold chain between them. "So you want me to make up a dead sibling?"

"I want you to make me *believe*," challenged Céleste.

Her balance was precarious. One strong gust of wind, and she'd be thrown into the river. She doubted the pocket watch's fob chain would be strong enough to save her. As it was, the mysterious smoke smell wreathed around her, joined by ribbons of Rafe's own shadow. The thief himself seemed to be drawing even closer.

"You want a fancy speech? Fine. I've been Enlightened for eighteen hundred and thirty evenings now. That's five years, if you can't be bothered with math. Five years of magic. Five years of living half a life—most days, it feels like I'm a shell of myself. And in the evenings? I have to lie to everyone around me to make ends meet. While Jean Cocteau and Pablo Picasso are upstairs creating masterpieces, I get sent to destroy them. Night after night after night, with no end in sight, with no one but my employer who understands what I truly am. As you saw, he's not the warmest of companions."

To put it mildly.

"So you're... lonely?" Céleste's hold on the watch softened a bit. "What, misery loves company? Is that it?"

"'*Solamen miseris socios habuisse doloris.*' That's the original line from Faustus, if you wanted the scripted version." Rafe was still tugging the watch—not away, but using its chain like a climber's rope, pulling himself closer and closer. "Although for what it's worth, last night was the first time in a long time that I *didn't* feel miserable. It was nice to laugh with you."

That could *be worth something*, Céleste found herself thinking, as the thief leaned in, wrapping them up in more shadows and smoke. His hand moved over hers, and Céleste's pulse began to drum hard enough to make her believe the pocket watch actually *was* ticking in their joined hands.

"Our employer might think I have a bleeding heart, but that's a hell of a lot better than none at all." She felt the growl of Rafe's voice through his fingertips. The gold between their palms began to feel warm, then warmer. "I don't want you to die, Céleste Artois. I want you to help me finish this job so we can both live long full lives with champagne and fish eggs and the world as our omelette. Is that convincing enough?"

"I'll take it," Céleste said, trying to ignore the heat of the pocket watch—and failing. The timepiece's gold was now burning to the point that if she held on much longer, she might end up with a winged hourglass singed into her palm.

She pressed the watch back toward Rafe's chest. "As for our

future, well, I suppose there's only one way to know for sure if our fateful hours are truly the same."

The thief smiled at this, the ink-drop tattoo under his left eye nearly disappearing. He unraveled his elbow from hers, tucked the timepiece into his vest pocket, and then threw himself off the balustrade. Céleste was too shocked to shriek. She peered down into the river. Muddy waters churned on, without Rafe. He'd landed on a second small ledge between the arches of the bridge instead, just beneath the *N* emblem wreathed in a stone garland.

"Come on, then!"

It looked like another dead end or a drop that would break Céleste's ankles, if she wasn't careful.

Hell, she thought, *the Mad Monk could just heal those too.*

Rafe waved up at her, and his shadow stretched from his sleeve—much like a street performer's silken kerchief—all the way to the balustrade. It felt like a solid hand when Céleste grasped it, strong enough to help lower her to the pedestal.

"What in the world are we doing down—" She fell quiet when she saw the boat moored under the arch.

Something about the sight demanded silence. It wasn't the craft itself—floating despite splinters and decades of peeling paint—but the woman who stood on its bow. She looked nothing like a figurehead from a pirate ship, though she was nearly as weathered. There was a net gnarled in her hands and a century's worth of wrinkles on her face. Her eyes were milky, but they fixed themselves on the pair of thieves anyway.

"I was wondering when you'd wash up." Her voice was water on stone.

Céleste wasn't sure which one of them she was speaking to.

Rafe crouched. "Hello, Seer. Lovely evening for lurking, isn't it?"

"I can't read your future from there, monsieur," she called back.

"That's fine by me," he answered. Then, under his breath to Céleste, he added, "Try never to board the Seer of the Seine's boat, and if you must, make sure your pockets are full of soil. That way she won't be able to touch you."

The Seer cast her net with a laugh. It splashed into the Seine, then sank. "Céleste Estelle Artois has enough dirt on her hands as it is. She became what ruined her, but she stands to become so much more—she's exactly where she needs to be."

A faint breeze slid downriver, blowing away the purple smoke that plumed from the boat's tin roof. The strings over the cabin door clattered too—not covered in beads, like Céleste first thought, but trash: shards of glass and fish skulls and rusted tin cans.

"Tell me, Seer, why did you send Céleste's glove to rue des Ombres?" Rafe asked.

"The same reason you go there night after night, dizzy fox." The Seer began tugging her net back in. "People so often think their futures are set in stone, that their stories are written in the stars before they're even born, but stone can be worn away, and stars will turn to dust if you wait long enough. I can find my way back to land again. And you . . ." Again, it was impossible to tell exactly where her foggy eyes settled. "You can cheat death."

"What is our employer searching for in the salon?" Rafe wondered.

"He asked me the same question." The Sanct's silver mask glimmered as she pulled the net back onto the deck. "I had no answers for him, and I'll have no more for you unless you lend me a hand, Monsieur García."

It wasn't the Seer the thief locked hands with then, but Céleste. When Rafe's shadow spread into wings, she was lifted with him over the river. They landed by the quai that lined the Latin Quarter. As Céleste clambered over a stack of crates, she could still see the Seer across the muddy waters, watching them. Her white eyes floated like the stars the fortune teller did not read.

Céleste tried her best not to shiver. "I thought our employer was collecting the dreams for their power." But that didn't make sense, did it? The reindeer with the lantern horns burst through her memory—a shower of sparks. "You think he's hunting for something?"

Rafe leapt down from the crate he'd landed on. "La Fée Verte stole from him, years ago. A memory? An idea? I'm not exactly sure what. He isn't either. But he's convinced she keeps it in that sparkly cave of hers. He's obsessed with getting it back."

"He wants a specific imagining?" Her heart yawned at the thought of how far the Vault of Dreams stretched. "That—that's a needle in a fucking haystack."

"Hence why I asked for help. I told you the job was big."

"'Big' is a word you'd use to describe an elephant... This is..."

"What?" Rafe quirked an eyebrow. "Were you going to say '*impossible*'?"

She had been.

But Notre-Dame's bells began to toll midnight—the enchanted hour. Their song shimmered through the air, along with a flock of emerald-feathered birds. Rafe's own wings pooled back at his feet as they passed overhead.

"At least you'll get a good long life out of it," he said.

The Door to Everywhere

Paris is a city famed for its doors.

Its doors are not just doors, you see, but works of art. They're meant to stop you in your tracks, like the brilliant entrance of Eight rue de Braque, where even the lion knockers have been painted blue. Other entryways are decorated with hanging brass hands or rings of intertwined serpents, inviting you to rap against wood lacquered with every color imaginable: turquoise, plum, crimson, yellow, pink, green...

But some of the city's most powerful doors are not painted at all.

If you stand in front of Notre-Dame de Paris long enough, its gargoyles might start to whisper, telling you the tale of the cathedral's devil doors. How a smith by the name of Monsieur Biscornet traded his soul to forge their intricate ironwork. Flourishing birds, scrolling vines, and budding angles—it was all so masterful, so unprecedented for its time, that Parisians believed he'd made a deal with Lucifer himself to finish the commission. It did not help that the locks wouldn't work until they'd been doused with holy water.

But a true devil's door lies at the end of rue des Ombres.

It does not need holy water to open, merely keys.

They hang from a chatelaine—that long set of chains attached to the nameless Sanct's jacket. When he moves, they sing songs of iron and gold and rust. The single door to his study whistles back. Air is always sliding through its ever-changing lock, filling the small room with strange scents: Melting snow. Hookah pipes. Salt from all seven seas and coal burning off the ships that crossed them. Sometimes you can smell fir trees—clean as stripped bone. Or berries ready to stain lips with ripe red bites. Or the sweet withered flesh of dates grown in far-off deserts.

This is the world.

It is at [redacted]'s fingertips. All he has to do is reach for a key, and the door's lock stops. Settles somewhere. This morning's selection is more ornate than most—the double-headed bird perched at the top of the key looks as if it has been dipped in gold. The sunlight that slants through the keyhole is the same color. Blinding. When the door opens, the young woman standing next to [redacted] tries not to shirk back from how bright things have suddenly become. A ballroom waits on the other side, with polished parquet floors and gods glaring down from the ceilings.

Another figure looms by the window. His monk's robes look much too ragged to belong here—wherever here is. The glass past his shoulder shows a park filled with plants you've never seen in Paris. Much less France.

This is a wilder kingdom.

The golden icon necklaces around the monk's neck tangle as he bows to [redacted]. His hairline is crooked. Too crooked. His blue eyes would be unsettlingly bright even if they weren't set inside a masque. They linger on the white-haired woman, pooling at the hollow of her throat. His own voice sounds as slick as oil.

"This is the Mad Monk," the nameless Sanct translates. "He is most pleased to welcome you to Russia."

PART II

THE FIGHTER

Once upon a time, there was a young woman
who stole her name from a grave.

This did not stop the rest of her past from haunting her.

She wore the hardest part of it on her finger—a silver dragon ring—and even though its teeth were now turned the other way, she still fought the beast in her sleep. She still woke up with scars.

She always felt one breath away from fire.

Chapter 8

Structurally Unsound

Honoré Côte had no more knives left to sharpen.

There were fifteen of them lined up in the grave dirt at her feet. Even the cheese knives were pointed enough to draw blood. She wasn't quite sure what to do now, except toss her whetstone back and forth between her palms. Back and forth. Back and forth. Céleste *still* wasn't back.

Honoré had a bad feeling about it.

To tell the truth, she'd been on edge ever since they'd gone to see that damn ballet. The riot was unsettling enough, but it was Rafael's appearance that really rattled her. And then his disappearance with Céleste. Honoré tried not to press the other Enchantress too hard after those first few nights when her friend was gone until dawn. Céleste was a grown woman, and she had every right to be where she pleased. Then a week passed. And another the same way. And another. There had been no new paintings in nearly a month. Céleste slept through the good morning light and most of the afternoon as well, and once she finally woke, she didn't seem to be in the mood to paint. Or talk.

This posed a problem.

When Honoré pointed out that the Enchantresses could not sell a blank canvas, Céleste didn't argue. She didn't pick up her pastels either. She simply rubbed her eyes and said she was tired.

"Of course you're tired!" Honoré growled. "Where have you been all night?"

Céleste's silence had scared her more than any answer could.

Five whole years they'd been partners in crime—each trusting the other, even in lies—but Honoré knew there was more than one job in Paris for a forger. Especially a forger as accurate as Céleste. Rafael himself had worked for years at the Caveau des Terreurs.

Vault of Terrors.

The bar was about as cheery as its sign—a play on the name of the gangster who'd owned it. Honoré's father had held court there, building a criminal empire with switchblades and false banknotes. He made Rafael draw fake deeds too in that sooty back room. It was a shitty studio, but it was one of Honoré's favorite hiding spots. Rafael used to whittle wooden knights for Gabriel to play with under the drafting table, and he'd leave his knives out afterward so Honoré could practice with them. It was the only place she could get away with such a thing, where she could learn how to slash and slice and stab. A rehearsal, of sorts. She'd always had an eye for fights, the way some had an ear for music, but this was because violence had been Honoré's lullaby for as long as she could remember. Too often her nights were spent in the closet, her mother's winter coats pulled down from their hangers and turned into a makeshift bed. Not that Honoré did much sleeping. Her hands had covered Gabriel's ears, while her little brother had clutched his knights.

You look just like him.

All that was coming back now, thanks to Rafael, and Céleste was still gone. Honoré had tried to be patient. She'd tried to sit around and wait, but her legs were starting to cramp, and she couldn't stand to keep staring at her friend's collection of empty dresses. *None of Maman's gowns were that fancy*, Honoré thought, as she picked up her four sharpest knives. They went into her boots and up her sleeves, reinforcing her hands and feet. She'd gotten so used to the weight over the years that, without them, she felt structurally unsound.

She retrieved a fifth knife and moved to Céleste's corner of the tomb.

She grabbed the nearest wig.

Sylvie perked up from her pillow, where she'd been staring at that book none of them could read. The green one. With the fairy on it. "What are you doing?"

Honoré wasn't entirely sure. She didn't wear wigs very often, and the hair on this one proved tough to cut. Chestnut strands fell to the floor in a ragged pattern. The hairpiece itself looked even more ragged when she fixed it to her head. Next was a Panama hat to shield her eyes and a moustache full enough to obscure the other half of her face.

"I'm going out."

"I'm coming with you!" Sylvie declared.

"Absolutely not."

"You can't just leave me here by myself!" the girl wailed.

"I'm going to check on something to do with Céleste and…it might be dangerous."

"She's not in danger," Sylvie said. "She's with Rafe."

"Céleste told you that?"

"No, the cats did," Sylvie said with a straight face. "I asked them where Céleste was going every night, and they said she follows Rafe into a disappearing alleyway…Maybe? Or an erased street? I'm still learning their language. Did you know they have ten different words for 'mouse'?"

Honoré clenched her jaw. Why must Sylvie be so *childish*? Granted, she was a child, but this whole bit about the cats had gone a story too far. And if it *was* true? If Céleste was following Rafael around Paris's darker streets and refusing to say so? Well, then, that just confirmed Honoré's fears.

She picked up a sixth knife.

"Rafael worked for some nasty people when we were younger." He might claim to be a penniless painter now, but Honoré knew better than to believe him. "I need to make sure Céleste doesn't get caught up with them too."

"Why do you keep calling him that?"

"Rafael? That's his name."

A frown drifted across Sylvie's face. "Well, the cats say—"

"Will you stop with the talking cats?" This was too loud, Honoré realized. The youngest Enchantress shrank into her blanket, her book tumbling to the floor. "I'm sorry, Sylvie—I just—this is no time for make-believe. Céleste could be in real danger. I have to go."

Belleville was a neighborhood of fighters.

It had been so for nearly a century...ever since Paris swallowed up the wine-making village and squeezed its workers dry with demands: *Bake all night. Fill our cups. What else are your short lives for?* It was as if the bourgeoisie hadn't learned anything from that first revolution at all. As if they didn't expect the working class to fight back again.

They had.

And while that second revolution was short, so short that it was nearly forgotten, it still scarred Belleville's walls. Bullet pocks. Defiant graffiti. There were small hand-drawn skulls all over the neighborhood, surrounded by the words VIVE LA COMMUNE 1871. Honoré had learned her first letters by tracing them. Her blood ran through these streets—literally. Legend had it that Honoré's grandfather had been shot right here on rue de Belleville, for daring to believe in better wages and women's rights.

Of course, that was merely a legend.

He could have just as easily been killed by gangsters, the way Honoré's *other* grandfather had. Or he may have been the gangster doing the killing. Honoré looked down at the silver dragon ring on her right hand. Her only heirloom. For five whole years, she'd worn it, until the metal had become another part of her. The bones of her middle finger were shaped by it, as was the pad of her palm, where the bottom kissed her closed fist. There were other marks too, passed down from when the ring had crowned her father's hand instead of hers.

It wouldn't be wise to wear the beast here, in its old lair. So she pulled the ring off and slipped it into the pocket of her trousers before she walked into Caveau des Terreurs.

The name hadn't changed, but the establishment itself was smaller than Honoré remembered—though it hosted the debauchery of almost a hundred people. The rickety corner piano was the same, right down to the sticky stains on its keys. Sand was still scattered across the dance floor, and the dozens of tables were covered—as always—with poker hands and glasses of spirits. Red and green oil lamps cast a sickly glow over the customers. Most wore the same outfit: Bénard trousers, a waistcoat fitted over a striped sailor shirt, a flat cap, a scarf, and multiple pockets for multiple blades. The men had a single blue dot tattooed under their left eyes. The women wore black ribbons around their necks.

She did not see Céleste sitting among them.

She tried not to recognize any other faces.

She knew the barmaid though. Eleanor had lived a few doors down and had always been serving tea to her rag dolls. *Playing like a proper girl*, Terreur once growled. She grew into a conventional woman too. Her breasts started filling out at the same time as Honoré's, but she didn't try to hide them, didn't hate the way they drew men's eyes. She treated the gangsters of Caveau des Terreurs much like she had her dolls—pouring drinks and talking to unhearing ears. She'd snuck Honoré lemonade on occasion, winking as she passed the bottle over the bar top. Honoré had always drunk it. Always tried hard to smile back, but not *too* hard, in case one of her father's men was watching...

"Excuse me." It wasn't difficult to make her voice masculine. Husky. Smoke from the lamps and every other memory here clawed down Honoré's throat. "Have you seen a young woman around recently? She has very fair hair—almost white—and she's about my height."

"No." Eleanor shook her head and went on polishing glasses. "No one like that here."

"Are you sure?" Honoré pressed.

A loud *CRACK* sounded across the room, followed by the

shattering of glass. Some drunk fool was using barware as target practice. *CRACK, CRACK!* Honoré did not jump at the sound, and she wondered if that was a mistake. Eyes were already beginning to drift in her direction.

"No one has white hair here," the barmaid said. "Most of us don't get old enough."

"She's young," Honoré repeated. "Twenty-four."

"You may not reach that age if you don't leave, monsieur. This is Apache territory, and they don't take to trespassers kindly."

But Honoré wasn't a trespasser at the Caveau des Terreurs. She was Fear's Bastard, and if she'd been his son, she would be seated at the tables over there, crying ink and never tears. *Men don't cry and bitches don't fight. (Back)*, her father had meant. *Bitches don't fight back.*

He'd been wrong on both accounts.

Honoré leaned farther over the bar top. Like the buildings outside, it was covered with signs of violence. Gouges where blades had been. A patina of splattered dark stains. Wine and blood were both difficult to get out of wood. Someone had carved up one of the largest red spots with what they thought was a witty epitaph: *Terreur is dead, long live Terreur!*

"Would you happen to have any lemonade?" she asked.

Eleanor almost dropped the glass she was polishing. The rag went limp in her other hand. "No," came the careful words, "I haven't served that in years..." Her gaze flicked over Honoré's shoulder, then back to the bar top. "What are you doing here? Did you not get my last letter?"

The scrap of paper tucked in the empty Château Robert bottle? Wedged against the buttresses of Notre-Dame-de-la-Croix like an offering? Her fingers had trembled when she'd opened it. Her lungs had seized when she'd seen the words. *Gabriel made his first kill today. Stay away, or you might be next.* She could still remember the sound of the bottle breaking.

She still felt its shards in her heart.

"I'm not looking for a fight," she lied.

"There's one looking for you," Eleanor murmured. "I swear on the saints, I haven't seen your pale-haired friend. Is that all you wanted?"

Of course not. Honoré could feel her heartbeat around at least three of her knives—faster and faster. Once upon a time, she'd sat here, admiring the way Eleanor moved like sunlight on water, even though neither of those elements could be found behind Caveau des Terreurs's bar. There was a mirror past the liquor bottles, and Honoré watched it now. The card games behind her had slowed.

"What about Rafael? Have you seen him around?"

The frown lines that appeared on Eleanor's face were deeper than Honoré remembered. "Who?"

"The forger."

The woman on the other side of the bar kept frowning. Could she really have forgotten?

"The García boy," Honoré pressed. "He stole all those travel posters from Gare de l'Est and put them up in the back room. Wouldn't shut up about Constantinople. You used to tease him that his imagination was always running in circles..." She glanced back down the bar, looking for that stupid sigil. "That's why he carved this."

The graffiti was far more elegant than the rest of the markings in the wood: a fox chasing its own tail. Eleanor hardly glanced at it though. She began polishing her glass again, even though there were no streaks left.

"There's been no hide nor hair of him. You should make yourself scarce too. The men are on edge, even worse than usual. The killings have spooked them."

Honoré lifted her eyebrows. "Killings?"

"You haven't heard?"

No, but murder didn't seem like it should be news here. Much less something to make an Apache quake in their gold-buttoned boots.

"Bodies have been turning up all over the city." Again, this didn't sound terribly suspicious. It didn't explain the tremble in Eleanor's voice. "Saint-Germain, Montparnasse, the Champs-Élysées."

"Could be another gang looking to expand their territory," Honoré reasoned.

That was a big expanse though. And the neighborhoods the barmaid had just listed were the province of the rich. Policemen *cared* there.

Eleanor shook her head. "The bodies... they're not normal. The first one they discovered made the police call the Louvre to see if the museum was missing a mummy. As if some sarcophagus had tumbled out the door and rolled all the way to the Champs-Élysées. But how else could you explain a corpse that looks like that?"

Honoré found herself shifting to the edge of the barstool. "Like what?"

"Dry as a desert. No blood. No stab wounds. No bullets either." Eleanor shuddered. "The police haven't even been able to identify the victims. The papers are keeping quiet too, but Séverin's cousin has an ear on the force. He says the killings keep happening every few weeks. So, yeah, the men are spooked."

Honoré looked back in the mirror. There were plenty of worn spots in the mercury—places where it was easy to see ghosts. This bar had more than its fair share, thanks to Terreur. Her father had made a name for himself, knifing his way to the top of Paris's fiercest gang, and even now that the fucker was dead, he wasn't gone. Not the way Honoré had wanted him to be, when she'd stabbed him. His blood scarred the bar. His moniker had become a title. His daughter looked just like him, and his son did too.

Gabriel.

Oh, Gabriel.

Her younger brother was sitting behind the piano, tinkering with its keys the way he sometimes had when he was little. "Twinkle, Twinkle, Little Star," he'd played on his own. He had the ear for music. His fingers were longer now. They moved more ferociously through the notes, playing the opening chords of "Valse des Rayons," which would soon get the patrons performing La Danse Apache. Horrid dance. Brutal dance, so brutal that it broke tables and sometimes left bruises on the women's necks.

Gunshots and murderous rumors hadn't made Honoré flinch, but this did.

"I'll keep my eyes open for your white-haired friend," Eleanor murmured as she put the glass back. "I'll write you if anything changes. I promise. Now go!"

Chairs were scraping back. Girls with ribbons knotted around their necks were getting pulled onto the sandy dance floor, and Honoré's own throat felt tighter and tighter. She knew the steps. Knew them all too well, outside the dance. Did Gabriel? If she hadn't plugged her little brother's ears, oh so many years ago, would he play this filth? Would he have chosen to stay?

Honoré should have left this place sooner—ten years sooner—with her mother and brother at her side.

As it was, she made a quick exit.

She walked away from the piano's wail, wanting so much to be different. At least she'd been wrong about Rafael. A relief. She wondered what kind of stuff he painted, now that he was no longer in Belleville. She should pay his salon a visit. For old times' sake. And to check in on Céleste. Maybe it was better for her friend to be spending so much time with other artists, to start working on work of her own instead of always selling herself as someone else. She had the talent. She'd needed the money to nurture it, back when they'd first met, which was why Honoré had suggested forgery. They had plenty of francs now. They could stop stealing anytime they wanted.

But if Céleste really had turned over a new leaf, why did her sketchbook stay blank? Why wouldn't she describe the salon Rafe took her to when Sylvie asked about their evenings together? Why did she always slip out of their tomb without saying goodbye? Why did she hail taxis at rue de Bagnolet so Honoré had no way to follow?

No...

Something still didn't sit right.

A restless red feeling stirred in Honoré's chest while she walked. Shadows fluttered on the other side of the street. The moon was playing tricks with Belleville's alleys—Honoré swore she saw someone there, a flitting presence at the corner of her eye. She refused to move faster. If someone *was* stalking her, she wouldn't give them the satisfaction of running. She wouldn't let her thoughts turn to bloodless corpses, much less vampires, because, of course, that was fucking ridiculous.

Wasn't it?

A cat darted across the lane.

Honoré exhaled.

Then she heard an unmistakable *click*.

The sound was tiny and tinny and followed by a voice that made her skin crawl. There was a drawl to the way the gangster spoke—sparks on silk. It set Honoré's neck hairs alight. "Leaving so soon, monsieur? You didn't even stay for a drink! The barmaid seemed quite upset."

Honoré knew that voice.

She knew that face.

She'd cut it in half herself.

It wasn't a vampire she found when she turned, but Rémy Lavigne. The gangster was standing several meters away, holding a golden revolver. Lazy weapon. Though maybe he'd been put off knives ever since hers carved that hideous line down his right cheek. The scar was puckered and purple—dragging off Rémy's chin and over his beetle-bright eye.

His gaze crawled over Honoré, but it didn't glint with recognition just yet. "What's your business here, eh? Fancy folk like you don't come nosing around Belleville after dark."

Fancy folk? Honoré fought back a laugh. True, her suit was bespoke, but Rémy's yellow boots had to be worth just as much, with their polished leather and gold buttons. They flashed as he stepped toward her.

Good.

Get him closer, just like last time.

"I was looking for someone," she said.

Night sharpened the edge of Rémy's cap as he paused. He was alone; Honoré guessed this—partly because the gun stayed pointed at her moustache but mostly because Rémy was notorious for doing his work solo.

His yellow boots flashed one more step.

Almost there.

She needed the element of surprise. Something to throw this hunter off-balance. "I was, in fact, looking for a Monsieur Rémy Lavigne. To pass on the news of his great-uncle's death. He was bequeathed quite a large estate, though I'm afraid that if I can't find him, these assets will go to the government."

This got the gangster's attention. He snagged on the sentences, his scar scrunching with confusion. "Estate? But… I don't have no great—"

Honoré struck.

She hit the revolver with her fist. It went spinning over the tram tracks. Honoré spun too, grabbing Rémy's red scarf in the hopes that she could use it to choke him to the cobblestones, but the fabric slipped out of her sweaty palm, and the gangster unraveled from it too.

Her knife was only half out when he lunged, and she bought more time by tossing her straw Panama hat into Rémy's face. His blade slashed it to splinters. Her own knife flashed. Her arm burned. Shit! Rémy had managed to land a blow. He'd gotten better over the past six years, since they'd last fought.

But she had too.

Honoré ducked and dodged and hit and stabbed. She dove for the gangster's kneecaps, aiming for a tendon. He kicked up, and the edge of her blade caught one of his boots instead. Three gold buttons scattered onto the street beside his gun. It might have been a worse wound than the tendon; Rémy cared far more about his clothes than he cared about any living thing.

He howled accordingly.

From there, the fight took on a bestial tone. Rémy's attacks turned erratic. Honoré too had to lean into her anger. Her hurt. The cut on her arm pulsed like a Gregorian chant: *Stab! Stab! Stab!* For so long, it had only been tree trunks and straw men and Céleste, who held knives like flowers. Now Honoré could let herself go into the wild thorny places that wanted to keep drawing blood.

It was too easy to see the past on these streets.

Her grandfathers were cast in the mercury shades of a daguerreotype.

Her father, always polishing blood off his ring.

Her mother, wearing a scarf to hide her cuts as she walked from the *fromagerie* with a basket of camembert.

Rémy, as a boy, breaking up stale bits of bread so he could lure strays.

The little black cat she'd never gotten a chance to name.

Herself. So small. So...

Shit. Honoré stuttered when she realized that the cat and the girl were solid, standing at the edge of a nearby alley. She lost her own footing then, tripping on Belleville's cobblestones. The entire street slammed into Honoré's spine. Then Rémy was on top of her, just like before, only there were no skirts to shove up. No skin to distract him. He wrenched Honoré's knife from her hand and turned it on her.

"You're going to pay for what you did to my boots," he said with a rancid breath. "They cost an eye. Maybe two. Tell me what you're doing here, and I might spare your sight."

She knew he'd do no such thing, if the truth came out.

The knife pressed hard into her chin.

Rémy's smile grew as he began to carve, but the cut didn't get very far. The blade stopped as soon as it caught the edge of Honoré's fake moustache. An entire end flapped up, and the sight of her facial hair peeling off made him stop. Stare. *See.*

His rotten grin vanished.

"Anne?"

Even as a child, she had found the name ill-fitting, as clumsy as the frocks she ruined in Belleville's muddy gutters. She'd left it behind when she escaped, drifting from place to place, name to name, because she knew the Apaches would be listening for any whisper of *Anne*. Any hint of the little girl with blonde braids and skinned knees.

Rémy grabbed her bleeding chin. "Oh...shit!" The gangster's lips twisted into a snarl. "It is you!"

"Anne is dead," she hissed.

Rémy laughed. "You will be soon, though your brother will kill me if I kill you first. He was quite a wreck after you left."

There was still a knife hidden up her right sleeve, and though Rémy had pinned the arm with his knee, Honoré found she was able to work the blade into her palm. All she had to do was keep him distracted until—

Rémy let out a shriek.

His knife jerked away from Honoré's face as a streak of fur flew into him. He fell back, clawing at this new attacker.

It was a cat.

It was *the* cat. From the alley entrance. Not black, like she'd first thought, but ginger. And tailless. It looked very much like the untamable tomcat from Père Lachaise, the one Sylvie liked to describe as a tiger. Given the way Rémy was screaming, the description was perhaps more accurate than Honoré had believed. The orange animal had its teeth sunk deep into the good side of the gangster's face.

"Honoré!" Her true name rang out over the cobblestones. She looked up to see Sylvie crouched between the tram tracks, reaching for the golden gun.

"What are you doing here?" Honoré untangled herself from Rémy's thrashing legs and scrambled toward the girl. "Don't touch that!"

Too late. Sylvie threaded her fingers through the knuckle-duster that doubled as the gun's grip. The pistol was cocked, and the little wavy dagger that served as its bayonet shivered when she tried to aim.

"It's pretty, for a gun! It feels light too! Like a toy!"

"A toy that kills people," Honoré reminded her.

"Anything can be a weapon!" the girl chirped back.

"Hand it here!"

Sylvie bit her bottom lip instead. "Are you going to kill him?"

Rémy was rising to his feet. The orange tomcat vanished back into the night, as suddenly as it had come, but the animal had left its mark. Several marks, in fact. Blood covered the gangster's cheeks, as if he'd been crying. Murder gleamed in his one good eye as he started toward the girls.

"Give me the gun, Sylvie," Honoré said urgently.

"You didn't answer my question."

"If I don't shoot him, he's going to stab us!" Honoré had her new knife in her hand, just in case, but the weapon felt different with an eleven-year-old nearby. It would be too easy for Sylvie to get cut. And she wouldn't bleed sugar here, that was for damn sure. "He's going to stab us, and we're going to die!"

"No," Sylvie said, as if this were simply an ending that didn't suit her.

She raised the pistol high.

Rémy paused. A wise move, since the barrel was aimed at his chest. Honoré's own heart thrummed with uncertainty. Was this a dream? It felt like a dream, as if she'd fallen asleep on her mattress, sprawled among her knives. That would make so much more sense than Sylvie playing target practice here in Belleville.

"Go away!" the girl shouted at Rémy, as if he were a fly hovering around some charcuterie. "Leave us alone!"

The gangster wavered.

Then he turned on his yellow-booted heels and ran.

"There," Sylvie said, as if she'd fixed everything.

If only.

Honoré watched Rémy round the corner, back toward Caveau des Terreurs, where the piano was still raging.

"Come on, *ma rêveuse*." Sylvie didn't put up a fight when Honoré confiscated the weapon. She took the girl's hand next and pulled her down the street. "We have to go."

Chapter 9

The Lobster Gargoyle

They took the long way back to their cemetery. Honoré liked her grave too much to let the Apaches scare her out of it, so she told Sylvie to walk south instead. Toward the Seine. It was a long enough detour that she'd be able to sense if anyone from Belleville was following them. Looking over her shoulder every few steps was something Honoré had sworn never to do, but it was different now that the youngest Enchantress was involved.

The girl was skipping—skipping!—down the street. As if they'd just left a dance hall instead of the territory of the most ruthless gang in Paris.

"That was very stupid of you," Honoré said.

"You're welcome."

"What were you thinking? Following me into a neighborhood like that? I *told* you it was going to be dangerous—"

"That's why I brought Marmalade," Sylvie cut in. "You should thank him. I'm pretty sure he saved your life."

"Marmalade?" Honoré echoed.

"He clawed up that thug's face, after I asked him to attack. You believe me now about talking to cats, don't you? I don't see how you can't."

The cut on Honoré's own face was now more crust than blood. But all the rage that Rémy had stirred up was still there, burning its way through her veins.

"You didn't save my life, Sylvie." She said nothing about the cat. "You put yours at risk, and now we're both in a hell of a lot of trouble."

"Why?" asked Sylvie.

Honoré considered being honest. *Because I was never like you. I* would *have killed Rémy if you'd let me. I stabbed my own father, years ago. I murdered him, but he didn't die, not the way I wanted him to. He cursed me with his last breath—loud enough for my younger brother to hear. Gabriel. Oh, Gabriel. He screamed when he found us, and Terreur's men came running. If I were a son, they would've kissed the ring I'd cut off. But here we are, fleeing. I hope you like sleeping with one eye open,* ma rêveuse, *because the Apaches will turn over every stone in this city to find us.*

But this wasn't the kind of bedtime story Sylvie was used to, and besides, it was nearly midnight. They were close to the river, on a street lit with electric lights instead of gas lamps. The younger Enchantress liked them because they glittered. Honoré liked them because they left nowhere to hide.

So far no one seemed to be trailing them.

"We may be safe to round back." Four solid walls would be good. Not to mention gates with locks and guards. "Let's head home."

"Oh...but can we at least walk by the cathedral?" Sylvie spun around, her palms pressed together as if in prayer. "I want to say hello to the lobster gargoyle! It's funny. What do you think the sculptor was thinking about, carving a lobster onto a church?"

"Thermidor, probably." Though Honoré doubted such a dish had existed in medieval times. "Are you quite sure it's a lobster?"

Sylvie nodded and darted toward the Seine. Honoré followed. It had been a long time since she'd been by this part of the river at night, and the sight of Notre-Dame rising to face the moon was daunting. As if God himself were seated at the top of the towers. Lots of people considered this place a sanctuary, somewhere to feel safe from the evils of this world, but Honoré felt her steps slow as she approached. She still smelled like smoke and sin.

She still felt like fighting.

Sylvie skidded to the church's left-most entrance, frightening pigeons from their shit-covered roosts. She pointed at the door's frame, where, sure enough, there was a lobster set in stone. It could have been a crayfish. Or even an anatomically unfortunate crab. But it was certainly some sort of crustacean.

"See?" Sylvie said triumphantly.

"I'll be damned."

"You shouldn't say that in front of a church." The girl scowled.

Honoré looked back up at the surrounding carvings: Kings with their scepters. The Virgin Mary swaddling her baby. Saints holding scripture. One unfortunate fellow was holding his own head instead. Honoré felt a begrudging kinship with him.

"The lobster doesn't really fit in, does it?"

"That's what makes it so wonderful," Sylvie said sagely. "If everything fit as we expected, the world would be dull, wouldn't it? Why... look at that green pigeon over there! He's the prettiest in the whole flock."

This time the girl was pointing at the edge of the square, which was lined with lamps and chestnut trees. The birds she'd disturbed were settling back down, all as gray as the gravel they roosted on.

"There's another!" Sylvie squeaked.

Honoré searched harder.

She saw nothing green, aside from the leaves. Sylvie started giggling, waving at the empty air, then patting her own head. Clearly, the girl needed sleep.

"It's time to go home," Honoré said.

"But..." The girl's stare drifted over the river, toward the Left Bank. "I think it wants us to follow."

"There's no green bird, Sylvie."

"You don't see it?"

Honoré rubbed her eyes until they danced with strange colors. Some greens. No birds. "I'm too tired to play make-believe. Let's just go back to the cemetery and get some sleep—"

"I'm not making this up!" Sylvie voice grew twice her size. "There really are birds, and they're calling me across the river!"

"You're hallucinating, then."

Sylvie broke out into a run toward the nearest bridge. She'd nearly crossed the thing before Honoré caught her by the elbow.

"You *never* believe me!" Her wail carried over the Seine's mud-colored waters. "Never ever! It's not fair! I wish Céleste were here!"

"Me too," Honoré muttered.

The other Enchantress would know how to coax Sylvie into bed without a fuss. Céleste acted far more maternal than Honoré. And more paternal, for that matter.

"Oh!" Sylvie's tone switched to slight surprise. "Our wishes worked! There she is!"

Honoré tightened her grip on the girl's shirt, but this wasn't a ruse. It wasn't a hallucination either. There, on the quai on the other side of the bridge, was Céleste, walking with Rafael García.

They were not holding hands, but they moved like a couple—closely. Honoré did not call out as they walked past the bridge. She couldn't. She heard Rafael's chuckle and then Céleste's echo. It was a real laugh. Not the kind used for marks, but one that meant her friend was truly amused. She usually only reserved it for picnics at Père Lachaise...

Honoré wasn't exactly surprised. She'd seen the draw between the two artists before *The Rite of Spring*, the way each of their gazes lingered on the other. What didn't make sense was the rest of Céleste's silence.

Why hide this?

"See?" Sylvie grinned wide. "Marmalade was right! Do you think she and Rafe are on their way to the vanishing street?"

The pair was already well down the lane, not looking over their shoulders even once. One could do that in the Latin Quarter. There were plenty of respectable folks on the streets—far more respectable than Honoré, with her sliced-up face, and Sylvie, chasing imaginary birds. Boulevardiers tapped their canes and doffed their top hats. A woman pulled a cart of slightly wilted flowers. And all along the sidewalks were café tables, filled with wine glasses and genteel conversation. The night was not young, but it wasn't over either.

"Should we follow them?" Sylvie asked, after Céleste and Rafael rounded the corner.

Honoré certainly didn't feel like going home anymore. If she did, she'd simply focus on that empty mattress and the fight that awaited her in the morning, when she'd try to convince Céleste to tell her what she could now see with her own two eyes.

She let go of Sylvie's sleeve.

They went down the quai, past barrels and moored steamers, before turning down a small side street, where Honoré caught a glimpse of Céleste's moonstruck hair. Back here was a maze of cobblestones, noisy with university students who certainly weren't studying, at least not the Latin this quarter was named after. A few took note of Honoré's face, and when she went to probe the cut there, she realized her moustache was only half attached. She ripped the thing off and tossed it to a boy who was drunk enough to be delighted.

She'd lost track of Céleste, but Sylvie—somehow—knew exactly where the other Enchantress was going. The alleys spit them out onto a larger boulevard, and the girl crossed it quickly before coming to a halt in front of a rather ostentatious fountain. Water trickled through a scene of Archangel Michael stabbing the devil.

Céleste and Rafael were nowhere to be seen, but Sylvie was staring at the statues, looking almost like one herself. Rapt. For some reason she focused on one of the abutting dragons. It didn't stand out as sorely as Notre-Dame's lobster, but something about the sculpture didn't completely blend in either.

Its eyes.

Its eyes were blank, and yet... not.

"Ma rêveuse?" That stare was giving Honoré the creeps. She reached into her pocket, where her own dragon lurked.

The fountain dragon blinked.

It was a reptilian sort of motion. The lids slid sideways. Unmistakable.

Sylvie gasped.

Honoré swore.

The dragon turned on its pedestal to face the Enchantresses. It snuffled at Sylvie's head, the way a horse might ask after an apple. Gentle but insistent. The girl giggled. Honoré started drawing her third knife. This weapon was barely longer than the statue's claws, claws that flexed as the beast stared down at her.

The dragon sat still long enough for Honoré to think that maybe *she'd* started hallucinating. Maybe it had always been cast that way.

But then the spell broke.

The dragon lunged.

Chapter 10

The Magical Heirloom of Mademoiselle Cake

Of all the foes Honoré had ever envisioned fighting—Prussian soldiers, rival gangs, Terreur, always Terreur—she hadn't thought to imagine a literal dragon.

The sculpture was the size of a stallion, so Honoré figured it had to be even heavier. A single bronze paw could crush her chest. Its fangs could slice her open. There were other sharp edges: Spikes jutted out of the wings and out of the creature's . . . stomach? There was even a pincer-type claw at the end of its tail.

By comparison, the knife in Honoré's own hand was laughable.

She dodged when the dragon leapt. Her blade struck hard enough to summon sparks, but it didn't so much as scratch the beast. *Ha, fucking ha!* What else was there to fight with? Rémy's revolver . . . The gun was folded tight in Honoré's pocket. When she went to reach for it, her finger met the cool bite of her father's ring instead.

It felt far bigger than she remembered.

"Oh!" Sylvie was wringing her hands by the fountain. "Please don't fight!"

Honoré wasn't entirely sure if the kid was speaking to her or the dragon. The statue was getting ready to lunge again, and there was no time to grab the gun.

She threw up her palms to defend herself.

Her ring *was* bigger; it was the most peculiar thing. The band's silver dragon had grown. Metal pooled out over Honoré's hand and the rest of her fingers so that they looked liquid beneath the moonlight. The jewelry's finer details—its ears and snout, its sharp eyes and sharper fangs—were moving. They gathered over her fist, growing and growing, until her ring met its bronze counterpart in midair. There was a magnificent twist of metal as the two dragons tangled together, and Honoré, standing below, felt the fight like she never had before. It wasn't like wielding a knife at all. The way the silver shifted was more like a limb, responding to Honoré's instincts by smashing the bronze statue into its own fountain.

Sylvie shrieked as water sprayed across the plaza. She seemed to be the only person who noticed that Honoré had a giant metallic dragon fused to her fist. The rest of the street was strangely complacent. Couples strolled past. Students too. Honoré recognized the boy who'd accepted her moustache. He took no further note of her or the shiny new addition to the Fontaine Saint-Michel. Honoré's dragon loomed over the water. The other statue was half-submerged, completely still again.

Sylvie crept to the fountain's edge. "What did you do, Honoré?"

A fair question. The strangeness of it all was starting to sink in. A statue had attacked her, and she'd used her ring to retaliate. Somehow. The silver was already shrinking back into the slim band she'd always known.

"You never told me you owned a magic ring!" Sylvie said, her tone accusatory.

"I— It's not—" Honoré faltered.

How could she say the ring *wasn't* magic, after what they'd both seen? All the younger girl's stories suddenly sounded plausible. Cats talked. Green birds haunted the midnight skies... Honoré realized, with a start, that she could now see them. There were dozens alighting on nearby trees and the fountain's remaining statues.

"Then how did it just come alive?" wondered Sylvie.

"You tell me!" Honoré waved at the fountain. "You're the one who led us here!"

"I was shadowing Céleste!" the girl informed her. "She and Rafe were following the green birds too! I just didn't want to say so because I knew you'd tell me I was being childish!"

Honoré's cheeks burned. She glared back at the birds, as if it were their fault she hadn't seen them to begin with. "Where's our friend?" she shouted at them. "Did you attack her too?"

"Goodness no."

The answer came from behind them. The dragon on Honoré's middle finger hissed back to life as she spun around—prepared for a fight.

Instead, she found herself face-to-face with the most beautiful woman she'd ever seen.

Her dress was green, and the surrounding streetlamps turned the color into something electric. The woman herself was glowing too. It looked as if there were sunbeams coming from her brow, gold filigree that pulsed and faded. Her eyes were a curious shade of amber, and instead of insects, they trapped time. She might have been twenty years old or twenty times that; Honoré had no idea. She only knew that her own insides flared wherever this other woman's gaze landed.

The ring closed its jaws when the newcomer paused to study it. "Are your thoughts always so violent?" she asked.

Her voice was like biting into a honeycomb, or seeing sunlight break through a storm, or smelling the first leaves of spring after endless winter.

It was enough to make a poet out of Honoré.

And render her speechless.

"Most of the time," Sylvie offered unhelpfully. "But Honoré's never made her ring move before!"

"I've never been attacked by a fountain before!" Honoré mumbled.

The green woman walked to the water and placed a palm on the overturned dragon. It began to stir. "My guard is more vigilant, these days. We thought you were one of *his* pawns." She looked over her shoulder at Honoré. "But you're not, are you?"

Honoré had no idea what this woman was talking about, but she felt compelled to shake her head.

Sylvie snorted. "Honoré would rather swallow a sword than work for a man."

The dragon of the Fontaine Saint-Michel shook water from its wings and climbed back onto its original pedestal as if nothing had happened. The woman turned and regarded Sylvie with something of a smile. "Is that so?"

"Of course! It's why we founded the Enchantresses. But up until now, we've never done any *real* magic." Sylvie tilted her head, taking in the newcomer's searing eyes, her very large folded wings. "Are you a sorceress?"

"Of sorts. The people call me 'La Fée Verte.'"

"I'm Sylvie! And this is Honoré!"

The other woman nodded. "A good name. One of my favorites, in fact. It comes from the patron saint of pastry chefs."

"Really?" Sylvie's grin turned impish as she looked at Honoré. "From now on I will call you 'Mademoiselle Cake'!"

La Fée Verte was watching too, and it was everything Honoré could do to hold her gaze. It felt too warm. To be fair, she'd never looked terribly long into reflections either. "Tell me, Honoré, what is it you are afraid of?"

"Nothing," she lied.

"Cats," Sylvie said.

"I'm not afraid of cats!"

"Then why do you hate them so much?" the girl asked.

"I don't hate them—I—" Honoré swallowed, thinking of the vision she'd had in the Belleville alley, when she'd mistaken Sylvie for her own innocent ghost. "I had a kitten, once. When I was your age. It—it didn't end well."

Sylvie opened her mouth, then shut it again. "Oh," she said, finally. "You never told me that."

La Fée Verte's gaze slid between the Enchantresses. Back and forth. Honoré wasn't quite sure what this magical woman was seeing, much less what it was that made her smile. "I can work with cats.

They can be quite useful if you manage to earn their trust. I'd like to work with you too, Honoré. Would you do me the honor of attending my salon this evening?"

Honoré held her breath. Her insides wavered. She'd just slammed this woman's enchanted statue into the ground. It didn't make sense that such a thing would merit an invitation, much less a job offer. This had to be a trap, somehow.

"I will!" Sylvie had no such misgivings. "Can you teach us how to do more spells, Madame Verte? Can we be sorceresses of sorts too? Oh! If I learn how to make statues move, I can make the lobster on Notre-Dame dance!"

La Fée Verte's smile faded then. "I'm not in the habit of inviting children to my salon, but I suppose I can make an exception if Honoré agrees to accompany me."

Sylvie clasped her hands together. "Oh, please, Honoré! Can we go? I swear I will never talk about talking to cats in front of you again. And I'll never again steal your cheese and blame it on rats when you ask."

"Why would you want to work with me?" Honoré wondered.

"Why wouldn't she?" Sylvie said. "You turned your ring into a dragon!"

"Fighting like that is a lost art." La Fée Verte swept an arm back to the fountain. "My guard here has served me well for the past thirty years, but shadows are starting to circle Paris once more. I'll soon need more than painters and statues to answer my call."

"You need a soldier?" Honoré asked.

"That's one word for it."

"She needs a knight!" Sylvie chirped. "Oh, Honoré, please say yes! Please, please, please?"

Birds rustled above the fountain's centerpiece. Its statues suddenly seemed much more urgent: The Archangel Michael hadn't moved, nor had the devil, yet Honoré wanted them to. She wanted the sword to plunge.

She wanted to feel her dragon's silver wings again.

The ring glimmered as Honoré held it up. "You can show me how to use this?"

La Fée Verte nodded. The beast seemed to be nodding too—its small ears flicked, and its tiny fangs sank shut.

"Well," Honoré relented, "I suppose one late evening couldn't hurt—"

"YAY!"

La Fée Verte smiled when the youngest Enchantress cheered. The birds around the plaza took off in unison, their emerald wings stirring the night air like the velvet insides of a magician's cape or the opening curtains of such an act.

Across the street, an alleyway appeared.

La Fée Verte's flock flew through.

"Welcome to the Quartier Secret," she said.

In the Quartier Secret, the smoke did not choke. The lamps were cheerfully bright. There were no incriminating bloodstains on the bar top—only a drink that turned silver when Honoré touched the glass. It smelled sharp: like frost on grass. She wasn't brave enough to taste it.

Sylvie's drink was a pink so bright, it made your eyes ache. La Fée Verte plucked the flute from the girl's grasp before she had a chance to gulp it down.

"This isn't for children." The skin around her eyes flashed an extra degree brighter. The glass in her hand vanished. "Perhaps when you're older, you can imbibe."

Sylvie sighed. "That's what Céleste always says."

Céleste. Honoré had been so caught up in this fever dream of a woman, she'd forgotten that this entire endeavor had been in pursuit of their friend. The first room in the salon was filled with similar distractions. A group of gentlemen played cards that kept changing suits—a game that proved impossible to win. A woman nearby was wearing a fur that turned out to be a living fox. She was feeding it bonbons.

But the third Enchantress was nowhere to be seen.

"Does this place go on?" Honoré nodded at the thick curtains around the room.

"The only borders here are your own imagination," La Fée Verte told her. "So, Sylvie of a Single Name, if you wish to drink something else, I suggest you conjure it for yourself."

"I can do that?"

"You can do anything you set your mind to in my salon."

The girl squeezed her eyes shut. "I'd like an elephant to pour me a cup of smoky cocoa so that I can drink it and make some fun smoke-ring shapes too."

Honoré glanced back at the card players—just now noticing the armada of ships and flying squid that swirled up from their cigarettes. No, this salon was nothing like her father's den of sins. She supposed she shouldn't worry about Céleste wandering off in such a wondrous place.

"Is it working?" Sylvie squeaked. "Did I create an elephant?"

There was no visible change on or around the girl. Her tunic was streaked with grave dirt and icing. It should have looked out of place with the room's gilded finishes, but Sylvie blended in here as well as she had on the outside streets.

One of the birds landed on La Fée Verte's arm, handing her a glowing string. She knotted this around her wrist. "I might suggest starting with something smaller," she told Sylvie.

"You said space wasn't an issue!" the girl protested.

"It isn't. But bringing an imagining out of your head takes faith on your part. You might find it easier to believe in a single cup of cocoa without the large land mammal serving it."

Sylvie set her shoulders back. The entirety of her tiny form shook with effort, and Honoré knew without a doubt she was still trying to summon an elephant. The girl hated to be told no. It was the only sure way to make her do something.

The bird on La Fée Verte's arm watched with interest, its jade head tilting back and forth. Honoré had seen nonmagical birds do the same after rain showers, while they hunted for worms.

A taut moment passed.

Sylvie scrunched her nose.

A single wild curl of her hair started to shine.

"There!" La Fée Verte exclaimed.

Sylvie opened one eye. "Where?"

The songbird swooped over her head, plucking the hair with its beak. Instead of flying back to La Fée Verte, the animal landed on Sylvie's shoulder, presenting the girl with her own idea. She cradled the glowing string in her palms. Her eyes burned bright with it.

"They grow from your head, of course. You can bring it to life by breaking it in half or you can save—"

The *CRACK* was almost as loud as the gunshots Honoré had heard earlier that evening. Only it wasn't a beer glass breaking. Sylvie had snapped her own imagining in two, and now there was a full-grown elephant spilling out. Honoré stumbled back, but the salon seemed compensate for the creature's presence, adding extra floorboards and growing the glass ceiling several more feet. The elephant's ears brushed a chandelier made of fireflies, scattering the insects like shooting stars. Beneath their light, Honoré could see that the animal wasn't gray but blue.

There was a teacup clasped in its trunk.

The cocoa inside was indeed smoking. These tendrils took the shape of tiny elephants who held even smaller teacups with similar steamy shapes. A picture inside a picture inside a picture. It was exquisitely detailed and dizzying to look at, but this didn't stop the entire room from staring.

"See!" There was triumph in Sylvie's voice as she accepted the hot drink. "I have faith."

A smile lit La Fée Verte's already-radiant face—so bright that Honoré couldn't help but smile too. Only, her cheeks weren't so used to the motion, and they immediately began to ache. So did the cut on her chin. "Try not to overexert yourself. The more dreams you wake here, the longer you'll sleep tomorrow."

It made sense now, why Céleste spent her mornings in a crumpled heap, white hair in disarray. Honoré wondered what sorts of things the other Enchantress pulled from her head. Sylvie's elephant, meanwhile, had gone on to wedge itself behind the bar and was making drinks for the salon's other guests. The girl was grinning so wildly, she could barely swallow her cocoa. Yes, she fit in well here.

Honoré couldn't say the same. She'd caught a glimpse of herself in a dress made of mirrors. The reflection was fast and fragmented, but enough to show exactly how much Rémy had sliced up her face.

Obviously, she wasn't expected to imagine elephants.

"What would you like me to do?" She turned to La Fée Verte, then thought of the first thing she always did, when she settled into a new place. "I could secure the perimeter."

"Honoré makes very good booby traps," Sylvie said, between sips of cocoa. Smoke poured out of her nostrils and ears, looking as swirly as a van Gogh painting. "I'll bet she can make them even better with magic."

Honoré glanced down at her ring. The dragon was back to its original size, but it was still awake. Blinking and yawning and flicking its silver ears.

"I don't think my salon needs any booby traps." The air around La Fée Verte hummed with birds as she fanned her wings. A fresh breeze caressed Honoré's face. "But there is something I'd like to show you."

Enchanted Mirrors

Most mirrors are made of glass.

Most mirrors will bear the sight of you picking spinach out of your teeth without much fuss—thank goodness—but there are others out there that have a little magic mixed with their mercury. To various effects. Some will answer the call *mirror, mirror on the wall* and act as windows. Others may show you your parallel reflection—a life you would have lived in a different world. There are even a rare few that serve as doors. Every one of these enchanted mirrors has a memory.

A memory that can be called upon, with the right spell.

On the night of May 29, 1913, a magical mirror was shattered in the Théâtre des Champs-Élysées. Most of the pieces that fell to the dressing room floor were too small to show anything, but there was one that spun beneath some hanging slippers—a single shard. A glimpse of what really happened at *The Rite of Spring*.

Mirrors do not have ears, so you cannot hear the clamor of Stravinsky's score. You cannot hear the ballerinas' tutus rustle as they step aside for the Ballet Russes performers, who stomp their way to the stage. You see only fragments of this exchange—tulle and hairpins and white-swan limbs. And then? A pair of wings. The Sanct bursts backstage. She almost looks like a dancer herself, all those peacock colors fanning out. Teal and purple feathers. A matching deep aquamarine light swims across her face. You cannot help but be mesmerized as you watch.

Then your breath catches.

Hers must too.

All that the glass shows of the Sanct's attacker is a single hand. A black...glove? It wraps around her throat and does not stop. What first were fingers become claws. Claws turn to vines—dark and choking. The Sanct struggles. Bruise-colored feathers drop from her wings, blowing away like autumn leaves. She withers, until there is nothing left but bone.

Chapter 11

Éclairs Make Terrible Swords

Honoré had seen a lot of horrible things in her twenty-odd years of life. Teeth wrenched from men's screaming jaws. Her mother's own skull cracked like an egg and oozing over the hearth. Black fur peeled away as if it were apple skin.

But she'd never before seen a horror like this.

La Fée Verte held the shard of mirror in her palm. The fizzing gold magic she'd used to summon the memory had faded. The glass was now black. Black and swirling. Honoré could no longer see the skeleton, but she couldn't shake the sight of its eye sockets nor the darkness that crawled through those holes like beetles, hungry for any final scraps of flesh. It was a testament to the steeliness of Honoré's stomach that she managed not to vomit when she opened her mouth.

"Who was that?" she whispered.

"A Sanct called La Belle. She was trying to establish herself in the Champs-Élysées—she'd put the blueprints for the theatre in Auguste Perret's head a few years back, and they'd just finished building it—"

"I meant the ... the ..."

"The black hand?" La Fée Verte's own hand closed over the glass.

Hard enough that Honoré kept waiting to see blood. "I don't know for sure. I have my theories, but even if they were correct, I couldn't tell you. Long ago, I burned his very name away."

Honoré's shiver had nothing to do with the ice-covered walls, which had frozen around the two of them at the other woman's command. She could see Sylvie's elephant silhouetted on the other side, along with the birds, swirling and swirling, like the frost from her own breath.

It was a far better sight than La Belle's corpse.

Dry as a desert. No blood. No stab wounds. No bullets either.

"So there's a real fucking vampire loose in Paris, huh?"

La Fée Verte didn't laugh, the way Honoré had in the alley near Foyot's. "Vampires are the stories your kind tell, the same way my imaginers call me a fairy. But the truth goes deeper than that. Magic does too. It goes all the way down through a person's marrow, past their beating heart, into the miracle that is being *alive.* Into that sacred space between body and being."

"A soul?"

"Many call it that, yes. A better term, perhaps, is 'anima.' It is the unique power of *you.*"

Honoré considered. "You're saying I'm magical?"

"Everyone is."

"So why isn't the whole world pulling smoky-cocoa elephants out of their heads?"

"Everyone is magical," La Fée Verte went on, "but only Sancts can cast spells. I use my powers to host this salon, where my patrons can dream of higher things, where they use their anima and shed it, as one might shed a hair." She nodded at the bangles on her arms. "It's not so different from prayer, in some ways. There are even Sancts who glean their magic at altars." She traced the bracelets—up, up, up—until her fingers hovered above her crescendoed collarbone. There was a musical curve to her lips too, as she smiled at Honoré. "My temple just so happens to have cake."

"And dragons."

"Yes. Cake and dragons—two very essential elements."

"I never figured those things could go together," Honoré admitted.

"Whyever not?"

Because éclairs make terrible swords. She glanced back at the wall, where Sylvie's silhouette sparkled past the frost. The girl had called her *Mademoiselle Cake* at least twice since they'd stepped inside the salon. It wasn't nearly as annoying as Honoré pretended it was—she'd never meant to christen herself after the patron saint of pastries, yet the name still fit in a way she couldn't shake. Just like the silver ring that slithered around the knuckles of her middle finger.

"None of the dragons I've met have had much of a sweet tooth." She tried to say this in a teasing way, tried not to remember Maman's swollen jaw or the rival gangsters with blood dribbling down their chins.

No, she looked back to La Fée Verte instead.

The Sanct was wearing only a thin green shift, but she didn't look the least bit cold, even with frost gathering on her eyelashes. She hardly blinked as she regarded Honoré. It felt strange to be stared at this way. To be studied, not as a threat but as something else. Something... softer. As soft as the smile that stayed on La Fée Verte's face.

"Well, you strike me as someone who could break the mold. Or at the very least recast it. Do you mind if I take a closer look at your relic?" the Sanct asked, when she reached out her hand.

Honoré stared at those fingers, so slender, tapered like candles. No wonder her own skin caught flame when they touched. Was it magic? It certainly felt like magic, glittering up her veins, as their hands joined. Her ring grew wings, and there was a matching flutter in her stomach. She could count La Fée Verte's breaths—one, two, three. Heat grazed everywhere the dragon was not.

"This looks like Revolution-era handiwork," the Sanct said, after a moment's examination. "How did you come by it?"

"Terreur."

"A Sanct?"

"My..." Honoré hesitated. It had been years since she'd spoken the word aloud, but better here than beneath Rémy's blade. She felt that she could let down her guard with La Fée Verte, just a bit. "My father."

The Sanct looked down at the dragon again. There was something in her eyes that told Honoré she knew about the marks the ring had left. How the bruises had healed, but the girl had not. How Honoré feared that if she ever peeled back her flesh, she'd find the beast engraved into her very bones.

"And how did he come by it?"

"His father, I expect." To tell the truth, she wasn't quite sure where this inheritance came from. Thank God her father had never figured out his ring was a magical relic—that he'd never truly turned its jaws on her.

The beast's fangs bared wide, as if it had heard what Honoré was thinking.

La Fée Verte released her hand. "The Fisherman of the Moon might be able to tell us more." She caught Honoré's quizzical look. "He's a merchant in Saint-Ouen who makes his living trading enchanted antiques: Glass slippers. Compasses that point to what your heart wants. Those sorts of things."

Honoré's own heart was twisting, spinning, trying to catch up with everything she'd discovered. "How many Sancts are in Paris?"

"Fewer and fewer these days." La Fée Verte looked at the mirror shard, which was back to reflecting her own face. A deeper sorrow shimmered just past the gold. "I drove this darkness out of Paris many years ago—since then it's become known as the City of Light—but he's grown stronger in exile. Strong enough to start trying to re-establish his territory here. He's failed to find a foothold in the Champs-Élysées, but he keeps testing my wards."

"In Saint-Germain and Montparnasse?"

She could tell her guesses were correct by the way the other woman's brow arched.

"I've heard rumors," Honoré explained.

"If that's the case, then it's not just Sancts under attack. He never did know when to stop..." Her voice drifted, in and out of some murky memory. "I have to protect my imaginers."

Honoré could see why. Even when she shut her eyes, she could see that dark hand reaching, taking...and when she opened them again, she saw the elephant's shadow. Sylvie was on its back, raising a cocoa cup high in the air. Was... had she sprouted butterfly wings? Honoré's chest ached at the sight, as if her heart had always been too small and now was trying to grow a size.

"I know you understand," La Fée Verte said softly.

Did she? "It's just—it's difficult for me to wrap my mind around. You. The Quartier Secret. All this magic. Even now it's hard to believe." Honoré swallowed. "I don't think I can give you any fancy dreams. I'm not like Sylvie. No one ever read me fairy tales when I was a child."

The wooden knights Gabriel had entertained himself with didn't count. Not after their father caught on to the fact his son was playing with "*dolls*." His boot stomped most of them to splinters. It had stomped Honoré's pinky too, when she'd tried to save one, so her finger was crooked from that day after. Forever changing the way she held her knife.

"I don't need your imaginings, Honoré. If you had been raised on fairy tales, then you'd know that no story is without its struggle. I chose you, at the fountain, because you used this dragon to protect not just yourself but Sylvie too," La Fée Verte said. "That is *your* power."

Again, Honoré wasn't so sure. She looked down at the long-broken knuckle. The ring—seeming to sense her thoughts about knights—spilled over to the old wound, covering her hand like a gauntlet. When she made a fist, she discovered the silver felt molten. When she pressed it into the opposite palm, she found the metal solid.

No boot could crush this. Bullets and blades wouldn't leave much of a dent either.

It bent only to her *will*.

If Honoré concentrated hard enough, she could shape the metal, guiding it just as she had during the battle. She could spread it up her arm and over her chest. She could sprout talons from her fingertips and wings between her shoulder blades. She could make herself strong enough to face demons—both old and new.

Chapter 12

Dreaming to Survive

The salon was always changing, but Céleste had managed to find a pattern to the place. Artists were creatures of habit and comfort. They liked to take their aperitifs in the front room and nibble on crystallized flowers while they reintroduced themselves—their memories as hazy as the surrounding smoke. Céleste had met Jean Cocteau nearly twenty times, and he'd herded her to the designers' tent after half of those, recalling only during her fitting that he'd dressed her before. *Never mind! What shall we wear this evening? A cape made of storm clouds? A scarf knitted with auroras? Trousers hemmed in honeysuckle?*

At least he remembered now that she preferred pants. And pockets.

These outfits became her touchstones, a way to tell this endless stream of evenings apart. Nights of fire, moonbeams, and furs. But every single one of these costumes paled in comparison to putting on Rafe's shadow. There was nothing quite like the feel of its darkness against her skin—sleek, but also crackling. Wearing his silhouette was like listening to a gramophone right after the needle dropped, waiting, waiting for the song to finally play. It reminded Céleste too of how winter air sometimes pulled itself tight around her fingers, turning her touches to sparks.

It felt like this all over.

Every night.

They met before the enchanted hour, sometimes at a café in the Latin Quarter, sometimes at a bench by the river—always approaching the Fontaine Saint-Michel together. Céleste still didn't trust the dragon to let her in alone, and Rafe didn't seem to mind being used as an imaginary shield. He played the part of romantic dreamer well. Almost too well. Whenever they stepped into the Quartier Secret, whenever he handed her an aperitif that somehow tasted exactly like dawn swallows swirling around a château's slanted roof, whenever his color-splashed fingertips tightened around his own flute, whenever he tipped its orange contents down his throat, Céleste could see an altogether different life.

She saw it in the painters' wing too.

Rafe liked to stop here, often after their costume change, when they were wearing moss or spiders' silk or a cape woven out of fables. Céleste looked down at these words, hemming her ankles, wishing she'd thought to ask for an invisibility cloak instead. The problem with relying on Rafe García's shadow was that it put her at his mercy. She could not go down into the Vault of Dreams until he finished painting.

Oh, how he painted.

Rafe's talent was raw. Her old art teacher would have been aghast at the way he held a brush, but the former gangster didn't seem to give a damn about form. He rolled up his shirtsleeves. He slashed. He slapped. He moved as if he were in the middle of a street fight instead of an all-encompassing canvas. It *was* a sort of battle—against the room's blankness. Rafe kept filling the white with frenzied strokes, summoning scenes that made Céleste forget his combative movements completely.

There were staircases that climbed into themselves, until you reached a ceiling of stars that could be picked and eaten like fruit. Balconies would become cliffside cities. Stained glass floors rose into rainbow-hued mountains, which rose into skies filled with colorful clouds, clouds that had castles tucked in their towering shapes, so that you had to paint wings on your own back to reach them. It was possible here. Artists often opened their exhibits toward the end of the evening, so that salon-goers could wander through one of André Derain's famed forests or get lost in a maze created by Pablo Picasso.

Rafe's landscapes felt like the beginning of something bigger though. You'd need more than one night to explore them properly... such as this ice palace. It sat on top of a slow-moving glacier, its walls threaded through with auroras. Green light grew like vines. Blue spilled through too. Bits of gold dashed up Rafe's forearms as he mixed a new borealis with his brush. It looked as if he'd plunged his hands into a vat of sunlight.

"Are you almost done?" Céleste called out.

"Never." He straightened, pushing some of the hair from his face to meet her gaze. The motion left trails of gold over his cheeks. "Why? Would you like to try?"

A satin sky yawned above them, crying out for more stars. Something yawned inside Céleste too, when Rafe walked over with the flaring brush in his fist. His shadow did not so much as touch her, and for a moment, she let herself imagine a life where she didn't need it. A night spent adding turrets to his castles and constellations to his skies and then drawing new horizons of her own. Nothing like those poorly painted backdrops at *The Rite of Spring*—who the hell believed that looked like Russia?

Céleste hadn't thought twice about this at the ballet, but she knew better now, thanks to her weekly visits to the Mad Monk. It wasn't quite like confession—there was no screen between her and the Sanct who posed as a priest. His head would bow, and his eyes would light, and a numbing blue would freeze her lungs, and it was all too easy to imagine snow blanketing the garden on the other side of the window.

She was due for another glimpse today, but only if she had dreams to burn first.

If they returned to [redacted] without any imaginings, he would be... displeased.

Céleste reached out and seized the brush. "We should go before we give ourselves frostbite."

Her voice felt ice thin.

Her fingers dripped with light. His too. Rafe was still holding the brush.

"I'd rather just paint you a coat," he said. "Fuchsia fox or silver sable? Which one do you want?"

Céleste did not want a coat. She didn't care what Rafe wanted either, or so she told herself. She tried to ignore the way their hands overlapped—tried not to think of more gold tracing their skin, of gilding each other's bodies like illustrations from a fairy tale. She didn't look at the divot on his chin. Nor did she let her gaze drop to the muscular ridges of his chest, even though his shirt made of sea fog did little to hide them.

"We already spent a tragic amount of time getting decorated by Jean this evening," she told him. "We can't waste any more painting snowflakes—"

"A waste?" Rafe's laugh wasn't funny at all. It shook them both, rattling the chains of his watch too. "Is that what you think this is? A waste? I spent my entire youth stuck in a moldy room, drawing whatever my boss wanted. Signatures, deeds, banknotes—nothing that was really worth a damn. I hated scribbling that uninspired shit, but I didn't have much of a choice in the matter. I drew the best I could in that dark closet. There wasn't even a window to look out of—so I found myself some posters to stick to the wall. The travel ones had the best landscapes. Athenian ruins. The golden spires of Constantinople. When I stared at them, I had something to look forward to." His gaze swept over the wintry chamber. "What's the point, otherwise?"

Céleste watched her cloudy breath rise. Fade. The palace he'd painted on the glacier looked a lot like the estate she'd spent *her* childhood in—ogival arches, matching turrets, a weather vane with a vain *A*. She wondered if Rafe had picked up those details from her own dark memory, when [redacted] had plucked it from her head. Did he think this was a place she wanted to escape to?

"When I was young, I lived in a château with lots of windows," she said. "My father was a rich man, but that didn't stop him from chasing fantasies. He lost our fortune to a swindler when I was seventeen, but he never told my mother and me. Instead, he found the highest window he could." Her eyes flicked to the tallest tower. Its walls were starting to sweat, and a puddle was forming on the snow below, where the Artoises' groundskeeper had found the body. "The house was shut up after that. My mother couldn't cope. She was sent to Charenton." Chunks of ice were falling now. "I lost everything."

"Careful," Rafe said sharply.

The whole castle was melting, sinking into its own glowing lake like some eerie Camelot. It swept Céleste's cape of fables around her ankles. It rose up to her knees, cold as grief. She couldn't stop it even if she tried, and God, how she'd tried. She took the train to Paris and didn't look back. She kept on taking. She'd swindled men as stupid as her father and buried their gold. Now she had to spend her nights trying to dig her way out of her own grave. *Céleste Estelle Artois has enough dirt on her hands as it is.* The Seer's words rushed back with the water. *She became what ruined her, but she stands to become so much more. She's exactly where she needs to be.*

Well, she would be. If she could just get Rafe to let go of the brush and hand her his damned shadow...

"I can't always be stardust," Céleste said. "I have to survive."

She'd spent five years turning this pain into profit, but she'd never spilled the truth of it like this. Not even Honoré knew the whole story.

Rafe's expression softened.

"I know," he whispered. "Believe me, I know, but dreaming is surviving." He let go of the brush then, to run a hand through his dark hair. This didn't just leave trails of gold but silver too—his ideas shimmered like tinsel. "If you go too long in the salon without creating something original, La Fée Verte will notice. She may not invite you back."

Shit. She hadn't considered this. Even though Céleste held the brush with perfect technique, it felt strange in her hand. Her calluses could no longer be called that, after three weeks without painting. The canvases in the Enchantresses' tomb were blank, and her mind felt much the same. The last time she'd sketched something that was truly hers, she'd been sitting in that melting turret.

As for shining hairs? Well, the green birds did not flock to her the way they bothered the other imaginers... Could they sense Céleste was sourcing her sense of wonder from Sylvie's storybooks? Forgeries seemed to be about the only thing she could conjure, apart from that first night following the dragon, when Rafe had stolen her hairpin. When everything turned glittering...

The thief was even closer now than he'd been then.

The gold on his face shimmered. So did the paint on his fingers, as he reached out to touch a strand of hair by Céleste's cheek. "After being locked away in that dark room for so many years, the light of this salon was almost too much. It took me weeks to finally paint something that *was* worth a damn." Rafe glanced back at the brush in her hand. "You *do* want to try, don't you?"

"Am I so transparent?" She certainly felt that way, as one of the castle's outer ramparts collapsed. As Rafe's fingers grazed her cheek. As her own hand tightened around the brush.

Want—yes, that was a word that spelled out Céleste's life. Only, she'd never felt it quite so keenly before. Instead of a hole in her belly, there was a fire.

"Go on," Rafe murmured. "The night's young. We have plenty of time to explore your landscape."

He was right.

Well, she *wanted* him to be right, and that was all that mattered as Céleste tilted her head closer to his. Rafe's hand traced down her jaw, tipping her chin just so, leaning in, in—

"OH!"

Both artists pulled apart at the sound. It had come from the outer edges of the landscape room, where the phosphorescent ice castle's water was sweeping past an elephant—of all things. The blue creature was balancing a tray of drinks on its trunk.

And on the animal's back...

"Were you about to kiss?" Sylvie called gaily. She was wearing a cape that unfolded into a large pair of orange butterfly wings, which she then used to balance along the beast's spine. "I didn't mean to interrupt. But I'm glad I did! We've been looking *everywhere* for you, Céleste! And I do mean everywhere! Isn't this place amazing? I can't believe you never told us about it before."

"*Sylvie?*" Céleste faltered in the frigid water, at a loss. "Your hair is . . ."

The girl finished triumphantly. "Pink!"

"Violently." Rafe looked as shocked as Céleste was, seeing her young ward with fuchsia curls, on top of an elephant. "It seems I should have nicknamed you 'Weasel' instead of 'Magpie.' How on earth did you manage to sneak in here?"

"I didn't sneak! La Fée Verte invited us inside because she wants Honoré to become a knight, just like Joan of Arc! Did you know her dragon ring is magical, Céleste? You should see her fight with it. She's supposed to learn how to battle shadows . . ."

"Shadows?" Céleste was thankful then that Rafe's silhouette was submerged.

The man himself appeared to be holding his breath.

"I think so," Sylvie went on. "La Fée Verte wouldn't say any more about it in front of me. They stepped into this castle and froze up the drawbridge a while ago and— Oh! Hello again!"

The last of the walls had washed away to reveal Honoré. Her friend looked changed. There was a nasty new cut on her face, but that was the least of it. Something about the way she stood *did* bring Joan of Arc to mind. Someone had conjured her a suit of armor . . . and there was a halo of light surrounding the other Enchantress, making her sharp features even sharper. Holier-than-thou. A war-banner image.

"*Mon amie!*" When Honoré started splashing toward her, Céleste saw the glow had come from La Fée Verte. She saw the armor was not a couturier's idea but her friend's dragon ring. Its band had rippled out from Honoré's fist, sheathing her skin in metal. "Can you believe it?"

No. Céleste couldn't.

She'd walked away from Honoré, dusk after dusk, because she thought she'd had no choice but to leave the other Enchantresses in the dark. Now—here under the light of La Fée Verte's stare—she saw what a mistake that had been.

"Honoré." It had never been so hard to say her friend's name before. "What— How did you find this place?"

"No thanks to you two." The other Enchantress's eyes cut to where Rafe was standing. "Why the hell did you keep this salon a secret?"

"It *is* a secret," Rafe explained. "No one who attends this place remembers it after sunrise."

"Everyone forgets all this?" Sylvie's pink brows knit together. "Every morning?"

La Fée Verte was moving toward them, but her steps didn't seem to ripple the water. "There are exceptions," she said. "I've invited Honoré to stay for the foreseeable future, so she can help me with some... security." Rafe's smile wavered at this. Céleste doubled down on hers. "Nothing for you to worry about, *mes rêveurs*."

Au contraire.

Her stomach twisted as she watched Honoré's ring crawl up her arm, until the dragon grew to the size of a hawk and perched on her shoulder. It reminded Céleste of the fountain statue—right down to the glint of its teeth.

"Isn't it wonderful?" Sylvie leapt off the elephant, her butterfly wings a frantic burst of orange. They were fresh and clumsy. She landed in a somersault, water splashing, her pink hair splayed across her face. "We can create anything we want! Did you paint this castle, Céleste?"

"Rafe did."

Rafe, who was eyeing the ring as if he expected it to bite him. Honoré seemed to notice his wariness, but she also seemed to understand. "It's all right," she told him. "I'm controlling it."

La Fée Verte raised her gilded eyebrows. "You know this piece?"

"I knew its former owner," he said tightly.

"I went back to the bar this evening, looking for you," Honoré said. "And then I found myself here." She looked back at the palace's dripping foundations. "You really are an honest artist now, huh?"

"I try my best," replied Rafe.

"His landscapes do liven up the place." La Fée Verte looked out over the glowing waters. "Rafe is one of my regulars. And you..." She glanced at Céleste, at the brush that hung from her hand. "I'm glad you've finally found your way to the painters' wing. Perhaps you could draw me another skirtless dress? The idea is probably well before its time, but I'd love to try planting it with one of the designers. Maybe Coco?"

"That's a fun name!" Sylvie took a sip from her steaming mug. "Speaking of names, did you know Honoré is the saint of cakes? Maybe you could draw her a coat of arms with éclairs and macarons." She laughed.

The other Enchantress rolled her eyes, and Céleste clenched her jaw so hard, her teeth started to ache. Her stomach kept turning, just as it had with that final bite of Sylvie's birthday tart. She wished she could go back to that moment—to the three of them sitting in their tomb—and make Honoré believe she was mad. That would be so much better than the alternative...

La Fée Verte smiled. "It's probably best to leave baked goods to the Sanct behind Stohrer."

Sylvie perked up at the mention of her favorite pâtisserie. Its windows displayed cakes with as much care as jewelry and had been smudged by her nose many, many times. "Stohrer is enchanted?"

"All bakeries have a sprinkle of magic, but if you go to Stohrer after hours, you'll find some extra-special treats," La Fée Verte told her. "The sweets I serve here pale in comparison."

"I'm quite fond of the baba au rhum," Rafe said. "Its syrup tastes like candlelight."

All at once, Sylvie started fluttering.

Up, up, and aw—

Honoré caught the youngest Enchantress by the ankle, before she could fly too far. "Where do you think you're going?"

"Where do *you* think?" Her wings kept flapping, layering Honoré's hair with orange butterfly dust. "To the enchanted pastry shop!"

"You can't just take off all on your own like that! It's dangerous!"

"So you keep saying. But I saved *you* from that gangster this evening—"

"There are worse things than gangsters out there, *ma rêveuse*."

Céleste didn't miss the glance between Honoré and La Fée Verte. She saw the way the Sanct's hand tightened over... an imagining? For a heart-stuttering second, Céleste feared it was one of her pieces, but no—it was nothing more than a shard of glass.

"Much worse," Honoré added.

"There are wonderful things as well," La Fée Verte said. "The bakery is quite safe—in fact it's one of the safest places in the city. You and your friends should go visit. Perhaps you'll find out that dragon of yours has a sweet tooth after all."

To Céleste's surprise, Honoré almost smiled.

"Great!" Sylvie called from above. "Let's go!"

A Sweet Escape

Stohrer is the oldest pâtisserie in Paris.

It is also the most magical.

The key is to go after hours—once the FERMÉ sign is turned and the overhead awning droops like a heavy lid. Pay no mind to these things, for as soon as you place your hand on the bakery door, you'll smell its invitation: Butter as rich as an evening sun. Folds of chocolate and caramel. This alone is enough to make you step inside, but then! You see that the glass chandelier drips with melt-in-your-mouth snowflakes. Pastries shaped like hot-air balloons float by—their tops made of spun sugar bubbles. Swallows with marzipan wings dive past towers of chocolate truffles.

"Can I help you?" asks a gentleman behind the counter.

The cases displaying his cakes need no light—you can see the macarons well enough when he bends down to show you their flavors. His masque glows over the labels: *Carols on a Snowy Evening. A First Kiss. A Second Kiss. An April Picnic by the River.* You choose Bastille Day Fireworks and an éclair filled with cloud crème.

"Make sure there's a ceiling over your head when you eat this," the baker says, as he hands you the paper bag.

Your mouth is already watering. "What do I owe you?"

What. Not *how much.* It's a question you've learned to ask, in such establishments. Magic is always give-and-take, but no Sanct is the same. This one seems sweeter than others—perhaps a side effect of working with so much sugar. His masque flashes when he smiles. "For my pastries? All you have to do is enjoy them."

It is not such a terrible price to pay, you think, as you hold the door open for a girl wearing a pair of butterfly wings. She's followed by a strange parade: a woman in armor, a man wearing an uneasy shadow, a woman with hair the color of starlight. As if she is always and forever dreaming.

Chapter 13

Fable and Lore

Céleste had plenty of chances to come clean about her new grift. She could have confessed with a mouthful of macaron—which somehow tasted *exactly* like stargazing on a Brun De Vian-Tiran blanket with a flask of hot cider. She could have said something at the café they passed, where tea was served to customers in cups with changing china patterns. Languages changed too, depending on the flavor of the leaves they sipped. English, Russian, Japanese...

Céleste didn't use any of these to tell Honoré and Sylvie the truth.

Nor did she slip in a word as the Enchantresses followed Rafe into a bookshop in the ninth arrondissement, where shelves wandered with as much purpose as an American tourist. Books were stacked on the floor as well, providing perfect perches for the shop's cats. Céleste spotted at least two—a tom with a bottlebrush tail and a beautiful cream-colored cat with cocoa markings—napping on leatherbound volumes. They seemed to know Rafe. The shopkeeper did too, uttering an exclamation when he saw who'd set the bells by his door chiming.

"I have just the thing for you, Monsieur García! A book from the ashes of Alexandria arrived only a week ago, and I thought immediately of your fondness for Egyptian myths—"

Why was it all booksellers wore spectacles? Surely the Sanct didn't need them to see. A silver masque scrolled his temples, flickering with whatever magic the bookseller used to summon the manuscript. The parchment was old and charred in several places. It would be hard enough to read even if it *weren't* written in a long-dead language, but this didn't stop Rafe from scanning the text, pausing every few lines to smile at some mysterious words.

It seemed he didn't need any special tea to translate them.

Honoré noticed this too. "I'm sorry, but where the hell did you learn to read hieroglyphics?"

"Cairo," he replied, his gaze still buried in the manuscript. "Where else?"

"You traveled all the way to Egypt?" Honoré frowned. "I didn't think the Orient Express went that far."

"It doesn't." Rafe unrolled the scroll a bit farther. "Thank you for this, Libris."

"The real thanks should go to Lore," the bookseller said. "He was the one who remembered your interest in embalming techniques. I hope this manuscript holds whatever it is you're hunting for."

Rafe looked up from the papyrus. His expression was still, so still, and his shadow was too, but Céleste could feel *something* shifting. It coiled almost as tightly as the scroll he tucked into the lining pocket of his jacket. This was exactly where he would've put the dreams they weren't forging. The perfect place for secrets.

"Your assistant is quite attentive," he said, with a smile that showed no teeth.

The bookseller smiled back. "I wouldn't call Lore my assistant. In fact, he'd probably consider the opposite arrangement to define our relationship. Is there anything else I can help you find before dawn, Monsieur García?"

"Do you have any fairy books?" Sylvie's butterfly wings kept brushing the bells by the door—she was unable to contain her excitement. "My rainbow is missing some colors."

"Which ones?" the Sanct asked.

"Lilac, I think."

"They're by Andrew Lang," Céleste explained. "The covers are very shiny."

Libris the Bookseller pushed his spectacles back up his nose. "Ah, let me have a look around. Feel free to do the same!"

But Céleste did not feel free at all as she explored the stacks. It should've been an exciting experience: so many stories waiting to be discovered while Sylvie flew from shelf to shelf and Honoré shouted at the girl to "watch your wingspan!" But the deeper Céleste went into the shelves, the more she felt the weight of so many unspoken words bowing in on her. It was hard to breathe, and it wasn't even morning yet. What would happen when the sun rose? When this cape of fables unraveled and no dreams spilled out?

Céleste would have nothing to show for her evening—and yet, she'd be exposed. Caught, not in a lie, but in her own terrible truth. Coughing blood.

She took a sharp breath.

Her hands wandered to her hair as she went deeper into the bookstore, inhaling the quintessential smell of *stories*—leather and ink aged with dust. It would be an interesting macaron flavor. Interesting enough for [redacted] to burn, at least. But try as she might, Céleste couldn't get the idea of this pastry out of her head. Nor could she stand the thought of going back to rue des Ombres empty-handed, so she kept twisting her hair into knots.

"What's wrong, *mon amie*?"

Honoré stood on the other side of the shelf, peering through a gap in the books. The titles framed her face in a way that called attention to the cut—short, but deep. She must have gotten the wound hours ago, but it hadn't stopped bleeding completely.

Céleste bit her own tongue. She'd taste red again, if she wasn't careful. "I—I was just trying to imagine something."

"I'm not sure that works without La Fée Verte," Honoré said.

Silence passed through their shelf, a stretch too long.

"I know why you keep going back to her salon, every night," her friend went on.

Another pause.

Somewhere, in another aisle, Sylvie squealed with delight.

"All this time we've been calling ourselves the Enchantresses when there was real magic out there, just waiting. If I could paint like you or Rafael, I'd absolutely choose castles over confidence schemes. You deserve this, *mon amie*." Honoré glanced toward the front of the shop, where Rafe was browsing. Then she looked back at her ring, which had spent most of the evening perched on her shoulder. "So do I."

"Sylvie says you're going to be La Fée Verte's knight," Céleste said.

"You know how she likes to romanticize things—" Patches of pink appeared on Honoré's cheeks. "But I figure, if you're going to spend your evenings at the salon, then I should too."

She tried not to tug on her hair, tried not to shrink at the thought of doing this every night. "What about when I forget in the mornings?" she asked with a dry mouth.

"You spend most of that time with Rafael anyway, no?" Honoré looked down at Céleste's gold-streaked fingers, her own flaxen eyebrows rising. "Our days don't have to be any different than they have been, lately. I suppose I could convince La Fée Verte to let you keep your memories too. She did make a concession for Sylvie—"

There was another squeal. A scuffle.

"And just what do you think you're doing, mademoiselle?" Céleste recognized the bookseller's voice then. "Can't you read?"

"Why else would I be browsing a bookshop?" came Sylvie's reply. "The sign says to ASK FOR ASSISTANCE!"

Honoré and Céleste exchanged glances and then hurried around the shelves. They found their pink-haired ward standing by a locked case—though locks had never been terribly effective where the youngest Enchantress was concerned. The glass door was hanging open, and the book that should have been behind it was now in Sylvie's hands. It looked rather plain compared to the other volumes on the shelves. Bare brown. There didn't even seem to be a title. Yet... as the girl clutched the book to her chest, Céleste saw gilding grow across its cover. Gold letters began to unfurl one by one:

The Enchantresses of Paris

"I think it's a story about us! See?" Sylvie flipped to the first page and tapped at the opening sentences. "'Père Lachaise was home to some very unusual ghosts.' It talks about you too, Céleste! You never told me you used to be Catholic. And is your tongue really made of silver?"

Céleste was biting it harder than ever, hoping there were no lines about how she'd lied, how she was still lying, how she was going to die if she didn't.

Libris the Bookseller also seemed distraught, fumbling for a pair of gloves draped by the case. Rafe grabbed the book instead. As soon as he touched the cover, its shining letters shifted into darker words: *The Unbreakable—*

But the title was interrupted, when Libris swooped in, placing the volume back behind the glass.

Sylvie made a face. "I was just getting to the good part—"

"Not much good comes out of reading your own story," the bookseller said shakily. "Hence the sign. I can skim some passages for you if you're willing to pay—"

"No," Rafe said quickly. "That won't be necessary."

Sylvie's brown eyes were glimmering. "Would it tell me who my parents were?" she asked.

"There's no telling *what* it might tell you," the bookseller informed her. "Everyone thinks they want to know how their lives will unfold, but I find that's rarely the case, even when it's a happy ending awaiting them."

"But, if you didn't like your ending, couldn't you just change it?" Sylvie wondered.

According to the Seer of the Seine, you could. But Libris did not say anything about dusty stars as he closed the case. He glanced back at the smallest Enchantress and—with a silver wink from his masque—added a second lock to the latch. "I'm afraid I must ask you to pay for the pages you've read."

Sylvie dug into her pockets.

She produced a ball of lint and a mashed macaron.

The bookseller sniffed the crumbling pastry. "I am fond of the

First Spring Leaf flavor, but I'll need more." He nodded at Honoré. "That ring might do." The ring in question bared its silver fangs. "Or your watch, Monsieur García? I've admired that piece for years."

Sylvie dug into her pockets again. "What about these?"

The dreams she pulled out shimmered pink—no surprise there. What struck Céleste was the fact there were so *many* of them and so much hair still left on the girl's head. The bookseller seemed fascinated as well. His spectacles glistened as he leaned down to inspect her offerings: A pod of white dolphins playing around a ship with seafoam for sails. Carousel horses galloping through a field of strawberries that were actually rubies. A princess and a pauper playing a game of chess.

"You're quite the daydreamer, aren't you?"

"I'll say." Honoré snorted. "She's convinced cats can talk."

"But of course they can." The bookseller glanced up at the gray tom, who was now perched on top of the display case. "Lore here has all sorts of fascinating tales to tell. I've tried my hand at translating over the years, and I've managed to record quite an extensive list of vocabulary. I can share it with you, if you're interested." He nodded back at the ideas in Sylvie's hand. "Hand over half, and we'll call ourselves even."

"Half?" Rafe raised his eyebrow. "Don't be such a shark, Libris! That's far too—"

"Deal!"

The tom watched closely as Sylvie handed over her imaginings. The bookseller didn't knot them into bracelets, nor did he toss them into a fire. Instead, he grabbed a nearby book and slipped the dreams between the pages, the way one might press a flower. Then he hurried down one of the aisles. Lore hopped off the shelf and trotted after him.

"Your dreams are worth more," Rafe told Sylvie. "Much more, if you save them. You should've haggled."

The youngest Enchantress shrugged. "I can just imagine other things. And it would be nice to understand what Marmalade is saying."

"Marmalade?" Céleste asked.

"The orange cat who has a taste for human flesh," Honoré clarified. "She named him after jam."

"He does have a sweet side," Sylvie said. "You've just never given him a chance to show it. Whatever happened to that kitten you had when you were a child isn't *his* fault, you know."

The other Enchantress's face didn't flinch, but her ring did. The dragon coiled around her neck, then spilled down her chest, covering most of her torso in silver. Her legs had to shift to hold the weight—moving into what Céleste recognized as a fighting stance. The first position of *défense dans la rue*.

Rafe mirrored this.

Céleste did not miss the way the thief placed himself in front of her and Sylvie.

"It wasn't Honoré's fault either," he said, eyeing his own reflection in the armor.

Both shimmered.

Then shrank.

Beads of sweat sprouted on Honoré's forehead. They rolled down to her nose as the dragon pulled back, retreating to its original perch on her middle finger.

"Here you are." The bookseller had returned, holding a volume almost as heavy as Sylvie herself. She nearly toppled over when he handed it to her. "*The Known Words of Fable and Lore*." The other cat's cream-colored ears perked up at the sound of its name. It yowled plaintively at Céleste. "Fable says to tell you that she likes your cape very much, mademoiselle." He glanced back at Sylvie. "If you're interested in other languages, I have plenty of guides. Flowers, clouds, bees, rivers, trees . . . Everything speaks if you know how to listen. Even houseflies hum in the key of F major."

"Sure," Sylvie said, as if this were common knowledge. "But I should probably just stick to cats, for now. They don't like sharing attention."

"You are wise, daydreamer." Libris smiled. "I expect you'll become fluent in cat-speak quite soon. I'll keep an eye out for that lilac fairy book in the meantime, and if you return *The Known Words of Fable and Lore* when you're finished, I'll buy it back by completing your rainbow."

Rafe did not seem worried at all when they exited the bookshop. He didn't bat an eye at the stars—which seemed to be growing waterier by the minute—nor did he try to turn toward the Quartier Secret. Even if they *did* wander back that way, there wouldn't be time to forge anything, Céleste realized. They'd wasted too many hours painting the ice palace and eating cake, and was she just imagining it, or could she already taste some iron on her tongue?

"What's next?" Sylvie sounded breathless, but that could have been because the book about cat-speak was so large. Large enough that she'd resorted to balancing the tome on her head instead of carrying it. "A mysterious meeting of owls? A secret garden party?"

"There *is* one of those at Temple de l'Amitié," Rafe told her, "but that's all the way over on rue Jacob. There are closer festivities. This way!" He waved them north, where the night wheeled over a distant hill and the almost-finished alabaster domes of Sacré-Cœur shone like the bite of an orchard apple.

"Isn't Sylvie a little young for Montmartre?" Céleste asked in a rusty voice.

"No!" the girl protested.

"I promise we won't get into *too* much trouble." Rafe looked back over his shoulder and winked. "We'll just go for a stroll up rue Lepic! Ten-year-olds can stroll, no?"

"I'm eleven!"

"Even better! Honoré and I snuck out here when we were that age!" Rafe whirled back on his heels with a laugh. Céleste was getting dizzy watching him, the gold paint on his face streaking like tiger stripes. Surely *he* wasn't planning on returning to rue des Ombres empty-handed. Was he?

It all turned to shit.

I was wrong to trust him.

Céleste glanced over at Honoré, remembering her friend's grave warning, but she seemed to be swimming in other memories. The dragon ring had swirled back up the Enchantress's shoulder, perching there like a hunter's falcon. Its gaze found Céleste first. Silver and separate.

Honoré's brown eyes looked cheery by comparison. "A short walk shouldn't hurt," she said. "Shall we?"

It was difficult to tell what was magical in Montmartre. The neighborhood already had a glittering otherworldly quality. Cabarets spilled up its liveliest street—rue Lepic—like a purse of loose jewels. There was a stucco elephant in Moulin Rouge's garden that was nearly a match for Sylvie's cocoa-dispensing dream—and as Céleste walked through the crimson puddles of light the club's sign splashed on the sidewalk, she couldn't help but think of Henri. Was the poor little rich boy inside the statue's belly, crying to dancers about con artists? Or was he still going on about vampires?

Again, such creatures didn't sound so far-fetched here. Up the lane sat a restaurant that used coffins as tables, and next to that was a place guarded by pearly gates. Cabaret du Ciel, it was called. The wings worn there were made of wires and harnesses, but a few doors down, you could find the real deal: feathers sprouting from bare shoulder blades.

Sylvie stopped in her tracks when more songbirds burst through the door of this establishment. Not green, but red as holly berries. There were yellow ones too—daffodil bright. "What's this?"

CABARET D'AILES, so said the sign. Céleste recognized the name from the moving posters. She recognized the birds as well. They swirled the same way they did on paper; red and yellow sparks curled into calligraphy. An elegant invitation over the street.

"A place where *want* can be turned into wings," Rafe explained. "Désirée and Plume will let you fly for an evening, if you offer them your burning desires."

This appeared to be true enough—a masque-less woman exited the cabaret with swan feathers swooping down her back. She smiled as she took off toward the steeple of Sacré-Cœur. Those weren't *gargoyles* perched on the church, cutting out jagged pieces of the moonlight with their wings...

Sylvie didn't seem to notice. She was too busy trying to get a glimpse through Cabaret d'Ailes's door. "I want to go inside!"

"That's the point," Rafe told her. "Want can be terribly powerful, if you know what to do with it."

This was true. It was the reason their fiddle games paid off so well and filled their graves with gold...but Céleste understood the other side of that coin. She knew *want* could be dangerous too. *You might go blind following such a feeling, seeing only its shine, wandering further and further from everything you've ever known, until you've fallen off the map entirely.*

It was too late for her, perhaps.

A glance at Rafe. The other thief was leaning against a lamppost, the gas flame inside leaping eagerly. His shadow seemed to do the same as he reached for his pocket watch. Céleste felt her chest squeeze tight, tight with the certainty that he was going to slip away and ditch her again. Somehow.

"No cabarets," she told Sylvie, firmly. "Besides, you already have a pair of perfectly good wings!"

"So? You have more than one dress, don't you?"

"Dresses are different," Honoré said. "They're clothes."

"Well, what about moustaches?" Sylvie argued. "You have at least thirty of those!"

Céleste edged closer to Rafe. He'd untangled the watch and was winding it, just like he had their first night together. And, same as it had outside the Vault of Dreams, the timepiece's gears began to grind. *No!* Her thoughts felt fanged as she reached for his shirtsleeve. She'd be damned if she let him vanish again—

Sea-fog fabric swirled under Céleste's fingers.

There was a hot hint of skin.

And then Rafe turned to run up the lane.

It was the songbirds Céleste noticed first. Both flocks were frozen in the sky, suspended midswirl. The revelers around the dome of Sacré-Cœur had gone still too. The air felt like the velvet lining of a jeweler's case, cushioning every motion as Céleste turned to see the other Enchantresses: Sylvie was statuesque; Honoré's eyes were stuck mid-roll. More guests were exiting the cabaret, caught with their bat wings snapping like umbrellas on a rainy day.

Céleste spun in a full circle, putting the paralyzed pieces together. She could see Rafe making his way up the street, his pocket watch swinging with every step. The thief hadn't used it to check his fateful hour...

Tonight Rafe García had stopped time entirely.

He didn't seem to realize Céleste had stolen this moment with him. He did not pause and look back before slipping through a small iron gate. The entrance was rusted over and almost unnoticeable, tucked between one celebration and the next. A snarled garden sat past it, so snarled that Céleste almost expected the branches to grow over the old stone staircase before she could climb it.

The windmill at the top of the hill looked just as forgotten: bleached boards, four skeletal arms.

A door, orbital and open. No bran was being sifted into flour inside. No spices were being crushed to make perfume. There wasn't even a millstone. When Céleste peered over the threshold, she saw a floor covered with plush carpets. Curio cabinets ringed the space, their shelves filled with oddities: dried flowers, bracelets carved out of jade, scarab beetles with their wings pinned open, a massive magnifying glass. At the center of the room sat a desk covered in scrolls, much like the one Rafe had borrowed from the bookshop, covered in centuries of dirt and lost languages. There were codices too, books that looked as if they belonged on chains in a monastery library, although Céleste wasn't sure the church would've wanted to keep a manuscript like the one at the top of the stack. A human heart had been painstakingly illustrated on the open page. Dissected. There was something sinister about the paper... That dark splatter on its edge might not be ink.

It made her bite back Rafe's name.

She hadn't seen the other thief enter the windmill, and there was no sign of him on the ground level. There were no stairs either, only rafters crisscrossing all the way up to the windmill's ceiling. Lanterns designed for desert nights hung from these beams—latticework and candy-colored glass. Blue, green, crimson... they lit a path to the desk.

The diagram of the heart didn't look any nicer up close. It made Céleste's own heart squeeze harder. Her throat turned into a straw, trying to drink the syrupy air. She stopped breathing entirely when she spied Rafe's sketchbook sitting at the corner of the desk. What had he been scribbling on the bridge? What had he been so eager to hide from her?

There were no cryptic notes on the pages.

No whimsical landscapes either.

Instead, Céleste found herself flipping through crude maps of Paris—made even cruder by the *X*s Rafe had slashed through certain spots. They appeared in almost every neighborhood, including the eighth arrondissement. She paused on this page, staring at the mark over the Théâtre des Champs-Élysées. What did it mean? What did *any* of this mean? Why was Rafe bringing scrolls to this windmill? Why was he researching human hearts and embalming techniques? The hair on the back of Céleste's neck began to bristle. An all-too-familiar feeling now...

His shadow was near.

"You shouldn't be here." The voice came from the rafters, from the darkness tucked between those hanging jeweled lanterns. This blackness grew into wings, and Rafe dropped in front of the door.

It was the only way out, Céleste realized as soon as the other thief loomed there. She spun around to face him, her back to the desk, her eyes searching the curio cabinets for anything that might resemble a knife. No luck. There were jars though, their glass tinted almost the same brown as Rafe's eyes. It was easy not to peer through it too closely, to tell herself that the shapes floating inside had nothing to do with her own heart. Beating faster and faster.

"What are you doing in this windmill?" Rafe asked, his voice a borderline growl.

"I should ask the same of you." The sketchbook was still in her hands, still open to the place they'd first met.

A change fell over the other thief's face, when he saw what Céleste was holding. It was much like the shift in the bookshop, only this time, his shadow started coiling as well. When Rafe took a step forward, she could see a beast crouched at his heels, far too large to be a fox. It didn't move.

Even when the sketchbook was snatched from Céleste's hands.

She didn't try to hold on—not the way she had with his watch. After seeing the *X*-slashed maps, it didn't seem wise to test how far Rafe García was willing to go. He stood close to her now, and through the thinning fog of his shirt, she could see even more scars, written across his chest in the language of knives.

"How did you manage to find this place?"

"I followed you."

"How?" One more step, and Rafe would have her against the desk. "How did you break into this moment?"

The spine of a book pressed into the small of Céleste's back; her silver tongue started to water. It was probably best to tell the truth at this point. "I saw you winding your watch, and I thought you were going to disappear on me again, so I reached out."

Dare she repeat the motion?

It would serve her better than a cheese knife, certainly.

"As soon as I touched you, the sky stopped." And now? Céleste's fingers landed on the other thief's bare arm. The windmill stayed still. Dust prickled the air. Iridescent insect shells watched from the shelves, and the candied lanterns did not wink.

Rafe's eyes flickered though.

"That's it?" He let out a breath. "A touch?"

Céleste nodded. It was hard to tell which pulse she was feeling in her fingertips—hers or his. Both were wild.

"I guess it makes sense the watch's magic could be shared that way," Rafe said after several beats. "I've never let anyone close enough to try before."

His shadow stirred back into the shape of a fox, though it still kept its distance.

He'd been afraid of her. But why?

"What about our fateful hour? Was that bullshit after all?"

"No," Rafe told her. "It's just the beginning." He pulled the watch from his shirt—which swirled so she could no longer see his scars. "The fateful hour is the watch's primary function, but it turns out it has another trick. If you wind the gears just right, you can stop time. I don't think the Sanct who sold me this relic knew about that fancy feature." He tapped the filigreed pattern on its face—now moving. The hourglass's wings were fluttering. Its sand was trickling too. Halfway gone. "When I discovered I could freeze a moment, I only managed to get away with a few seconds at first. Now, on good evenings, I can steal an extra hour."

And quite a few other things, by the looks of it.

"Is that what you're doing with your time? Stealing?"

"Depends on who you ask."

"I'm asking you," Céleste said.

Rafe's fox peered around his boots, its ears folded back on its head. "I hunt down secrets."

"What kind of secrets?"

"The key to immortality."

"You want to live forever?"

"Our employer does," Rafe said delicately. "But our employer is... not easy to please. He can't know about this place." The shadow fox shuddered a little and hopped onto the thief's muscular shoulders. It reached up to the nearest lantern and opened the orange glass. There was no fire inside.

No, Céleste realized. The lights above them were shining with dreams.

Rafe's dreams.

She recognized the sweep of his landscapes when the thief handed some to her. "This isn't the first time I've had to entertain a daytime acquaintance," he explained, grabbing several more dreams to slip into his own pockets. "It's easy enough to grab what I need from this stash while they start sprouting feathers at Désirée and Plume's establishment. Far easier than what would happen if I failed to return to rue des Ombres."

It made sense then, why Rafe had acted so laissez-faire all evening. Why he was currently so on edge. The windmill was his safety net. His contingency. *Theirs* now. She wouldn't have to go back to [redacted] without an offering.

"Always have a backup plan," Céleste murmured.

"What?"

"Oh, it's just something the other Enchantresses and I say."

"Enchantresses?"

"That's what we call ourselves—Sylvie and Honoré and I." Céleste felt a needle of pain, straight at the center of her damned heart. "They're more than just acquaintances."

"Clearly." Rafe shut the lantern and looked back at her. "Will that pose a problem?"

Céleste glanced back at the dreams she was holding.

You shouldn't let Sylvie think we can just make believe our way out of mistakes, she remembered Honoré saying. *We lie, yes, but not to each other. Not to ourselves.*

So much had changed since that night.

"It will get tricky, if Honoré stays Enlightened." She would need a good reason to disappear with Rafe. "But she already knows I've been spending my evenings with you. She believes we're involved..."

"Aren't we?"

"I meant romantically."

"Ah." A hint of a smile edged his lips. "Would that be such a difficult performance, *mon amour*? We've already set the scene, after all. Sylvie was convinced we were about to kiss in the landscape room."

She wasn't the only one.

Céleste had never stopped noting how close Rafe had her to the desk, though now it felt less like a threat and more like a promise. His fox shadow wove through the rafters above them. The thief himself was still, watching her with those burnt-sugar eyes.

"It's just... I've never had to lie to them before," she said quickly. "I'm not sure I can pull it off."

"Well, then, perhaps we should practice." Rafe took a step forward. He lifted his hand to her cheek, just as he had in the landscape room. The gold paint was still glimmering on his fingertips, and when he touched Céleste, it felt as if her skin had become one with the sun. "Kiss me, Céleste Artois. Kiss me like your life depends on it."

That wasn't too far from the truth. Neither was the way Céleste leaned in. She'd kissed plenty of men before—viscounts and nouveau riche businessmen who'd needed more than a sliver of ankle to distract them. She considered herself quite good at it. Better, when there was champagne involved.

But this... this was different.

This was Rafe.

She knew the curvature of his lips, knew how to tilt her own just so, knew how to melt into him the way his shadow sometimes did. He tasted like a murmur at midnight. Like spiced smoke and sea fog and, somehow, the tail end of a sunset. Céleste let herself linger for several seconds before pulling back.

"Good," Rafe whispered. "That was good, but we can do better, I believe."

He leaned in, one hand sliding up the nape of her neck, the other curving around her waist. There was more heat to this kiss. It flushed through Céleste's cheeks. It curled down her spine, lighting up each heave of her caged lungs. It slid between her thighs and trembled there.

And, *Dieu*, oh *Dieu*, she *liked* it.

Rafe broke away, his scarred eyebrow raised with a wordless question: *Shall I go on?*

Céleste reached up and pressed her thumb into that perfect chin divot. She drew his lips back down to hers, only vaguely aware that the desk was still there. No, most of her was focused on the feel of Rafe. All over. The graze of his tongue inside her mouth—just a taste. The thief's hands slipping down, leaving gold paint spatters across her collarbone. Skimming the crescent moon of skin where her corset became breast. Céleste was starting to feel stars too. She wanted them to shine brighter, wanted to be blinded by the light of it all, wanted Rafe's hands to wander even farther, wanted him to hoist her onto that desk covered with secrets, dark secrets she could keep behind her for a while longer—

But then Rafe pulled back.

His hair was wild, and his watch swung, keeping time with his heavy breath. "That was…convincing. Though I think it might be *too* much of a show for young Sylvie."

"Probably," Céleste said, swallowing her disappointment.

"We need to be getting back to Cabaret d'Ailes so your Enchantresses don't think we've vanished." Rafe nodded at the lanterns, which had oh-so-slowly started to flicker. The moment they'd stolen together was nearly gone, confirmed by the tiny hourglass engraving on his watch. It was down to only a few grains of sand. "We'll tell them we're going home together before sunrise, and then we'll take these dreams to rue des Ombres. No one will be the wiser. Though you may want to wipe off that paint for the sake of congruity."

Céleste looked down at the edge of her corset. Yes, the other Enchantresses would notice if it was suddenly sparkling gold, but the paint proved hard to rub away, even with the handkerchief Rafe handed her.

"What about tomorrow evening?" she asked. "Sylvie's going to want to keep exploring."

"We'll just kiss our way into a corner, until we find the right dream." Rafe eyed the fading shine of her décolletage and bit back a smile. "That should be easy enough."

Céleste wasn't so sure. The paint was coming off in flakes, glittering on the ground between them. It was messier than she'd expected. And now, standing across from the thief whose touch still glowed under her skin, whose secrets still lurked at her back, she had a feeling things might get even messier.

Chapter 14

More than the Rot

La Fée Verte did not look any less brilliant in the daylight.

In fact, Honoré mused, as she and Sylvie followed the Sanct through the booths that made up the flea market of Saint-Ouen, the woman almost appeared brighter. Her feathers were the color of fresh leaves, and the rest of her had the glow of a hazy spring day. Never mind that this late June morning was already sweltering, so sweltering that most of the ragpickers hadn't bothered setting up shop. One or two sat napping in chairs, exhausted by an evening spent rummaging through garbage piles, their boots propped next to their latest finds: candlesticks, dishware, mismatched earrings, stuff too sad for even Sylvie to consider stealing.

The youngest Enchantress was too busy trying to teach Honoré feline vocabulary anyway. "Their tails are tonal! They use them to accent certain words! That's why I couldn't understand Marmalade when he was talking about Céleste and Rafe and the strange alley..."

What more is there to understand? Honoré wanted to ask, as she wound around a booth of jars filled with things like buttons and musket balls. *They found the salon.*

They found each other.

She wanted to be happy for them. She really did. Honoré wanted to believe she'd found something too, as she followed La Fée Verte through the labyrinth of trash. Somewhere here was a Sanct who might know more about Honoré's ring, who could tell her why the silver was suddenly thrilling up her arm, sprouting claws and wings. She no longer needed knives to fight. Nor did she need a cabaret to fly—as soon as Céleste and Rafe had said their goodbyes and left Montmartre, hand in gold-smeared hand, Honoré had used her ring to launch into the lightening sky with Sylvie. She'd even managed to get her dragon to carry *The Known Words of Fable and Lore* in its jaws without denting the cover. The metal was easy enough to manipulate. Sometimes a little *too* easy. Honoré hadn't meant to get so defensive about the kitten comment in the bookstore, but she was more than making up for it now.

"Oh! And I was wrong. Cats have *fifteen* different words for mice!" Sylvie nearly bumped into a table covered with glass fragments. The owner startled awake at the clamor, but he didn't seem to see the cause. "I can't wait to tell Céleste! Though I suppose I'll have to."

Honoré paused to examine the scattered glass. Not broken, she realized. The pieces were slides for a magic lantern—painted with bouquets and polar expeditions and dancing skeletons. If she blurred her eyes just right, they resembled a smashed vase again.

The whole world seemed like that now.

And La Fée Verte? She was the magic lantern itself, the light that made Honoré's insides tremble like moth wings. No, there was no need for Cabaret d'Ailes at all. Her steps already felt floaty as she followed the Sanct to the outer edges of the market, to a stall that was just as cluttered as the others. Empty perfume bottles, a telescope, and so much other bric-a-brac held down a worn blanket. There was plenty more piled high in a cart on the opposite side of the booth. The ragpicker who'd gathered it all was slouched against the wheel, a hat placed over his face.

La Fée Verte called out to him across the table. "Long night?"

"Not nearly as long as it should be, in my opinion."

The hat slid off with a grunt, and Honoré saw the ragpicker had bright bronze markings all across his face. Without that, it would be easy to mistake him for a beggar. His gloves had no fingers; his coat had no lining. The inside was covered with keys instead. Keys and pocket watches and necklaces and monocles and all sorts of other small trinkets that chimed like alarm bells when he stood. "It's been a time since you've visited my booth, Verte. What brings you to the realm of moonlight sinners?"

"A relic."

"Got plenty of powerful objects here—" The other Sanct paused, when he saw Honoré and Sylvie. "Ah, so the rumors are true."

Sylvie sidled up to the table, her pink hair spilling over a tangled rosary and a half-burnt map. "What rumors?"

"Libris told me he met a daydreamer who tried to steal her own story. I didn't quite believe it." The Fisherman of the Moon cast a glance at La Fée Verte, then looked back at Honoré. His stare was appraising. It lit up even more when he noticed the ring wrapped around her wrist. "He also mentioned a dragon."

"This is Honoré Côte and Sylvie of a Single Name."

"A pleasure. I hope," the other Sanct amended. "Try not to let your fingers get too sticky here, daydreamer. Some of these objects . . . well, their magic can stick to you the wrong way if you don't handle them properly."

Sylvie backed away from the table then, leaving the rosary coiled like a snake. The charred map was no longer next to it.

Honoré broke in before the Fisherman of the Moon could notice. "La Fée Verte says you can tell me more about my ring."

"It's a ring, is it?" The Fisherman of the Moon plucked one of the many chains that hung inside his jacket. There was a jeweler's loupe on the end. It made his eye the size of a small planet as he stepped around the table to get a better look at Honoré's hand. "Ah, yes. I see now. What interesting metalwork! And that *spell*work! You'd be hard-pressed to find a smith who can do either nowadays."

"La Fée Verte thinks it's from the Revolution," Honoré said.

"It very well might be," answered the Sanct. "The magic certainly holds echoes of that era, but I can't say for sure."

La Fée Verte pressed her lips together. "You've never seen a piece like this before?"

"Not exactly." The Fisherman of the Moon kept orbiting the ring, until his nearness made Honoré bristle. The dragon did too. But instead of shrinking back from the ring's fangs, the Sanct leaned closer. "Tell me, mademoiselle, what does it feel like to wear?"

Honoré wasn't entirely sure how to answer this question—mostly because the ring fit her so well. Aside from her return to Caveau des Terreurs, she hadn't removed the piece in years. Without it she just felt warped.

"It's a part of me," she said, finally.

"How long has the ring been in your possession?"

"Five years." She skipped the part where she'd had to cut the beast from her father's dead hand because his finger had grown too far into it. "But I didn't know it was magical until last night."

"After my fountain guard Enlightened her," La Fée Verte explained.

"I'm surprised you managed that. This metal... well, let me test something." The Fisherman of the Moon set down his loupe, still staring at the ring. The bronze markings around his eyes started to glow. More glittering light left the tops of his fingerless gloves, winding toward Honoré. *A spell.* It never hit her skin—the dragon expanded. Motes of the Sanct's magic disappeared into its scales. "It seems this ring was designed to shield its wearer from enchantments."

"I wasn't wearing it at the fountain," Honoré remembered.

Strange, to think that if the ring had remained on her finger, she'd be back at her tomb now, rolling her eyes at Sylvie's stories about green birds, waiting for Céleste to stumble through the door after a night at *who knows where.*

She knew now.

She could feel La Fée Verte's gaze—all that candlelit warmth she'd wondered about before. So it wasn't magic that had made Honoré's skin sing at the Sanct's touch, but something more.

"That's right," Sylvie interjected. "You pulled the ring from your pocket, and the dragons fought each other! It was legendary."

The Fisherman of the Moon tipped his hat. "Who won?"

"Well, Honoré's ring smashed the other dragon back into the fountain, but then La Fée Verte was so impressed that she asked Honoré to become her knight, and now I'm allowed inside the salon," said Sylvie. "So . . . everyone."

"A knight, eh?" The vendor looked at La Fée Verte with a surprised expression. "She hasn't taken a shine to someone like that in years!"

The other Sanct seemed ruffled by this. A few birds stirred out of her feathers and flew to the booth's red tarp, which was so sun-bleached that it had faded to a coral color. La Fée Verte's cheeks quickly started to match.

The Fisherman of the Moon kept on speaking. "That's quite the tale, young daydreamer, but I sense it is only the start." He glanced back at Honoré's silvered arm. "If you mean to fight even bigger battles with this ring, take care. Relics are almost never what they appear to be at first glance. Or second. Even I have trouble seeing every layer. I once sold a watch for a pittance because I believed it was nothing but a fortune teller's bauble. But Nicolas Flamel was no fortune teller. And I was a fool who let time itself slip through my fingers." He glanced at La Fée Verte, Sylvie, and Honoré in turn. "Try not to be fools."

"All right!" Sylvie chirped.

Honoré pushed the metal back into the shape of a ring. No sweat sprouted from her brow, as it had in the bookstore. She was grateful for that. "What else do you think this relic could be capable of?"

"I'll have to do more digging," the Fisherman of the Moon told her. "Libris has a mountain of Revolution-era letters he's been begging me to come collect. If this was forged during that era, I may be able to find documentation of it."

La Fée Verte lingered by the table, running a hand over a music box. "My wards are failing, Fisherman."

"I've heard those rumors too," he said.

The other Sanct made a wry face. "Gargoyles are such gossips."

"It's not just statues whispering these days. One of the ragpickers found a husk while they were digging through a trash pile—now most of them are too afraid to go out at night. Say there's an even worse sinner loose in the moonlight." The Fisherman tilted his head. "You need to cast your own net wider, Verte. Keep more dreamers awake."

"I won't let history repeat itself."

"Ah, but that is what history does," the other Sanct said, as he glanced over his wares. "To fear such a thing only makes him stronger, Verte. He may not knot your shadow with it, but he doesn't need to, so long as you choose to keep your own hands tied." He picked up a carnival ticket—**ADMIT ONE**. "We are more than just the rot that happens around us."

"Fine words, for a magician who picks through garbage," Honoré said.

The Fisherman's coat jangled as he gave a short bow. "You credit me too much, Mademoiselle Côte. It was La Fée Verte herself who said such a thing, the night she handed me this."

The other Sanct stared at the ticket. There was something tattered in her expression, as worn as the paper itself. "Dreams weren't enough to stop him, last time."

"Who are you talking about?" Sylvie asked.

"No one," the Fisherman of the Moon told her. "At least for now."

Over the next several weeks, Honoré Côte found herself picking through her own fair share of trash. Not for candelabra that lit with a snap or spoons that made your soup extra savory or any of that nonsense. No, she was searching for signs of a killer.

A vampire, really.

There was no arguing with the term when she came across her first corpse—the one that had frightened the ragpickers. Honoré couldn't blame them for swearing off their search for treasure after unearthing this: Skeletal limbs arranged like matchsticks. Lips peeled back in a horrible wordless scream—the same kind Honoré had watched taking shape in that shard of mirror, when La Belle was killed. Whoever had drained that Sanct had done the same to this soul. Again, a mystery. There was no telling who this body belonged to. This wasn't for the rot, strangely enough. It was the thick of summer now, the time of year when people lingered a few minutes longer underneath café awnings to avoid the high noon sun. This corpse had no such cover. It should have decayed quickly. There should've been a maggot or two, paired with some unholy stench, but as Honoré knelt over the remains, she smelled nothing. She found no marks on the skin, which had the consistency of a dried-out corn husk. *Husk*—wasn't that what the Fisherman of the Moon had called the body? An apt term. This looked more like a discarded vegetable than a person.

Honoré found more as June slowly crawled into July, as she spent more and more evenings patrolling the city with the help of her dragon ring. She used its silver wings to soar over Montrouge, Austerlitz, the Marais, the glittering lights of the Champs-Élysées. There was no rhyme or reason to where the husked bodies turned up…only rumors. Bar talk. The kind of stories Honoré would've ignored while she canvassed for the Enchantresses' next long con.

It amazed her, how quickly life could tip on its head, like an hourglass reversed. How she now spent her nights flying, honest-to-goodness *flying*, with the wings of the ring her father had once used to beat her. It was a heady feeling. **Powerful.** Far more powerful to Honoré than sitting in a salon while an elephant served her smoky cocoa. Or pasting on a moustache and fleecing a few francs from a foolish businessman.

If she could really use this magical relic to battle true monsters? To make sure this damned "Black Hand" didn't touch La Fée Verte or the rest of her dreamers?

Well, then, she would fight.

She just had to find the fucking vampire first.

None of the rumors went this far, unfortunately. The trail went cold with each of the corpses. Honoré marked them on an imaginary map in her head—*X*, in lieu of any names. As far as she could tell, their enemy was still just circling the city, picking off people where La Fée Verte's wards were weakest. So far, the Quartier Secret was safe. As was the rest of the Latin Quarter. No inebriated university students had stumbled into a shadowy end. A few were gathered around the mist-shrouded entrance of a nearby bakery, where Honoré had stopped to buy a bag full of fresh croissants. It was too late to swing by Stohrer, and flying always made her hungry for some reason. Even the drained corpses made her want to sink her teeth into something—probably because she needed a reminder that she was alive. Bread would do. Yeast, wheat, butter, and yes, a little bit of sugar.

Not enough for Sylvie to notice. In fact, the girl would likely complain at the lack of chocolate if she snatched the bag. Honoré should probably steer clear of the salon if she wanted to eat her fair share of breakfast.

Most of the dreamers were already exiting the alley. Across the street, Honoré could see Céleste walking hand in hand with Rafe. Had they seen her? She wasn't sure. The pair paused beneath one of the opal-lit lanterns and kissed under the shifting rainbow light. It wasn't exactly the kind of thing Honoré wanted to interrupt for the sake of croissants...

She was about to slouch over a nearby café table, when she felt a small breeze.

Green fluttered onto her shoulder.

It was a songbird.

"Oh, hello." Honoré felt her hand crumple against the paper bag. A few years ago, Sylvie had gotten her into the habit of tossing stray bakery crumbs to pigeons, but this wasn't some innocuous gray bird.

This was an extension of La Fée Verte.

It wasn't hard to read the songbirds' body language. The way this one hopped and fluttered... it was asking Honoré to follow it over the zinc rooftops. Across the river. Up to the closest bell tower of the looming cathedral.

La Fée Verte was leaning against one of the stone balustrades, her emerald wings quite a contrast to the surrounding stony sculptures.

The songbird slipped back into her feathers when Honoré landed on the walkway beside her.

"What are you doing up here?" She patted the banister as her dragon ring shrank back into a band. They weren't quite at the top of the cathedral, but that did nothing to diminish the view. Apart from the salon's parting fog, Honoré could see all the way down to the curve of the Seine, where the Eiffel Tower was starting to pull out of the night's darkness.

"Waiting..." There was an open-endedness to the way the Sanct said this. Honoré figured it could mean just about anything: For the sun to rise. For her enemy to appear. For a young woman with an enchanted ring and a bag of still-steaming bread.

"I found a husk over by Montparnasse this evening. A man, judging by the clothes," Honoré said.

La Fée Verte tilted her head, taking in Honoré's trousers and loosely buttoned shirt. Her own gown was gold, matching her masque light, along with the mists starting to crawl out over the river. Dawn was very close.

"Montparnasse," she said slowly. "A fair number of my artists live in that neighborhood."

Down on the bridge, Honoré could see several salon guests gathered to watch the approaching sunrise. More than a few were wearing *tails*. The drained corpse had been lacking extra appendages, but that didn't mean anything if he'd been attacked before midnight.

"It's the second body that's turned up there," Honoré said. "Could that mean something?"

"It means I must refresh my wards in the fourteenth arrondissement." La Fée Verte sighed. "Every victim is making him stronger."

She sounded tired, and there was a heaviness behind her eyes as she looked out over the river. Honoré wanted to be something other than the bearer of bad news, so she lifted the bag of pastries.

"Do you eat?" The question felt clumsy, coming from her lips.

La Fée Verte's bangles glittered down her wrists as she straightened. "What?"

"Do you eat bread?" Honoré clarified. Despite all their talk of cake, she'd not once seen La Fée Verte take a bite of the confections in her salon. "Or do you just live off air and ideas? I don't have any sonnets to share for breakfast, but I did manage to get some croissants. If—if you want one, that is."

The Sanct laughed. She looked surprised but happy. "I would love nothing more, Honoré Côte."

The croissants were still warm, flaking off onto Honoré's fingers when she drew them from the bag. Her mouth watered as she handed the first pastry to La Fée Verte. Several of the Sanct's birds peeked out of her wing feathers, their beaks twinkling while they eyed the bread.

"You know, I once worked at Stohrer," she said. "Croissants are deceptively difficult to bake. You have to let the dough rest each time you fold in the butter—and there are so many folds. It really is an art."

Honoré was already halfway through her pastry. She paused, looking down at all the layers she'd just bitten through. "I never thought of bread that way. I did once try to use a *ficelle* to teach Sylvie how to fight with a knife, but she just ended up eating it."

"A battle with baked goods? That's imaginative!" La Fée Verte laughed again and lifted her croissant. "What would this be in your arsenal? A pistol?"

Honoré chewed through the rest of her croissant, trying not to think about the actual golden gun Sylvie had waved around. "I think I prefer it as breakfast food."

"Me too." The Sanct took a bite of bread, her eyelids fluttering. "This tastes even better than poetry."

"Well, certainly any of *my* poetry," Honoré added, though she still thought of every beautiful comparison she'd made at the first sound of La Fée Verte's voice. Honey on her tongue and sunlight pouring through storm clouds.

There were no clouds on the horizon now, as the Sanct turned to look at her. "No one has ever brought me breakfast before."

Dawn light spilled across the river. It matched the color of La Fée Verte's eyes—amber and gold. Honoré could see the imaginers' tails burning away, swirling up in a column of glowing sparks as their memories evaporated.

"Seems to me not many people have had the chance," she answered.

Several green birds flew out into the sparks, swooping like a flock of swallows as they guided the light back toward Notre-Dame's south bell tower. As soon as the sparks hit La Fée Verte's face, they melted into her masque, making it glow even brighter. It made Honoré think of what the Fisherman of the Moon had said: *She hasn't taken a shine to someone like that in years!*

It made her own insides glimmer with hope.

"It's not easy to trust others when you have a history," La Fée Verte said, looking back down at Honoré's ring. "But even before I stole my enemy's name, there was no one who brought me croissants without expecting some magical favor in return."

Honoré looked back at the dragon relic too. She thought of all the effort she'd poured into the metal over the past three weeks, how she'd learned to shape its wings and jaws and tail, how she'd hardened these things over herself, how incredibly strong she felt, but also how incredibly scared—scared that all this magic was too good to be true.

Too good for *her*.

It was the same with the shimmer she felt even deeper inside.

"I don't— I've never let my guard down easily either. You can't, when you grow up the way I did." Honoré thought of all the bottles of lemonade Eleanor had shared. All the smiles Honoré had needed to swallow back with them. "But the moment you Enlightened me at that fountain, I knew I wanted to fight for you."

"I knew too," the Sanct murmured softly.

The last of the imaginers' sparks were settling into her masque, and salon-goers on the bridge had scattered. Honoré stayed right where she was, her hand on the balustrade. Only her heart leapt when La Fée Verte's fingers brushed against hers.

"Thank you for the bread," she said.

The Mapmaker

There once was a mapmaker who drew places.

Yes, you might say. *Isn't that what cartographers do?*

Yet this mapmaker did not call himself a cartographer. He did not employ compasses or sextants or even a telescope. He did not climb mountains or sail coastlines or cross deserts. In fact, it was a rare occasion that he even left his attic workshop. He could see most of Paris from the circular window by his drafting table—mazes of mansard roofs that spelled out strange alphabets. It was easy enough to copy. He'd seen it take shape over the years, spilling out of the river and growing through the marshlands, while men's hands carved out catacombs and conjured cathedrals.

This was one way to build a city.

The mapmaker had mastered another. He worked by the light of his own eyes—there was no need for a lantern as he bent over the parchments, etching spaces into existence. An alley here. A palais there. An island that drifted up and down the Seine. Places that could only be found if you knew to look. There were many who came searching for his workshop, who climbed up flight after flight of creaking stairs, who knocked on the mapmaker's door to ask for a space to call their own.

Perhaps you also wish to do this?

Sorry to say, but you are too late. The mapmaker was too late too. He tried to erase the worst of his work, but *places* are not like pencils. They last long after the people who name them are gone. Longer even than the names themselves.

Chapter 15

Shadows Circling

Lying to the other Enchantresses should have felt worse than this.

Céleste had more energy than ever—despite her long nights wandering around Paris, she woke up with no need for coffee. She would stop at the magical café across from the opera house later, to order a pot of tea and listen to a world of conversations unfurling around her. Spanish, Italian, Mandarin, Russian... she'd always thought this last language sounded like an axe splitting wood for a bonfire. There was a smoky taste to the tea, a sharpness across her tongue when it slid down, but then the words began to bloom in her ears. *Hello. Goodbye. How is the tsarevitch? As well as he can be. And the boy's mother... have you really fucked her? No need. She hangs on my every word as it is, and her husband too. All of Russia will be ready, when the time comes.*

There was still a hint of hatchet in the Mad Monk's words.

Céleste stared at the saints chained around his neck—their rapturous expressions a reminder to keep her own face pious. [redacted] and his disciple might not speak so freely in front of her otherwise, and even if she couldn't cast spells of her own, knowledge was power.

"How goes your search?"

The ballroom seemed to darken at the Mad Monk's question.

Not a cloud creeping across the palace gardens, but her employer's masque. It rarely flickered like this. Even rarer? His annoyance. He did not frown, but he didn't have to. The corners of his lips twitched like a clock counting seconds. "It will go faster if you keep her fresh."

This *did* make Céleste shudder, hearing [redacted] describe her like a slab of just-cut meat, ready to be stuffed away in an icebox. The Mad Monk's magic was frigid, fortunately. Cold enough to play her disgust off as a shiver.

But she did feel fresh in the days that followed such visits. She woke up in her grave, stretched, and breathed deep. She'd started taking long afternoon walks to get out of the mausoleum. Not that Sylvie and Honoré spent much time there anymore, but things became awkward when they did. How was Céleste supposed to pretend she didn't see the youngest Enchantress's growing collection of wings? Or the enchanted knickknacks she'd started collecting under her bed?

Ignoring Honoré's dragon was even harder.

The ring hardly ever looked like a ring anymore. It was always moving up and down her friend's arm, or perched on her shoulder, or climbing on her back so that she might fly. Though Honoré never tried to do this when she thought her friend had magical amnesia. No. The great irony was she treated Céleste like a convalescent. As if she were nursing a hangover.

"Sleep it off!" Honoré liked to say. "We'll go looking for a new mark this evening."

But Céleste could only lie on her mattress for so long.

She pretended to paint, instead.

She didn't work on the drowning woman. She left Ophelia floating over in the corner as she packed up a much smaller easel. Honoré and Sylvie seemed to believe Céleste when she told them she was going out to sketch the city. That, or they were too busy tending to their own secrets to bother following her to Montmartre.

She found herself, most afternoons, walking to Rafe's windmill.

It was the perfect hiding place.

If the other thief was to be believed, he'd found it only after seeing the structure sketched on an old map of the neighborhood. The building was much like a trap street. Imaginary, until it wasn't. Hidden, unless you knew exactly where to look. Even the Sancts who ran the cabaret next door didn't seem to notice the windmill. No one but Céleste and Rafe had opened the garden gate in years, and when the sun was shining so baldly in the sky, she was the only soul who could step foot in this place.

It looked different in the daylight.

Sunbeams shot through warped boards, revealing that the amber jars were filled with flower bulbs. Not organs. The page with the dissected heart was stained with soot. Not blood. The rest of the desk's scrolls remained unrolled. Rafe probably figured she couldn't read them, and in this case, he was right. There was no tea for translating ancient Aramaic or hieroglyphs. At least, none that was sold in Paris. But most of the items in this windmill didn't seem to come from the city. Hand-carved nesting dolls, jungle insects with their wings splayed wide, geodes that had been cracked open to show their spiky purple insides…Céleste wasn't sure how any of these items related to immortality. Unless there was something she wasn't seeing. That might very well be the case…When she picked up a magnifying glass, she noticed there was a strange script written on the scarab beetles' iridescent shells. Secrets. Again, they were too hard for her to read.

She started to sketch them instead.

Still life. No life. *Everlasting* life.

Her mind hummed with the possibilities; her fingers wandered freely. It had been years since Céleste had drawn something without a mind to sell it as a van Gogh or a Monet—and now she sat at the heart of the old masters' neighborhood, trying to settle on her own style. Just the right balance of shadow and light. Darkness was easier to draw. She didn't have to worry about erasers or pressing too hard—no, she could throw herself into the page. She could lose hours trying to perfect the lines of Rafe's shadow.

She'd thought the other artist would be simple to sketch from memory. He'd branded himself there, after all, with his burning stare. But every time Céleste tried capturing his profile, she felt something was missing. The ink-drop tear? No. The day-old stubble darkening his jaw? No. The brow scar? The chin divot? The way his lips quirked—not quite smiling, but not scowling either? No. No. No.

Every single element was there, but Rafe's face never leapt off the page.

Not the way his fox shadow did.

She drew it apart from him. A separate series: Leaping. Prancing. Napping with its nose tucked beneath its tail. Slinking. Céleste's pencil could hardly keep up with the creature, so she set it to chasing its own tail. Around and around.

"What do we have here?"

Céleste jumped when she saw Rafe standing at the windmill entrance. The sky just past his shoulders was purple with dusk. The other thief hadn't meddled with time—an entire afternoon had slipped away while she worked. How long had it been since that last happened? Her hand was tender from holding the pencil when she set down the instrument. She wanted to close the sketchbook too, because now that Rafe was here, the portraits of his shadow suddenly felt too personal.

For him, or for her? Céleste wasn't sure. All she knew was that her insides flickered when the other artist's eyes alighted on the page. He leaned closer over her shoulder, so close that she had no choice but to let him see what she'd been sketching.

"Nothing," she said quickly.

"That doesn't look like nothing," Rafe murmured, taking in the picture of the fox running in a fluid O shape. "It looks like you've finally tried to capture something other than a boiled lobster. Color me impressed!"

"They're just scribbles." It was hard to keep her own cheeks from coloring as she said this. Rafe's face remained very close to hers. "I wasn't trying to steal your sigil."

"My what, now?"

"Your sigil. Honoré told me you used to draw foxes chasing their own tails. I was attempting to build my calluses so the other Enchantresses will believe I'm out—" Céleste paused as she felt Rafe stiffen. "What's wrong?"

"Nothing," he said.

But it didn't look like nothing, the way his hand shook when he reached for the paper, the way his fingers barely traced the fox, grasping at some long-lost muscle memory. "My sigil," he muttered under his breath. "*My* sigil. *Mon Dieu*. I'd forgotten all about that..."

His true shadow circled them then.

Around and around.

The goose bumps that sprang on Céleste's arm had nothing to do with fear and everything to do with how Rafe kept staring at her drawing, the way he finally looked back up at her. "This piece—" He faltered. "It's—it's more than just a scribble, Céleste."

Praise. She'd sought it so shamelessly in Gertrude Stein's salon, but to hear it here, in the darkness of Rafe's windmill, made her feel almost naked. Seen in a way she was rarely used to.

"A doodle, then," she said, trying to make her voice as light as a 9H pencil.

"Yes, well, it's a doodle of *me*." He ran a finger over the page, right along the sketchbook's spine. Softly, so softly. A shiver went down Céleste's back as she watched. "Would you mind if I kept it?"

The request surprised her. "I had no idea you were so vain, Rafe García."

"Neither did I," he replied. "But a man should be allowed to have some hidden depths..."

"Being vain is the opposite of hiding," Céleste pointed out. "If you want to display this piece, I'll trade it for a few of your dreams." She glanced up at the overhead lanterns. "Sylvie wants to visit some floating island in the Seine tonight, so we should probably fill our pockets before we meet up with the other Enchantresses regardless."

Rafe tore the page from her sketchbook with gentle fingers, his expression uneasy. He didn't seem to like dipping into his lantern stash. Curious, that. Was he worried [redacted] might catch on to their backup plan? Or was there more to it? Céleste hadn't seen him use his dreams as currency at any of the shops—so what else would he save them for?

What were they worth?

Enough for Rafe García to haggle over. "Île du Carnaval shouldn't take long to explore. It's just overgrown rides and tents."

"Well, you know Sylvie. She'll want to go to Stohrer afterward, and if we let her wander there alone, Honoré will get upset." The other Enchantress was too busy "patrolling," as she put it, and she didn't want Sylvie flying over the city with her. She also didn't want the girl sneaking out by herself, for reasons she refused to discuss with Céleste. It was just as well. Céleste couldn't exactly explain that *she and Rafe* were the reason La Fée Verte was so on edge.

"Nothing will happen to Sylvie at Stohrer," Rafe said. "That shop survived the Revolution. It will probably keep serving pastries until the end of time. And maybe even after. Ha! I wouldn't be surprised if Nicolas made macarons for ghosts."

The idea of ghosts wasn't quite as humorous as it had once been—those evenings when Céleste and the other Enchantresses had set out to spook the cemetery guards. "Well, something *will* happen to us if we disappoint our employer, and I don't want to have to waste your extra hour scrambling back here."

The other artist placed her folded drawing in his pocket. He reached for the nearest lantern and set it down on the rug between them. "We shouldn't get too comfortable with this arrangement."

That was the thing, Céleste thought as she watched Rafe open the lantern's orange glass hatch, dream light spilling across his face. It *was* comfortable. Some of the best nights of her life had happened inside these last three weeks. Watching Sylvie try to talk to the flaming Blake tyger in cat-speak, then trying to convince Honoré to take the plagiarisms out on patrol with her. Or flying with the youngest Enchantress to the top of Notre-Dame to feed stanzas of poetry to a pelican statue, who gulped up the lines like fish. Or standing in the middle of the landscape room while Rafe painted flowers the size of trees. Or sinking into a vine-draped corner to kiss him... drowning in the heady scent of jasmine, tangled up in his touch, heat blossoming all over her skin...

The point of these kisses was to convince the other Enchantresses that the pair needed privacy, which allowed them to steal away and start stealing dreams. It worked well. A little *too* well, sometimes. For Céleste found that the deeper they went into those fantastical landscapes, the harder it was to pull herself out. Instead, she found herself looking forward to the moments when Rafe would trace her lips with his thumb, when her whole body went taut and then melted into his, when the kiss tumbled into something hungrier and Rafe drew her into the depths of his shadow. The shock of this was usually enough to make Céleste pause and catch her breath. To remind her that they had darker work to do.

Was it just as hard for Rafe to pull away?

Céleste wondered.

He certainly didn't seem miserable.

His shadow fox sat on his shoulders now. It looked almost solid in the dream light—watching Céleste. She both loved and hated how much she'd come to depend on it. "Perhaps we wouldn't have to rely on your stash so much if you taught me how to shape my own shadow."

"I can't." He pulled out several dreams and handed her half. "Not until you learn how to conjure some imaginings of your own."

Oh, so he was going to hold that over her too, was he? As if there weren't already enough to juggle. As if Céleste hadn't tried her best to copy Sylvie's constant glow—but coming up with creative ideas was much harder work than building back calluses.

"I know, I know. Dreaming is surviving."

"It can be more than that." Rafe closed the lantern then, his gaze alighting on where her own silhouette was stretched across the rug. "*You* can be more."

At first glance, the Ilê du Carnaval looked like an overgrown spit of land in the center of the Seine, but if you watched the island long enough, one would see that it floated. Slipping under bridges, sliding by quais and the other three islands that dotted the river, passing the Eiffel Tower's iron stance again and again. In the hours it took

Céleste, Rafe, and Sylvie to explore it, they drifted from one border of the city to another. Then back against the current. Twice, Céleste looked past the phantom tents to see the Seer's houseboat. It was anchored under the Pont Saint-Michel, as always. She stood on the prow, her white eyes prying through the passing leaves.

Sylvie didn't seem to notice.

She was too busy clearing vines from the carousel, only to find that the ride no longer held horses. The wooden animals now roamed freely through the abandoned carnival. Around a giant steam-whistle organ and a lagoon scattered with swan boats. In and out of tents that once held wonders—according to an old poster Céleste found fluttering by a game booth.

Who knows what dreams may wake at the Carnaval des Merveilles? The text was flowery. And green. Much like the drawings of the birds that roosted inside its letters. Or the leaves that choked the island in its current state. It was a far cry from the festivities that unfolded on paper, where the grounds lit up with a cloud of fireflies that scattered for trapeze artists while spectators feasted on fistfuls of fairy floss as pink as Sylvie's hair.

"This carnival must have been amazing." There was a hint of sadness in the youngest Enchantress's voice when a carousel horse shied away from her outstretched hand. "I wonder why people stopped coming."

It was hard for Céleste not to entertain this question as she walked with her ward through the carnival. Even harder when they found the tent of the fortune teller—Madame Arcana, according to the sign—who'd left her cards facedown on a table. Céleste couldn't help but peek at the spread. Death, the Devil, and the Fool. She flipped them back over quickly, telling herself that they hadn't waited all this time for her. And, of course, the face she saw reflected in the crystal ball just beside them belonged to her . . . despite the fact its eyes were fogged over.

She tossed a tablecloth across the entire ensemble before Sylvie could see.

"Sometimes magic loses its shine," Rafe was saying, as he ducked into the tent. "There are sites like this all across Paris, you know.

Versailles was so covered in enchantments during Louis XIV's reign that you could hardly stare at it without crying—it's one of the reasons he was nicknamed the Sun King."

Sylvie listened, rapt. "Really?" she asked.

"Where did you learn that?" Céleste wondered. "An ancient scroll?"

"No. This was a firsthand account. Told to me by one of the cherubs in the palace itself."

Sylvie's eyes widened enough to catch the overhead stars. "You went to a *palace*?"

"Anyone can. It's much like this place now. Most of the power has been plundered, but you can still catch glimpses of what it was, in the Hall of Mirrors—"

"I want to see it!"

"Not tonight," Céleste said hastily. "It's too far."

"We can *fly*!"

"I would have to borrow wings," she reminded the youngest Enchantress.

"So? We can go visit that cabaret place! You and Rafe could trade them a kiss for some moon moth wings! Or I could lend you some. Though we'd have to go back to Père Lachaise—"

"There isn't enough time." Céleste cut her off, trying to speak before Sylvie could spill the location of their camp, but it was too late.

Rafe's interest was piqued. "What's in Père Lachaise?"

"Our tomb, of course!" Sylvie chirped. "And lots of dead people."

The other thief arched his knife-nicked brow at Céleste. As much as she'd visited his windmill lately, she'd never once mentioned the Enchantresses' mausoleum—if there were still going to be secrets between them, she preferred that one belong to her. At the very least.

"Oh, Céleste! You'll love flying! It's so fun! Did you know Honoré laughed, her first time? She even did a loop the loop!"

"Honoré?" Rafe's eyebrows rose that much higher. "Doing acrobatics with that dragon? Surely you jest!"

Sylvie shook her head. "No! I'm telling the truth! She makes it look easy. I got too dizzy when I tried."

"Well, we certainly won't reach Versailles before sunrise if we zigzag." Céleste tried her best to veer the conversation back on course—after all, she had another palace to visit. "It's probably best we return to the salon."

The girl wrinkled her nose as she looked around the shrouded tents. She wanted to keep exploring, obviously, but to Céleste's surprise, she didn't beg to stay. "What happened to this place . . . it won't happen to the Quartier Secret, will it? History won't repeat itself," she added in her parrot tone. "Right?"

"There's nothing to worry about, *ma rêveuse*," Céleste said.

It was the worst lie she'd told yet.

This dawn began just like all the rest.

Céleste had taken to lingering in Place de la Concorde so that the sun would erase all traces of the night's festivities, from painted tattoos to crowns of poetry. She'd forgotten about a stanza woven into her braid once, and her employer's reaction had been . . . unpleasant. Now she let them burn in the sunlight, instead of [redacted]'s hearth. Golden sparks fizzed up the façade of Hôtel de Crillon as she disappeared into the trap street below. Rafe pulled his own dreams from his pockets. Again. Céleste had tried her best to get them back to the salon early enough to steal away—they might have been able to manage it, if Honoré hadn't returned from some mysterious errand while they were trying to excuse themselves from Sylvie's hair-coloring party. They might have managed still, with Rafe's watch, but the other thief shook his head when Céleste looped her arm around his waist, tugging one of the chains. He'd leaned in too, his whisper grazing her ear: "Time's up."

He must have used the extra hour earlier, before catching her at the windmill.

Mysterious errands, all around.

This one seemed straightforward enough. The door's lock settled as soon as Rafe's shadow slid beneath it, opening to the usual scene. [redacted] sat in his wing-back chair. His fire waited. Its light licked across the Sanct's cheeks; they appeared more sunken tonight. Carved a bit too sharply. His reach looked the same, when he took their offerings. As if there weren't fingers fitted beneath those black gloves but claws, closing over Rafe's horizons.

[redacted] did not so much as look at them.

"Would you care to explain how you spent your evening?" he asked, as he tossed the imaginings into the fire. "Obviously you cannot be bothered to do your job, since you keep bringing me the same worthless drivel, night after night after night."

Rafe flinched.

Céleste's breath became like a knife's edge.

"Is something wrong, Monsieur García?" The room went darker. Walls bent at the edge of Céleste's vision, and Rafe's shadow spilled across the floor. It twisted—in and out of its fox shape—clawing at the Persian rug as it was dragged into [redacted]'s waiting arms. When the Sanct touched the darkness, it split into dozens of rope-like strands, which wound their way back up Rafe's legs, over his torso, to his neck.

"No," Rafe gasped.

"Do not lie to me, Monsieur García."

"I'm not—" Words got cut off as the shadow wrapped around his throat.

The Sanct's nostrils flared. "Oh, but you *are*. Do you think that I am so easily deceived? Hm? That I can't taste your wanderlust in these pathetic wonders?" The flames in the fireplace reared higher, causing the fox shadow to stretch and twist. It looked more like a part of [redacted] than Rafe now. "You think I don't know about your little excursions?"

Shit. The Seer must have spied them through the Ilê du Carnaval's underbrush after all. She must have tipped their employer off again. Céleste's thoughts grew as brambly as the carnival's leaves when she watched Rafe García get lifted off his feet. The thief grasped at the shadow wrapped around his throat, but his hands kept slipping through. The scars on his arms looked like waning moons.

Pale slivers, growing paler. He couldn't breathe, and she couldn't just stand here watching—

"Please!"

Céleste knew this was the wrong word the moment it slipped off her tongue. Their employer's stare turned on her. His eyes were about as merciful as a starved wolf. The masque around his temples spread like a night fog, and suddenly she felt her own shadow slipping, pulling away from her feet just as it had during the opening notes of *The Rite of Spring*. Tauter than a cello's strings.

"Go on," [redacted] told her. "Beg."

The fire kept flaring behind their employer, and in its terrible light, she saw Rafe... His neck veins bulged, crawling up to his eyes, until Céleste could see every ounce of blood there. The rest of the thief was getting chiseled away. His cheeks hollowed. His chest started to cave. His skin withered like fruit left too long on the vine.

"We couldn't slip into the Vault of Dreams tonight, so we had to improvise." Easier said than done, with her own lungs crumpling. "It was my idea to use Rafe's ideas—"

"It was, was it?" Their employer's face had changed. A black cloud still pulsed around his eyes, but Céleste could have sworn the Sanct's jowls had filled in. Enough to cushion a snarl. "Let us see."

Rafe made a strangled sound when [redacted] reached for Céleste's hair.

There was no lost castle in the strand the Sanct plucked.

Just the specter of the windmill.

"My, my," clucked their employer, as he examined it. "You two *have* been busy. Though I expected a more magnificent lie, given your reputation, Mademoiselle Artois." He tossed this memory into the fire as well. "You'll have to do better than this if you want to save yourself."

Céleste's cough came on cue.

Blood spattered her palm like an ellipsis. Rafe's breath stuttered.

"And what is it *you* want?" She looked back up at the Sanct. "For both your forgers to die?"

Their employer sighed.

Their shadows went slack.

There was a gasp from Rafe.

"A fair point," said [redacted]. "I only need one of you."

The Sanct was still holding on to their silhouettes. Rafe's fox hung like a limp dishrag—seized by the scruff. Céleste's stretched from her feet to his black glove. She swallowed back more red. *Shit.* It was all going to turn to shit if she didn't think faster. How could she spin this?

"That's not true," she managed. "Not anymore. La Fée Verte has a new guard, someone who knows me and Rafe." The other thief was recovering beside her, his black hair hiding his face. "She's been watching us closely the past three weeks, and we only managed to slip away because she believes we're sleeping together. If you let one of us die now, the other won't last much longer."

"La Fée Verte has taken on a protégé?" The Sanct's hands tightened over the fox shadow.

Rafe could only nod. There seemed to be tears in his eyes—visible only because they reflected the fire so. [redacted] stared back into the flames as well. He stared and stared and then stood before walking to the door and pulling out his ring of keys. They jingled as he sorted through them—a sound that set Céleste's teeth on edge. She wasn't surprised when he let the gold key that unlocked the Mad Monk's palace fall back with the rest.

The one he used today was mostly rust.

The door's hinges were too. They gave a laboring groan.

"Come," their employer called.

Céleste jerked to her feet, although she wasn't quite sure how much of the motion was *her* and how much was her shadow—the thing [redacted] seemed to be able to pull like a string. Rafe was getting dragged back across the rug as well.

"Clever of you to use Moulin's old windmill as your bolt-hole, Monsieur García. I'd forgotten about it, thanks to the Mapmaker. Do you know, I used to have a perfect view of that courtyard? See?" [redacted] paused at the threshold. "Don't worry about the daylight, Monsieur García. I'll keep you Enlightened. I want you to watch every second of this."

Past their employer's shoulder, Céleste could see an attic loft. An *artist's* loft, though it somehow felt more like a tomb than her own cemetery set-up. No broom had been over the floor in at least a decade. Drawings were pinned all over the walls, and even though their lines were soft, they had a frenzied feeling. Obsessive. Most featured the same young woman with an operatic pose: Mademoiselle Leroux, according to one of the penciled titles.

None were signed.

Perhaps they had been, once. Streaks of soot marked the lower-left corner of each piece, where signatures traditionally sat. Several papers fluttered to the floor when [redacted] slipped out of the wardrobe door. He stepped on them uncaringly and went to the window, which opened onto a familiar scene. Montmartre, once more. The glittering spell of its night was broken, as were the shards of glass a man was sweeping up from the sidewalk below. The rest of the street was as stark as a spine.

Céleste could see their secret garden, tucked between the neighboring buildings. If she jumped off the wrought iron balcony, she just might touch one of the windmill's arms. Or she would fall. And Rafe's shadow wouldn't be there to catch her this time...

The Sanct was still holding the fox by the scruff, still controlling Rafe with it. The other thief came to a halt at the railing beside Céleste. His face was no longer shriveled, but his eyes remained desperate. Bruised. The veins their employer had almost burst wreathed around his brow—a deep purple that smudged into the blue dot of his tattoo.

The masque around [redacted]'s temple licked the air as he leaned over the railing. "It was impossible to get a good night's sleep here. Painters wandered in and out of that mill at all hours. Flying, flirting, screaming, singing." A breeze blew through the window, scooping up several sketches of the prima donna. It must have been the Sanct's spell—for when the papers swirled past his head, they burst into flame. "All that joie de vivre. They thought so highly of themselves... they believed in the power of their dreams."

Céleste could see the lanterns' rainbow glimmer through the mill boards. Lost, when the burning sketches landed on weathered wood.

"Most of those artists are dead now. The rest are dying, their soft hearts rotting away even as they beat in their chests." Disgust curled their employer's lips. His glove also curled, deeper into the shadow fox's fur. "Fantasies will not save you."

The fire caught quickly.

A hot roar. Sparks spitting. Rage. So much rage. It beat Céleste's body with all the force of a smith's hammer. She couldn't help but tremble as she watched Rafe's dreams go up in flames. Ghosts of lands that never were. Mountains and seas and so much more. Where would she hide from the other Enchantresses now? How would she survive?

A scream needled her ear, but when Céleste looked at Rafe, she saw the other thief's jaw was clenched. The rest of him stayed just as rigid—except for the tear rolling down his bruised cheek.

The sound had come from his shadow.

The fox was thrashing in [redacted]'s grip, evanescing with the rest of the inferno's smoke. Its tail was a snuffed candle, ribboning out. The legs vanished next. Then the rest of the animal. Until all that was left in its place was a formless black. When their employer let go of Rafe's shadow, it fell flat at his feet. Stagnant. Spent. The thief crumpled into it like a marionette whose strings had gone slack.

Céleste's own knees felt shaky when the Sanct released her silhouette.

"Play lovers. Be lovers, for all I care. But do not try to deceive me again, or I will be worse." The Sanct's eyes darkened as smoke rose over the neighborhood. "I will be so much worse."

Chapter 16

The Knight and the Hellcat

Honoré Côte stood by a heap of ashes.

They were darker than the usual fireplace soot, marking out a perfect square. None of the surrounding plants had caught fire, though they were beginning to drop their leaves, as if it were October instead of July. The air held an extra chill too. There was a grayness to the day that had nothing to do with clouds. Or smoke. The pillar witnessed by the owners of Cabaret d'Ailes had vanished by the time they summoned La Fée Verte.

The message had come by bird—not green, like the rest of the creatures roosting in the misty reaches of the Quartier Secret, but red. The animal trembled when it landed on the loveseat where Sylvie had fallen asleep, *The Known Words of Fable and Lore* splayed across her chest. Honoré was tired too, after an evening spent patrolling Paris's streets, but she didn't want to shut her eyes when La Fée Verte was lounging in the opposite chair, her wings draped over the rest of her like a lazy morning robe.

This pose didn't last long, after the bird said what it had come to say: "Montmartre is burning."

They flew to the eighteenth arrondissement, but there was no fire brigade to greet them. Only two Sancts. The winged women stood in front of a small gate, their arms outstretched, the flash of their red and gold masks easy to mistake for flames. When Honoré landed, she saw they'd extinguished the fire, but something sinister was still spreading from the ashes. Leaves kept dropping down the stone steps, as if some invisible rot was slouching its way toward the gate, determined to seep into the rest of Montmartre.

It might have, if not for La Fée Verte.

She landed by the other Sancts. Her magic joined theirs. Her hand touched the gate, making the iron glow gold, creating a cage for whatever shrouded the hill. The pall wasn't just drying up leaves but the posters pasted on adjoining buildings too—Honoré could see the ends of a Tournée du Chat Noir advertisement starting to curl. Its iconic black cat looked about ten shades blacker.

"I smelled it about an hour after sunrise," the red-winged Sanct told La Fée Verte, as the messenger bird slipped back into her feathers. "I thought a guest had left one of their desires on a settee, but then I saw the windmill."

Windmill? There were a few left in the neighborhood, Honoré knew, but she'd never seen one here. She still didn't.

"Is there a body?" she asked.

The yellow-feathered Sanct shook her head. "No Sanct has used this place in years."

"I thought it was erased after Moulin disappeared." Her companion's ruby wings trembled. "I thought our magic was strong enough to keep him out."

"It is." La Fée Verte pushed through the gate. There was a flash of gold from her eyes, and a wave of warmth as she fanned her wings. Leaves began to bud on the surrounding bushes—quickly unfurling into lusher summer shades. New moss coated each step as she climbed. "You were right to summon me, Désirée. His curse hasn't spread too far. We can keep your claim on Montmartre if we act quickly."

The other two Sancts stayed close—their wing tips touching, their halos shining. Their magic braided with La Fée Verte's as they followed her to the base of the windmill. Honoré also edged toward the scorched earth, close enough to nudge the burnt ground with her boot. No grass grew back. It was so dark that she started to see shapes—the way one did when one sat in a lightless closet for hours on end. Like when Gabriel's head had been heavy in her arms and her mother had been trapped on the other side of the door and there had been nothing Honoré could do but stare. She saw bursting stars and wriggles that reminded her of maggots and circles that smeared like spilled blood.

"Honoré?"

She started at the sound of her name.

"Go guard the gate while Désirée and Plume and I seal the breach," La Fée Verte said gently. "We don't want our backs exposed."

To what? Honoré wondered. A street sweeper? The couple sipping coffee in the cane chairs of a nearby café? There wasn't much for her dragon to do. La Fée Verte's magic had already taken root, and the path back to the gate was wreathed with flowers. Magnolia, cherry blossoms, wisteria—blooming all out of order. Beautiful. She even paused to smell them.

The scents were sweet but faint.

It was hard for Honoré not to wonder if she was missing something. She hadn't heard anything more from the Fisherman regarding her relic, but she'd had three weeks to mull over his words. *This ring was designed to shield its wearer from enchantments.*

Was that why she still felt so out of place in La Fée Verte's salon? Honoré knew it was odd that she felt more comfortable around desiccated bodies than a party full of painters and poets. She wished it weren't so hard to blend into the Quartier Secret. Céleste and Sylvie and Rafael had no problem making themselves at home—why, just last night, she'd come back from patrol to find an entire room of imaginers trying to copy the youngest Enchantress's hairstyle. The most notable of them was Duchess d'Uzès, who picked up a paintbrush and splashed pastels into her own graying locks.

The paint was as purple as these wisteria blooms when she waved the brush at Honoré. "Would you like to try?"

"You'd look ravishing in violet!" Jean Cocteau swept his own pale pink fringe to the side as he said this. "No, no. Forgive me. I misspoke. You'd look ravaging. Especially if we went a few shades darker—"

"I'd look like an Easter Egg!" Honoré snapped.

Her dragon ring did too.

The rainbow collective scattered, leaving Sylvie there to look at her as if she'd just committed murder. So much...so much like Gabriel. It made Honoré want to roar even more. But then she caught Rafael staring too, his arm wrapped around Céleste, watching her ring, and damn...was that fear flashing through his eyes? Or was it Terreur? Either way it had made Honoré's nostrils flare. Deep breath. *Keep the fire in.*

Don't let history repeat itself.

She sniffed La Fée Verte's resurrected blossoms again.

She twisted her ring.

It didn't come off as cleanly as it had on her last trip to Caveau des Terreurs, but it certainly wasn't as messy as when she'd tried to take it from her father's finger. There was no blood staining Honoré's hands when she slipped the relic into her pocket.

The flowers *did* smell brighter without it.

The gate glittered as Honoré pushed through, doing another quick sweep of the street beyond. Sequins were scattered on the sidewalk alongside flyers for a variety of vices: gin, cards, skirts hiked high. Harmless enough, all things considered.

She crossed her arms and leaned against the wall, studying the Tournée du Chat Noir poster again.

Its edges were still curled.

But the cat's tail was not.

Honoré frowned.

The cat inside the poster smiled. A Cheshire grin that twisted into a snarl as the creature leapt out of its advertisement. Black fur blurred to the size of a panther as it landed on the sidewalk.

"Oh shit," Honoré swore.

The...drawing...moved like spilled ink, but it sure felt solid when it lunged at her. Fur glossed Honoré's arm as she sidestepped. Claws raked the opposite wall. The cat splashed against the stone; dark drops rolled down bricks, causing the weeds that grew through the sidewalk's cracks to wither wherever they landed. Honoré fumbled through her pocket as the monster rounded back on her. The ring! The ring! *Fuck.* The cat sprang again. She kicked it with her ash-smudged boot, and even though this action pushed the creature back, it seemed to *pull* something too. Dark and stringy. It unraveled from her foot, latching on to the cat like a second tail.

Honoré could feel her dragon latching on as well. Her ring roared from her pocket, up her arm, over her torso, ready to tear apart the cursed drawing still tethered to her boot. Silver rushed down her leg—she was almost fully armored.

But the cat had transformed too. It no longer looked like the drawing from the Tournée du Chat Noir. It no longer resembled a panther either. It was her kitten—the one she'd found in a lifeless heap in the alley behind Rémy Lavigne's apartment. Next to a saucer of soured milk.

Her stomach curdled again.

Her dragon froze. Honoré couldn't bring herself to strike the skinless creature, even when it stalked toward her with bloody paw prints, even when it seemed to be lapping up her shadow so it could grow larger and larger and—

There was a flash.

A blade that was not a knife cut through Honoré's shadow. One of La Fée Verte's imaginings. The Sanct had removed a bangle from her wrist and was now holding it like a dagger, sawing through the second tail string that connected Honoré and the cursed creature. It snapped from the Enchantress's leg. The rotting kitten shifted into a hellcat—with abyssal fur and flames for eyes. It should've been an easier foe to fight, but when Honoré reached out for her dragon, the ring felt slippery. She couldn't make it move. She almost couldn't move her arm either under so much dead-weight metal.

The hellcat hissed.

A black tongue uncurled from its teeth, lashing out at La Fée

Verte. This caught the edge of the Sanct's wing, causing several feathers to fall. Her masque flickered. She pulled more dreams from her wrist and turned them into blades.

"Here!" She tossed one to Honoré. "Use this!"

The imagining felt heavier than Honoré had anticipated.

Sharper too.

When she stabbed the demon—dream blade to skull—it didn't splash apart into a puddle of ink. Instead, the creature became ash, swirling past its empty poster and over the garden's blooms.

"You told me you weren't afraid of cats," La Fée Verte said, as she watched them vanish.

"That wasn't a cat," Honoré managed.

"No," the Sanct agreed. "It's one of his tricks: pulling dark thoughts out of people's heads. Fears are hard to fight. Memories can be even harder." She kept staring at the rooftops, her gaze narrowing on an empty balcony, where curtains fluttered on either side. "The Fisherman of the Moon was right. It was a mistake for me to rely too much on your ring. I should have armed you with more hope. Hope as sharp as hurt. Most people wouldn't be able to wield a dream that way, but I can tell you've had practice..."

Somehow, Honoré knew she wasn't talking about *défense dans la rue* lessons. Croissant pistols be damned. No, the Sanct was talking about actual *hope*. That brute force Honoré felt as she stared at the Sanct's bangles—evening stars and fields of fireworks. Her own insides burned. She didn't want to be a mistake, especially to La Fée Verte. There had to be a better way to start blending in...

She needed something else to fight with.

To fight for.

"Give me dreams, then," she said.

Honoré had never been one for wearing bracelets.

Like so many other feminine accessories, they felt designed to constrain. Metaphorical shackles. When paired with corsets and tight shoes, they were unbearable. She wasn't sure this sensation would change much, even if the bracelet happened to be a sliver of someone else's soul. Even if they looked oh so beautiful on the arms of the woman guiding her into an underground room that reminded Honoré of a cathedral. It wasn't just the shape of the space, its vaulted ceilings dripping with dreams, but a holy feeling. The sensation that she'd set foot on sacred ground. There should be hymns chanted here, or incense burning in censers, or altars spilling over with fruit.

Honoré felt more at peace here than she ever had inside a church.

"It's beautiful," she whispered.

La Fée Verte's cheeks went the same color they had at the Fisherman's booth. "Thank you. I've never shown any of my guests this space before. It's precious to me. Really, it's my life." The Sanct's arm sang with light as she lifted it. Her wings stretched too. Green feathers materialized into birds and began unknotting the bangles one by one, flying them up to the ceiling. "I've spent years mastering the magic of art. Every night I invite the brightest minds of Paris to my salon, and every night I take a small spark in return—"

"That's a lot of nights," Honoré said, as she looked around the cavern.

"I suppose so. The best ideas often need time to grow," the Sanct said. "And sometimes they must stretch outside their original imaginers' heads. This is a safe place for them to do just that. I've grown several inventions here. Neon lights, scooters, pneumatic tyres..."

"And women's trousers?"

"I'll try again, as soon as your friend paints me a pair." La Fée Verte smiled. "She seems slow to warm."

Was she? It was difficult for Honoré to say—their own first meeting had been at knifepoint on a winter evening, when she'd tried shaking Céleste down for francs. But all the other young woman possessed was a damn good poker face and an art portfolio.

"These are all I have," she said when she handed the papers over. "And I was just told they're worthless."

Many of the drawings inside were done in pencil, as gray as the young artist's eyes. Notre-Dame de Paris, the Panthéon, the Arc de

Triomphe. These were the sights of someone fresh to Paris... Céleste Artois, according to the signature on the bottom. The *A* looked like the Eiffel tower—slender and ambitious and not necessarily to everyone's taste.

Honoré kept flipping through the drawings, her knife forgotten. "You drew them?"

A nod.

"Use them for a fire, if you'd like. Or stuff some down your clothes to keep warm. It's all the same to me," Céleste said.

Snow started to fall, catching the edges of the sketches. Honoré shut the folder quickly, to keep them from ruin. "They're wrong." She handed the papers back to Céleste. "The person who said that. I've seen men only half as good as you, and they live like kings, drawing their own money."

"Really?"

"It's how I'd steal," Honoré admitted, "if I could draw. It's a hell of a lot nicer than mugging people for pocket lint."

To her surprise, Céleste laughed. "Then it's a good thing you tried to rob me."

They warmed instantly after that—not by burning Céleste's drawings, but by erasing her name from the bottom and replacing it with a signature that could pass as Monet's. At least in the eyes of tourists who didn't mind parting with some coins. The sketches sold quickly. Céleste drew more. She purchased paints. She bought tickets to Musée d'Orsay and the Louvre. She studied the masters' canvases. She mimicked them well, but when Honoré had looked at the paintings, she couldn't help but feel like something was missing, that snow-swirling, breath-catching wonder that had made her lower her knife.

The spark she knew now. The magic.

"It's good that you've been inviting Céleste here," Honoré said. "She needs room to grow too. But... do you have to take her memories every morning?"

"Yes," La Fée Verte said.

"Why?"

The other woman's lips pinched. "To keep this place safe."

"Isn't that why you're keeping *me* Enlightened?" Honoré wondered.

"Yes," the Sanct answered again. "But you're different."

"I'm not a dreamer, you mean."

Honoré raked a hand through her chopped hair. Tempting, still, to blame its dullness on her childhood's lack of fairy tales—but Rafael had grown up right alongside her. He'd sworn, he'd stolen, he'd stabbed. He had even more scars than she did. And yet, somehow, he managed to paint over them. Was it because he'd gotten the hell out of Belleville when he had? Leaving Honoré with nothing but a note that said *MEET ME IN CONSTANTINOPLE* and a pile of shit?

It was hard not to see the irony.

Rafael had risen above the Caveau's rot, while Honoré had continued to spread it. She'd lured Céleste into a life of crime. Years of her friend's art—her power—had been wasted on fiddle games. Thank goodness Rafael had managed to get her excited about painting again. Honoré could almost *see* sparks flying between the pair when they were in the landscape room together.

She wanted to be happy for them.

She really did.

Even more than that, she didn't want to get left behind again.

"You may not be an imaginer," La Fée Verte replied softly, "but you, Honoré Côte, have an unwavering heart. It has been tested and found true. You battle fountain beasts and bring bread to the hungry. The world has been ugly to you, yes, but you still *care*. You care so fiercely...I know, with my deepest anima, that I can trust you, and that is worth more to me than ten thousand dreams."

More birds swirled out of the Sanct's wings, rising in a column to the ceiling. Each one grabbed an imagining in its talons and returned to La Fée Verte's feet. Shard after glowing shard was spread out, fit together, until Honoré saw the outline of a sword. Sharp, sharp hope. Oh, this was so much better than a baguette or a bracelet! She itched to pick up the hilt, but La Fée Verte grabbed it first, lifting the blade to Honoré's shoulders.

She shirked automatically, but it wasn't an attack.

It was a knighting.

Honoré recognized the gesture from an illustration in one of Sylvie's books, where an elegant willowy woman touched a man on the shoulder with a broadsword. The drawing had looked archaic. The thought of knights felt much the same. Until now, she couldn't have imagined swearing such fealty to someone.

She knelt for La Fée Verte though.

Her knees touched stone, but everything else in Honoré Côte soared as she stared up at the golden woman. *She who wakes the best in us.* Honoré could see even more dreams from this angle. They shone over the Sanct's head like a halo, but as Honoré locked eyes with La Fée Verte, she no longer felt like a sinner.

She was Fear's Bastard, yes.

She was his murderer too, but La Fée Verte saw past that. She must, if she was asking this of Honoré.

"Would you like to go by 'sir' or something else? What title should we use for a knight who is also a lady? 'Dame' perhaps?"

"Dame," Honoré declared. For though she'd taken a male name and wore men's clothes, this was more to deter them than to become one.

"I dub thee 'Dame Honoré, Defender of Dreamers.' May your hope be bold and your justice be true." The sword switched shoulders, but La Fée Verte's eyes did not waver. She held Honoré's gaze, pouring light into it. "May you fight for a better world. May you make it so. Be thou a knight in my name."

"I will," Honoré said, breathless.

Her veins felt full of molten gold, as if the armor were *inside* her. She looked down and was surprised to see that she was not, in fact, glowing. Only her dragon hand shimmered. The beast's wings gave an excited flap when La Fée Verte handed over the sword. Honoré cradled the blade, taking in its details like a mother meeting her infant child for the first time. So much shone beneath the surface: Sea monsters. A map of a lost continent. A reindeer with lanterns sprouting from its horns.

Her dreams now.

La Fée Verte smiled down at her. "Arise, Dame Honoré."

Black Cat Fears

A cursed cat wanders over the rooftops of Montmartre. It would be impossible for you to follow without wings, and even if you borrowed a pair from Cabaret d'Ailes, you wouldn't be able to keep up with the creature. It is mostly ashes, swirling over chimneys—every which way—before blowing into an open attic window. From there it slips into the keyhole of a locked wardrobe. If you peered through, you'd be surprised to see that there are no coats.

The ashes settle back into a vague feline form in front of a fireplace. It leaps onto the arm of a wing-back chair. The man sitting there doesn't pet the cat. He picks through the ashen fur instead, as if searching for fleas. He isn't, of course. It's hard to say what he finds. Even harder to say what makes him smile.

The cat jumps to the floor and saunters back toward the door. The man follows. He does not have your limitations. He hardly has any at all—anymore. He's walked this world ten times over, digging up its oldest secrets. He has feasted on kings and pulled stars from the sky to try to fill the hole inside him.

And it is not enough.

It is never enough.

The chatelaine at his waist jingles, but he has no need of its keys.

The cat slips through the lock and twists the door open for him. He's seen many things past this threshold—palaces, jungles, streamliners—but the sight that greets him now doesn't belong on a postcard. It's a hole-in-the-wall tavern. There are several holes in the walls as well as in the furniture. Sappy spots of liquor make the man's boots stick to the floor as he follows the ashen cat to the bar. He already feels more solid here than he has in years. Why might that be?

He pulls a stool up to where the cat is perched. The animal dissolves. When ash scatters away—finally—the man sees a bloodstain in its place. His smile grows as he presses his hand to the wood.

It's an old wound.

It tastes nothing like Mademoiselle Artois's sickly blood. There's a violence here that makes his mouth water: anger and oak and the lightning that felled the tree well over a century ago. The man's own fingers dig as deep as roots, pulling the stain up into his own veins, spilled life spilling through him—

The wood is almost dry when he's interrupted, some fool sidling onto the adjoining stool, holding a gun as if it were a threat. "You aren't welcome here. This is *my* bar," he snarls. "Caveau des Terreurs. Didn't you see the sign over the door?"

The man hadn't seen the sign, of course, but he sees other promising things. That name... it's carved in the bar top just under his fingers, waiting to be claimed. The men who answer to Terreur are waiting too, playing with knives and their own violent egos. It wouldn't take much to turn them into an army.

The man reaches out.

The gun goes off.

Another hole has gone through the Sanct's chest, scarring the wall behind it, but the dying gasps that fill Caveau des Terreurs do not belong to him. The tavern itself will be in his possession soon enough, and while it's a far cry from the bold avenues of the Champs-Élysées or the dizzying colors of Montmartre, it is, nevertheless, a piece of Paris.

It is a start.

Chapter 17

Where Poverty Is a Luxury

Céleste could not go back to her grave.

She couldn't even make it as far as Place de la Concorde's obelisk. She was coughing up too much blood, filling handkerchiefs at a rate that sent her heart racing. Did most people waste away this fast? Or was this simply all the time she'd stolen coming out in thick garnet clumps? Ruby streaks. Vermilion edges. She'd never realized before how much blood was like fire. Its colors consumed your vision so that you could not look away. Why were endings so mesmerizing? She thought about the book Sylvie had snatched from the case. Céleste was glad the youngest Enchantress hadn't read much further... that she didn't have to see... this...

Rafe was watching though. He watched her the way he'd watched that windmill inferno. His eyes were almost the same color as his shadow when it spilled onto the stones of Place de la Concorde. And just as flat. Again, Céleste thought of a snuffed candle, though she was fairly sure the other thief remained Enlightened. [redacted] had made no move to reverse any of the curses he'd placed upon the pair, nor did he stop them when they limped back out onto the rue des Ombres. They were lucky to be alive.

For now, at least.

"Guess I don't need those enchanted rubies you promised," she croaked, when Rafe fished a fresh handkerchief from his pocket. A paper fluttered to the ground as well. "My lips are bright enough."

The other thief did not laugh. He knelt to pick up the paper—it held the sigil she'd sketched not even a day ago. That damn fox running around and around, never quite catching up with itself.

A sob escaped Rafe's throat when he saw the drawing.

He crumpled onto the stones, into his too-still shadow.

His wingless shoulders shook.

Those weren't the tears of someone who'd parted with a few enchanted knickknacks. No, this was rawer. It was... *real.* The same kind of grief Céleste had felt when she'd told the other thief about her parents' château: *I lost everything.*

Had they?

She balled the handkerchief in her fist as she sank onto the stones beside Rafe. The backs of their hands touched. "I'm sorry." She couldn't remember the last time she'd said those words out loud. Much less in earnest. "I—I didn't mean for him to see the windmill."

He took a shuddering breath.

At least he *was* breathing.

It was hard to forget the image of him hooked like a cow's carcass at a butcher shop. Going all leathery. His complexion was much improved, despite the red rimming his eyes.

"It's my fault." The artist's fingers crunched the borders of his sigil. "I let you in."

Somehow, Céleste didn't think Rafe was talking about the building that had just burned. He was probably wishing his lines about tangled fates *were* bullshit, right about now. If he'd just left her bleeding on the steps of the Théâtre des Champs-Élysées, none of his dreams would have gone up in smoke.

"Monsieur!" It was the doorman from Hôtel de Crillon, wandering down the sidewalk to check on them. "Is this woman bothering you? Should I flag down a cab?"

Rafe folded the fox sigil and stood. "Yes."

Céleste coughed. She must look a sorry sight—did the doorman think she was a beggar or a prostitute? Either way, he'd probably try to call the police if she lingered on the curb. She didn't think it was a good idea to slink back into rue des Ombres either, not while the passage still smelled so thickly of smoke. Better wait for [redacted]'s anger to cool. But wait where? Père Lachaise was out of the question, and Rafe's windmill must be nothing but ashes by now. Thanks to her. He'd be a fool to invite Céleste anywhere else...

"Christopher Marlowe was full of shit, wasn't he?" she said, looking up at the other thief.

His mouth quirked at this—the shape looked strange amid Rafe's bruises. "If by 'shit' you mean legendary plays that are still quoted centuries later... Then, yes, I suppose the playwright of *Doctor Faustus* was full of it."

"Misery does just fine without company." She waved her crimson-covered rag again. "Go on, then."

"You're coming back to my studio with me. Obviously. I'm not going to let you sit here and wallow."

"You're not?" She faltered. "But you just said you were sorry for letting me in—"

"I never said I was sorry." Rafe's voice had a fierce edge. "You saved me in there, Céleste." He looked down at the folded fox in his hands, his words going softer. "I need you, still, and thanks to your Enchantresses, that arrangement is mutual. If one of us fails, both of us do. Like it or not, we're in this together. We're in deep. Might as well go a bit deeper." Rafe tucked her drawing into his pocket and offered a hand to help her stand. "Come, *mon amour*. Let's go home."

Two Passage de Dantzig was not a house.

Nor was it a windmill.

Rafe García lived in a building designed by Gustav Eiffel. It had stood by the engineer's tower once, serving as a wine pavilion during the Exposition Universelle of 1900. After the fair, the structure was dismantled and rebuilt off a much quieter street. It sat behind a set of ivy-strewn gates, though these were almost never closed. La Ruche was open to all and had been so named because it resembled a beehive. In shape, yes, but also in the constant hum of activity. Its honeycomb rooms buzzed with artists, models, clochards, anyone who needed a roof over their head.

A category that now included Céleste.

"I used to dream of a place like this," she said, as Rafe led her past a sculptor hammering away at a piece of stone in the courtyard. "My acceptance letter to Académie de La Palette arrived just before my father died, so I came to Paris after the funeral, but, of course, there was no money for tuition. No one would take me seriously without it." Not even the academy's director, who'd twisted the ends of his very real moustache as he explained there were no scholarships available. Perhaps she should try to find a patron?

His suggestion had sounded simple enough.

The reality was that Paris's salons were crowded. Especially Twenty-Seven rue de Fleurus. Countless artists clamored for Gertrude Stein's attention. To be hung on her wall was a crowning achievement. She was a kingmaker. *King*, Céleste had soon learned, because there were no paintings by women on display. There was hardly any space for women in the main foyer either. Wives and girlfriends and mistresses were shuttled off to a separate room, where they were entertained by Gertrude's partner, Alice.

Céleste managed to escape this fate, elbowing her way to the chair by the white-tile fireplace. Madame Stein didn't throw her sketches into the fire, but her words burned the young artist's ears: "I'm afraid you don't have what it takes. Though you do have a fascinating face . . . perhaps you'd let Matisse try to capture it?"

She fled the Twenty-Seven rue de Fleurus shortly after.

She might have abandoned Paris altogether, if she hadn't been held up in a nearby alley.

"No one except Honoré," she amended. "But Honoré takes everything seriously."

"You still could have come to live at La Ruche," Rafe said. The cab ride from Place de la Concorde had seemed to revive him a little. "They don't charge rent to stay in the building."

"That sounds too good to be true," Céleste replied.

"Well, there are enough leaks in the roof to make up for it, but those help with the fact there's no running water. As our friend Jean likes to say, 'Poverty is a luxury here!'"

Céleste didn't see Monsieur Cocteau inside, but she recognized several other guests from La Fée Verte's salon as she followed Rafe to his studio. There was Guillaume Apollinaire—a poet who'd taken to smiling at Céleste every time they passed in the leafy corridors of the Quartier Secret. It was not the same, in these crowded halls of turpentine. The large man had to shift his muscular frame to let Rafe and Céleste pass. He frowned as they did.

"Rough night, Monsieur García? I had too much wine myself, I think..."

Not wine, Céleste thought wistfully. *Smoky cocoa.* The blue elephant—like all of Sylvie's other imaginings—did not disappear with the mist each morning. Instead it had become a fixture in the Quartier Secret, pouring drinks behind the bar, which had stretched its space accordingly.

Rafe García's studio had no such leeway. The room was the size of a closet, but, unlike some of La Ruche's other nooks, it had a window. A pot of geraniums sat underneath to catch the aforementioned leaks. Their petals would be impossible to paint without cadmium. It was the most expensive shade of red. The most poisonous too.

Céleste coughed into her handkerchief yet again, wishing she could still blame hay fever.

"Welcome to my sunlit life." Bright rays washed over Rafe's face as he stepped into the room. The light *was* glorious in here. "I'm usually not Enlightened during the daytime, so I spend most of those hours sleeping. And painting. I know it's not much."

And yet, it *was*.

Every available inch of wall was covered with landscapes. Saw-toothed mountain ranges. Sand-whipped deserts. Jungles growing over ancient cities. A sky full of stars falling into a vast blanket of snow.

Waterfalls misting out into rainbows. There were more localized scenes as well, mostly churches and catacombs. Céleste could even see their ill-fated windmill—it wasn't the focus of the piece, but it was there, its blades peeking over Montmartre's poster-splashed storefronts.

The lower-left corner of each canvas was signed *Raf.*

"Your name is missing an *e*," she pointed out.

Again, he did not laugh. He pulled her picture of the fox from his pocket and pinned it up on the wall, smoothing out its wrinkles with care. "As I said before, there's no indoor plumbing, but you're welcome to stay as long as you need."

Generous, considering the fact that Rafe's bed was a mattress shoved into the corner. Too small for the two of them to use without touching. Not that Céleste had much room to be picky... her body was starting to feel as crumpled as the handkerchief in her fist. She sank into the pile of blankets and coughed again. The geranium was close enough to tremble.

"It might not be that long," she told the other artist, when he sat next to her.

The mattress dipped beneath his weight.

It was less fire, she felt, when their shoulders touched (*Mon Dieu*, she didn't want to think of flames. Not now.), and more light. They both sat awash with midmorning sun—bright enough for Céleste to notice that Rafe's bruises had vanished. His tattoo was back to a single tear.

"You underestimate yourself. If you go back to rue des Ombres tonight, he should let you drink from his cup," Rafe said. "That silver tongue of yours saved our lives. If you hadn't spoken up when you did..."

What?

Céleste wondered. It was curious that Rafe hadn't made any move to salvage his stash. If their employer wanted the key to immortality so badly, then couldn't Rafe have traded the secrets he'd hunted down for the rest of the windmill? Why had he chosen to let all those curio cabinets and manuscripts *burn* instead? Was it because he had no other choice?

"Why do you work for him?" she asked. "There are easier ways to get diamonds."

"I work for myself."

That was rich. Even if *he* wasn't. Céleste looked around the rentless studio. "So, what? After you find our employer's missing idea, he'll hang your paintings in the Louvre?" [redacted] was probably a kingmaker too. For artists and actual emperors. She'd certainly heard him discussing Tsar Nicholas with the Mad Monk often enough. "Raf García and the enchanted landscapes! Art historians can't resist a good mystery, you know. They'll eat up that missing *e*—"

"I don't want to be famous." He cut Céleste off, sharp as a pair of sewing scissors. "I want to be *free*." There was anger in Rafe's voice, but it wasn't directed at her. It went deeper. It made the thief clench his hands into fists. His eyes strayed to the fox painting. "Free of this half-life spent forgetting who I am over and over and over again. I'm so goddamn sick of being a husk!"

Most days it feels like I'm a shell of myself. He'd worded the sentiment differently that night on the bridge, but Céleste understood. She thought of Monsieur Apollinaire, who'd just now tried to introduce himself to her in the hall—even though he'd dedicated a poem to her two nights ago. The man recited it after sipping smoky cocoa, the stanzas taking shape in ribbons of cloud. They'd faded, after a few hours. Same as Jean Cocteau's ram horns or Duchess d'Uzès ever-changing hair colors.

Rafe's own hair remained black—a raven-feather shade. She'd never seen it in such full sun before. Like everyone else, they'd stayed strangers this side of sunrise, stuck that way until his midnight memories returned at dusk.

"You want to be completely Enlightened."

"That would help." The thief sighed.

"Why doesn't our employer let you see magic in the daytime?" Obviously he could, if Rafe was sitting here on the mattress talking about such things.

"He claims it's because he doesn't want La Fée Verte noticing me, but really it's about control," Rafe told her. "I'm at his mercy every sunset. Life would sure be a hell of a lot easier without my regular bouts of amnesia."

Céleste bit her lip. She wasn't so sure. She used to feel free with

Honoré and Sylvie—but things had gotten strained since the other Enchantresses had been welcomed into La Fée Verte's salon. Now that the windmill was gone, it would be even worse. She no longer had the luxury of relying on Rafe's spare dreams, which meant there would be no more midnight macarons at Stohrer. No flying off to explore the gilded halls of Versailles. No learning the basic conjugations of cats.

If Céleste and Rafe were going to finish this job, they would have to keep using each other as an excuse to disappear.

Play lovers. Be lovers, for all I care.

She did care.

She'd said she was sorry on the curb, but the apology didn't feel like enough. It didn't convey the ache Céleste felt as she looked around Rafe's studio, where colors bloomed in the most inventive ways. "Are you sure I can stay? I—I wouldn't want this place to burn."

"It won't," Rafe said, nudging the potted geranium with his foot. "There are too many damn leaks."

Her laugh was bloodless.

His smile caught sunshine.

"What happens when you forget me, tomorrow morning? When you wake up and find a strange woman in your bed?"

She was suddenly very aware that they were sitting there, on the edge of Rafe's mattress. Their shoulders were no longer touching, but that was only because the other thief had turned to take her in. Brown eyes twinkled above his tattoo. His grin had gone a bit sideways—cheeky.

"I expect I'll be utterly delighted," the thief said. "And I doubt it will be difficult to convince me to share this studio. For you, Céleste Artois, I'm an easy mark."

So very, very easy.

She wasn't even sure who leaned in first, only that his lips were there. They'd rehearsed this scene so many times, beneath opal streetlamps and shooting stars and flowering ceilings. It felt second nature to Céleste. Then again, it always had. But Rafe surprised her by moving past her lips, instead kissing the soft skin just beneath her earlobe. His breath grazed her neck, catching the curve of her collarbone. Céleste's chest started to sparkle just like a lit fuse.

The feeling went down, down, down...

This was usually the part where Rafe's shadow swept over them, where the pair pulled apart and disappeared into the Vault of Dreams. But the other thief's silhouette spilled across the mattress, moving only with his body's own motions, kissing the arc of her neck, wrapping his hands around her waist, pulling her so close that their outlines melded together on the bedsheets.

We aren't pretending anymore.

Céleste reached for the buttons of Rafe's own shirt. The top ones came undone quite easily, revealing scars that only made the muscles beneath that much more impressive. *The language of knives.* What story did they have to tell? She might have asked the other thief, but there was no room for words in her throat, only a moan, as Rafe's kisses followed that lit-fuse feeling, down, down, as his fingers traced the outer edges of her thighs, moving slowly but surely inward. Céleste's spine curved like those carnival swan boats. Her chin tilted up. Her mouth parted with a gasp.

"Oh!"

The geranium shuddered again as Rafe pushed off the pot to reach for the laces of her corset. Céleste's thoughts went poison red.

"Oh!"

Her exclamation was sharper, sharp enough to make Rafe stiffen. "What? What's wrong?"

"The blood."

Rafe's eyes found her lips. There must be stains there—she'd been coughing up so much—but he didn't flinch. It took every ounce of Céleste's strength to push the other thief away.

"I could...I might make you sick."

"I don't have to kiss you on the mouth." His voice simmered. "There are plenty of other places to explore."

Oh, Céleste was well aware. The ache she felt beneath her belly had nothing to do with his paintings. One touch there and she might explode.

"What if I cough?" She hadn't since coming to rest on Rafe's bed, but it was only a matter of time. "We have to be more careful."

Blood, after all, was far messier than paint. As much as Céleste wanted to lose herself in these bedsheets, she knew it was dangerous. Rafe might get consumption, yes, but it could be even worse than that.

I will be so much worse.

"You were right. In the windmill. We got too comfortable with our arrangement, and I slipped up today, when I saw our employer killing you. I—" She swallowed. "I don't want that to happen again."

The other thief looked ready to argue.

He sighed instead. "Our employer isn't omniscient. It is possible to hide your thoughts from him…It's like the stardust trick, but opposite."

"And you didn't think to tell me before?"

"I've been distracted," Rafe said, working his jaw back and forth. His gaze burned almost as hot as her *want*. "As loath as I am to admit it, you have a point. We've got to stay focused. We have to find that goddamn dream."

Céleste almost didn't return to rue des Ombres that evening.

Rafe's mattress was comfortable despite the sleeping arrangements. Or maybe, perhaps, because of them. The pair had settled into the bed back-to-back, but sometime during their dreams, they'd turned to face each other. She woke in dusk's violet light to find their foreheads touching. White hair tangled with black, but the pillow beneath remained crisp.

She hadn't coughed once.

Céleste's consumption caught up with her when she climbed out of bed. Fresh wet in the crusty clots of the handkerchief. Rafe stirred at this sound, his fob chains falling across his vest. The top buttons remained undone. Céleste wondered if he normally wore such shirts to bed—complete with a magical watch tucked in its pocket—or if he'd made an exception for her.

She wished he wouldn't.

She wished for a lot of things. It would've been nice to have more of a warning, about how ruthless [redacted] could be, though Céleste supposed that wouldn't have made much difference. Better to go back to the last time Sylvie blew out a birthday candle—so all three Enchantresses could discover magic together. Again, that might not have changed things. She'd still been dying then, and try as she might, Céleste couldn't just *wish* her consumption away. Dreaming might be surviving for someone like Rafe García, but no matter how much she wanted to stay in bed with him, she knew [redacted] was right.

Fantasies would not save her.

Unless she kept taking them to the nameless Sanct.

So Céleste found herself slipping out of La Ruche's ivy-wound gates and returning to rue des Ombres. She'd never entered the tunnel by herself before. Was that why the door at the end looked so different when she knocked? Reddish light cast through the keyhole, and there was . . . piano music.

Céleste wasn't sure who was more surprised when she walked out of the tavern's supply closet—herself or the barmaid. The woman almost dropped the carafe she was pouring. Her face paled to the point that Céleste almost offered an apology: *Sorry for bursting out of your barware cupboard.*

But then she saw who was being served.

[redacted] sat at the end of the bar. He looked more human than before—his cheeks rounded and ruddy—but Céleste's basest animal instinct warned her that she could not be sorry. Not the way she'd been with Rafe. An apology followed by skin touching skin. So bare and exposed . . . She pushed back this thought too, wishing the neckline of her gown weren't so plunging. That it didn't make her neck look so swanny in the bar mirror.

"Ah, Mademoiselle Artois, welcome to my new territory."

"It doesn't look that new." Cobwebs fluttered from lamps. The piano cried out for a tuner. The stool wobbled when Céleste took a seat beside her employer.

"New to me," the Sanct amended. "Eleanor, would you pour some wine for my guest?"

"Yes, Terreur."

A name! Céleste tried not to look surprised as the barmaid reached for an unopened bottle of Chardonnay. This was harder to manage, when her employer snapped his fingers and Eleanor froze. Strained. The black ribbon around the other woman's throat looked far too tight.

"No, no. Céleste here deserves the special reserve." The Sanct gestured at the carafe that sat on the bar top. Eleanor moved—immediately—to pour it. Was it the same wine he'd served Céleste at the first meeting? The color was similar. The tavern's crimson lamplight left a strange sheen on the liquid. Stabbing shapes. "She's had quite the day. As have I." Terreur turned toward her. "I stumbled across this quaint place not long after our last encounter. They serve the most delicious vintage." He nodded toward the glass. "I think you'll appreciate it."

Thanks to years of pulling confidence schemes among the upper crust of Parisian society, Céleste knew you were supposed to swirl older wines. Smell them. Sip. Savor.

Instead, she swallowed as fast as she could.

She only paused to breathe when the glass was empty.

When her lungs were better.

"Are you hungry?" the Sanct asked. "Of course you're hungry. You're always hungry. You know, you're much more suited to this work than Monsieur García. He tried to run from this life, but you sought it out. You took a damn taxi."

Céleste ran her tongue over her teeth. She didn't feel like eating, but she didn't think that was the type of hunger her employer was talking about. It wasn't what set her on the edge of her stool when he reached for the ends of her hair.

His touch was nothing like Rafe's.

It was hard not to shrink back, especially when the strands in the Sanct's fingers turned black.

She could see Château Artois and herself locked outside its gates, but this wasn't the only memory. There were others: The time she'd broken into her father's office and sipped enough whisky out of his crystal decanter that she vomited. A night at the opera, where she'd gotten a visiting British viscount good and drunk off champagne before convincing him to invest in a "newly discovered van Gogh." Her last lunch at Foyot's, where she'd feasted on caviar before she sold the fake Eugène Delacroix painting to a fellow diner. Herself bragging to a statue as she'd buried the coins.

Terreur smiled at these sights.

"You're a taker, Céleste Artois." He let the thoughts fall back. "I don't have to pull your strings to get you to steal. It's already in your nature. You're the one I would have chosen."

Not to kill, he meant.

"I will take some dinner, if you're offering," she said lightly, trying to ignore the feeling that she'd already bitten off more than she could chew.

The Sanct next to her laughed. "The food here is shit, but I'll be moving on to better venues soon enough." Every word he spoke made her think of a wolf's fangs—how sharp they were after that first taste of flesh. "As soon as you find what it is I've forgotten."

"The thought La Fée Verte took from you?"

His laughter vanished.

His toothiness stayed.

Humans were born with holes inside them—so said her thieves' creed—but Céleste was beginning to believe Sancts were too. All the power of gods, and they still sat at bars, drinking and devouring.

"Do you have any idea what it looks like?" Céleste pressed.

"It's . . . large," the Sanct said. "Other than that, I cannot say. I only know what it is not. The place it should fit in my mind . . . It echoes."

So does the Vault of Dreams, Céleste thought, but for all its vastness, the cavern did seem to have some sort of order. The songbirds strung the dreams up newest to oldest, and so far, she and Rafe had been staying close to the stairs. "How long has it been gone?"

"Thirty years."

"Thirty?" She'd have to go deeper into the cavern, then.

Much deeper.

A Message in a Bottle

Mon amie—

I told you I would write [redacted]

Yours truly,
Eleanor

Chapter 18

Caveau des Terreurs

"Have I caught you admiring your own sword again?"

Honoré looked up from her lap to see La Fée Verte standing at their regular morning meeting place. The statues perched on the edge of Notre-Dame's south bell tower were still dim, waiting for dawn. The sun was rising later and later these days, now that summer had slipped into September. The pastries in the bag next to Honoré's knee were steaming more too, thanks to the drop in temperature.

La Fée Verte didn't seem to notice the chill. This morning she was dressed in a gown of green lace woven to look like leaves. It would've been hard to see where her wings ended and her dress began, if not for the hints of skin peeking through the fabric.

Honoré forced herself to glance back at the object in her lap, lying just next to her unsheathed blade. "Not my sword. Not this time, at least."

It was true that she'd spent an inordinate amount of time admiring the weapon the Sanct had forged for her. The dream sword was far sharper than any of the other knives she'd owned. There was also a lightness to it. Whenever Honoré pulled the blade from her scabbard, it felt even better than flying. It felt almost as good as La Fée

Verte coming to sit beside her for yet another sunrise. This meeting had become their morning ritual. The Sanct would stand by the balcony, welcoming a shower of sparks, while Honoré kept her company. She always brought bread, along with news of the previous night's patrol.

Her findings had been scarce, as of late. There were no more bloodless corpses, no strange fires, no theatre riots, no demon cats. Things had quieted down since Honoré's battle with the poster in Montmartre, but she knew she shouldn't count this as a victory. The vampire wasn't defeated. He'd just gotten better at hiding.

Honoré *had* discovered something this evening though.

"I found a message in a bottle."

"Oh?" La Fée Verte leaned over to get a closer look. The scent of flowers burst through the autumn air, and Honoré felt unseasonably warm. The same way she had when Eleanor once poured her drinks from similar Château Robert containers.

This time, though, Honoré did not shrink back.

No one was watching them up here, after all. Even the gargoyles were turned away, and Honoré figured they were controlled by La Fée Verte, who also seemed to relish their closeness. Her masque light beamed against Honoré's cheeks when she looked up.

"It doesn't have any enchantments inside, if that's what you were wondering," La Fée Verte said softly. "What does the letter say?"

"I'm not sure."

Though it wasn't for lack of unrolling the parchment. Honoré had fished out the paper as soon as she'd spotted the bottle by the buttress of Notre-Dame-de-la-Croix. There was no telling how long Eleanor's message had been sitting there. Days? Weeks? More? Enough mornings for the dew to do some damage. Only the edges of the letter had been spared. The rest was one watery stream of ink.

"My friend who first told me about the killings, she promised to write with any news. Maybe some new husks have turned up. Maybe I'll find a fresh trail that leads us straight to that bastard!"

La Fée Verte frowned. "You don't have to sound so hopeful about it, my dame."

This honorific the Sanct had created for Honoré had sounded strange to her immediately after the knighting, but like these sunrise visits at the top of the cathedral, it was now a bright point. Yes, it fit her differently than her other stolen name—but that wasn't such a bad thing.

"Don't I?" She looked back down at the blade resting over her legs. *Hope as sharp as hurt.* The reindeer with the lanterns was munching contentedly on fiery blossoms. Of all the imaginings inside the blade, that one was Honoré's favorite. It reminded her that there were beautiful ways to hold fire inside herself too. "I'm not excited about the bodies, obviously, but this monster . . . he's haunted you for a long time. I know that struggle. I've fought that fight. That's why you gave me this shiny new sword, isn't it? If I sound excited, it's only because I want the chance to swing it at him. I—" Honoré almost swallowed the words, but then she decided to be brave instead. "I want you to be happy too."

La Fée Verte regarded her for a lingering moment.

A smile bloomed on rose-colored lips.

"He hasn't stolen all my joy. Hardly." The Sanct grabbed the brown pâtisserie bag by Honoré's knee and started to open it. "Ooh, is that chocolate I smell?"

It was. In Honoré's excitement about the note, she'd decided to celebrate by buying *pains au chocolat* instead of ordinary croissants. A good choice, judging by the way La Fée Verte sang with delight after her first bite. Honoré let out an appreciative grunt too as she ate her own breakfast and watched green birds swirl out into the sunrise.

Caveau des Terreurs seemed different.

Honoré couldn't say why for sure as she stepped into her father's old haunt. Her hand curled around the scrap of paper she'd shown La Fée Verte that morning. The one covered with Eleanor's blurry penmanship.

I'll write you if anything changes.

So much *had* changed since the barmaid's promise. Honoré was fairly sure none of the gangsters who glared from the tables could see the sword of dreams hanging from her side. She hadn't bothered with a wig or a false moustache this time. She hadn't removed her ring either, though she kept that hand in her pocket as she took a seat at the bar.

Eleanor was wiping it down with a rag, leaving beads of water across the scarred wood. Sweat rolled down her temples too, making swirls of her dark hair. She did not look up, but kept polishing one spot, over and over.

"I got your message," Honoré said. "Well, I got the paper. Most of the words were ruined."

Eleanor's lips thinned.

Her rag slowed.

Honoré understood then why this particular patch of wood was so bothersome. It was too bright. There should have been a stain there . . . a gauge . . . a crudely carved phrase . . . something to mark her father's timely end.

But his blood was gone.

She could feel the dragon stirring around her fist as she examined the rest of the bar top's graffiti. Yes, there was the ode to Madame Lavigne's breasts. And the fox chasing its own tail, so artfully carved by Rafael. And the many different scars from many different knives.

"It said someone new is running the place," Eleanor said, still without looking up. "He's . . ." She scrubbed harder. Shuddered. "He showed up six weeks ago. I've never seen anyone like him, and I've been seeing all sorts of other strange things . . ."

The dragon had almost coiled up to Honoré's elbow now, impossible to hide. She didn't miss the way Eleanor's eyes caught it.

"What kinds of things?" she asked.

"Your white-haired friend for—oh!" the barmaid exclaimed.

There was a blur of fabric. Honoré's windpipe burned shut. She could see the red scarf around her neck, in the mirror, being used as a garrote. Rémy's scarf. "You must have some balls stuffed away in those trousers, coming back here without that kid and her cat. When I'm done gutting you, I'll find them next, make myself a nice new pair of boots out of that orange hide."

Traces of Marmalade's assault still scabbed the gangster's face. Honoré smiled at the sight in the mirror. She grabbed at the twisted silk, not the way a suffocating person might—all flailing arms—but with sharp silver purpose. The dragon ring's fangs cut through the scarf, freeing her as Rémy went stumbling back into some chairs.

He swore.

Honoré stood.

The dragon rose up her shoulder, swelled over her chest. Its jaws opened as she walked toward the gangster. Rémy scrambled backward. A necklace spilled out of his striped shirt—the golden charm of a saint dangling from its end. Odd. Rémy had never struck her as the religious type. *He'd sure as hell better start praying now.* Honoré snarled with both sets of teeth, and a dark stain spread over the crotch of the gangster's trousers. He reeked of fear. Her ring felt magnetized. She leaned down... closer, closer... close enough to realize that the scabs around his good eye weren't scabs at all. Marmalade's scratches were gone. The tattoo on his cheekbone—that singular dot that all her father's men marked themselves with—had spread. As if the ink had found a vein and was slowly poisoning the rest of him...

It was the same with the other Apaches' faces, Honoré realized.

The entire bar was watching her.

They made no move to help Rémy, to jump between him and the teeth of her father's ring, even though it was obvious they could see it. Their eyes followed the dragon. The rest of their bodies sat unnaturally still, their hands folded in their laps like fancy dinner napkins, even though Caveau des Terreurs had never served much more than greasy meat.

"Go on," came a voice from behind her. "They're waiting."

Honoré kept the dragon trained on Rémy when she turned. She found a stranger sitting at the spot Eleanor had scrubbed clean, his fingers drumming the wood. "Who are you?"

"You don't know how long I've been waiting to answer that question." His fingers drummed faster. "Imagine my surprise, when I followed your fear to this establishment, when I found a name just waiting for me like an overripe plum on a branch... heavy and juicy and *there*." He knocked on the wood again. "Terreur is dead. Long live Terreur."

Honoré felt her stomach twist.

The dragon exploded then—to the size of its more mythical counterparts. Scales shoved Rémy Lavigne back into a chair leg. Wings wrecked chandeliers. The piano screamed as a tail smashed it to splinters. Collateral damage. Honoré focused her talons on the Sanct. They sank into his arm, nailing it to the too-clean bar top. She waited for the red to spread—just as it had before—but no blood spilled from the holes she'd made. They looked like tears in paper.

Even more so when Terreur ripped his arm away.

She aimed for his chest next, but the silver fangs that sank there came back clean.

The Sanct was... empty.

He could not die.

Not the way Honoré's father had.

Not the way she'd wanted him to.

The Sanct smiled then. Red and green oil lamps flickered. Every gangster around the dragon stood in unison, their chairs scraping altogether off-key. Even Eleanor stiffened behind the bar, the whites of her eyes straining as her hand throttled the neck of a bottle. She seemed to be fighting herself as she broke it against the sink, sending sharp glass everywhere. Rémy—on the other hand—looked more than happy to pull a knife from his boot. To lunge. His shadow seemed to leap before he did, the thinnest black strand tugging all the way to the newest Terreur's fingers. His hold on these men was nothing like her father's had been. It wasn't just fear.

It was puppetry.

Rémy was on her then, stink-breathed and stabbing, but the gangster didn't stand a chance. He *did* bleed when Honoré crashed her dragon through his chest. Crimson globbed onto the floor. Something left his eyes—not light, since there wasn't much of that—but the warped tattoo marking. It snaked off the man's face, gathering his spilled blood with it, before slithering back to the

Sanct on the stool. Honoré's own insides scrambled as she watched his chest wound close, as she heard another one of the gangsters take a crunching step forward...

Her dragon faltered then.

For Gabriel.

Oh, Gabriel. He'd emerged from the remnants of the piano—splinters in his fair hair. They reminded Honoré of the carvings their father had crushed. So did the expression on her younger brother's face.

"Gabriel..." She hadn't spoken his name in so long.

It left her tongue tasting ashes. That was the flavor of the dark Sanct's magic too—she remembered from her battle with the hell-cat. She could see another black memory taking shape on the sandy floorboards between her and Gabriel. It belonged to her brother, guiding him into the exact same spot where he'd stood all those years ago, where she'd left him screaming at the sight of their father's corpse.

"Gabriel, listen to me, this man...he's not a man...He's—he's a sorcerer. He's got you under some sort of spell—"

Her brother took another step forward.

Honoré stepped back.

Words hadn't worked last time either. She'd tried explaining—*Our father was going to beat me to death because he found Rafael's note; he said I was trying to steal you away*—but Gabriel only screamed louder. She tried to cover his mouth, but her hands were dripping with blood, and she made him *taste* it. He spit. He sobbed. *It was an accident*, she'd wanted to say, but that was the same lie Lucien Durand had used when Anne found her mother crumpled by the hearth. Blood had stained its stones, stained the dragon ring, stained everything from that evening forward...

"I don't want to hurt you." She stumbled over Rémy's limp arm as she said this.

Behind her, the Sanct laughed.

It didn't matter. It didn't matter that Honoré had a shield for curses. It didn't matter that she'd spent the past two and a half months trying to master the dragon—stretching the ring's wings and retracting its fangs and learning how to push through that paralysis she'd felt when facing the hellcat. This was so much worse. Terreur might not be able to manipulate Honoré's thoughts directly, but he didn't have to. Not when he had so much control over her brother.

The shadow tether at Gabriel's feet shuddered, up, up to his arm. He pulled out a pistol—the kind Sylvie had called *pretty*—and aimed the golden barrel straight at his sister's heart.

A lemonade bottle smashed to the floor.

Eleanor.

The barmaid had a bullseye aim, Honoré knew. She meant for the glass to shatter at Gabriel's feet, cutting across the shadowy memory that guided them. Her brother's gun went slack the same moment this string did, when the Sanct pulling it turned back to the bar. Gabriel blinked. Eleanor gasped. Her hands went to her throat, to the black ribbon she'd never, ever worn before.

It's not a ribbon. Honoré felt her own breath shrivel as she watched the barmaid's face. Dark curls swirled around Eleanor's temples—more than mere hair—binding Eleanor back under the Sanct's control.

"You may try to fight me," the Sanct said coolly. He was still facing the barmaid, yet his eyes found Honoré's in the mirror. "But you cannot win."

Her father had thought much the same.

Honoré didn't think this reflection was enchanted, but there was an eerie echo to this moment: The dragon ring slick with blood. Gabriel stock-still. The other Apaches closing in on her with their knives.

Her own sword shimmered at her side. Dreams she'd somehow forgotten all about...

He may not knot your shadow with fear, but he doesn't need to, so long as you choose to keep your own hands tied. We are more than just the rot that happens around us.

The ragpicker's words didn't sound so trite anymore.

The Sanct in the mirror wavered when Honoré unsheathed her

blade. The weapon was far more golden than the pistol in her brother's hand. She couldn't stab Gabriel, of course, but she didn't have to. If a single dream could sever the hellcat's tail, then surely this sword could do more.

She could cut her brother free.

She could show Gabriel her truest self: the heart that was worth more than ten thousand dreams, despite the shards left by leaving him here. She was stronger now than she'd been then. She was Honoré. *Dame* Honoré. The knight who could not be crushed to splinters. She would save her brother from Terreur again—only this time they'd escape Belleville together.

The thought burned bright. The sword of dreams burned brighter as Honoré aimed the blade at the shadow string tangling her brother's feet. She swung with all her hope and might.

She watched—in disbelief—as it shattered.

Pieces sprayed across the sandy dance floor, reduced to glass and dust. Gabriel's boots crunched over them, and another lemonade bottle smashed into her dragon armor. Eleanor's aim had gone wrong again. It had all gone wrong.

"I must admit, I expected more from La Fée Verte's protégé," the newest Terreur mocked from her father's seat.

Honoré had as well.

Her ring roared. Her heart did too. The rest of the Apaches were circling—a tightening noose of scarves and blades—and her armor could only do so much. There was nothing to be won here.

Something was wrong with Honoré's ring.

The dragon flew well enough out of the Caveau des Terreurs, out of Belleville, over Paris's lacework streets, across the river. She even managed the tight landing into the Quartier Secret's open-air gardens, where someone had imagined a bottomless pool. Sylvie, most likely. Hers were the only creations that didn't disappear with the morning mists. The sun was high now. Honoré's reflection shivered when she plunged her hands into the teal waters. Rémy's blood turned purple before it washed off, swirling down, down. She tried to push her ring back into a band after she scrubbed it clean, but some silver streaks refused to budge. They sank into her skin, following her forearm's veins in a toothy, all-consuming pattern. *Like roots*, Honoré thought, as she scoured her skin.

She thought of other things too.

Rémy's dead-weight arm. (He would have killed her.) Gabriel's stare—black with hatred and something far more sinister. (He would have killed her too.) (And she would have let him.) The Sanct's smile—as empty as the hole she'd put though his chest. (*Long live Terreur!*)

How the hell could she fight something like that?

"Dame Honoré?"

La Fée Verte was standing barefoot in the garden, her wings blending with surrounding vines. Her masque melted into the sunlight. There was such a *fullness* to her that Honoré had never appreciated before: The pink flush of her cheeks. The whir of her birds. The rush of Honoré's own blood when the other woman knelt at her side. The tiger heat of those eyes. The honeyed warmth of her voice.

She wiped a single tear from Honoré's cheek. Her hand lingered there. Soft, so soft, just like her question. "What happened, my dame?"

"You shouldn't call me that." The honorific hadn't fit as well as Honoré hoped. She was fairly sure the armored heroes in Sylvie's storybooks didn't cry. Nor did they shatter their swords or abandon their brothers in their darkest hour. Twice. "I'm a shit knight."

The story came out in fragments, like the letter stuffed inside that first lemonade bottle, like the rest of the barmaid's glassy resistance. Honoré told La Fée Verte about the too-clean spot at the bar. About the name that used to be carved there. How no new blood stained the wood after her first attack. How Rémy's wounds had slithered across the floor, after the second assault, knitting the new Terreur's flesh back together.

"He...he *was* like a vampire." She shuddered at the memory. "My dragon did nothing to him."

La Fée Verte's hand fell from Honoré's cheek to her arm's silver-streaked skin. "And your sword?"

"I—"

More fragments.

She kept replaying the moment her weapon went to pieces. Cloud kingdoms and fluorescent leviathans. That beautiful lamplit reindeer, smashing to the sandy floor. "I believed I could free my brother—" The shame of it all was thick in her throat. "But I must not have believed hard enough. The blade broke."

"Broke? That's not right."

There was so much disappointment in La Fée Verte's voice. Honoré could hardly bear it. "Like I said... shit knight."

The Sanct was silent for a long moment.

"Your shattered sword had nothing to do with your willingness to fight, my dame. Believe me." Her touch on Honoré's arm went even softer. "None of this is your fault."

Rafael had said something similar about the kitten—nice of him, sure—but again Honoré felt like she was being placated. Why else would things keep breaking around her, unless she herself was broken?

"Your enemy has a foothold in Paris now because of me," she said. "He has a *name*. He said it was my fear that led him to those things."

"My wards should have stopped that from happening." La Fée Verte stood. Birds rushed around her head as she pulled aside a curtain of vines. There, by some trick of folded space, was the corkscrew staircase. "They should have prevented the fire in Montmartre and *The Rite of Spring* riot too. I thought they were failing because his attacks were growing stronger, but I'm afraid it's worse than that."

Honoré's dragon arm felt extra heavy as she followed La Fée Verte down into her cavern. Lights chimed, and green birds flew through their midst, plucking random imaginings.

She examined each one as it was delivered, back and forth with the tilt of her palm.

She threw them to the ground.

There was no light.

Again.

There was no newborn beauty.

Again.

There was nothing but glass on stone.

Again.

"You did not fail my dreams, Dame Honoré." La Fée Verte's whisper echoed across the broken pieces. "It was my dreams that failed you."

Even if this was true, it didn't make Honoré feel better. No, the numb disbelief she'd felt at Caveau des Terreurs only spread.

"There is power in an idea." La Fée Verte dashed another chime against the ground. "But these are not ideas. They're copies. Whoever conjured these replacements is a talented forger. That is why your sword shattered, Honoré. Someone is stealing my powers from me."

Yes, they were.

And Honoré knew exactly who.

PART III

THE DAYDREAMER

Once upon a time, there was a girl who wanted, more than anything, to be a part of a story.

Not just any story, but a proper Tale, filled with magic and adventure and endings that made everything sad untrue.

From the introduction of
THE KNOWN WORDS OF FABLE AND LORE
by
Libris the Bookseller

Cats are creatures with short tempers and long memories.

Very long memories.

Lore tells stories that can be dated back to the Eleventh Dynasty, when his ancestors were worshipped as deities. It's little wonder that the ancient Egyptians regarded felines this way—of all the members of the animal kingdom, cats are the most comfortable with magic. To those who aren't, it must seem strange, how they stare at *nothing* in a way that sends chills up your spine. Or how they disappear for days on end, only to return with frost on their whiskers at the height of summer. Where exactly did they slip off to? What wonders have they witnessed?

One can wonder.

Or one can ask.

Perhaps I am writing myself out of a job... for if you take the time to understand *Felis catus*, you may never need to set foot in a bookstore again. Their knowledge is encyclopedic. Their adventures can be Odyssean. (Hence the need for very long and luxurious naps.) They may choose to share such things with you. Cats will talk quite a lot, once they deem you worthy. This test varies from cat to cat. I won Fable's trust by scratching her under the chin three times a day. Lore claimed me by peeing on my finest rug and then staring as I scrubbed the spot clean. I did not shout. He did not repeat the offense.

Find your cat.

Earn their respect.

Learn their words.

And listen.

Chapter 19

Here There Be Monsters

Sylvie of a Single Name did not mind being an orphan.

Or so she told herself.

It hadn't been such an easy role when she was younger, constrained to the gray halls of Saint Francis's Home for Children. There was no one there to tuck her into the sterile white sheets of her dormitory bed, or kiss her softly on the forehead, or read stories about toads who turned into princes and stars that sang lullabies. She hummed such things to herself back then, to keep from thinking about food. Glorious food. It was better than listing all the things she could not have—the way Noelle always did in the adjoining bed. *Croissants. Pain au chocolat. Cheese. Leg of lamb. A yule log. A mother. A father.*

Children in fairy tales rarely had parents either, but this didn't seem to make them sad. Au contraire—those orphans were free to explore. They could stow away on ships to the New World, or live in seaside caves that could only be accessed at low tide, or become a member of a wolf pack and howl at the moon anytime they pleased. They could answer adventure's call without a parent's worried inquiries to the police.

Sylvie had learned to avoid such authorities, thanks to Honoré and Céleste and their less-than-legal lifestyle. She ran free through Paris's streets, picking pockets while pretending to be the lost daughter of a raja. She liked the idea of being a princess, and the lie was so bold that people sometimes believed her. A few even reached for their purses to help her buy a train ticket, but by the time they looked up, Sylvie was gone, running away with the coins they would have given her.

That had been before.

Now the coins she slipped into her pockets sported the Sun King's face—fished out of a wish-granting fountain that had long gone dry. Would the Fisherman of the Moon have traded for them? Sylvie felt a little bad for stealing from the Sanct's booth, but she probably wouldn't have found the fountain's courtyard without the map she'd snatched. It showed Paris, mostly. Paris as she'd never seen it. The fourth island floated up and down the Seine, always sketched in a different spot. There were catacomb entrances dotted over arrondissements that weren't supposed to have tunnels. There had been a faint gray windmill in Montmartre when Sylvie first stole the parchment, but somehow the spot had since been blotted with ink. Or soot. Sylvie wasn't sure what the markings were, but they were all over the map, spattering almost every section of the city aside from the Quartier Secret.

Sylvie spent most of her hours there—sleeping in a hammock of vines until La Fée Verte's guests arrived. Plucking their hairs was much more fun than picking pockets. Even if the imaginers saw her, they didn't seem to mind. But the green birds were territorial, taking up her airspace in a mad rush, until Honoré had intervened.

"You can't steal from La Fée Verte," the older Enchantress said with a sigh.

"I'm not," Sylvie replied.

"Don't be cheeky—"

"I'm not," she repeated. "The ideas are growing out of the imaginers' heads."

"Because of La Fée Verte's magic," Honoré explained. "She needs their dreams to power this salon. It's like Céleste said: 'We do not steal from local boulangeries if we want them to keep selling us *pain au chocolat*—'"

"Stohrer magical pastries are so much better!" Sylvie chirped back, mostly to see Honoré roll her eyes and to see her tiny silver dragon do the same.

Sylvie had taken more care after that, only taking her own dreams—the way Rafe García did whenever he explored the landscape room, placing them alongside that shiny pocket watch of his and then slipping away to kiss Céleste. Sylvie wasn't sure what happened next. More kissing, probably. That was what people did when they were in love. Right?

But what did Rafe do with his ideas?

Your dreams are worth far more, especially if you save them.

Sylvie tried her best. Every time she pulled a shining strand from her head, she wrapped it around her wrist—the way La Fée Verte did—and when her arms ran out of room, she started stashing them away. Not in the songbirds' salon. There was a far safer place on the other side of Paris.

La Banque d'Ossements.

It had been weeks since Céleste or Honoré had made any deposits in Père Lachaise's graves. They hadn't made any withdrawals either; there were still francs hidden all over the cemetery. Sylvie buried the Sun King's golden face alongside them. She didn't want to get dirt on her dreams though... Those she stored in Honoré Côte's mausoleum. The other Enchantresses had been visiting this campsite less and less—once Céleste had moved to La Ruche to take up art in earnest, Honoré had seen little reason to stay there. Marmalade made up the difference, claiming much of the tomb as his den.

I shall allow you to store your things here, oh hunter mine. Especially your spare cans of pâté.

The bookseller's guide had cleared up their conversations greatly, now that Sylvie knew about tail accents and whisker inflections and the mice-carcass offerings that signaled undying loyalty. She'd tried not to wrinkle her nose at the tiny gray bodies Marmalade brought her. The proper response—according to *The Found Words of Fable and*

Lore—was to offer something of "reciprocal value." Sylvie settled on an enchanted macaron.

Marmalade *did* wrinkle his nose.

They'd been fast friends ever since.

The tomcat was still difficult to understand at times, since he'd been born without a tail. The rest of the strays in Père Lachaise used to make fun of his accent—so he'd had to be defensive to make up for it. Hence his tattered ears and quick bite. Or, as Honoré so sarcastically put it, his *taste for human flesh*. He never scratched Sylvie though. He told her stories instead. About men who twisted shadows and women who shone like the sun—who'd been given titles like Osiris and Rah. Or Hades and Apollo. About young children like Sylvie, who'd slipped through the cracks of the world, who'd gone missing and discovered magic.

She'd found plenty herself. Most of the pink ideas Sylvie pulled from her head, she stored here. Under mattresses. On shelves meant for boxes of ashes. Inside the cracks in the central tombstone. By the beginning of September, the mausoleum had run out of room. She was starting to see why La Fée Verte's salon was so infinitely spacious...

Sylvie was starting to notice other things too.

She was no longer so tired come dawn, even after she spent an entire night dreaming. There were no dark circles around her eyes when she caught glimpses of herself in mirrors. Sometimes there were even sparks... a trick of the light, surely. Or the glass. She'd learned not to trust reflections after discovering a compact that showed Sylvie other Sylvies. The girls who'd stared back were caught in different lives. One was starving in her orphanage uniform, still. Another had cheeks plump from a mother's cooking. Sylvie had tried not to watch her too long—it was just the magical version of Noelle's sad chorus. Better to focus on what she *did* have.

Wings. A talking cat companion. A whole magical city to explore. A glass roof over my head... and lots and lots of dreams.

Sylvie lay back on the main gravestone and stared at them, the way she and the other Enchantresses used to watch stars, making up new constellations to add to the observatory ceiling. Honoré's were mostly shaped like knives.

The memory made Sylvie laugh.

Then sigh.

Marmalade curled up next to her.

What's wrong? he purred.

"I miss my friends."

But you see them every night.

"I know, but... it's like they don't see *me*."

Because you wear an invisibility cloak?

Céleste had asked Sylvie to imagine a pair of these a few weeks back—and she loved the idea so much that she'd conjured another for herself. And then another. And then another. It was easy to lose them—there were at least ten identical garments crumpled in various spots around Paris.

"Even when I'm not wearing the cloak," Sylvie said. "Honoré is too busy trying to be a knight, and Céleste is too busy disappearing with Rafe."

After their visit to the lost circus, the oldest Enchantress had insisted on staying close to the salon. Unfortunate, given Honoré's rule: *Never go out alone! It's too dangerous!* Sylvie figured she wasn't breaking it, technically, if Marmalade came along with her to explore Versailles. She also figured Honoré would figure differently, which was why she failed to disclose the fact that Céleste and Rafe were... busy.

She's not disappearing with him. The cat paused. *Not yet. Her soul is still whole. Her name is still hers.*

Sylvie frowned. The night past the glass pressed closer. "What are you talking about?"

Rafe's curse.

"Curse?" Sylvie paused at this word, not because she didn't understand it, but because she'd never really thought too much about the sour side of magic. She always walked extra fast over the Saint-Michel bridge whenever that old wrinkly Seer called to her—*Daydreamer! Daydreamer! Give me some days, and I'll tell you if your dreams come true!* Certain objects made her shiver too. The compact mirror—after she snapped it shut—or the way Honoré's ring sometimes stared a little too hard.

But Rafe didn't make her feel like that.

Rafe was funny. He brought her cloud crème éclairs. He painted her whiskers and giant piles of sugar she could make snow angels in. He let Sylvie hold his pocket watch and see her fateful hour—half past twelve, precisely.

The man is . . . not himself, Marmalade said.

"Is that what happened to my last name?" Sylvie wondered. "A curse?"

It would be a better story than being forgotten. Or worse, discarded on the orphanage steps like an order of milk. If there *had* been a note tucked in her baby blanket, Sylvie had never seen it. She'd seen other records though, tossed into a wastebasket with the remains of the headmaster's midnight snack: bitter orange peels.

I doubt that, Marmalade said. *You're only getting brighter.* He tilted his nose at the overhead imaginings. *You're becoming more Sylvie. Rafe is shadowed.*

Cats could be cryptic sometimes. Sylvie suspected it was entirely on purpose. "Shadowed?"

Like the spots on your map. The cat hopped off Sylvie's lap and padded over to the unrolled parchment. *Rafe goes to this one every morning.* His paw hovered over a sooty line in the eighth arrondissement, small enough to look like the slip of a pen.

"Well," Sylvie said, "if Rafe is cursed, then we'll just have to figure out a way to break that curse . . ." It sounded like something a plucky heroine with butterfly wings and a talking cat companion would set out to do. "I know he and Céleste have already kissed, so it's probably not that."

Probably not, Marmalade yowled. *Besides, it would have to be true love's kiss to be magical.*

On the map, the shadow road looked like the exact right place to start an adventure. Now that Sylvie was standing in front of the Hôtel de Crillon, she wasn't so sure. The dark arch before her seemed to suck up the light of the nearby gas lamps. It made Sylvie pull her invisibility cloak even tighter around her shoulders. Her cat companion stared at her anyway. His eyes were as orange as the heart of a candle.

"What's back there?" she asked.

Marmalade growled—more of a feeling than a word.

He hissed when Sylvie stepped closer to the alley. *Cats do not go there.*

"I'm not a cat." She wasn't a coward either... She couldn't be, if she wanted to find the best bits of magic.

So she hugged her invisibility cloak close and tiptoed into the tunnel. It looked like a dead end, at first. But when Sylvie's eyes started to adjust to the darkness, a door took shape. It kept taking shape—the keyholes changing again and again. When Sylvie knelt to peek through, she felt as if she were watching slides from a magic lantern. A study with a roaring fire. Icebergs floating in an ocean. Piano songs playing from a tavern. Desert sands piling into dunes.

She sat back, dizzy. Normally, when Sylvie came across a lock, her fingers grew greasy. It was the only reason she wore pins in her hair—to bend and twist them until she heard that oh-so-satisfying *click*.

But this looked far too big for a bobby pin.

Just then, Sylvie heard footsteps. Not from the *everywhere* side of the door, but hers.

"How long do you think La Fée Verte has been harvesting dreams? How far does the cavern go?"

It was Céleste. Sylvie smiled and nearly waved, before remembering she was invisible. She paused instead, watching as the oldest Enchantress walked with Rafe. They weren't laughing or holding hands, the way they always did when they slipped off to the salon's leafier corners. No. They looked tired. Rafe looked even more than that. He looked... less.

There was something about both artists that made Sylvie stay silent. She pressed herself flat to the side of the tunnel as the pair passed.

"There's no telling with Sancts," he said. "They don't age the way we do."

"It must be nice, having a key to immortality."

A steely look flashed over Céleste's face before she knocked on the door. *THUMP. THUMP.* Sylvie's heart hammered too. She wasn't sure why she didn't just throw back her cloak and announce herself.

But then the door opened.

Sylvie crept after her friends. She didn't step into a vast desert or a desolate sea, but there was something overwhelming about the space, something that kept her pressed into the corner, watching in silence while Rafe and Céleste walked to a wing-back chair. What were they doing? Pulling dreams out of their sleeves, handing them over to some dark hand, which then tossed them into a fire.

Sylvie shrank back as the imaginings flared—sparks turning to sparks. It didn't make sense. Rafe had said she should save her ideas, so why was he letting these burn? And what about Céleste? This was far worse than stealing bread from a local boulangerie...

She must be trying to break Rafe's curse. That was it. The oldest Enchantress never did anything without good reason. Her costumes were chosen with care. Her paintings were precisely flawed. Her bedtime stories always had a surprise twist at the end...

The man rose from the chair.

Sylvie of a Single Name knew what hunger looked like. In Saint Francis's Home for Children, it had been ladder ribs and lips licked dry. Feral stares. When she'd escaped to Paris's wider streets, she hardly recognized her reflection in the shop windows—sharp, ready to break. Not so much inside as outward. Smashing glass. Sinking her teeth into fresh crust. Ripping. Tearing.

This man was all that. Only, he wasn't a man, Sylvie realized, as she saw the black Sanct masque around his eyes. He was the kind of darkness that made stars pale. He looked like he could *eat* stars with those incisors. Bones too. *Snap, crunch.* So why not names? Why not the souls themselves? It was a silly thought, Sylvie knew, but terrifying too. Far more terrifying than rifling through the old headmaster's wastebasket.

Céleste was watching the exit. Sylvie didn't like her friend's locked-in look. She liked it even less when the hungry Sanct pulled a set of keys from his belt and started moving toward the door.

Was *he* the reason Céleste had asked for those invisibility cloaks?

Sylvie huddled by the coatrack, hoping hers would hold up. Her lungs burned. The key ring jingled. Stars grew in Sylvie's eyes as she squeezed them shut. *Don't eat them, don't eat me, don't, don't, don't—*

Hinges squealed.

A cool breeze tickled Sylvie's cheeks. She cracked an eyelid. Gold. So much gold splashed carelessly over doorframes and ceilings and windows. This must be Versailles; its gardens sat shrouded in mist, waiting for the sun to wash over them with yet another gilded layer. Sylvie had gone exploring here, a few weeks back, fluttering beneath god-vaulted ceilings while Marmalade marked his scent across the Hall of Mirrors. *Mine now.* The palace wasn't a long flight from Paris. She could get back to the city quickly enough with the butterfly wings she was wearing.

Sylvie slipped into the ballroom.

The hungry Sanct had paused at the center of the parquet floor. Flames danced onto the candelabra as he snapped his fingers. Strange... Sylvie didn't remember Versailles being so dusty. Or so cold. She shivered as Céleste crossed the space to meet with a second Sanct. He was striking. Not beautiful, but charged. His eyes, and the surrounding masque, were electric blue. They flared when he raised his hand in the sign of a cross. His monkish robes did too—revealing wings that reminded Sylvie of a cockroach.

His voice skittered.

Her skin crawled.

What were they doing? *Praying?* She'd have to ask Céleste later, when the hungry Sanct wasn't breathing down their necks.

Sylvie exited the ballroom, into another that looked just like it. Then another. Then another. Until she found a set of crimson-carpeted stairs that led to a large pair of doors. *Freedom!* She threw herself into the sky—fast enough that the hood of her invisibility cloak flew back. A streak of fuchsia. A dash of orange.

She began to notice other colors as she flew higher.

The last time she'd visited Versailles, she'd been so overwhelmed by its gold that she hadn't paid much attention to the rest of the building. This morning, the palace was achingly blue. The same bewitching shade of the priest Sanct's eyes. Had he enchanted the stones somehow? Had he stripped all the gilding too? The outside ornamentations had dulled to a drab olive color, matching the surrounding trees. There were far more of these around the palace grounds than Sylvie remembered, and as the sun rose higher, revealing more of her surroundings, the truth dawned on her.

This was not Versailles.

She swung back around a series of spires, rooftops shaped like foil-wrapped bonbons. She'd never seen crosses like that in France—with three crossbeams instead of one, the bottom bar hanging on by a thread. Panic flickered in her chest, matching the pulses of masque light from a nearby window. Céleste was still there. The priest Sanct was still chanting. The door with the changing locks yawned behind them. Still open...

But then the prayer ended.

Wait! Wait for me! Please! Sylvie didn't dare scream this as Céleste turned. She didn't even whisper. All she could do was watch through the window as the oldest Enchantress exited through the magical portal. The hungry Sanct followed.

The door didn't just close when he shut it.

It vanished completely.

Sylvie's map of Paris would be no help now... She watched with a sinking heart as the priest Sanct stepped through the opening into the blue palace's next room. She knew then that she'd chased this adventure just a little too far.

Here there be monsters.

Chapter 20

In Somnis Veritas

Living at La Ruche was a bit like staring into one of those enchanted mirrors—Céleste could see herself in another life here. A life with open windows, where she woke up to the chatter of other artists in the courtyard, composing poems or sharing bowls of the vegetable stew constantly simmering in the nearby soup kitchen. Free to anyone who was hungry. Céleste often was, by the time she awoke in the late afternoons, awash in buttery sunlight. But she usually chose to stay in the sheets, where she could trace the lines of Rafe's face on the pillow beside her. A warm-up. It was getting harder and harder to get out of bed these days. The air grew ever colder. They'd slipped into autumn, somehow. Three and a half months had passed since their first fateful meeting, and it was hard not to wonder if she'd be alive otherwise. If she'd gone straight back to the cemetery after *The Rite of Spring*, would Céleste be there? Still? Six feet under?

But that was a darker diversion.

The life that Céleste entertained at La Ruche had more colors to it. Cadmium, sure, but also yellows and pinks and greens—hues that most of the old Romantics wouldn't be caught dead mixing. This was partly because of Rafe's palette. But also because she'd run out of charcoal, and the other artist had pushed his collection of paints on her. *Please, use whatever you need! What's mine is yours!*

Her rendition of the shadow fox still hung above the bed.

There was a painting of the geranium too, her first stab at proving she deserved to stay here. Rafe was right—one didn't have to pay money to have a studio at the "beehive," but like La Fée Verte's salon, it was understood that you would fill the space. Art was their honey; thus, flowers seemed like a fitting inspiration. Céleste drew the blooming iron lamps of the Métropolitain entrance next, sketching the alleyway of the Quartier Secret just past that. Her third painting went further, capturing the fuchsia blossoms that grew around the salon's green door. *In somnis veritas.*

Rafe was particularly entranced by this piece. He stood in front of the canvas, watching its paint dry. "You must be stealing my dreams," he murmured.

Céleste eyed him carefully. He was a different person these days, back to his normal rhythm of forgetting midnight's magic at dawn. Sunlight made Rafe more artist than thief—and he believed that was all they were. This was partly why she'd begun to paint so much. It was easier to stand easel to easel than try to talk around the truth of their relationship.

Not that she was entirely sure what that was anymore.

They still kissed in the salon, and she still enjoyed it. She *more* than enjoyed it. But they were both careful to stay inside the boundaries of their performance. No matter how much Céleste wanted to push Rafe down into a bed of beaming sunflowers after the Enchantresses left them for the evening, she pushed away instead.

They had to stay focused.

(Ha! As if she could focus with the taste of *him* lingering on her lips.)

They had to steal that goddamn dream.

(Again, ha! There were still thousands of imaginings to sort through.)

The man Céleste shared an art studio with had no memory of how far they'd gone together, but there were moments like this, when she could sense glimmers of his true self fighting to break through. "Stealing your dreams? What makes you say that?"

"I don't know." Rafe's fingers traced the Latin letters, too reverent to actually touch. This was also them before dusk. After dawn. Céleste had certainly entertained thoughts about pushing him onto *this* mattress—and she'd had ample opportunities to flirt—but when it came down to it, the idea of being with Rafe when he wasn't *Rafe* felt wrong.

So she always woke up before him, in their shared bed. She always studied his sleeping face long enough to remind herself that this would not last forever. She rose and put on her robe and turned her *want* into colors on a canvas.

She'd become quite prolific over the past month and a half.

"I don't know," Rafe murmured again. "I just... It seems as if I've seen this door before." He glanced back at the drawing of his sigil. "Your work always sparks something in me."

"Déjà vu?" she suggested, as she set about cleaning her brushes. The memories of magic were still there, somewhere in his head. They had to be, if they kept reappearing. All the salon's imaginers eventually remembered their previous evenings there... though sometimes it took several hours after midnight.

"It feels like more than déjà vu," Rafe declared. "It feels like... a candle being dropped into a giant cavern."

A strange image, Céleste thought. But perhaps it was more déjà vu coming through. They'd spent so many hours in La Fée Verte's Vault of Dreams, going deeper and deeper every evening. It was easier for them to lose each other there, now that Rafe could no longer cloak them both with his shadow. For some reason he'd lost that ability after the windmill had burned. He couldn't shape his silhouette into wings either. The fox had been scarce too. Once, when they'd stopped in the landscape room to paint an upside-down garden for Sylvie, Céleste had thought she spied the creature hiding in a tangle of honeysuckle.

But that could have been her own imagination.

She still hadn't managed to pull any of her own dreams from her head. They must be growing though. Twice Céleste had felt the green songbirds pluck *something* and fly off to the Vault. Wouldn't it be ironic if she ended up stealing her own idea? Possible, but not probable. She and Rafe went well past the established path of the birds now, far enough from the stairs that there likely wasn't much need for the invisibility cloaks they wore. Sometimes Céleste could go most of the evening without seeing him.

She missed that closeness.

She missed a lot of things: Fighting lessons with Honoré. Bedtime stories with Sylvie. Waking up each day without wondering if it might be her last.

Rafe too battled a lingering dread, despite his amnesia. "I dreamed I went back to Belleville, last night," he'd told Céleste, their second evening at La Ruche. "No one knew me though—no one but you. And I tried to run, but my feet wouldn't move. I was trapped in my own shadow, and I couldn't get out."

It's all right, she couldn't say. *You're awake now.*

At least he had a few hours where Terreur was a nightmare. Céleste wished she could say the same. She wished she could be as charmed as the rest of La Ruche's artists, who found themselves gazing out to the ivy-throttled gates most midnights. *Oh, look at that bird! I've never seen such emerald feathers!* A magical migration usually followed—from Montparnasse to the Quartier Secret.

Rafe's Enlightenment often found him earlier, during the blue hour. Céleste had mistaken the magic for a bat at first, because it was so dark and frantic through the studio window. But as soon as it flew into the back of the other artist's head, it vanished. His eyes widened, then flashed as he checked his pocket watch's fateful hour. This was always the first thing Rafe did, once he became *her* Rafe.

There were still several hours before that would happen on this autumn afternoon. Céleste lay next to Rafe on the mattress, watching the September sun highlight his sleeping face. Wanting to capture it. To bottle not just the light itself but the warmth of his body beside hers and the scent of woodsmoke whispering through their window and the stir of an even closer fire beneath her belly—

Tap-tap.

A soft knock on the studio door jarred Céleste out of bed, though

Rafe did not so much as stir. It was probably Guillaume Apollinaire. Or one of the commune's many other artists who loved to pop in to see the painting she was working on. Flame-striped tigers. Dresses made of leaves and mist. Dancing on a floor filled with stars... This last piece was only half-done, constellations still unstrung as Céleste pulled on her robe and opened the door.

It was Honoré standing in the hall.

Céleste hated how her heart caught when she saw her friend. *"Mon amie?"*

"I found myself in Montparnasse, and I thought I'd drop by." Honoré's eyes flicked over to the mattress, where Rafe was lightly snoring. "How are you taking to the penniless life?"

Céleste wasn't quite sure what to say. She'd memorized her lines at night well enough, when it was understood that they all understood magic. But now *she* was supposed to be blind, her sight wiped clean. She wasn't even sure how much of her friend she was supposed to see. Surely not the shining dreams stuffed like knives into her belt. The rest of her clothes looked plain enough. Trousers. Half-rolled tunic sleeves. Her arms were crossed. Why were her arms crossed? Why was her brow furrowed? *Shit.* Céleste had been quiet too long...

"It's richer than I'd anticipated," she answered. "I've never met so many people eager to give so much away."

"Are you painting?" Honoré didn't push, but there was something forceful in the way the other Enchantress stepped past. There was something aggressive too in her examination of the studio's canvases.

"I've been trying to establish my own style," Céleste said quickly. "Delacroix was getting too depressing, and Sylvie's been spinning such fantastic stories lately—I figured I'd try my hand at illustrating them."

What other reason could she give for the scenes Honoré was now scouring? Bears that breathed fire. A painting of Duchess d'Uzès painting her own hair purple. Gardens made almost entirely of green birds. Surely the other Enchantress recognized these moments, but the painting that finally gave her pause was one of Rafe's, where the windmill peeked over Montmartre's rooftops. Honoré stared at its blades, her eyes going smoky. The sleeve over her right arm stirred, and Céleste tried her best not to notice.

"And what about the rest of your work, *mon amie*?"

Céleste knew then. She knew the other Enchantress knew.

"I really did believe you were becoming an honest artist. I bought all your bullshit. La Fée Verte even turned it into a sword for me... and that shattered when I most needed it." Honoré pulled a dream from her belt and threw it on the floor. It smashed to pieces near the potted geranium.

Rafe groaned.

Honoré pulled out another forgery.

"I can explain," Céleste said, before her friend could break it.

"Explain what? Why you've been stealing La Fée Verte's power for a vampiric megalomaniac? Why you've been lying through your teeth for three and a half months? Why Eleanor said she saw you at Caveau des Terreurs? Why I walked into an ambush there this afternoon? Fuck, Céleste! This isn't some fun little fiddle game. I almost died today!"

Over on the mattress, Rafe kept stirring. He wouldn't understand what they were saying if he woke, but he might, if he remembered their words after sunset. Céleste reached out to grab Honoré's hand so she could draw her friend away from the studio. But the other Enchantress was hot to the touch—silver and red rage.

Céleste gasped as the dragon's fang sank through her palm. It hurt, but it was so much more than metal piercing skin. It was Honoré—her friend, her *sister*—stabbing her. It was the understanding that Céleste hadn't escaped the blood on her hands. Not at all. She'd simply made things that much worse. She'd betrayed Honoré.

She deserved this.

But the other Enchantress gasped as well, pulling her arm to her chest as if *she* were the one who'd been wounded. "Shit! Are you all right, *mon amie*?"

"No." The word unraveled from her.

Then she kept unraveling.

She felt like a piece of tatting that had snagged on a gate. One catch—one *truth*—was all it took for her lacework lies to disintegrate. *I'm not all right.* Céleste knew she should have admitted this back in the hay fever days. At least then she would have had a shoulder to cry on, instead of a bite wound. Honoré had pulled herself back, was staring at Céleste as if she were a stranger. There was truth in this too, and that was what hurt so badly.

"I'm dying, Honoré."

This confession was one of Céleste's longest, lasting the entire walk from La Ruche to the river. She did not relish it. She didn't smile the way she had while burying some rich fool's gold. She couldn't brush the dirt from her hands and walk away. But there was something freeing about telling Honoré everything. The disease's hay fever stage, last spring. The crimson gloves, at the ballet three and a half months before. The dreams she'd traded for long summer days. The slow nightmare that had unfolded from it all.

"I didn't know what he was." As soon as Céleste said this, she wondered if it was another lie. She had gone searching for the Balkans on their employer's globe, after all. Right after she'd sipped that...wine. "I didn't want to know. I just wanted to be able to breathe again. Then you and Sylvie found the salon, and everything has gotten so knotted up. If I stop forging dreams for this Sanct, he'll kill me."

"Shit," Honoré said at the end.

An apt summation.

It got even shittier, when the other Enchantress told her side of the story—when Céleste understood the full meaning behind her employer's new name. His recently acquired tavern territory. His plans to keep swallowing Paris. What that truly meant for the city... Her stomach churned when Honoré described the corpses she'd discovered in almost every arrondissement. Entirely exsanguinated.

Just like the poor soul from the tale Henri had told at Foyot's, fueled by far too much champagne, but *mon Dieu*, if it wasn't starting to sound prophetic.

"I didn't know about the husks." Again, Céleste wondered if this was entirely true. Not just because of the blotted-out Balkans, but thanks to a different map. Those slashes in Rafe's sketchbook...was that what they'd marked? Murders?

Was she really sharing a bed with such a calculated killer?

Céleste thought back to their first encounter there. The blood staining her lips that ruinous morning hadn't bothered Rafe nearly as much as it should...Was that because he'd simply told himself it was a fine red Bordeaux?

The same way she did.

They were both very good liars, after all. Even to themselves.

She stopped at this thought, her lips tasting far more acid than iron. There was no blood in her bile as it splashed to the sidewalk stones.

Honoré looked back over her shoulder as Céleste retched. "Are you all right?"

"No." She coughed bitterly. *Not unless I keep drinking other people's blood.* That had to be the key to immortality, right? It was how their employer gave himself such ruddy full cheeks every few weeks. "Why didn't you tell us that's what you were finding on your patrols? Sylvie figures you're just blowing smoke about the streets being dangerous, and I thought..." She straightened, realizing how close they were to the Fontaine Saint-Michel.

I thought I was the danger.

The thought wasn't stardust, but the salon's bronze guardians did not stir.

Honoré gnawed her lip. "La Fée Verte asked me to stay quiet. She doesn't want fear of the slayings spreading through her imaginers," the other Enchantress explained. "If they're too afraid, they won't dream. And if they don't dream, she'll have no power to push back Terreur. Her stores are already scarcer than they should be..."

Because of Céleste and Rafe.

Fuck. Her friend's earlier sentiment came echoing back. *This isn't some fun little fiddle game!* Céleste's thoughts started to spin—as wobbly as the globe by her employer's chair. *The stakes are much higher than that.* The Balkans. Russia. And Paris, now. What would the city come to, if Terreur finally got his missing wish?

What about the rest of the world?

She stared off at the fountain. It wasn't quite late enough for the pedestal dragon to wake, and the other statues kept warring as they always had. They made quite the spread: angel, devil, Céleste, and Honoré. Each of them bound to the other.

The other Enchantress stared at the sculptures too. "I haven't told La Fée Verte yet," she said.

"Will you?"

Céleste could see Honoré was struggling—not just with her own dragon, but even deeper ties. "I'll ask her to heal you."

Céleste let out a breath, relieved. Her friend had already forgiven her, which was a miracle in itself because Honoré Côte held on to more grudges than she did knives.

As for the consumption?

"I don't think it's that easy, *mon amie*," she said. "Rafe says she doesn't heal imaginers—she didn't even heal *you* when you agreed to become her knight." Céleste nodded at her friend's chin. There was a faint mark there, almost as silvery as her ring.

"That was just a scratch," Honoré growled. "Besides, I told you Rafael's full of shit."

Right. Tigers and stripes and all that. Céleste still had a difficult time imagining him as an alleyway killer—though she probably shouldn't try *too* hard this close to the fountain. "He was trying to save me, I think. He noticed the bloodstain on my opera gloves after the ballet—"

"Do you think it's a coincidence that *The Rite of Spring* was the first night you coughed up blood?" Honoré's voice was as pointed as her knives. "Have you seen what your 'employer's' magic does to people? He drains them. He . . . he . . . controls them."

Yes. Céleste had seen. More than that, she'd *felt* it, the tug of her shadow and the squeeze of her lungs. *I will be worse. I will be so much worse...*

"I don't want to work for Terreur. I'm not sure Rafe does either." It occurred to her then that the other thief might not be exsanguinating people willingly. "But if he *was* telling the truth, then my confession to La Fée Verte would be a death sentence."

"Let's test her, then." Honoré nodded down at Céleste's bloodied palm. "I'll ask La Fée Verte to mend your hand. That way, if she says yes, we'll know she has the power to save you."

Chapter 21

Feral Creatures

Honoré Côte had gotten good at dressing wounds over the years: Meat from the icebox for bruises. A splash of spirits in a gash. A needle over flame. Never mind that embroidery nonsense—her mother had taught her a different kind of stitching. Showed her just how much hurt a human body could take.

The slice in Céleste's hand was clean, but it hardly felt that way.

Honoré's feelings seethed through the ring, shivering where the metal ribboned its way into her veins. Flecks of her friend's blood had dried on her dragon's fangs. The bite had happened too fast to tell if Honoré had truly lost control of the beast. Or not. Both possibilities scared her. She'd never thought she'd face someone worse than her father—who'd thrashed and hit and broken the people she loved. But this new Terreur, the way he twisted loyalties... How could you fight demons if they were your friends? Your family? Yourself?

Honoré tucked her dragon hand in her pocket and watched La Fée Verte examine Céleste's wound.

"You don't need magic," the Sanct told them. "Only time."

Céleste sank back into the front room's settee and stared at the ceiling, where Sylvie had grown a hammock nest in the vines, empty at the moment.

"Please," Honoré pressed. "I— The wound was my fault." It felt dangerous, saying this, looking from La Fée Verte's amber eyes to Céleste's sterling ones. "I don't want Céleste to suffer. Can you heal her? Is that even possible?"

"It is," the Sanct said.

Céleste straightened in the settee. "But?"

"There's a cost."

Her friend paled then. "I'm guessing it's not a pair of painted pants."

"No." A faint hint of amusement danced across La Fée Verte's face, before her expression grew dark. "One person's flesh can only be mended with another's."

The memory of blood across the Caveau des Terreurs's sandy floor came slithering back. Honoré shut her eyes, trying to unsee that terrible image of Terreur's empty chest wound closing. He hadn't needed a needle or thread to sew himself back together—only Rémy. And La Belle. And countless other corpses, left out to dry like a tanned cow's hide.

"It's not a pretty magic." La Fée Verte's voice echoed against the delicate glass ceiling. "I've watched other Sancts travel too far down that path—taking lives to strengthen their own. I find it best to avoid the temptation altogether."

When Honoré opened her eyes again, she saw Céleste staring. *You see?* Her gray eyes seemed to say. *It's not so easy,* mon amie.

"Use my hand," Honoré said. "Use my hand to heal hers."

"Are you sure, my dame? Her wound is so small."

If only it were...

"Yes." Honoré was sure about this because she was so *un*sure of everything else. Eleanor's note was still bleeding ink in her pocket, and despite Honoré's best efforts, no one had been saved today. La Fée Verte was weaker than ever. Gabriel was a shadow puppet. Rafael too, albeit in a less obvious manner. Céleste was dying. The new Terreur *couldn't*. And the harder Honoré fought, the worse things got.

Fuck.

Her ring hand started to shake, but it was the other palm that

La Fée Verte lifted. She placed it over Céleste's wound and then put her own hand on top of it. There was a wash of golden light from her face—and a moment of candle-warm peace. Then, the sting. Honoré gritted her teeth.

Céleste did not look relieved.

She was waiting for Honoré to tell La Fée Verte the truth of why they were really here. But that cost? It was more than a scratch. It was lungs. A life. It was more than even Honoré was willing to pay.

"There." La Fée Verte stepped back. "All better."

Honoré let her hand slide away. She looked up at Sylvie's hammock, her own stomach fluttering again, sick with the thought of the happy ending she'd started to believe in: La Fée Verte at her side every dawn. Céleste healed. The salon safe. Paris too. So that Sylvie could fly over the city's streets without landing in a morgue—her only name replaced by a question mark on the toe tag. What a terrifying thought. Honoré had only been able to keep it at bay because she'd believed Céleste and Rafe were entertaining Sylvie in the salon every evening, painting rainbows and...*shit.* They'd been lying about that too, of course. And if they weren't keeping an eye on Sylvie at night, then the girl was almost certainly out playing explorer.

Or worse.

La Fée Verte's green wings fanned wide. "What's wrong, my dame?"

Everything. Everything is wrong, and the worst thing is, I can't tell you...

Honoré tried not to clench her wounded hand. Harder still? Keeping her face blank. She'd shared so much with La Fée Verte in their golden sunrise moments, now a secret felt like sacrilege. What kind of knight used armor against their lady?

What kind of Enchantress abandoned her friends to die?

"Have you seen Sylvie recently?" It was hard to keep her voice level, to stop her thoughts from spiraling. Her last pink-hair sighting had been several nights, several days ago, but Honoré had just assumed the girl was in some hidden corner of the Quartier Secret.

"I don't sense her in the salon." La Fée Verte's wing feathers began to swirl, a gust of green joining the leaves on the ceiling. "I can send birds to the other Sancts and ask if they've seen her around their establishments."

"She's probably camped out at Stohrer." Céleste's declaration sounded light, like powdered sugar, but Honoré wasn't fooled.

Not anymore.

This search was different from Honoré's usual patrols.

She did not fly, for one thing. Instead she kept the dragon close at hand, hardly trusting it in the air, much less with Céleste at her side. The other Enchantress had followed her out of the salon and over the Seine, staying silent until they reached Notre-Dame de Paris's doors. The lobster gargoyle wasn't dancing. Nor were the many saints next to it. Honoré stopped and stared at them, trying to muster up some kind of prayer. *Please, please, don't let anything happen to Sylvie...*

But the kid shouldn't count on saints to protect her.

That was Honoré's job, and she'd failed.

Again.

She looked over at Céleste, who was taking in the height of the bell towers, her hair gleaming under the lamplights of the surrounding square. It was so easy to be angry—so often—but Honoré was finding it hard to fault her friend. She knew how persuasive Rafael García could be. She knew how far he'd go to get what he wanted. She'd almost followed him there herself, even though she knew next to nothing about Constantinople or artists' colonies or what have you. The only thing that had stopped her was Gabriel.

She sometimes wondered what their lives would've become if she'd *dared to dream*, as Rafael so loved to say. What if she'd run to catch that train with her brother, instead of staying another few disastrous days at the Caveau? What if *she'd* left the note for her father to find? *SEE YOU IN HELL—FEAR'S FIRST BASTARD.* She thought of this and then, immediately, of Sylvie's scowl: *You shouldn't say that in front of a church.*

Honoré knew better. Sculpted saints didn't give a shit about curse words. They didn't seem to care much about her prayer either.

"Sylvie's going to be all right." Céleste's voice chiseled at the ancient stones.

Honoré shut her eyes. She wanted to believe this, but even if she did, what difference would it make? Her father was in hell, while the devil was in Paris, and no amount of hope was going to change the fact someone she cared for would die soon. Céleste's survival depended on La Fée Verte's demise. And vice versa. The choice was impossible, and it was *hers*, and goddamn if she didn't just want to step up onto the church and become a statue herself.

But really, this just made her think of La Fée Verte standing on the south bell tower at sunrise, those wings fanned wide and her smile so bright and her shoulder so warm against Honoré's, so that nothing about the Enchantress felt like stone at all. No. She was flesh and blood and *magic*…

"Oh," Céleste murmured beside her. "I think the gargoyles are whispering."

Honoré might have mistaken the sound for wind, if she'd felt a breeze on her face. It was faint and gray, too gravelly for her to make out many words. "What are they saying?"

"I'm not sure… something about a door?"

"Great." Honoré cracked an eyelid, sounding wry. "That narrows down our search."

"Maybe the bookstore has a guide to gargoyle speech?" Céleste suggested.

But when they reached Libris's shop, the Sanct shook his head. "Statues don't usually speak enough to warrant a translation—but if it's Notre-Dame's statues you're listening to, I can tell you what they're saying. They repeat the same story over and over about the devil door—"

Lore meowed.

Fable hissed.

Libris frowned. "You're searching for the daydreamer, yes?"

"Word must travel awfully fast, by cat," muttered Honoré.

"It does," the bookseller told her. "Your friend hasn't been here since she tried to steal her story, but if you do track her down, tell her I found the lilac fairy book she was asking after." Libris pulled the volume from a nearby shelf. Its binding was similar to the color of the Easter egg hair the imaginers had wanted Honoré to wear. Embossed wisteria blossoms scattered across the cover, along with a golden fairy dancing on the tail of a shooting star. "It's a first edition, and one of the last..."

"What makes you say that?" Céleste asked.

"Andrew Lang died last year."

Of course, he fucking did, Honoré mused darkly.

"I'll hold it here until Sylvie returns," Libris promised. He glanced again at the two cats perched on the locked glass case. *Meow, meow.* "Do you know a tom by the name of Marmalade? They tell me you should talk to him about the daydreamer."

Of course, they fucking do. "Where can I find him?"

"Ha!" The bookseller laughed. "You don't find cats. Cats find you."

"Well, that didn't simplify anything. Now we're searching for *two* feral creatures," Honoré grumbled as she and Céleste departed the bookshop. The other Enchantress turned toward the second arrondissement. "Where are you going?"

"Stohrer."

"I doubt they have Marmalade there. Jam, maybe."

"Sylvie goes to that bakery every single night," Céleste said. "If we ask its Sanct when he last saw her, we'll know how long she's been missing, at least." The other Enchantress no longer sounded so sugary—or sure—and Honoré realized then that Céleste's declaration in front the cathedral had been her own version of a Hail Mary. She was quite talented at hiding her fears, even from herself, but Honoré had always known her friend's habit of talking to statues after their fiddle games spoke to something deeper. More than just your typical lapsed-Catholic guilt. "We should pick up a pastry while we're at it. It'll soften the blow when we tell her about Monsieur Lang."

And what about you? Honoré couldn't bring herself to ask this question because she knew the answer depended on her. Honoré Côte, Defender of Dreamers.

The Shit Knight.

None of this is your fault, Honoré.

No, but it would be, if she didn't sacrifice her best friend. Losing one Enchantress for a single evening was bad enough, and to make matters worse, it sounded as if Sylvie had been missing even longer than that.

"Ah, yes, the daydreamer. She's got quite the spark!" said the Sanct behind Stohrer's pastry cases. "She gave me an idea for this most curious cake three nights ago! A pie filled with candy butterflies. It's been a joy to make—their wings are like stained glass, only made with melted sugar. I haven't had such fun baking since my days as a pâtissier for the Beloved King himself! 'Son of the sun,' we called him. Well, a great-grandson, in truth, but he had enough shine to hold the throne. Couldn't say as much for his own son—"

"Three nights ago?" Céleste interjected. "Has she been back since?"

The Sanct shook his head. "I'm surprised. I've been saving the first bite of this cake for her, but perhaps it was meant for you two instead—you both look like you could use some cheering up."

He wrapped up the butterfly pie and handed it to Céleste. The other Enchantress made no move to open it. Why would she? No amount of sugar could coat the fact Sylvie had been missing for *three whole nights*. Honoré couldn't shake the feeling that something was terribly, terribly wrong. Her dragon ring was shaking too, when she stepped out of the shop, enough for Céleste to keep her distance when she followed suit.

Honoré didn't blame her.

She didn't even trust herself to move, so she stood on the curb. "What do we do, *mon amie*?"

Céleste—who always had a plan, who'd once talked her way out of a gendarme's handcuffs—simply shook her head. Brown paper crinkled under her newly healed hand, and if Honoré squinted just right, she could pretend they were preparing for a picnic. Oh, what she wouldn't give to go back to the mausoleum, to cut Sylvie a great big slice of *tarte au chocolat* and listen to the most ridiculous of her stories.

They could return to Père Lachaise, she realized.

If only to search.

"We should go home," said Honoré. Céleste's face pinched at the word, reminding her that they no longer lived there. Together. "Back to our grave, I mean."

"I can't," the other Enchantress told her, her eyes foggy with worry. "It's too dangerous. Rafe will be missing me, and so will Terreur if I stay much longer."

And yet, Céleste seemed to be waiting. *She's waiting for me to stop her*, Honoré thought faintly. *But if I take her to the grave with me, it will bury her…*

It wasn't her dragon hand she reached out with. "You should probably leave the cake with me, then."

Honoré Côte's tomb was not empty.

She'd fully expected it to be—but there was movement behind the doors when she stepped over her alarm bells and into the clearing. Light shone from the mausoleum's roof as well—the rosy shimmer of a lantern.

"Sylvie?" Honoré's voice was hopeful as she called out into the crisp air, but she had her knives ready—both dreamed and steel. "Is that you?"

No answer.

A shadow darted beyond the entrance.

Honoré crept up the steps and kicked in the scrolling iron door.

"OWWWWWWWWWWWWT!"

The noise was ghastly. If she'd been the more superstitious sort, she might have expected to see her namesake sitting on his tombstone. Instead, Honoré found herself facing down the orange tomcat.

That explained the movement, at least, but the lights… Honoré halted, trying to understand what she was seeing. Dreams. Dreams stuffed into mattresses and hanging under the glass stars. She knew Sylvie had *said* she was saving her imaginings, but she'd claimed the same thing about a bag of bonbons she'd once wheedled Céleste into buying. The sweets were gone in less than an hour, so Honoré had assumed the girl's dreams would suffer a similar fate.

She'd been wrong.

The mausoleum had been transformed. It reminded Honoré of a smaller—*much* smaller—version of La Fée Verte's cave.

"OWWWWWT!" The tomcat hissed again when she stepped inside.

The beast looked larger than life against the dreams' reflections—almost tigerlike.

"You've made yourself at home here, haven't you?" Honoré caught herself. "*Mon Dieu*, I'm talking to a cat."

Marmalade looked even less pleased than Honoré at this turn of events. His tail stub twitched irritably as he let out a long, low, continuous growl.

"You haven't seen our mutual pink-haired friend lately, have you? Fable and Lore asked me to ask."

The tomcat fell silent and tilted his head. Orange eyes narrowed.

"She's been missing for three days." Honoré felt the youngest Enchantress's mattress for any stray sign of warmth. Her hand came back covered in cat fur. "I'm worried."

Marmalade let out a plaintive *meow*. With all the magic of this place, Honoré could've sworn she heard a *me too* tucked inside its echo.

"That girl acts as if she has seven lives or something!" That was the saying, at least when it came to cats. Honoré knew it wasn't true, but this hadn't stopped her from wishing it when she was younger.

Marmalade hopped down from the tombstone and wound himself around Honoré's ankles. The fur was as soft and warm as she remembered. If not brighter. Honoré stood very still as her trouser legs became flecked with orange.

There was no flash of teeth.

No sudden sink of claws.

The cat seemed to be... comforting her.

Slowly, slowly, Honoré knelt and scratched Marmalade between his ragged ears. "You're not such a nasty old bastard after all, are you?"

The moggy began to purr.

"He says he'd like you to move just a little bit to the left, thank you very much—"

Honoré spun around, and Marmalade darted between her legs, straight into Sylvie's waiting arms. The girl stood in the doorway. It looked for all the world as if she'd grown. Her hair was still garishly pink but mostly covered by a hat. The style was strange—earflaps lined with fur. Honoré had a feeling the headpiece hadn't been made in Paris.

"Where the hell have you been?" she asked tartly.

"Oh, Honoré!" The girl sounded breathless, as if she'd run a very great distance in a very short time. "You're never going to believe what happened... I met a princess!"

Chapter 22

A Girl Who Slipped Through the Cracks of the World

Sylvie of a Single Name waited a very long time for the magical door to reappear.

She waited through breakfast and well into teatime, hovering around the blue palace's windows. Each room looked more pastry-like than the last—crown molding icing, clotted cream walls, crème brûlée amber everywhere. Would lunch be served soon? She'd already scoured the crumbs from her pocket and was broadening her search for a kitchen she could plunder. A dining room she might raid.

No one seemed to live in this palace though. There was no king. No queen. There weren't even servants. Only the priest Sanct prowled the halls, his robes dragging back and forth.

The sun was high in the blue-bolt sky when he finally stepped outside. Sylvie retreated to the highest cross of the chapel's gold domes. She stayed cloaked as she watched the priest Sanct walk the park grounds. Was it just her imagination, or did the trees he passed drop some extra leaves? Their branches were definitely thinning—enough for Sylvie to see where the priest Sanct's path led.

A *second* palace sat on the other side of the trees.

She flew toward it to get a closer look. This palace was smaller than the first and had been painted a pale yellow. Guards stood by the entrance. They could see the Sanct, eyeing him uneasily, but they didn't cross their bayonets to deny him entry. He was known here. He was . . . welcome? As Sylvie soared toward the door, she saw four girls flocking to the robed figure. The youngest hugged him as if he were Père Noël, come to bring them Christmas gifts. The guards began muttering. Their words were strange, and their tone was dark, and Sylvie knew they felt the same way she did. They understood the wrongness of it.

What happened next was even worse.

The priest Sanct was greeted by an older woman, and though she wasn't wearing any jewels, Sylvie somehow knew she was a queen. She led the priest Sanct upstairs to a room with drawn curtains. Sylvie couldn't see anything through the window, but she could hear someone sobbing.

The queen said something, and the priest Sanct replied in kind.

The weeping started to fade.

Sylvie wished she could wish for a translation, but she was too far from La Fée Verte's salon. She fluttered to the adjoining window instead, peering into one of the most elaborate playrooms she'd ever seen. A giant dog on wheels paraded by a river of model ships. Teepees and canoes lined the plush carpet. Honest-to-goodness airplanes were strung from the ceiling. The floor was littered with trains and cannons and other tiny tools of war.

None of the princesses were playing with these.

Sylvie figured that was what the four girls had to be—even though their clothes weren't nearly as nice as their storybook counterparts. Servants would be a little less obvious in their eavesdropping, not pressing their ears to the door, the way these princesses were. The youngest was flat on her stomach, trying to peer beneath the crack, pearls askew around her neck. She looked close to Sylvie's age, close enough to be her friend in a different life.

Or even . . . in this one.

It was silly, Sylvie knew. It was probably even stupid, considering the priest Sanct's closeness with the royal family, but she figured she had to ask *someone* where she was.

Why couldn't that someone be a princess?

The girls scattered all at once, the youngest rolling over a regiment of toy soldiers and yelping as the door opened. The priest Sanct stepped out. Past his shoulder, Sylvie could see a wall filled with tiny gold pictures of saints. A camp bed sat beneath them, but it was too dark to tell who might be lying in it. The queen was crying as she shut the bedroom door behind her, but her lips were fixed in a wobbly smile. She touched the priest Sanct on the shoulder and planted a kiss—a *kiss*—on his palm. More words were exchanged. Then the priest Sanct raised his hands and made the sign of the cross.

Just as he had with Céleste.

But there was something different about this rite. Something more . . . unholy. Sylvie could see his fingers plucking strands from the queen's frayed countenance. Not imaginings. These strings were darker, and they didn't break when the priest Sanct pulled them to himself. Merely faded, a little. If Sylvie squinted—just right—she could see thousands of these ties between the priest Sanct and the queen. So many that their shadows blurred together on the playroom rug, over its scattered tin soldiers.

Apparently, being a royal wasn't all crowns and gowns, the way it was in stories. Princesses still had to sit for lessons like any other child. Well, the teachers were fancier here than they'd been at Sylvie's old orphanage. Plus, they actually *taught*. Though the youngest princess seemed entirely uninterested in whatever her tutors said. She wriggled like a newly hatched tadpole during French lessons, tugging at her pearls and casting furtive glances toward Sylvie's window.

Sylvie was still invisible. Her cloak stayed tight around her shoulders, but even without it, she wasn't sure the princess would see. Neither she nor her sisters seemed to notice the gathering shadows around their mother.

The queen reminded Sylvie of a marionette show she'd watched once. Her smile had hooks. Her nods were one second off. The movements wouldn't look so jerky without the priest Sanct standing as close as he was, smiling and nodding while he knotted more strings from Her Majesty's head.

There was no storm cloud hanging over the youngest princess, though, when the tutors released her. She dashed out onto the sunny grounds with a joyous yelp, her long chestnut hair streaming every which way. There was a brown spaniel too, running with her to the nearby lake, where a rowboat waited. The wooden craft was meant to carry them to an island with a *third* palace. A play palace, Sylvie realized, as she flew toward the pale blue structure. It was only four rooms—built for royal children to escape to on lesson-free afternoons.

The princess placed her dog in the vessel and then climbed in herself before rowing over to the opposite boat landing.

Sylvie landed nearby.

Her cloak slid onto the ground.

The spaniel barked, but when the princess looked up, she only frowned, wagging her finger at the dog. Sylvie was disappointed, but she wasn't surprised. She was so drenched in magic that only Sancts and Enlightened people seemed to see her these days, imaginers who wandered Paris past midnight or children who grabbed their mothers' hands and pointed whenever Sylvie flew past. She was a gleam in their eyes, whereas their parents saw only empty blue sky. Sylvie had hoped the youngest princess was young enough to fall into that category. Oh, how she wished they could be friends.

Oh!

The wish must've been stronger than she'd thought. Strong enough to grow outside La Fée Verte's salon. She'd never had an imagining do that before! Nor had one of Sylvie's dreams ever broken while it was still on her head—but there was a flash. The air shimmered pink. The princess gasped and dropped the rope she'd been trying to tie to the dock. It slithered off into the water as she stared at Sylvie.

"Privet. Kto ty?"

Sylvie still wasn't sure what language this was. She didn't quite know what the dog was saying either, but soon the spaniel stopped barking—its tail wagged as it sniffed Sylvie's hand. Licked.

"Hello," she greeted. "My name is Sylvie."

The dog's tail wagged harder.

This seemed to set the princess at ease.

"That's a fitting name for a fairy." The other girl's French was very good, despite how wriggly she'd been during lessons. "Though I've never met one before, so I could be jumping to conclusions."

She was, of course, but Sylvie wasn't quite sure how to explain her sudden appearance otherwise. Much less her monarch wings and magenta hair.

"Well, I've never met a princess," she said, instead.

"I'm a grand duchess." The other girl drew herself up into a pose fit for a postage stamp. "Anastasia Nikolaevna of the House of Romanov."

"Is that a country?" Sylvie wondered.

"No, silly!" Anastasia giggled so hard that she snorted. "Romanov is my house!"

"Oh." Sylvie glanced across the water, where the second palace presided over a well-trimmed lawn. "The blue one or the yellow one?"

The princess's laughter made her lean back on the boat post. The sound was merry, pealing like church bells through the autumn landscape. "Oh! I like you. You're funny."

Sylvie hadn't meant to be, but it was just as well, if the princess liked her. Already she had visions of them drinking tea and riding horses and doing other regal things together. Going to a real live ball, perhaps? Though it didn't seem as if either one of Anastasia's houses had hosted such a gathering in years...

"Why don't you use the blue palace?" she asked.

"It's called Catherine Palace," Anastasia informed her. "My sister Maria thinks it's haunted, but Mama says it's just too big for us. That's why we live in Alexander Palace instead. The yellow one," she clarified. "I live there with Mama and Papa and Maria and Tatiana and Olga and Alexei. And Shvybzik, of course." She nodded down at the spaniel sitting contentedly at his mistress's side. "Where do you live?"

"I used to camp in a cemetery," Sylvie said, "but now I stay in an enchanted salon. In Paris."

"Paris!" The princess's eyes lit with the word—blue, but not at all like the priest Sanct's. "I've always wanted to go! But what are you doing all the way here in Tsarskoe Selo? Have you come to be my fairy godmother?"

It was Sylvie's turn to laugh. "I'm not really a fairy."

"Oh..." Anastasia's brow creased beneath her fur cap. "Are you a ghost, then?"

"I hope not," Sylvie said.

"So what are you?"

"I'm just a girl." Sensing the other girl's disappointment, Sylvie went on. "But I can grant you a wish, if you want!"

"Really?"

She hoped so. She hadn't tried to conjure outside the salon before—the act was easy enough when she was surrounded by firefly lanterns and storybook smoke—but the fact she'd wished this meeting into existence was proof Sylvie could imagine something else. "Do you want a pony?"

Anastasia shook her head. "I already have one of those."

"What about a fur coat?"

"I have a lot of those too," the grand duchess said. "This is Russia."

"I mean, a coat that grows fur when you step through snow! That way you'll never have to wear layers!" It sounded lovely enough to Sylvie, shivering out here under the afternoon sun. Russia *was* much colder than Paris. "I could make us some smoky cocoa too!"

A hair began glowing before Sylvie even finished her sentence—she'd forgotten how hungry she was—and when she broke the strand, a steaming thermos appeared on the ground. As Anastasia knelt to touch it, the smoke shaped itself into a double-headed eagle and drifted up into the baring branches. For a moment, just a blink, it was easy to imagine them blooming.

The grand duchess's smile grew back too when she examined the flask. "You...you made this out of thin air? But...how? I thought magic was just for saints and holy men!"

The mention of saints made Sylvie think of Honoré—the patron of pastry chefs. They'd need cakes to go with the cocoa, of course, so she set about plucking more hairs. *POOF!* Some croissants. *FLASH!* Some éclairs. *CRACK!* A fur coat that doubled as a picnic blanket.

"I just picture things and then believe them with all my heart," she said, setting the plates down. "Sometimes saying it out loud helps."

"Praying." Anastasia nodded, tugging her Spaniel into her lap so he wouldn't help himself to the pastries. "That's how 'Our Friend' heals Alexei."

Our Friend. She was talking about the priest Sanct.

But Sylvie didn't mention him. Instead she asked, "Alexei?"

"He's my younger brother. The tsarevitch. He's supposed to be emperor one day, but he's...well, if Alexei even gets a paper cut, he'll bleed and bleed and bleed. The doctors can't help him, but whenever Grigori Rasputin starts praying for my brother, the bleeding stops. The bruises vanish. Mama says he's a miracle worker!"

Sylvie fought back a frown. This Rasputin must not be so bad, if he healed people. So why did chills crawl down her spine when they were in the same room? Why did she need another sip of cocoa, even now, to keep from shivering?

"That must make your mother happy," she said carefully.

"Oh yes." Anastasia nodded. "Mama worships the starets—that means 'holy man' in Russian. She listens to everything he says. Alexei isn't happy though." Anastasia stared back at Alexander Palace, toward the window with drawn curtains. "He gets sick of being sick. I wish I could change that..." She stared back at Sylvie. "Do you think *you* could?"

Suddenly the pastries felt flaky.

The cocoa clumpy.

"I don't know," Sylvie admitted. "I think your friend's magic is different from mine. He's...he's a Sanct, and I'm just a daydreamer."

"But that's exactly what my brother needs! Some dreams! You'll be perfect!" A thrill went from Sylvie's ears to her wing tips at the grand duchess's declaration. The fantasy of their friendship grew even stronger. "Oh, please, can I take you to meet him?"

How could she say no to that?

So it was that Sylvie of a Single Name found herself in the Alexander Palace playroom, enchanting a regiment of tin soldiers. Most of them were still spilled on the rug where Rasputin and the tsarina had stood—hours earlier—casting their conjoined shadow. This had been washed away by moonlight and by the faint pink pulse of Sylvie's imagination. It was easier to conjure outside La Fée Verte's salon than she'd first believed—probably because she'd been practicing on the Children's Island all afternoon. After a picnic on a shedding fur coat, she'd imagined a snakelike rope that slithered out to Anastasia's drifting boat. After it slithered *too* far, she imagined a bridge of ice that nearly melted when they were halfway over.

The soldiers were more manageable. They were small, designed to follow an imagination's orders. Sylvie made them march toward the tsarevitch's bedroom.

Anastasia stood by the door, her nightgown long and bright. "Alyosha?" she called.

The room was dark until Sylvie stepped in with her dreams' light. The golden icons above the tsarevitch's camp bed began to glow. Something about the saints' eyes made Sylvie want to flip their frames around, but they'd been nailed too firmly to the wall. Instead, she tried curtseying when Alexei Nicholaevich sat up.

Both motions were clumsy.

The newly healed prince wasn't at all what she'd expected. His skin was so pale, it was hard to tell where the sheets covered him. Or where the bleeding had been stopped. There were no bruises on his arms or legs, but his eyes had sunken into dark circles.

"Nastya?" His gaze drifted from his sister, to Sylvie, to the soldiers. "Is this a dream?"

"Yes! But you're not asleep! I've brought someone to cheer you up!"

Suddenly, Sylvie wasn't so sure she could. Her magic felt like a candle here—shuddering enough for a sudden breeze to snuff. What good would marching metal soldiers do when the tsarevitch himself seemed barely able to walk?

Alexei swung his feet to the floor, then knelt to examine the regiment. He giggled when they saluted him. Sylvie began to understand then why the Sanct at Stohrer gave away his pastries for the joy of them—a policy she herself was all too happy to take advantage of. The smile on Alexei's face was worth it. So was his sister's.

"This is Sylvie! She's a not-fairy from Paris," Anastasia said.

"What's a not-fairy?" her brother wondered.

"She believes things and they come true!" the grand duchess told him. "Show him something else, please?"

They moved to the playroom then. The tin-soldier regiment marched behind the giant stuffed dog on wheels, which Sylvie enchanted to serve as Alexei's steed. She plucked another hair—and the airplanes hanging from the ceiling cut loose from their strings, doing loop the loops and nose dives. She sent the model ships sailing across the carpet too, their cannons firing tiny gumdrops. A toy soldier speared one of these candies with his bayonet and brought the treat to Alexei.

"It tastes so real!" the tsarevitch declared, after swallowing the wintry spice. "How?"

"I tell myself stories," Sylvie said. "And then I believe them to be true, but I can only do it because a *real* fairy taught me how." That had to be the deciding factor, right? She'd spent so many years picking up sticks that never turned to swords, talking to cats who only meowed back, exploring tunnels that merely turned into dead ends.

"What are real fairies like?"

Sylvie thought of all the Sancts she'd come across over the summer: The baker. The bookseller. The bric-a-brac vendor. Rasputin. La Fée Verte. The hungry man. They were all so different. "Most have wings, of some sort."

"So do you." Alexei nodded at her butterfly wings.

"I wasn't born with these," Sylvie explained. "I made them up."

"Maybe that's how fairies *are* born," the tsarevitch said. "Through stories. Isn't that why they're called fairy tales?"

One of the airplanes stuttered before crash-landing into the giant teepee. Sylvie could only stare as toy soldiers rushed to the scene. Was it really as simple as that? She had a hard time imagining La Fée Verte without her effervescent feathers, but maybe those *had* been imagined. Maybe—once upon a time—the Sanct had been just a girl too. A girl who'd slipped through the cracks of the world.

Something glimmered in the corner of Sylvie's eye.

Not pink, but bronze.

She turned to see one of Anastasia's hairs shining.

The grand duchess looked almost as surprised as Sylvie when she pulled the strand from her head. "Oh! I was just thinking about one of my favorite fairy tales..."

The phoenix had two heads—just like the bird that had flown out of the princess's cocoa. It was small enough to roost in the playroom's green fireplace, where it burned without coal nor logs, crooning a song that made Sylvie's heart soar. Everything else inside her felt bigger too. What did it mean, that she'd taught the grand duchess magic?

"A firebird!" Alexei whispered. "A real firebird!"

Anastasia stared into the humming fire. More of her hair started to spark—hot, hotter. Pocket-sized bears danced there, next to toadstool tea parties and a zebra with color-shifting stripes.

Funny, that a princess's dreams should look so much like an orphan's.

Soon the tin soldiers were riding around on tiny ostriches and unicorns. The frigates were floating, firing bubbles out of their cannons. These popped against the bougainvillea blossoms that bloomed from the ceiling, then became butterflies, swirling into the firebird's smoke. If Sylvie squinted, the playroom almost looked like a corner of La Fée Verte's salon. Was this how the Quartier Secret had started? With a handful of dreamers? She'd never thought too hard about its beginnings before, but now that she was sitting here, it seemed important.

Was every Sanct once a human?

Was Sylvie still "*just*" a girl?

The grand duchess was having a grand time pulling imaginings from her head. Her brother watched raptly, clutching the ears of his stuffed-dog steed.

"What about the train, Nastya? Can you make it move too?"

"Why don't you try, Alyosha?"

The tsarevitch squeezed his eyes shut. His breath teetered. The firebird's light flickered against his drawn face—making the hollow spots even more hollow—and Sylvie was suddenly afraid the boy might fall onto his own soldiers. If one of their bayonets made him bleed, what would she do? What would Rasputin do, if he found Sylvie here? The Romanov children said the Sanct was their friend, but what kind of friend tangled a mother up in dark strings? What kind of friend only healed someone halfway?

Alexei—as wobbly as he looked—did not fall.

The train didn't move either.

"Is it working?" he asked after a moment.

"No." His sister sounded deflated.

"How about now?"

"You have to *believe*," Sylvie insisted.

"I do!" Alexei opened his eyes and stared sadly at the train. "Maybe my hair is too short..."

Sylvie wasn't sure that was it. One of her favorite designers in the salon was practically bald, and he still managed to pull outfits out of his head every evening. The tsarevitch's hair stayed dull, the back parts matted from spending all day in bed.

"You're probably just tired," Anastasia reasoned. "You *did* nearly die this morning."

"I don't want to be tired," her brother croaked.

"Then you should go back to sleep," the grand duchess said, glancing at Sylvie. "We can try again tomorrow. Can't we?"

Again, it felt hard to say no. Bubbles popped. Bougainvillea butterflies spun into the fire, where the double-headed bird was nestling itself into embers. Sylvie looked back at the train stalled on the carpet.

"I have to go home to Paris," she said. "My friends need me."

"We need you too!" Anastasia exclaimed.

Sylvie wondered if this was true. She could see darker knots in Alexei's hair, far darker than his inherited brown. It was almost the same color as his mother's. What was Rasputin's magic doing to them?

And Céleste... what was it doing to her?

Sylvie had set out to break Rafe's curse, but the shadows Marmalade had mentioned seemed to stretch further than that. Much further.

"Don't leave us," the princess said.

"Please," added Alexei, his face forlorn.

An idea started to take shape as Sylvie stared at the siblings. It was impractical, maybe even impossible, but this wouldn't stop her from trying to pull it from her head. "I think... there may be a way for me to go *and* stay."

The journey back to Paris would have taken Sylvie nearly a week by train. Over one month as the crow flew. She didn't bother testing this distance with her own wings. The best method to get home, she figured, was to go back the same way she'd come.

By magical door.

The portal still hadn't reappeared in Catherine Palace, despite many more peeks through its frosty-dawn windows. It was just as well. What Sylvie really wanted was a secret passage of her own—a place where she and the grand duchess could meet. Not halfway, but *both* ways. At the City of Light and the Children's Palace.

The play palace was the perfect location for an enchanted door, seeing as the Children's Island was ignored by the rest of Tsarskoe Selo's residents. Rowing a boat was too much trouble for the adults, and the three older grand duchesses considered themselves too grown for such a small building. There wasn't much room for them regardless, since Anastasia and Sylvie had filled the house with toys they could no longer keep in the playroom after that first magical night. Boats that still spat out the occasional bubble or gumdrop. Most of Alexei's soldiers. A whole menagerie of miniature animals. It wouldn't do for Rasputin to get bitten on the ankle by a thumb-sized tiger.

There were doors everywhere now too.

Sylvie had spent the past two days pulling over a dozen doors from her head, but they led nowhere, opening to walls if they opened at all. She'd forgotten to add knobs to the first and hinges to the second. Minor details. The major one—the distance she was trying to compress into the space of a step—was harder to wrap her head around.

"We do need a place to put brooms," Anastasia said, after the thirteenth try led to a shallow closet. "The tiny animals are messier than I thought they'd be."

Sylvie looked down at an elephant that was giving itself a bath in a teacup. She wondered how her other elephant was doing. Was it still serving smoky cocoa to the salon's guests? Had any of them even noticed she was gone?

She shut the thirteenth door. "The magic is too big, I think. I can't—it's hard to believe I can go back to Paris in a single step."

"Isn't that how you got here?"

Anastasia and Alexei had listened to the tale of Sylvie's arrival several times. Each version changed—ever so slightly—becoming truer as she added in her talking cat and invisibility cloak.

She never told the Romanov children about the curses though. Or the dark strings she kept seeing around their mother.

"Yes," she told Anastasia. "But I didn't make up that door."

"Someone must have, once!" the princess pointed out. "So you know it's possible!"

This was hard to argue with. Also, it looked like they'd need a place to store mops as well as brooms. The teacup the elephant was bathing in had tipped over, spilling amber liquid that the tin-soldier regiment was marching straight through, leaving scores of tiny tea prints all over the wood.

"I just don't know if *I* can do it," Sylvie admitted.

"You can." Anastasia sounded so *sure*. Her voice did not waver. Neither did her arm, when she reached out and took Sylvie's hand. "I believe in you, Sylvie."

There was something distinctly magical about hearing a princess say her name this way. It felt almost like a spell. A wish come true! They *were* friends! And they could stay friends if Sylvie could manage to conjure this door...

She squeezed her eyes shut.

She squeezed Anastasia's hand.

She squeezed her thoughts through a keyhole, imagining home on the other side. Late-night bakeries and endless bookshops. A lobster gargoyle wriggling to the chime of its cathedral's bells. A stone pelican ruffling its feathers several stories above. An overgrown island drifting down the Seine, past the Seer's smoking houseboat. Sylvie wanted—so badly—to show these things to Anastasia.

The princess wanted this too. Sylvie could feel the other girl's wish, as hot as a firebird, blooming between their palms, burning in a way that she could hold. Use.

I believe in you, Sylvie.

And Sylvie finally believed in a door.

It was unlike the others she'd pulled from her head. There was a *FLASH*, bright enough to trace the veins through Sylvie's lids, and when she opened her eyes, she saw the door standing there. Brightest pink. There was a key in the lock, already turned. Ajar. Flaky scents of *pain au chocolat* slipped through the crack, and when Sylvie pushed it open, she found herself standing beside her neighborhood boulangerie—a tiny shop on rue de la Réunion. The lane was a thoroughfare from Père Lachaise's south gate to more crowded streets. Until now, there'd been nothing magical about it.

Sylvie stepped out to study her door.

It was just as pink on the Paris side, where a second key dangled from the lock.

One, she noted happily, for each of them.

She handed Anastasia's over with a smile. "Welcome to Paris, Your Majesty."

Chapter 23

The Key to Immortality

"You Enlightened the princess of Russia?"

The three Enchantresses were back in their tomb again, sitting in their respective corners. To Céleste it felt just like old times, aside from the fact that several of her opera gowns were beaded with dreams. The ledge of her easel was covered with imaginings too. As was the gap beneath Honoré's pillow where she normally kept her knives. Sylvie had also copied the bookseller's method: pressing dreams between the pages of her fairy books.

But of all the stories tucked away inside this mausoleum, the one Sylvie had just shared was the wildest.

"Anastasia is a grand duchess," the girl said, taking a generous bite of butterfly pie. It had been almost twenty-four hours since Céleste and Honoré had acquired the pastry from Stohrer, but the cake hadn't staled. Its candied insects were as lively as ever, whirring around the tomb's glass dome, while Marmalade watched from Sylvie's lap. Entranced.

"You Enlightened the grand duchess of Russia?" Céleste repeated faintly.

"She's not *the* grand duchess. She has three sisters."

"Oh," croaked Honoré. "Did you Enlighten them too?"

"No." The girl shook her head. "Only Anastasia. I showed magic to the tsarevitch, but I think he was already young enough to see it. It's hard to say...The whole family is friends with a Sanct."

"The Mad Monk?" Céleste asked.

"Anastasia told me his name is Grigori Rasputin. He gives me the creeps, but he heals the tsarevitch almost every week."

Céleste couldn't help but glance toward Honoré's corner then. One day had passed since their own exchange of blood, and the other Enchantress was still wearing a thin bandage on her palm. She hadn't wanted to think too hard about the deeper implications of La Fée Verte's statement that each breath her lungs drew had once belonged to someone else. That the vintage wines she'd sipped weren't the kind poured into a communion chalice, unless your priest happened to be the Mad Monk...

"Rasputin?" Honoré echoed. "I've read about him in the papers—he's that mystical priest from Siberia, no? It makes sense that he's magical. But how did *you* cast a spell, *ma rêveuse*? I thought only Sancts could Enlighten people."

"I thought so too," Sylvie said. "But it's more complicated than that. Have you noticed that all the Sancts have started calling me 'daydreamer'? I thought it was just a nice nickname, but Marmalade tells me it's a title. It's what you call a person who can conjure dreams during the day." The ginger tom let out a yowl. "He says it's an in-between stage. Like a cocoon."

Céleste could feel her own insides fluttering—she couldn't tell if her stomach was ill or excited or a strange combination of the two. "In between *what*?" she asked.

Marmalade meowed once more.

"Humans and Sancts," Sylvie translated. "Turns out if a person stays Enlightened long enough, they can collect their own dreams and gather enough power to allow them to start performing larger spells." She waved at the dreams around them. "That's why I was able to Enlighten Anastasia!"

"You?" Honoré let out a flabbergasted breath. "You're a Sanct?"

Céleste's exhale was sharper. This theory might have been easier to dismiss if it weren't for Sylvie's shining face. There was an undeniable glimmer around the girl's eyes—a sparkle that had nothing to do with the rose-colored dreams strung from the ceiling.

Or perhaps . . . everything.

"I'm not a Sanct yet," Sylvie told them. "I'm still a daydreamer, but if I keep collecting dreams, I'll eventually become like La Fée Verte."

Céleste had been Enlightened for over three and a half months, but she was starting to see just how blind she was as well. "That's why Rafe told you to save your imaginings," she said slowly, remembering the thief's other hints: *Dreaming is surviving. You can be more.* His devastation about the windmill was far worse than she'd first thought. It wasn't his contingency that their employer had burned but Rafe's potential *power.* His shadow had fallen so flat because he'd had no magic left to shape it with . . . "That must be why La Fée Verte snuffs out her imaginers' memories every morning. To keep them from keeping their own dreams."

If a priest from Siberia could become a Sanct, then so could an orphan from nowhere. So could thieves from the streets of Belleville and the castles of Provence. So could painters and poets and princesses . . .

A thrill went up Céleste's spine, just sparkling enough for her to imagine wings there.

"She told me she erased their memories to keep the salon safe," Honoré said.

"When I gather enough magic, I can help you with your patrols!" the youngest Enchantress exclaimed. "I can fix everything! I'll find a way to break Rafe's curse. I'll help the Romanovs too—"

"Curse?" Honoré interrupted. "Rafael is cursed?"

Céleste's nostrils flared with another razored breath. Again, she felt blind. Or rather, like a candle falling through a cavern, as Rafe had so eloquently put it. "He hates that he can't remain Enlightened. Is that what you're talking about?"

"No." Sylvie frowned. "I thought you knew—"

She was interrupted by the clamor of bells. They were too tinny to belong to Saint-Germain de Charonne or any of the other nearby churches. Someone had—finally—set off Honoré's perimeter alarm.

The other Enchantress shot up from her mattress, arming herself with one of Sylvie's dreams and padding toward the scrolled iron doors.

Something flickered over the roof, quick as Céleste's heartbeat. She grabbed one of the imaginings from her easel, holding it like a brush as she followed Honoré to the tomb's entrance. There was no sign of anyone outside. No stray mourners. No spooked groundskeepers. No bright eyes peering through leaves. Those belonged to Sylvie alone, as she joined the other Enchantresses on the mausoleum steps—flashing more rose-tinged light across the clearing. A spell. It lit up the surrounding foliage, enough to show the stray shadow that sat at the center of the Enchantresses' camp, over a paint-splattered picnic blanket. It looked almost like another stain. Flat. Black. Fox shaped.

Céleste's heart felt like a struck match.

Her veins became fuses.

Rafe was hiding in his own shadow once more. Hiding from *her*. She wondered where his new stash of imaginings was located. What other secrets was he keeping so close to his scarred chest...?

"How did you find us?" She spoke to the darkness.

Their secrecy wasn't one-sided. Not by a long shot. She'd been so careful yesterday evening, trying not to tip Rafe off to the fact Honoré knew about their operation, trying not to show her own awful revelations. The key to immortality: blood on her lips, blood on his hands. She struggled—still—to envision Rafe as a vampiric killer. He just didn't seem to have that *in* him. At least not in a way that could be splashed onto a canvas at La Ruche or conjured in the Quartier Secret.

But Rafe García was a hunter.

Céleste could see that now, as the dark air over the paint-splattered blanket began to shiver into a man. Rafe had tracked her back to Père Lachaise. How long had he been prowling outside Honoré Côte's grave, watching her with those broken brown eyes? It was still impossible to tell what shade they really were as he stared at the three Enchantresses.

"Oh!" Sylvie waved brightly. "Hello, Rafe! We were just talking about how to break your curse."

"So I heard." His voice was coal dust. His dark hair was unbound and wild, wild like the rest of the cemetery's shadows, wild like the fox twisting at his heels. He took a step toward the mausoleum. "I can see why you consider La Ruche an upgrade, *mon amour*." Céleste wasn't sure what to make of the fact that Rafe was still using their false terms of endearment—that her skin still prickled with something more than danger when he edged closer to her on the step, squinting up at the tomb's bold granite letters. "Is...is that your name, Honoré?"

To Céleste's great surprise, the other Enchantress did not raise her dream blade, nor did she stop Sylvie from taking Rafe by the hand and pulling the thief through the doors, showing off her hoard as if she were a proud baby dragon.

"See? I saved all these! Just like you told me to! Now we can become Sancts together!"

"One day. I hope." Rafe's eyes glittered even more as he gazed up at dreams and glass stars. There was a faraway look on his face—not distant, but wistful. The kind of expression the original Honoré Côte must have had whenever he peered through a telescope. "You're a good deal closer to that goal than I am though, Magpie."

"Ma rêveuse." Céleste's hand tightened over the rosy imagining she was holding.

Honoré's gaze narrowed.

Sylvie's eyes stayed wide. "What?"

"He's not who you think he is. He's—" Céleste licked her lips; she couldn't just *kiss* the truth of Rafe García away this time. She didn't think she could stab him either, but she could at least put herself between Sylvie and danger. The girl's butterfly wings fanned out in surprise as Céleste pushed in front of her. "He isn't safe."

"None of us are," Rafe replied. "Not if Terreur finds out about... whatever this glitzy grave situation is."

"The Enchantresses!" Sylvie's wings kept fluttering, so she managed to poke her head over Céleste's shoulder when she spoke. "That's the name of our gang because Céleste said that lying well was the closest thing she could think of to magic. That was before she found the salon, of course!"

"What do you mean he's not safe, *mon amie*?" Honoré's dragon coiled up her arm and spread its own silver wings so wide that it blocked the doorway. Again, Céleste was reminded of the bookshop, as Rafe stiffened into the first position of *défense dans la rue*.

"He's the one who's been husking people to keep Terreur alive," she said, her own heartbeat high in her throat.

The other thief's eyes flashed. "Is that the kind of man you think I am?"

"I don't know," Céleste admitted. "Are you a man? Still?"

When Rafe flinched, his fox shadow did the same. It was growing, growing on the opposite wall, to the same size it had been their first evening together in the windmill. Right after she'd opened that sketchbook of his, plucked from a desk filled with literature on sliced-open hearts and embalming techniques. "I found maps of every arrondissement in his possession. When I asked Rafe about the *X*s that covered them, he said he was hunting down the key to immortality for our employer." It hadn't been too hard to piece the rest of the puzzle together, after she'd learned about the bodies from Honoré.

Rafe cursed under his breath.

The silver dragon snaked from the doorway, wrapping itself around the thief's hand, causing him to drop the watch he'd been palming. Two gold chains shimmered from his vest pocket—had he been planning to escape with the timepiece? Céleste's heart kept thunderstorming through her. The entire tomb felt charged.

"Is this true?" Honoré hopped up onto the central gravestone. The way her ring was moving made it look as if the dragon had pulled her there. "Don't you dare try to bullshit me, Rafael Martín García."

The other thief shut his eyes. "Elements are."

"*Which* elements?" pressed Honoré.

"Don't hurt him!" Sylvie squealed, as the silver kept clawing around Rafe.

The other thief was barely able to nod toward his vest pocket. "I have the maps here, but they aren't what Céleste believes them to be." He paused, as Honoré pulled the sketchbook from his garments. "They don't mark the murders."

"Murders?" Sylvie squealed again.

Honoré flipped through the pages. Once, twice, three times. They must not have matched the locations of the corpses she'd discovered, because when she finally shut the book, she asked, "So what do they mark?"

Rafe hesitated. It wasn't Honoré his eyes had settled on, but Céleste. "I…I'm not trying to keep Terreur alive. Trust me, there's nothing I want less. He's made my life a living hell for the past five years. I've been searching for a way to escape him."

Something soured on Honoré Côte's face. "Why don't you just hop on a train again?"

"It's not that easy—"

"No. It's *not*," the other Enchantress snapped. "But you left me and Gabriel anyway. You left that note…Did you know my father was the one who found your letter? He was so fucking furious because he thought I was going to steal his son away. I was only a few hits away from ending up like Maman, and then…"

The dragon shuddered.

Rafe did too.

Honoré went on. "I thought about you a lot afterward, about that better life you'd set out to build for yourself, painting the golden spires of Constantinople in person and washing off Belleville's muck in a hammam. I always hoped you'd actually made it happen, despite everything. After we ran into you at *The Rite of Spring*…and Céleste started talking about your work. Well, I was *inspired*. I figured if you could escape our past, then maybe I had a chance at shedding it too. But it was never true, was it?"

"*In somnis veritas*," Rafe replied.

"What's that?" growled Honoré. "A curse?"

"It's the inscription above La Fée Verte's door," Céleste recalled. Rafe's eyes were still locked with hers. It wasn't a plea that shone through them, but something stronger—the shiver of flame, the glitter of stardust. The longer she stared, the more her heart took the shape of moth wings. "It means..." Céleste's mind whirred. She'd had a Latin tutor, long ago, before her father had stepped out that tower window, without any wings of his own. "It means 'in dreams there is truth.'"

Rafe nodded. "I didn't understand the inscription, when I first darkened her threshold, but dreams are the only true thing for me now. I know you feel the same, Honoré. I can't think of anyone in Paris more fit to be La Fée Verte's protector."

Another shivering moment.

Honoré's dragon began to retreat. Her face looked stricken. "So why are you still doing Terreur's bidding? Are you dying as well?"

"No," Rafe told them. "I'm damned."

Excerpts from
The Unbreakable Curse of Raf[redacted]e[redacted] García

There once was a young man who dreamed of faraway lands, and so he went to see them.

He did not get very far.

His journey began in Paris's Gare de l'Est, on a platform filled with steam and brass-latched luggage. The Orient Express wasn't the type of train that would suffer a forged ticket or even one purchased with dirty money. Its compartments were too gleaming for a runaway gangster with a tear inked under his eye. But he figured he'd see the same sights from the baggage car. Vineyards and castles and olive groves. Europe's holy buildings—cathedrals that would shift into the mosques featured on the travel posters. He sketched as much as he could: Strasbourg, Munich, Vienna, Budapest.

That was the end of the line.

Not for the train itself—that kept chugging onward, toward Constantinople's shiny spires, but only after a porter discovered the stowaway camped among the Louis Vuitton suitcases. The Ls *and* Vs *were stained with charcoal marks. The offending artist was tossed out into a strange city with bone-colored stones and roofs as red as blood. Buildings that turned to bodies of work in his sketchbook.*

He drew quite a few, before a devil found him.

He was too focused on the saints of Saint Stephen's Basilica to see the shadow fall over his sketchbook pages, to turn around and find that no one was casting it. A no one who preyed on other no ones—drifters and runaways, the types of people other people would not go looking for. Forgotten even before they were fed on, drained to the very dregs of themselves.

A person's life is made of many things: blood, yes, but memories too. Power is threaded through the tiniest moments, such as when your name first leaves your mother's lips. Rafael Martín García. This devil started there. He swallowed a vowel, savoring the flavor of the a *while he sifted through other memories.* Migas *for breakfast—not with tortas, but croissants. Strange. The name tasted Spanish, but there was something distinctly French about this artist's childhood. He'd never felt fully at home on Paris's streets, which was why he'd so often wandered to their edges, pulling down travel posters from train stations' walls. It was a petty crime compared to some of the others that unfolded around him. Attacks in alleyways. Money laundered like clothes. Murders ordered by a man with a silver ring. It was a vicious cycle—around and around and around—and the artist thought he'd finally escaped it by coming here.*

This thought was too hopeful for the devil's taste.

Too much like a dream.

He spit it back out and swallowed an l *instead. Shadows began to merge on the plaza's concentric stones—around and around and around—one life draining into another. Raf*[redacted]e[redacted] *García did not notice the way his own silhouette flinched. It was only when he went to sign the sketch of the church that he understood he was losing himself.*

Raf—

His pen paused.

The devil over his shoulder paused too—looking more closely at a memory of his victim's studio. Those weren't paintings drying on the drawing table, but banknotes.

Monsieur García wasn't just some struggling artist.

He was a forger.

He was exactly what no one had been looking for.

Most people think working for the devil is a choice.

Would you call it a choice to keep your heart beating? To stop yourself from being unmade*? Monsieur García could not say no. His sketchbook had fallen to the plaza stones when he finally saw the extra shadow stretching out from his feet, when he followed its twisting lines to the willowy man. They were bound together already. Raf*[redacted]*e*[redacted] *could see scenes from his childhood knotting the air between them—like some oily umbilical cord. Later, he would learn that this comparison was not correct at all. It was more like a noose. Or a leash. Depending on how he answered this devil's deal.*

Steal me dreams, *he'd said.* Serve me, and I will give you the rest of your life.

Raf[redacted]*e*[redacted] *had laughed. "What? No kingdom to go with it? You should work on your pitch—" The pitch of his own voice cinched tight then. His throat closed in on itself. He felt his mind going blank, blank like the sketchbook pages blowing across the square. None of the passersby stopped to pick them up. No one stopped for the artist either as he fell to his knees, seeing stars that spelled out his immediate future.*

Dying without living. He was only nineteen, and, like any other nineteen-year-old, he'd thought his horizons were endless. There would always be another train to catch or another border to cross. There would always be another day to sit down and try to draw what he really felt *inside him—soaring skies and snow-gripped mountains and sunlight as potent as wine. He'd never quite been able to capture that magic on a page, but that failure hadn't frightened him.*

Until now.

Darkness closed in, turning that vast yearning into a void, showing Raf[redacted]*e*[redacted] *just how much more this devil could take from him.*

Everything he was, is *and,* could ever be.

"You'd prefer a more biblical proposition?" The Sanct relaxed the shadow between them. Raf[redacted]*e*[redacted] *gasped. "Become my disciple, and I can show you the way to life everlasting. You don't have to die here, Monsieur García. In fact, you do not have to die at all. As for kingdoms... some of my followers control empires. Serve me well, and you'll have your pick of palaces. Palais du Luxembourg. Palais de la Cité. Palais de L'Élysée..."*

All in Paris.

Raf[redacted]e[redacted] shook his head. He couldn't care less about those castles—he'd seen most of them before.

"What do you want, then?" the devil asked.

He wanted to go. He wanted to get away from this predator, but the thought only made the shadow around his neck grow tighter. "My name..." Raf[redacted]e[redacted] gasped.

"That's it?" the devil scoffed. "Two letters?"

Yet it felt like so much more was missing... Raf[redacted]e[redacted] didn't quite understand what, only that when he reached inside himself, he felt... hollow. Husked. The towering mountains were no more. He didn't even want to draw the steeples of Saint Stephen's. He couldn't think of a prayer, though there was one inscribed on the building: ego sum veritas et vita. *He figured it was a prayer, anyway, or some sort of smart saying, smarter than anything he could dredge up at the moment.*

So he turned to an old quote from his father instead: "All a man's got is his name."

"That's not true," the devil said. "I don't have a name."

"You're not a man."

This got him a laugh. "I was, once, but then I became more. Do you know what I could do with those letters I took? I could make the sun go dark at midday. I could drag someone into sleep for a decade. I could turn my shadow into wings. I could teach you to do these things too. I can show you the world as it truly is: without end."

A slightly better pitch—but it still reminded Raf[redacted]e[redacted] of a sermon he'd heard once when his mother had dragged him to mass. Hadn't Jesus chosen to starve in the desert instead of accept Satan's offer? What does it profit a man if he gains the whole world, yet loses his soul?

What should a man do if his soul was already lost?

He could feel himself *hanging from his bones like a half-gnawed chicken leg. Cut into pieces in the exact sharp shape of the devil's teeth. White teeth. Too white. His smile turned everything upside down.*

Raf[redacted]e[redacted] smiled too, even though he did not want to.

It was like looking into a warped mirror.

In the end, the devil did not have to force him to kneel. Despite all the Bible verses he was now remembering, Raf[redacted]e[redacted] García was no saint.

"Bullshit!" Honoré's voice cut though Rafe's story. Her ring raised its head once more. "Your name is Rafael."

Again, that faraway look flashed over the other thief's face. "I was surprised when you called me that at *The Rite of Spring*. No one else is able to."

Céleste realized he was right—when she tried to twist the name from her own silver tongue, the *a* and the *l* kept slipping away. They seemed to do the same for Sylvie, whose cheeks were starting to match her hair from the effort.

"Why?" Honoré asked, after a moment of struggling stutters. "Is it because we grew up together?"

Rafe shook his head. "No one at the Caveau has recognized me, not even Eleanor, and you know how she never forgets a face..." His eyes glinted off her ring. "My best guess is that it has something to do with your relic. You can shield yourself from enchantments with it, no? If you did take the ring from your father right after I left for Constantinople, it means you were wearing it when I was cursed."

"So why don't you just claim a new name, then, like I did?" Honoré asked. "There are plenty around here. Just throw a rock, and you'll hit a gravestone. Hell, this dark Sanct did it when he claimed my father's old title."

Sylvie's pink eyebrows popped up. "Wait, your dad was called 'Terreur' too? That's confusing."

"It's not ideal," Rafe agreed. "The history behind that title only lends my employer more power over the Caveau and its Apaches.

When it comes to magic, names are so much more than what you call someone. It's not just letters that I'm missing...it's...well, this new Terreur took pieces of *me*."

"Your anima," Honoré said.

"What's an anima?" asked Sylvie.

It was another Latin word, Céleste realized. One that tied in all too well with Henri's very first story about vampires: *Says they don't take just your blood but your soul too.* "It's his essence."

"La Fée Verte says it's a person's power," added Honoré. "Their unique magic."

"Oh." Sylvie considered this for another moment. "That's why the cats say you aren't yourself."

It was also why Rafe had claimed he was *working for himself.* True words. Too true. Céleste hadn't thought to interpret them so literally. "So Terreur devoured your soul?"

"Not all of it. I still have enough anima left to dream," he explained. "As long as I'm forging ideas for our employer, he won't swallow the rest. I've been trying to steal back pieces of myself. I even gathered enough dreams to start shaping my shadow—a small way of resisting his control." Rafe glanced down at the fox weaving in and out of his ankles. "I find that when it looks like this, it doesn't bend to the dark Sanct's magic quite as quickly. Of course, he's very strong, and I've encountered a few... setbacks."

"The windmill," Céleste clarified.

Honoré's eyes narrowed once more. "That was yours?"

"It was what I hoped to be," Rafe said sadly. "Spending all that time in La Fée Verte's salon—pouring what's left of me onto a canvas—it's helped me see that souls aren't stagnant. They grow."

"Like hair," Honoré said.

A strange analogy, perhaps, but it seemed to Céleste that Rafe appreciated it. "Exactly! Our employer doesn't like imaginings though. They weaken him. I figured if I gathered enough of my own dreams, I could find my true self again." He glanced back down at the fox peeking out between his boots. "I figured, after that, I could help others do the same." His eyes alighted back on Céleste when he said this. "I got sloppy though."

"You met me."

The way he stared reminded her of every distracted touch, every edged whisper. How much of what they shared was actually true? She wondered this as she watched his fox. If Rafe was able to shape it again, it meant he must be gathering a new stash of dreams somewhere, a place he didn't dare invite her to. Céleste couldn't exactly blame him. It wasn't as if she had much to offer on that front.

She looked back up at the sunrise hue of the dreams above them.

A horrible thought came to her then: "Is that the reason I haven't been able to conjure any imaginings at the salon? Did . . . did Terreur take my soul too?"

Marmalade meowed on the central stone below.

Sylvie chimed in as well. "It's still whole!"

"Yes," Rafe answered, "but Terreur sped up Céleste's disease when he was . . . *feeding* backstage at *The Rite of Spring*. His attack was mostly concentrated on La Belle, but everyone in the theatre was touched by his magic."

"*That's* why everyone's shadows went stringy," Sylvie realized aloud.

"Shadows can show all." Rafe's fox spun in a circle as he said this. "Our employer's favorite magic is controlling people using their own fears—a form of compulsion. Most of his victims aren't even aware he's doing it, but if you happen to see your shadow twist into a string, the best thing to do is dream. It loosens Terreur's grip when a person can see past their fears."

"That's what you've been trying to do with your fox!" the youngest Enchantress surmised.

Rafe nodded.

Céleste thought of that night in the theatre. She could still remember the shock of seeing her own blood on her glove, of feeling her shadow become a riptide beneath her. She remembered her employer's smile too, after he'd made the stain disappear. It made her own teeth grit together—the thought that she'd been taken in so carelessly.

She wondered how much worse Rafe felt.

There was some relief in the fact he wasn't a wanton murderer, but damn if the alternative wasn't much brighter. No wonder Rafe had quoted Faustus that evening on the bridge. He was cursed to a half-life, forced to plunder heaven on hell's behalf. And Céleste?

Well, misery loves company, no?

Her fellow grave-mates certainly looked despondent. Sylvie was frowning—not the question mark expression she usually wore, but a worse crease. Honoré kept standing on the slab that spelled her name.

"What about my brother's soul?" she rasped. "What about Gabriel?"

Rafe's voice fell. "I've seen him around the Caveau. He doesn't remember me, but as far as I can tell, your brother is still your brother."

This didn't seem to bring the other Enchantress much comfort. "I saw him at the Caveau too. There was a shadow string wrapped around his arm when he tried to shoot me."

A pained look crossed Rafe's face. "Terreur is hard to fight," he said with a heavy sigh. "He's a heartless bastard."

"Just like his goddamn namesake—"

The other thief shook his head. "Not *this* kind of heartless. Your father didn't carve his beating heart from his chest and lock it away. Other blades won't touch him so long as it's hidden. That is the key to Terreur's immortality." He nodded at the sketchbook Honoré was still holding. "That's what I've been hunting for all this time."

"His heart?" Céleste's pulse started thundering again.

"Or what's left of it," Rafe said. "I've had to do a lot of digging to learn more about the spell Terreur performed. There wasn't a great deal written about it. There's even less now." The ash in his voice made Céleste think of the windmill's desk. All those papyrus scrolls, the diagram of the dissected heart...it all suddenly made so much more sense. "But, as far as I understand it, once you remove that muscle with magic, it transforms into something else. An animal, a flower, a talisman."

That would account for the curio cabinets as well: scarab beetles' shiny wings and amber jars filled with root bulbs and crystals formed in far-off mountains. No wonder Rafe had been so upset when Céleste first discovered them. No wonder he'd let the windmill burn without a fight. What would have happened if Terreur had taken a closer look at the building's contents?

She shuddered to think.

Over on the gravestone, Marmalade meowed.

"Really?" Sylvie perked up. "In ancient Egypt?"

"Is he talking about the embalming techniques?" Rafe ventured. "Those were the earliest examples I could find—some pharaohs were able to mummify pieces of themselves and lock them away in pyramids, while the rest of their bodies walked the earth."

Honoré glanced down at her dragon, a hard look passing over her face. "This mystery flower-animal-mummy heart... is it something I could stab? Would Terreur die?"

Rafe nodded.

"Good," said Honoré.

"That's why he's taken pains to hide it so well. That's why I've been hunting for it ever since Budapest," the other thief said. "The letters of my old name are lost for good, but I can take back the rest of my life. I figure if I kill the bastard, I'll have an actual future. The search has been regrettably slow—"

"Probably because you've been filching dreams," Honoré snapped.

"That," he admitted. "And there's the sheer *scope* of the search, not to mention its secrecy. My pocket watch has helped—I've even been able to use the Door to Everywhere without Terreur noticing. I figured having a second forger around would help divide his attention too."

"Why didn't you tell me any of this?" Céleste wondered.

Rafe hesitated. His ink teardrop looked darker somehow. "You saw how easy it was for our employer to pluck the windmill from your head. I couldn't risk you knowing about my hunt for his heart. Plus, I didn't suppose you'd be an advocate of killing the Sanct who's keeping you alive."

Touché.

"So...what? You swooped in and saved me after *The Rite of Spring* so I could be a damn distraction?" she asked sharply. "All that talk about bleeding hearts and dreaming to survive was just horseshit?" A surge of anger, not just at Rafe, but at herself, at the way she'd fallen for him—hook, line, and sinker.

Rafe almost looked like he was falling too, as he pushed off the wall of the tomb. His shadow swirled around his ankles as he moved over to Céleste's corner. Past all her old opera gowns and the never-finished Ophelia piece—now barely visible through all of Sylvie's dreams stacked on the easel. The other artist didn't stop to study it anyway. He was too focused on kneeling at the edge of her mattress.

"You're more than a distraction to me, Céleste Artois," he said.

"What, then? A whim?"

"The night after we met, you asked me for a fancy speech—and everything I told you on that bridge was true. When I saw your bloody gloves after the ballet, I knew I had to do my best to save you." Rafe reached out and took Céleste's hand. Again, she noted how well their calluses matched. "I thought you could help me too. There was the hope that you'd distract our employer, yes, but as the evenings kept unfolding and we spent more of them together... well...I started seeing myself in a whole new light. Because *you* see me, Céleste. You call me out of the shadows even when I'm damn near invisible.

"Picasso, you know, he can be full of himself, but he once told me that 'the purpose of art is to wash the daily dust of life off our souls.' Ever since Budapest, I've been trying to excavate mine. Painting and dreaming and digging as deep as I can for my own magic." Céleste pictured him in the landscape room then—the battlelike movements of his brush. Rafe *was* fighting for something every time he painted. Every time he sculpted his shadow into a fox. The silhouette had started circling the pair on the mattress, chasing its own tail. "I'd been struggling for so many years, but then you came along and caught it all in one little sketch."

The sigil. *His* sigil. The one still hanging over their bed at La Ruche. "That was just a scribble," she managed.

"Don't." Rafe shook his head. "Don't be so dismissive. You're worth more than that. So am I."

Tears sprang into Céleste's eyes then, but they weren't angry. All her rage had melted into a gold feeling—one that matched the electric current Rafe García's shadow always traced across her skin.

"It would've been easy to give up after our employer destroyed the windmill," Rafe went on. "Five years of work, gone. But my sigil was still there, and so were you, sitting on that curb, coughing up more blood. I decided to keep going. To do something worth a damn. So, no, Céleste Artois, you aren't a whim. You are my salvation, and I pray to whatever god might be listening that I can return the favor. I promise I'll do my best to find Terreur's heart, and then I'll find a way for both of us to be free of him."

Easier said than done, but Céleste knew she needed to believe these words.

What was the point, otherwise?

"You're getting better at monologues," she said, squeezing his hand.

The thief smiled and ran his thumb over her knuckles. "Yes, well, you seem to be rubbing off on me."

Honoré let out an impatient grunt. "What about your search? Do you have any leads on where the heart might be?"

Rafe's hand fell away from Céleste's. His smile shrank. "It's not inside his study. I know that much. I wondered for a while if it could be that globe he keeps so close to his chair... I've searched through many of the blacked-out territories too. But I've come to believe Terreur's heart is hidden somewhere inside this city," the thief told them. "Why else would he be so fixated on Paris?"

"Could that be what you two are searching for in the salon?" asked Honoré.

"I doubt it," Rafe said. "If La Fée Verte had Terreur's heart, she'd be able to control him."

"So could we," Céleste said.

A heart—no matter what shape—was leverage. She tightened her fist and imagined Terreur's life force beating against those faded calluses. *Him* squirming on his barstool. *Him* frozen with fear. *Her* fingers picking through those fair hairs, finding something black to bind him with, to force him to heal her, to release Rafe García's shadow...and then?

She winced, realizing her nails had dug too deep, cutting a fresh mark into the hand La Fée Verte had mended.

Honoré crouched on the tombstone, her eyes narrowed. "Are you suggesting we blackmail Terreur?"

"It seems like the best solution to all our problems," Céleste reasoned. "The *only* solution, really."

"We still have to find the heart first," her friend pointed out. "And if our search is anything like Rafael's, that could take years. Paris doesn't have that kind of time. La Fée Verte's wards are already weak."

"So we take a different approach," Céleste said. Terreur didn't strike her as the type who'd leave his most vulnerable parts sitting above the fireplace mantel like a candelabra or a clock. He was more guarded. He probably even thought he was invincible. *That* would be her angle. "I can try to fish some clues out of him. Stroke his ego. He'll let something slip. Men always do."

Rafe went rigid on the mattress beside her. "He's not some rich fool looking to buy the Eiffel Tower—"

"Oh!" Sylvie grinned. "That con was fun."

It had also failed. Not because of the deed Céleste had forged on government stationary nor the story Sylvie invented about how city officials wanted to sell it for scrap because it didn't fit with Paris's other monuments. Honoré even found some businessmen who almost bought it. They hadn't managed to go through with the grift though—it had been impossible to make Honoré look old enough to pass as the deputy director general of the Ministère des Postes et des Télégraphes.

The Enchantress's upper lip twitched—perhaps with a memory of that ill-fated gray moustache. "Rafael is right. We can't just waltz into this the way we would play any other fiddle game."

"Why not?" Céleste wondered.

"Because he's not a man!" She'd never seen fear play out so plainly on Honoré's face. "He's an evil sorcerer who can strangle you with your own shadow!"

Céleste thought of all the other times they'd sat around this tomb, pinning on wigs and hemming up stories. The Eiffel Tower had been ambitious, certainly, but she had no doubt they could've pulled off the con with a pinch of magic. A few wrinkles, à la the Seer of the Seine. A paintbrush to turn hair silver. Such things were possible now, thanks to Sylvie's daydreams. Thanks to the salon Honoré so valiantly fought for. Thanks to Céleste's lies that led all three of them there in the first place.

How much more could they do if they believed—not just in themselves but in each other again?

"He might be an evil sorcerer," she said with a smile, "but *we* are Enchantresses."

The Fisherman of the Moon

There is plenty of trash to be found at the flea market outside Les Puces.

There are plenty of treasures as well.

Wander over to the farthest booth outside the old city gate, and you'll find yourself an audience with the Fisherman of the Moon. He resembles many of his fellow stall-keepers—men whose hands are permanently scuffed from digging through piles of garbage. There appears to be dirt on his face too, but if you stare hard enough, this takes on a glittering bronze cast. It glistens even more as you look over his wares. Music boxes, magic-lantern slides, masquerade masks. An opera program from 1880 catches your eye. It must not have been so yellow when it was handed out to the ticket holders—over three decades ago. It must not have felt as fragile in their gloved hands as it does in yours.

"That was the final performance of Mademoiselle Leroux. They found her body in the Palais Garnier's basement the next morning—dry as a mummy. None of the police could figure out what had happened to her, but that's only because they could not see." He tapped the program. "The opera house was the haunt of a Sanct who grew too hungry. He used to harvest inspirations from his private box, but that evening he stole the prima donna's voice. The show was cut short. As was her future. It was the last anyone heard her."

You shiver and put the program down.

It lands beside a bell jar full of teeth—too dull to belong to an animal.

"Dark times followed that year," the Fisherman of the Moon goes on. "There were other victims. People became too scared to go out at night. Dreamers stayed behind closed doors, and all of magical Paris went to war."

The molars in the jar begin to rattle.

You can almost hear words—*skritch, skritch*—scratching behind the glass.

The Fisherman of the Moon sees your own teeth clench. He tosses a handkerchief over the whispering bones—and its embroidery blooms into morning glory patterns. "We've had a good long peace since then, thanks to La Fée Verte. An age almost as shining as the Sun King's. Would you like to see some of those relics?" He opens a case to reveal a tiara of golden vines—always growing—with pieces of sunlight lodged in the center of the flowers. "The Sancts who kept court at Versailles had an eye for beauty. One could argue it blinded them."

"What happened?"

"To Versailles's magic?"

Yes, you want to say. But your question feels bigger. *To the owner of those teeth. To the Sanct who stole the opera singer's voice. To the head that wore that crown.* When you reach out for the tiara, its tendrils reach back, curling in the shape of your finger.

"It grew too wild. There's no telling how magic will age inside inanimate objects. After a few generations, the jewels of Versailles soured. New rings were forged by revolutionaries, but from what I've been reading, I gather most of those spoiled as well." You notice there are no rings on the Fisherman's grimy fingers as he prods the exploring vine back inside the case before snapping it shut. "Some Sancts think me foolish for hunting through garbage heaps, but the more I dig through the past, the more I find myself able to see the future."

He glances at a different program. The paper is fresh; the ballet was far more recent: just this past May. "I'm nothing like the Seer of the Seine, of course, but I can read other currents. There's a pattern to people, you see, to the flow of our fears and hopes. We are, all of us, terrible. We are, all of us, beautiful."

You nod as you browse his other pieces: A postcard from Cairo with an extra pyramid in the background. A ship in a bottle, with a thunderstorm too. A spare button that changes to an exact match of the ones on your jacket. A box of matches that always catch at the first strike—although the color of the flame is never the same.

It is these you leave with, the promise of light in your pocket as you wander off into the night.

PART IV

THE HUNT FOR A HEART

Once upon a time, there was a young woman
who wanted to be a muse.

She grew this idea into a pair of wings, and then
she grew her wings into a flock of birds.

She sent them far and wide, waking the brightest minds in Paris.

She woke up something else as well.

She did not think to put it back to sleep.

Until it was too late.

Chapter 24

The Ones Who Wanted Wings

The Enchantresses were better together.

Honoré Côte could not argue with that, but she knew they were better with La Fée Verte too. It wasn't just personal preference. The group's plan to defeat Terreur wouldn't work without the Sanct's blessing—without a steady flow of dreams to burn, night after night—so it was agreed that they must confess. Honoré couldn't remember the last time she'd been this nervous. Her pulse beat all over her body—with the singular silvered exception of her right arm—evidence that she was not heartless. If anything, she had *too* much heart. It stuttered through Honoré's veins as she stood before La Fée Verte. In front of Céleste. Between the two women. Her power was supposed to be protecting people—so why didn't she feel like a shield? Why was her skin so flushed? Why had she insisted on bringing all of them here, to the salon's garden with the bottomless pool, where she'd washed her hands of Rémy's death, where his blood must still be swirling. Down, endlessly down.

Rafael lingered by the water's edge, staring at the stars' reflections, as Honoré told his story. Then Céleste's. She stumbled over the words. Sylvie would have done a better job—but the youngest

Enchantress was hearing many of these details for the first time. The leaves of the branch she was perched on shuddered when Honoré described the extent of their friend's disease.

La Fée Verte's wings shuddered too. Her golden face held no trace of anger, only sadness, as she gazed across the garden at Céleste. "I thought I sensed a deeper hurt," she said, once Honoré finished her explanations. "You hide it well.

"And you..." She turned toward Rafael, kneeling and holding out a hand to the young man's shadow. Slowly, slowly, it moved to meet her—a fox that sniffed the Sanct's fingers. "I am sorry."

Rafael still hadn't looked up from the pool. "Why are *you* sorry?"

"The Sanct who stole your name and broke your soul..." La Fée Verte lowered her hand. "I created him."

Sylvie's tree shook again.

Céleste's eyes narrowed.

Shock. Honoré felt it too—rushing up to join the rest of her nerves—as La Fée Verte met Rafael by the pool. One of her birds slipped from her wing and plucked a strand from her head. When the Sanct cast it into the waters, the sky gave way to a different scene. A long-ago Paris—without automobiles or electric lights. There was no light around the eyes of the fair-haired woman who sat on the curb either. A bedraggled shawl hugged her shoulders instead of feathers.

"I know what it's like to watch your future die," La Fée Verte began. "I know what it's like to hide in plain sight—to throw my family's jewels in the Seine and my accent into the gutter. I understood why so many people were so angry too. No money, no bread, no hope... it's no wonder they started a revolution."

Suddenly, a moth landed on the young woman's shoulder. Its wings were made of marzipan, but she didn't eat it. She simply laughed as the confection fluttered around her head.

"There weren't many Sancts left in Paris, when I was Enlightened, but Stohrer was still standing. Barely. Nicolas took me in." Honoré recognized the baker in the unchanged doorway. "He fed me. He taught me how to see the good in people. He showed me how to share it." The next memory saw La Fée Verte inside the shop—her hair powdered with sugary snow. Her feathers too. Green birds gathered in the glass chandelier, watching customers as she passed them pastries. "I was never a terribly talented baker though, so I set out to find my own magic."

The pool swirled, showing a daydreamer hunched over scrolls, reading by the shine of her own eyes. "Many ancient Sancts—the powerful ones—gathered worship. Prayers and bent knees. They set themselves up as gods. Others chose to be seen as kings, but it seemed to me that France had already had enough of those.

"When I was a girl, my parents used to host these beautiful salons. They made a space for philosophers and artists and anyone who wanted to talk of higher things. There was even an aeronaut, once. I didn't meet him myself, but I listened from the staircase as he told stories about his balloon. That night, I dreamed I was flying, and I woke up with my heart in my throat, not because I was afraid, but because I wanted it to be true... so badly..." La Fée Verte's feathers stirred. The waters at her feet did too. Honoré recognized the Sancts from Cabaret d'Ailes—simply women then. They seemed to be walking through a carnival, wandering past a merry-go-round with galloping horses. Pegasi, actually. Wings moved in time with their wooden hooves. "I never did meet that aeronaut, but I found others who wanted wings. People who wanted to dream with me. Most were children of the Revolution. They wanted to build something better than the world their parents had left.

"I found power in their ideas. I learned how to take songs and poems and paintings and make them soar... make them magic. I discovered ways to make other imaginers magical too, to give them the very same gift Nicolas had given me." La Fée Verte glanced up at Sylvie's tree as she said this. "Daydreamers ruled Paris—some saved enough of their imaginings to become very strong Sancts, but we were, at heart, a democracy. Each interwoven with the other, strengthened by our shared idea of sharing magic. We built cafés and cabarets and carnivals."

"Like the one on the floating island?" Sylvie asked.

Honoré frowned. She'd seen the drifting landmass—it was hard *not* to notice with how often she flew over the Seine—but she'd never seen a carnival there. Certainly not one as shimmering as the memory inside the pool, where La Fée Verte was handing out tickets. **ADMIT ONE**. The letters read far more crisply under the torchlights than they had at the Fisherman's booth.

"Yes," La Fée Verte said. "The Carnaval des Merveilles drew many talented dreamers to me: Désirée, Plume, Libris, La Belle, Madame Arcana, Moulin, the Fisherman of the Moon . . . Their imaginations were brilliant enough to turn them into Sancts. Some stayed with the carnival. Others went on to establish magical corners of their own. Libris built his bookstore, and Désirée and Plume started their cabaret. Moulin had a windmill where she hosted artists."

The windmill's blades looked much like they had in Rafael's painting—except they were moving. Honoré recognized the blooming vines that wreathed the hill as well. Men tossed off their top hats when they reached the top of the stone steps, revealing glittering hairs.

"Montmartre looked different then. The neighborhood was a haven for artists who could not afford rent. They were hungry—not just for food but for meaning. They wanted to paint and write and sing. They wanted their lives to matter," La Fée Verte said, with a hint of sadness. "There was one young man who visited Moulin's windmill every evening. He did not speak much, she told me. He preferred to listen to the prima donna who came to give an encore after her performance at the opera house every night. He liked to sketch this woman as well. There was something especially striking about his drawings. Powerful. They commanded the eye so that you almost could not look away." La Fée Verte stared into the pool, where Honoré could see a man taking shape. *Man*. That was the main difference from the monster she'd faced in the Apaches' bar. He had no black masque yet, but his fair hair and blue eyes were the same. "The artist had this air about him too. Everyone at the windmill seemed to gravitate in his direction. Even Moulin herself. She started to teach the young man how to harness his own power—he was a quick learner. Eager. Too eager, now that I look back, but when he came to the Carnaval des Merveilles, I had yet to learn the difference between want and obsession. I didn't understand how dark his dreams would become...how all-consuming...Perhaps if Madame Arcana had warned me..."

"The fortune teller?" ventured Céleste.

"She vanished, the night that devil joined my carnival; she didn't even clear out her tent." La Fée Verte seemed unsettled. "I suppose that *was* a warning in itself."

"So you taught your enemy magic?" Honoré said.

"He claimed he wanted to become a muse, so I showed him how to harvest other peoples' imaginings, how to take just enough so that their souls stayed untouched, how to sow magic back into dreamers' minds to make sure more inspirations would grow. Again, he learned quickly. Once I'd shown him all I could, he established himself at the Palais Garnier."

"The opera house?" Honoré asked. She and the other Enchantresses had been there several times to find wealthy marks.

"It was the perfect place for a new muse: rich with inspiration, freshly built itself. The Palais Garnier hosted lavish performances that filled well over a thousand seats. He should have been satisfied there, with so many sparkling minds, but no..." She shuddered. "He focused only on the star soprano. He took and he took and he took, until there was nothing left of her." La Fée Verte glanced back at Rafael's fox. "By the time I realized what he had done, it was too late. He'd vanished as well. I'd almost begun to believe he was gone, when other drained bodies began turning up across the city. Artists from Moulin's windmill. Moulin herself. Victims piled up and fear started to spread, and I could not weed it out of my own dreamers' minds because they were too afraid to even come to Île du Carnaval."

An empty carousel spun inside a ring of gutted tents.

A bookstore with too much dust.

A café with cold cups of tea.

"It was the same with other magical establishments. Daydreamers' powers faded as his shadow grew—darker and darker across the city. Some Sancts decided to join him. Even more, after my fortune teller turned up by his side. They feared that this meant the future of Paris belonged to him.

"I was afraid as well." La Fée Verte swallowed. "I tried to reverse his Enlightenment, but he'd grown too powerful to forget his magic. He'd become too powerful even to kill." The pool began flashing with visions of a battle. Shadows tangled with spells. Gargoyles peeled themselves off Notre-Dame's bell towers, diving at the shadow-bent man just as Honoré's dragon had. Many were smashed to dust. Claws and beaks evaporated. So did the marks they'd left on [redacted]'s flesh. "Imaginings slowed him, but they did no lasting damage, and the more we battled, the stronger he grew. Blood only seemed to feed him. I don't think it was a coincidence that he forced the Mapmaker to carve out a space for him by Place de la Concorde—where my mother and my father were guillotined. It was difficult for me to dream there. So I turned to a different magic."

The cathedral had vanished. La Fée Verte stood in front of an obelisk with an army of Sancts on the plaza behind her. Masques winked like stars over the cold stones. Honoré recognized a few: the bookseller, the baker, the dancers of Cabaret d'Ailes again. But there were so many others. A Sanct at La Fée Verte's right side held a scroll—no, he held a map. His hands shook.

La Fée Verte's eyes blazed.

Stones around them began to burn.

Smoke choked out the rest of the memory.

"Just the whisper of his name was enough to plant fear in people's hearts, so I took that first. I took and I took and I took, but no matter how hot the fire got, he would not die. The spell started burning through my followers instead... They gave up too much of their magic for this final push. I knew that if I stopped, their sacrifice would be in vain. I knew that if I kept going, more would fall."

The dark clouds parted to show La Fée Verte and her enemy interlocked, their magic sulfuric. His shadows pulled at her feet. Her birds clawed at his head. Some got tangled in the sorcerer's hair, trapped and swallowed, while others managed to steal strands.

"I could not make him forget his magic, but I didn't need to, in the end. His dream was to devour all of Paris—to become its shadow king. That was the vision I found in his head."

One of La Fée Verte's songbirds pulled away—the idea in its talons looked wormier than most. Not glowing, but gray. The color of ash and long-cold corpses. [redacted]'s eyes began to dull as well, their fire smothered. "After I stole it, he faltered. I pushed him out of Paris and set up wards to ensure he could not set foot on the city's soil. Nor any of his disciples. He's found ways to test these boundaries over the years—the Seer wasn't always the Seer of *the Seine*. I would have that traitor gone altogether, but water has its own rules, and most of my power is tied to tightening the rest of my defenses."

"The Fontaine Saint-Michel's dragon..." Honoré thought back to the bronzed beast's attack that first night.

"My gatekeeper." La Fée Verte nodded. "There was a time when I might have Enlightened anyone with a hungry heart, but this enemy taught me what Nicolas Stohrer did not—to search for darkness in people. Everyone has shades of it, to some extent, but I trained the statue to weigh those against their brighter thoughts. This doesn't always work, of course." Her gaze swept from Rafael to Céleste and finally to Honoré. "So I established a second safeguard to prevent any darker magic from growing: a spell that makes every imaginer in Paris forget magic at sunrise."

"You stopped creating daydreamers," Céleste murmured.

"Again, this doesn't always work." Golden eyes glanced up at the tree, where Sylvie was crouched.

The youngest Enchantress stared back. Unabashed. "But... doesn't that just hurt you?" she asked. "If you'd invited Rafe to your salon before he ran off to Budapest, he might have stayed! He could've become a daydreamer and helped strengthen your power instead of stealing it. Right?"

La Fée Verte stayed silent, her masque wavering like a lantern down to the last of its wick. It was hard to see what the Sanct was thinking—outside the pool—but Honoré had a feeling it wasn't as black-and-white as the battle that had played out there.

It never was, was it?

"There are many things I would have done differently," the Sanct said, finally. "Given the chance."

"Me too." Rafael's gaze found Honoré when he whispered this.

She stared back. He didn't look so different from the young man she'd grown up with at the Caveau. *A firebrand with his head in the clouds*, according to Eleanor. While no one had ever read fairy tales to Honoré, she'd known about knights even then, thanks to him. His carvings. His whittling knives. His quiet corrections on how to hold a blade just so. His even stronger silences. Rafael never breathed a word about the two siblings crouched under his drafting table whenever their father's boots came into view, prowling past wood shavings and crumpled drafts of banknotes. How many bruises had he spared Honoré then? How many cuts? *Tigers don't change their stripes*, she'd told Céleste, and she could see now just how true her saying was.

Curses be damned.

Rafael's magic *had* reached for the clouds. The stars, even. But Honoré knew that if he could figure out how to turn back time with that fancy watch of his, he'd choose to stay in Paris, not for La Fée Verte's invitation, but to keep Lucien Durand from finding that note, because, at his core—in that sacred space between body and being—Raf[redacted]e[redacted] García was a protector. This was the real reason he hadn't left Céleste bleeding on the theatre steps. It was the reason he stayed standing here now. Rafe might have been missing a few letters from his name, but he wasn't nearly as lost as he thought.

None of them were.

"We do have a chance," Honoré said. "We can defeat this bastard, but only if we believe in each other—"

"Dreams weren't enough to stop him last time," La Fée Verte broke in. "The only thing that's changed since our visit to the Fisherman's booth is that Terreur has claimed a name. He has enough power to hold a piece of the city. I fear he'll soon swallow more."

"You shouldn't be afraid!" Sylvie piped in. "That way he can make you a puppet! Just like the tsarina! Besides, Honoré wasn't talking about our imaginations. We're going to find this evil sorcerer's heart and stop him before he takes over Paris again!"

"His heart?" La Fée Verte blinked.

The pool at her feet went dark.

Rafael stared back into the black water. "He cut it out from his own chest and buried it away. It's why you couldn't kill him before. It's why Terreur drains people's blood along with their souls... The anima, he uses for power. The blood, he must drink to keep his own body from withering."

Silence again.

La Fée Verte's skin had paled to the color of candle wax.

"Don't worry!" Sylvie chirped from her tree. "We have a plan."

A plan that had been pieced together over a gravestone, under the wavering light of dreams and stars. Admittedly, it felt as fragile as glass. Honoré glanced over at Céleste. Her friend hadn't said much in her own defense, so how could she be expected to talk their enemy into confessing the location of his heart? And even if she did, would it be in a place Sylvie could steal through unnoticed, so she could bring the heart back to the other Enchantresses? Honoré had no doubt that she herself would be able to stab it... if they got that far.

"Fighting Terreur outright will end poorly." Céleste smoothed her skirts; the hem around her ankles swished. "But, as powerful as he is, he is not invincible. His heart is still out there somewhere. I can trick him into telling me where it is, but the only way I'll be able to manage that is to keep playing my part as his forger—so that Terreur believes I'm absolutely on his side."

"Are you not?" La Fée Verte asked simply.

Honoré's chest tightened far more than it ever did when she bound her breasts.

"I'm here," Céleste replied. "Offering you the last chance at victory you have left. Terreur might not remember his exact vision for Paris, but he feels the hole of that dream. He's not going to stop chasing it. Trust me."

"That's the thing," the Sanct answered. "I don't trust you."

Céleste didn't flinch at this the way Honoré did. Her friend held herself like one of those marble statues that could be found in a wealthy person's foyer, chin tilted high. "I can't fault you for that, La Fée Verte, but you shouldn't fault yourself either. Or your dragon guard. Even I don't know how much stardust I truly have inside. I've spent so long painting without it…"

Honoré flinched again.

Céleste's storm-gray gaze met hers. "But if there's one thing I've learned in my years as a forger, it's that Honoré Côte is someone you can trust with your life. She is your best defense. Without her, I'd still be down in your vault, stealing dreams for days, but now I see there's a better way."

She reached up to pluck a star-white hair from her head.

It shimmered as she held it out to La Fée Verte.

Inside? A dress with the skirt sewn into trousers.

It was—Honoré mused—the perfect peace offering. But she'd expect nothing less from Céleste Artois. "Instead of forging, I'll focus on dreaming. I'll try my best to conjure imaginings," Céleste promised the Sanct. "You won't lose any more power on my account. I'll replace whatever imaginings I take to Terreur each night with my own ideas. Once we locate that bastard's heart and defeat him, you and I can split hairs."

Which was just a fancy way of stating that she wanted to become a Sanct.

La Fée Verte's hand hovered over Céleste's imagining.

Her lips drew tight.

Her wings folded in.

She's still afraid, Honoré realized. Each of them was in their own way. They all wanted the same thing—Terreur dead and gone—so why did this moment feel so tangled? Why did Honoré feel as if she were walking a tightrope when she joined the two women and grabbed the dream floating between them?

Céleste's imagining had an edge to it.

A weight.

If Honoré yanked her own heart out of her chest at this very moment, she figured it would have similar proportions. Heavy.

Sharp. The shape of a blade, but a blade forged by hope instead of a hammer. A weapon made of stardust—not steel. Truer, even, than the sword La Fée Verte had first knighted her with.

She wondered if the Sanct was also remembering that scene as Honoré held the other Enchantress's dream in her palms. "Céleste might be slow to warm," she said, "but she is right. She's standing here with you now. With *us.*" Honoré lifted the glowing imagining, like some ancient offering. "This is our only path forward. Together."

La Fée Verte's face shimmered.

A few birds slipped from her wings and alighted on Honoré's fingers, examining the idea, but none flew away with it. The Sanct herself reached out to accept the trousers—her palm resting over Honoré's. Her touch trembled.

"Very well." She exhaled. "I'll give Céleste and Rafe the dreams they need to continue their charade with Terreur—but that pattern won't hold much longer. He's gaining strength in Belleville."

"I'll work as quickly as I can without tipping him off," Céleste promised. "It's a delicate balance."

"To that end, Rafael shouldn't be hunting for the heart," Honoré said, looking back at the other thief. "I'll take over that search so you can focus on your dreams." *And Céleste's.* The sparks between them weren't just chemistry, she knew. "The more you can conjure, the better our chances."

Chapter 25

Straw and Gold

Dreams were harder to pull from one's head than forgeries, as Céleste discovered later that night. Her pantskirt had been simple enough—but that idea had had weeks to simmer, growing in the back of her mind like one of those stubborn dandelions that popped up among Père Lachaise's tombstones at the tail end of autumn. Now that she'd uprooted it, the rest of her mind felt bare. As white as her surroundings. She and Rafe were back in the landscape room, but this time, they both held brushes. A songbird was perched on Céleste's shoulder, tiny gold talons digging into her shoulder as it waited for another dream to grow.

No pressure.

Rafe had several birds on his jacket too. They were less stationary, swooping in and out and around and around, gathering ideas. He was one of La Fée Verte's best imaginers, after all. He hadn't been lying about that.

But Céleste?

"Did you ever hear the fairy tale of the miller's daughter who was forced to turn straw into gold?" she asked, as Rafe began to paint. Orange streaked from his brush—bright as the fur between a tiger's stripes.

He shook his head. "No, but that sounds like a handy talent to have."

"On the surface, certainly," she said. "I always figured she'd spend the rest of her life looking twice at a coin, never really knowing its worth." Or burying it beneath a stranger's grave, never to be touched again. "If everything *could* be gold, can't it all be straw too?"

"Is that how the story ended? With the heroine stuffing francs into scarecrows while she questioned all of existence?" Rafe wondered.

The image made Céleste laugh. "Not exactly."

"Good," Rafe said, with the twirl of his brush. "That'd be pretty damn bleak."

His landscape, on the other hand, was looking fluorescent. A sunset took shape over lines of vineyards. Their leaves—Céleste noted with a smile—weren't green or straw-colored, but gold. *Cheeky, that.* Or just Rafe. He'd used the shade plenty of times before, going well beyond the walls of the ice palace or the outlines of her corset. Though those were certainly the most memorable instances...

She let her gaze linger on the other artist. His brushstrokes were no longer frantic; now they reminded her less of a street fight and more of the way his touch had moved along her thigh that first afternoon in La Ruche. A careful yet eager caress. It made Céleste clutch her own brush more tightly.

Somehow, their encounter on the graveyard mattress had felt even more intimate. *I'm damned. You are my salvation.* That was a lot of pressure to put on someone, but Céleste found she preferred it to the alternative: *Good, but not good enough. I'm afraid you don't have what it takes.*

Her art mattered to Rafe García.

Her awfulness too.

It was a rare thing, Céleste knew, to have someone who treasured every part of you. The straw *and* the gold. Rafe had stayed by her side in the darkest of places. He hadn't flinched away when she'd been coughing up her lungs or stealing to survive. He wasn't shrinking back now either.

Rafe had come so close that Céleste could count his eyelashes.

She could see herself reflected in his gaze—her white hair almost, but not quite, glowing. "If I might offer my two cents, I don't think you have to worry about barnyard vegetation. Try not to worry at all. I know that's easier said than done when our lives are at stake, but it's amazing what a little cognitive dissonance can do."

She swallowed. "How *have* you managed, all these years?"

"I didn't, at first," he said, his voice husky. "After Budapest, I was . . . well, frankly, it's a miracle I managed to get past the Fontaine Saint-Michel's guardian statue. I spent the first week of midnights getting shuttled around the salon by Jean. He taught me how to embrace the ephemeralness of this place, how to remember the beauty in my bones, if not my mind. That's the trick, you see: Focus on the light. The joie de vivre. The things that make life worth living."

"And when you're with Terreur?"

Rafe shook his head. "I try not to think of him here. I can't."

Céleste understood. "Then what do you think of?"

"A fresh set of pencils. My first sip of morning coffee. Cherry blossoms in the spring. Laughing with you . . ." He added this last item so quietly. "I've gathered more of my own imaginings since June than I did all those years prior. My magic's even stronger now than it was before the windmill burned."

She felt her own cheeks start to burn at this, flushing all the way up to the roots of her hair.

"Don't hold yourself back, *mon amour*." Rafe reached out and touched her brush hand. "Just start painting."

Céleste took a deep breath as the other artist stepped back.

She lifted her brush and started sketching fruit on the vines.

Garnet grapes.

No, that made her think too much of wine, so she turned them into stars instead. Small every-colored orbs of light that could be plucked and squeezed into a glass—oh! Céleste felt a gentle tug and watched as the songbird launched from her head, soaring into the bright orange sky. Beyond. Her thought streaked from its talons like a comet. Her hand tightened around her brush. The calluses were back—thanks to her days at La Ruche—and they had hours yet before dawn.

It wouldn't hurt to keep going.

She painted a flock of paper cranes that swirled past a winking moon. On the far hill, she called up a cathedral with windows that winked back. Rafe, meanwhile, was painting a train. It would have been an exact match for the Orient Express—if its carriages hadn't been crested with a circling fox. Gold as well.

Bits of the color remained on the brush as Rafe tucked it behind his ear. His shadow leapt onto the gleaming car with him, curling into one of the first-class seats, while the artist himself swung from the steps. One arm stretched toward Céleste.

"Care to join me for a ride?"

Again, she didn't think it would hurt. She tucked her own brush behind her ear and grasped his hand. "Where are we going?"

"We can go wherever we want—it's one of the perks of an imaginary landscape." A smile lit Rafe's face as he pulled her onto the steps. The train began gliding forward.

The edges of the grape leaves blurred, melting into each other. Rafe's body swayed with the car as he held Céleste close. She could feel the tautness of muscles through his garments. His bicep fit oh so well around her waist—the only thing between Céleste and the growing rush of the tracks. The engine kept picking up speed, but the other artist made no move to go inside.

The vineyards turned molten.

Rafe's eyes gleamed as he stared out at the fields. "I spent a lot of time studying travel posters as a young man, so I thought I knew what I was in for when I stole away on the Orient Express, but that second evening...well, there was this sunset." Fiery light washed over his face as he nodded at the horizon. "It was beyond incredible. It was wild. Too wild to capture—and I didn't have any of the paint colors, besides—so I put down my brush, and I stuck my head through the open window of the baggage car. There was this rush of wind, and for one moment, I became a part of the sky, and damn if I haven't been chasing that feeling ever since."

Wind whipped through Céleste's hair. She understood now why so many of La Fée Verte's early imaginers had been entranced by the idea of wings. "Flying?" she asked.

Rafe looked back down at her. "Freedom," he said.

She could see the painted tracks wavering ahead. Soon, very soon, these would come to an end, but she didn't want to think about that. She couldn't. No, instead of the mess, Céleste would choose to focus on the beauty. To be in this moment. Fully. She let herself fall with the next tilt of the train so that Rafe's chest met hers, and his arm tightened around her waist. His own *want* was thinly veiled by his trousers. It pressed into Céleste's navel, and she felt those familiar fires stir to life.

At La Ruche, she would've turned over on their mattress and bit her lip. Now there was no reason to hold herself back. There were no Enchantresses to impress and no dreams to steal. If Rafe was to be believed, their kissing would not be a distraction but a way to summon the shiniest parts of her own soul. Why stop herself? Why not stand on her tiptoes and press her lips to his?

Céleste could not think of an answer; she wasn't really thinking at all as she rose to kiss Rafe. This wasn't their first kiss. Hardly. That had happened in the windmill. Dozens upon dozens of others had followed—their lips meeting in secret gardens, flowers everywhere, hot and blooming—but none of them had felt quite like this.

This wasn't their first kiss, but it was their truest.

Raf[redacted]e[redacted] García and Céleste Artois.

Together.

At the edge of their world.

Rafe's braced arm was the only thing that kept Céleste from slipping off the steps. The ground rushed below her heels. Wind tugged at her skirts, but neither of these compared to the soaring sensation of his mouth on hers. It was as if she'd just discovered magic for the first time again—velvet curtains drawn back to shock and delight. Stopped in her tracks by the understanding that this was just the beginning. The beginning of something much, much bigger...

There was a jolt.

Rafe's lips parted from hers as the floor tilted beneath them. His arm tightened around her waist. When Céleste followed his gaze over her shoulder, she saw why. The painted tracks *had* ended, but instead of stopping, the locomotive kept climbing, over the spires of Céleste's cathedral, toward the fire-splashed sunset.

Into it.

Rafe let out a delighted laugh that reverberated in Céleste's own chest. She understood why: They were becoming a part of the sky. None of her short trips flying to the top of Notre-Dame compared to this. Neither did any of Paris's sunsets. How could they? Clouds prowled like jungle cats: orange, pink, purple—blazing. A shower of falling stars sparkled across the scene as well.

"Shit," she said, as reverently as she could. "I thought we'd wrecked."

Rafe shook his head, and there was a new burst of light, followed by a flurry of green feathers—oh! Those weren't meteors. They were the couple's imaginings brightening the sky.

"I told you, *mon amour*," he murmured. "We can go wherever we want."

The train kept climbing through the neon roar of clouds, so high that Céleste could no longer see the vineyards. The moon she'd painted had grown from the size of a thumbnail to a smile.

She was grinning too as she looked back at Rafe.

"I want you," she said.

The artist inhaled. His nicked brow quivered. "Are you sure?"

Rafe wasn't really asking about Céleste's desire, she knew. It was Terreur looming behind his words. But that bastard didn't belong here, so she nodded. Then she took the other artist's hand and led him into the dining car.

The tables were set to serve a first-class feast—but Céleste brushed the plates and goblets away. She ripped at the laces of her own corset. Rafe peeled off his shirt, letting it join the cloth napkins and their politest knives. He shoved these aside as he lifted Céleste to the table's edge, kissing her lips, her throat, while tracing her hips, her thighs, the burning parts between them. There were no secrets here, no need to be careful in this wild sky, so Céleste wrapped her arms around Rafe's neck and kissed him back, so long and so fiercely that she saw stars. There were stars behind her eyes—matching the brilliance of his touch *down there*—but she spotted actual stars too, floating just outside their closed carriage windows. Her lunar landscape hovered there, orbited by emerald birds unable to find their way inside the train. Rafe's hair was so threaded through with silver that she could hardly see its original color. Hers glowed too—more shooting stars on this side of the glass.

Rafe looked over his shoulder to see what had caused her pause.

"Ah." The artist didn't pull back the way he so often had before. Instead, his shadow rose from its seat and stretched so that the fox covered every one of the cabin windows. "Call me a prude, but I'd rather not be on display."

"Prude?" Céleste arched an eyebrow at him. "That's certainly not the word that comes to mind."

"A poor choice. To be fair, I'm hardly thinking with words at all." Rafe shifted so that his bare chest was over hers. So that his imaginings spilled around her face. Skin to skin. Dreams to dreams.

Céleste pulled him even closer.

He was *in* her.

Oh, the fullness. Her entire body flushed with it. Her skin felt like the sky on Bastille Day—bursting with colors and heat. She dug her fingers between Rafe's shoulder blades, where a pair of wings might go. Her hips rolled in time with his. He held her gaze with such intensity, such tenderness, that Céleste couldn't help but gasp. Then moan. Rafe bit his own lip at the sounds, then leaned back in to kiss her on the neck. She shut her eyes, focusing on the thrilling heat of him inside her, building and building. She took Rafe's lips, his hands, his hope, until every single one of her hairs shone, and Céleste was lost inside the light of it all.

No words.

Just stars,

stars,

stars.

Finally she landed back inside herself, and Rafe curled into her chest, his scars pressed into her page-pale skin.

They lay this way for as long as they dared.

Until the train began to slant down and stray silverware came clattering back toward them. Soup spoons and cheese knives and two loose fob chains belonging to a pocket watch. Céleste caught them both. Rafe sat up with a sigh.

"I don't want to go back to the Caveau," he murmured. "I— There's so much more to hide from him now."

She understood what he meant, especially after his fox fell away from the carriage windows. The night was nearly over. She could no longer see her moon, and their train was falling back through a thick mist, broken only by La Fée Verte's birds. Her fist tightened over Rafe's pocket watch—tempted to squeeze out an extra hour. Céleste knew that as soon as she stepped off this train, the birds would hold up her end of the bargain, flocking to her head like it was a wheat field.

She knew too that her dreams were worth something.

They had to be if she already missed them.

"We've come this far." Though the thought of Rafe's windmill burned even more now. Along with the memory of [redacted] pulling it out of her head. "Besides, you told me Terreur isn't omniscient, remember? He only scents our fear. If we just keep thinking about how much we want to survive, that's the only thing he'll see." Besides, it's like she told Sylvie: "The best lies are rooted in truth."

Rafe's ink-drop tear crinkled as he pulled his shirt back over his head. "I prefer the Latin version."

In somnis veritas.

"It *is* more poetic."

Instead of winding the pocket watch, Céleste flipped it open: *8:45*, the hands read. Still. They stayed that way, even after she handed the timepiece to Rafe. Their fateful hour hadn't changed—even after all this.

There were no more dreams growing from Céleste's head as she walked down rue des Ombres—strangers' ideas rattled inside her pockets instead. She focused on darker thoughts as she approached Terreur's door. *It's like the stardust trick, but opposite.*

That had been Rafe's advice, all those mornings ago. She could tell the other thief was trying to heed it by how stiffly he moved beside her, how silent he'd been on the taxi ride here. His fear was thick. Real. The same as Céleste's. Conjuring the feeling was easy enough. The real trick was reining it in so that their employer wouldn't follow the threads and catch wind of the Enchantresses' plan. So Sylvie and Honoré wouldn't get tangled in his web any more than they already were. Céleste's pulse fluttered like the day-dreamer's butterfly wings. Her heart felt sticky. *This is just another costume change*, she told herself. Just like slipping on an opera glove or a mourning veil. Just like pinching her skin to summon tears. *Believe yourself and he'll believe you.*

Be the taker or be taken.

Céleste's motto turned into a mantra, circling through her head over and over again as she turned the door's knob. It opened to Caveau des Terreurs. She saw the space with new eyes, not just because it was a glimpse into Honoré's past, but because it might hold hints of their fate as well. Was her employer's heart tucked away in the piano? Was it one of the flies alighting on the sticky bar top? The barmaid wasn't there to wipe it down or to greet Rafe like a stranger.

Terreur was pouring his own drinks.

Red wine.

If it was wine...

Rafe paused. "Where is Eleanor?"

"Gone." Terreur snapped his fingers, and the decanter tipped itself over his empty glass. "She proved difficult to work with, so I no longer require her services."

What's the opposite of stardust? Céleste wondered. *Rust? Iron? The smell that's swimming from that wine glass?*

"What about you?" their employer asked. "Have you brought me my dream?"

Rafe had to be smelling the same scent, but his nose didn't wrinkle. The rest of his face remained stony as he set several ideas on the bar. None showed Paris, of course. In exchange for the power La Fée Verte's birds had harvested after their train ride, the Sanct had given them a smattering of imaginings—seahorses with saddles and that sort of thing. Images that made Terreur twist his lips. This expression didn't shift with Céleste's offerings, but he did push his drink toward her.

"For your trouble," said Terreur.

Céleste's stomach sloshed too.

Her lungs were fine—she wasn't due to visit the Mad Monk for another few days. So what was this? A test? Was he suspicious? He would be if she kept sitting here, staring into the drink, trying not to see its oily sheen, the way ghastly images floated across the top. She recognized the barmaid. What was her name? Eleanor? The young woman's life flashed before Céleste's eyes: Mud-pies served to dolls and kisses wrangled from boys in back alleys. The same alleys she used for target practice. Throwing darts and knives and bottles. *Just in case.* The second-to-last bottle smashed past Honoré's feet. The final one on her friend's dragon armor. She'd wanted to scream when those silver wings spread to fly away, but her jaw would not move, and her throat kept getting tighter, tighter, tighter, and—

"Is something the matter?" their employer asked.

Céleste's hand tightened around the glass's stem. She'd done this before, she reminded herself. [redacted] had served her La Belle's blood after *The Rite of Spring*. Eleanor herself had poured that *special reserve* at this very bar. It was harder to swallow, now that Céleste knew what it cost to keep her alive.

Or, rather, *who*.

"Is this not rich enough for your taste?" the Sanct wondered. "You have been spoiled, I suppose. I usually save royalty for special occasions."

It was hard not to think about Sylvie's story—of the tsarevitch in his playroom. The boy's blood didn't truly vanish when Grigori Rasputin "healed" him, she realized. It was just transfused to the

Mad Monk's masque. And then to Céleste. All under the guise of prayers...

Mon Dieu.

She focused in on her own prayer then: *Be the taker or be taken.* She brought the goblet to her lips. The taste—ugh—was like horseshoes, but she forced herself to keep drinking. Down, down. Until there was no longer a ghost in the glass.

Céleste slid the drained cup back toward Terreur. "I want more."

The Sanct arched his eyebrow and reached for the decanter.

"I want more than days," she went on, before he could pour a second serving. "I want to become like you."

It was her employer's turn to pause, his hand clenching the glass neck. "Monsieur García has told you about my heart, I see."

Rafe stayed very still at the end of the bar, staring at the sandy floor, just as he'd gazed into the garden pool. Céleste focused her own eyes on Terreur's—their thirsty blue. He didn't seem to be staring at her hair or any memories lurking beneath their surface. He didn't *really* see...

Yet.

"He told me about hermits who live forever in mountain caves and pharaohs who locked pieces of themselves into pyramids. If there are eternities to be claimed, then why should I settle for days? I want more."

Terreur smiled then.

His lips were a terrible red. Hers were a perfect match, according to the mirror behind the bar. It looked almost like rouge—another piece of costume. She hated how damn convincing it was, how Rafe still couldn't bear to look in her direction.

"Leave us, Monsieur García. We don't need your bleeding heart here."

It was hard to tell if Terreur's words were a command or a spell—there were so many extra shadows in the Caveau that Rafe almost had to wade through them to reach the exit. The door shut and locked behind him, becoming a storage closet once more. "I'm surprised Monsieur García spoke of such things...he's never shown much interest in following my footsteps."

"He's a wanderer," Céleste said.

"A wonderer too. He believes La Fée Verte's magic is better than mine."

"Prettier, perhaps. All smoke and mirrors and vines, but I want something that lasts past sunrise. Something more potent." She made a show of licking her bloodied lips. "Could you show me how to become immortal?"

"If you were willing to go that far," the Sanct said. "Few are. Even the Mad Monk hasn't been able to bring himself to remove his heart, though he's come up with an inventive substitution system. Tell me... about your arrangement with Monsieur García... Do you really love him?"

The question caught her off guard.

"No." Céleste wasn't quite sure if she was telling the truth. Wanting to kiss someone was not love, nor was sharing their bed, nor feeling fireworks at their touch. Love was... well, it was the sort of thing that kept Sylvie turning the pages of whatever story she was reading. The girl was always so determined to see whether or not the characters would ride off together into the sunset.

Ah shit.

Terreur's eyes narrowed. "He's grown attached to you, I think," her employer said. "His heart is too soft. It snagged when he saw your bloody glove after *The Rite of Spring*—so I doubt he could remove it without dying. The spell I performed requires you to sever yourself from everything, leaving not even a string... That way no one can break your heart." There was something strange in his voice—beyond its coldness and rust. "Nothing can touch you because you have nothing to lose."

"How did you cut it out?" She glanced at the top buttons of his shirt. There were no scars peeking through. But why would there be if he had the power to erase them all? "Did you use a knife?"

"A comb."

"For... hair?"

"It was symbolic."

"Did it hurt?"

"Nothing hurts anymore." His voice kept stretching into some unknown distance. Silence followed, until Terreur looked back at the dreams at the bar's end. "But if you want more of my power, you're going to have to earn it, Mademoiselle Artois. Find me my lost dream, and I'll show you the way to life everlasting."

A curt dismissal.

Céleste had gone as far as she could, so she rose from her stool and went to the door behind the bar. Usually, when she twisted the knob, the lock shifted back to the rue des Ombres. Not this morning. This morning she stepped into darkness. No cobblestones. Something softer. No sunrise at the end. Merely a wall papered with the remains of an Orient Express poster, aged to the point that Constantinople's spires no longer shone gold.

The body at Céleste's feet looked brittle too.

Fingers snapped like straw beneath her boot as she flinched away. *Eleanor.* It bore no resemblance to the barmaid, but somehow Céleste knew this was her skeletal husk. She felt this truth in her own bones. She bit her lip until their blood mixed, forcing her thoughts back to straw and gold, straw and gold. The story of the miller's daughter and the king who would have killed her at dawn, if she failed her impossible task. The young woman had survived—not by dreaming but by making a deal with a demon, who then came, many years later, to claim what was his.

A bleak ending.

Or rather, it would have been, if the miller's daughter had been less cunning.

Chapter 26

The Point of No Return

Once upon a time, an orphan, a princess, a knight, and a tomcat broke into an opera house...

This time, the lock was small enough for a hairpin. Sylvie still had a few on hand as she stood outside the Palais Garnier. She'd always thought it funny that some Parisians called this building a grand wedding cake, but as she broke open its doors and stepped inside, she could see why: Layers upon layers of marble. Tiers of gold. Even the air tasted sweet, blooming with dozens of perfumes left over from audience members who'd gone their separate ways hours before. It was well past midnight, and aside from Honoré, there was no one to stop the two girls from running up the vestibule's grand staircase and sliding down its polished bannister.

Well, there were the statues.

A pair of women stood at the bottom; the lamps in their arms were switched off, but Sylvie could still feel sparks inside them. It was the same with the metal salamander curled at the bottom of the column. Sylvie knew now that she could wake the sculptures if she wanted. She could make them sing or stand guard or spill secrets...

"Anastasia!"

The grand duchess paused at the top of the stairs—a strange sight in her nightgown and magical fur coat. "Yes?"

"Do you want to practice another spell?"

Sylvie and Russia's youngest princess had been meeting every night over the past week to do just that. They unlocked the pink door and stepped into each other's worlds. Paris, mostly. Their very first night had been spent on top of the Eiffel Tower, eating cloud crème éclairs while Sylvie pointed out the electric-lamp constellations that made up her city.

"Montmartre is that way! You can borrow wings from one of its cabarets. Oh, and down there in the Seine is a floating island where a magical carnival used to be. The carousel horses run wild now. They like to eat the silver-skinned apples that grow in the corner of the Jardin du Luxembourg over there." She noticed something strange as her finger traced over certain arrondissements. The Champs-Élysées did not look as bright as it should, even though the neighborhood's lamps were lit. Belleville—on the distant horizon—was even darker.

Sylvie skipped these explanations.

"What happened to the carnival?" Anastasia asked, through a hefty bite of cloud crème. It was a good thing they'd knotted their gowns to the Eiffel Tower's iron, or the princess would have drifted away.

"Well..." Sylvie's answer drifted too. She wasn't quite sure. It didn't make sense—why La Fée Verte had so easily abandoned her old dream of sharing magic. What would Paris look like if she'd kept on creating daydreamers after she banished the evil sorcerer?

This was their chance to find out. For seven midnights in a row, the two girls had wandered the city, sharpening their imaginations. Double-headed firebirds flew around cathedral towers and accidentally melted the feathers of Stohrer's chocolate swallows. Anastasia was getting better at pulling ideas from her head, although the princess almost always broke hers, for the delight of watching them swirl to life. Glass snowflakes and rainbow parrots and even larger things that would not fit through the door back to Russia. It was just as well. None of these dreams disappeared at dawn, so it was better if they didn't go swirling around Rasputin's territory. Sylvie could manage the princess's imaginings in Paris.

She managed most of their bigger magic too, spells Anastasia was all too willing to practice with her. "I think we can make these statues wake up!"

"Why?" Honoré had finished scanning the perimeter and was eyeing the torch-bearing women warily.

The grand duchess skipped down the steps to join them. "Why not?"

"They could attack us," the other Enchantress pointed out. "Or they could turn on their lamps and alert someone that we're here—"

"Or," Sylvie said, "they could give us some clues about where to find the treasure."

A snort from Honoré. "I'd hardly call the disembodied heart of an evil sorcerer a treasure."

It could *be made of gold*, Marmalade added as he sniffed the salamander statue. *That's what King Tutankhamun entombed. But it could just as easily be a ball of yarn. Or a mouse.*

"A mouse?" Sylvie squirmed.

I love mice.

"What is he going on about?" wondered Honoré.

"The shape of a heart," answered Sylvie.

"It's like this, right?" Anastasia traced a Valentine's Day heart through the air, her fingers kissing.

"Real hearts don't look like cupid's ass," Honoré said, as she rolled her eyes. "They're meatier."

"What about magical hearts?" the princess retorted.

They're mostly made of what you love, Marmalade meowed.

Sylvie wasn't sure that helped their search much—from what Céleste had told them, it seemed Terreur didn't love anything at all. He'd cut off every attachment. Had it happened here at the Palais Garnier? According to the memories La Fée Verte had shared, this was where the Sanct's path had veered off into darker magic. His point of no return. When Sylvie had studied her charred map of Paris, it had seemed like the most sensible place to start searching.

But once again, things appeared different in person. Standing here, Sylvie was struck with the true scope of their mission. The opera house was huge—mosaic ceilings, chandeliers dripping with crystal, staircases sweeping up and down. One building could take *years* to search, if they didn't have any solid leads.

"Maybe the statues can tell us more." Sylvie turned back to the torch-bearers balancing on the right bannister.

She reached out, both with her hand—joining Anastasia's palm—and with her...well, she didn't know what to call the force she felt rising in her chest. Anima, perhaps? It poured out like light. It caught the sliver of energy she felt inside the sculptures, and the lamps in the women's hands began to flicker.

"Oh!" Sylvie pulled back. Honoré was right—they didn't want to attract attention. She wasn't worried so much about stray sopranos or managers, but if Terreur somehow found out they were searching... "Not so bright, please!"

The lights dimmed.

The statues began to blink.

Anastasia's hand tightened in Sylvie's. "They're alive!"

It did look that way. The sculpture of the lower woman shifted, and the salamander scuttled around the column. (Much to Marmalade's delight.) Sylvie was happy too. She'd tried the spell several times before on the lobster who graced the Portal of the Virgin, but this was the first time she'd managed to make a carving move.

"Um, hello!"

Both bronze women tilted their heads. It seemed she hadn't given them quite enough life to speak, the way Notre-Dame's gargoyles sometimes did.

"There used to be a Sanct who lived here, about thirty years ago. Do you remember him?"

The salamander suddenly curled in on itself.

Glass lamps shuddered in the women's hands.

Sylvie took this as a yes.

"We...we're trying to find his heart," she explained. "Would you happen to know where it is?"

One of the statues shook her head, but the other woman raised her lampless arm and pointed. Up.

The heart hunters climbed the stairs and paused, taking in the vestibule from a slightly higher angle. Sylvie's initial excitement faded as she looked around the landing. The statues below had shifted back to their original pose—of course, it couldn't be as easy as that.

"See anything?" Honoré asked.

"There's a cupid's rear end." Anastasia pointed to two small cherubs hovering above the entrance to the auditorium.

The other Enchantress let out another exasperated snort, but there was a hint of admiration in her words. "You're quite precocious for a princess, you know."

"Not really," the grand duchess told her. "You should meet my older sister Olga. She's cheeky too! But I guess most people see us the way they view hearts: Too sweet. No meat!"

This got a full-blown laugh from Honoré.

A rare sound. So rare, it startled Sylvie. The cherubs over the auditorium entrance jumped at the same time she did, and as she walked closer, the statues started jabbing their chubby fingers down at the door.

Beyond this was overwhelming darkness, until Anastasia pulled a firebird from her head and sent it soaring around the theatre's seven-ton chandelier—flaming wings gleaming against an abundance of gold. Sylvie imagined scores of fireflies to join in. These twinkled over the seats. A few even formed a halo over Honoré's head as she strolled down the aisle. She moved the way she always did in theatres—on the prowl.

"I don't think Terreur left his heart lying under a seat," Sylvie said, as the other Enchantress scoped out the premises.

"Maybe it *is* a seat!" Anastasia chimed in.

"Céleste said he cut his heart out so he could be untouchable," Honoré said, "not so people could sit on it every evening listening to women who try their best to sound like dying cats—" This got a hiss from Marmalade. "Fine. Angry teakettles."

"I like the opera!" Anastasia twirled in the aisle. Far above, her firebird did the same. "It's the perfect place to eat chocolates—you don't even have to wash your hands afterward because you're wearing gloves! Mama always fusses about it, but Papa doesn't mind. He even sneaks me treats sometimes."

"See, Honoré? The tsar of Russia thinks it's fine to eat sugar!"

"An emperor can afford new teeth," Honoré replied wryly.

"So can we!" There was all that La Banque d'Ossements gold they never spent, but also... "We could just wish new teeth back in if they fell out!"

The other Enchantress's jaw clenched. "That's not how magic works."

"Sure it is," Sylvie said, flapping her butterfly wings. "Remember that leopard's tail I gave you a few weeks ago? And Monsieur Cocteau's ram horns?"

"Those are... accessories. Teeth are different." Honoré sounded hesitant. "You can't just *wish* yourself better, Sylvie."

"You have to pray," Anastasia told them cheerfully. "And use saints! 'Our Friend' put up a whole wall of icons over Alexei's bed to guard his soul."

Sylvie looked up and saw more angels carved into the ceiling's corners, their meaty fingers holding trumpets instead of torches. These pointed toward the stage, past the painted trompe l'oeil curtains, which did not stir. Still, she felt a shudder in her chest that made her want to change the subject.

"My heart would be a stack of good books," she said as they made their way backstage. "Or flying through a midnight sky. Or biting into a warm croissant. Or opening a can of pâté for Marmalade. Or palming the perfect diamond. Or making up stories with Céleste." *Or seeing Honoré smile at the green birds perched on her shoulder. Or watching La Fée Verte shine a bit brighter every time her knight walks into the room.* Sylvie didn't say these last lines aloud, but they still counted.

"What about your parents?" the princess asked.

"Honoré is my mother," teased Sylvie. That was another thing she loved—making the other Enchantress's eyes roll. It never got old.

"Really?"

"I'm her *guardian*." Honoré put an undue emphasis on the word. "We're both orphans."

The princess's lips pinched, as if trying to take back the words they'd already said. "I'm sorry. That—that would be awful. I don't know what I would do without my family. They're my heart... Snowball fights with my sisters. Long summer days on the *Standart*, running barefoot on the deck and pretending there are pirates in the distance to entertain Alexei. Oh, and reading aloud with Papa in the evenings. I love Mama too, of course, but she gets so wrapped up in worrying about my brother..."

Sylvie's turn to swallow. They were in a less gilded section of the opera house now, a space filled with levers and ropes and trapdoors. It was hard to know where to go, even with their dreams lighting the way.

"What about you, Honoré?" she asked.

Shadows from the ropes crossed over the other Enchantress's face as the Romanov's firebird flew through them. "Mine would be made of Camembert," she said.

After a bit more wandering backstage, they came across some fauns—painted with panpipes against a background of spring hills—who guided the heart hunters through the Foyer de la Danse to the dressing room of a star soprano. It was clear the door hadn't been opened in years. Long enough for patina to eat away at CHR[redacted]TINE LEROUX's placard. Long enough for a fine layer of gray dust to cover every inch of the space inside. Nothing had been disturbed in decades. Pots of makeup still sat on the vanity—along with a crown that must have been a part of Mademoiselle Leroux's costume. Faded dresses were tossed over a washed-out couch. A bouquet of long-dead flowers had been placed not in a vase but in a wastebasket.

"There's no cheese heart here," Anastasia announced. Her firebird perched on her shoulder as she began rifling through jars of rouge that now looked like the bottom of a dried-up lake bed. "But that's probably good, given the state of things."

"Some cheese gets better with age," Honoré said as she walked around the room.

"And stinkier," added Sylvie. She was inclined to agree with Anastasia. Nothing here looked much like an evil sorcerer's heart.

A piece of art did catch her eye: A framed charcoal drawing of Mademoiselle Leroux herself. Onstage. Midnote. As Sylvie studied the woman's pose, the soprano stopped singing and pointed toward the dressing room's mirror. It was large, stretching from ceiling to floor.

It was also enchanted.

Sylvie could tell because she did not see herself in the reflection. She also knew due to the fact the room looked brighter inside the glass: its furniture and wallpaper, those gowns, even the trashed roses. They still had their petals, blooms that shifted from white to pink to red to black. Mademoiselle Leroux did not spare them a glance as she burst through the door. She was in costume—wearing a headdress of crystal-studded stars, her eyes lined with thick kohl. The makeup must have been applied carefully, but it was streaming down the prima donna's cheeks, her tears falling as loosely as her black hair. The look in the woman's eyes was pure panic. Her hands kept fluttering to her throat. Her mouth kept opening. Choking.

"Oh..." Anastasia set down the perfume bottle with a thud. "What's wrong with her?"

Not *what*, Sylvie knew.

Who.

Mademoiselle Leroux's hair didn't move the way it should when the opera singer bent over her vanity. Long black strands tugged toward the open door. The soprano's hands scattered through her costume jewels. She grabbed a comb topped with an opal crescent moon, but instead of brushing her unruly mane, she palmed the piece. Sharp silver teeth jutted through her knuckles. Tears kept blackening her cheeks. Her hair kept pulling away.

Sylvie felt her own hairs stand on end when the hungry man appeared.

He looked different—more man than hunger, back then. All the same, he didn't bother knocking. He didn't stop when the prima donna tried to shake her head, only jerked the dark strings between them, causing Mademoiselle Leroux's entire body to go stiff, stiff enough that the silver comb started to stab her hand. Even so, she did not drop it.

The Sanct paused when he saw the roses blooming in the wastebasket.

Mademoiselle Leroux struck.

Her comb raked his cheek, drawing a few lines of blood. Fury. The hungry man's lips curled back, and Sylvie thought again of how he must swallow stars as the soprano's headdress disappeared in a swarm of darkness. The crescent-moon comb dropped to the carpet, and the Sanct leaned in, as close as a kiss, only he wasn't so tender. His mouth was unhinged. His—

"Enough!"

The mirror cracked under Honoré's dragon fist. Sylvie wasn't sure if her friend meant to hit so hard—but she had—and now all the heart hunters could see were their own fragmented faces.

"But..." Anastasia kept staring at the glass, her cheeks pale. "What happened to her?"

"You're better off not seeing." Honoré's voice softened, but her silvered hand was still gripping the mirror's edge, choking off its enchantments. "Trust me."

"I *have* seen strings like that before." The firebird on the grand duchess's shoulder flickered. Her voice did too. "They're all around my mother."

Sylvie bit her lip. She wasn't sure exactly what Rasputin was doing to the Russian royal family, but it was clear to her that the Mad Monk's magic wasn't good, even if he did heal Alexei's wounds. She supposed it was only a matter of time before Anastasia understood this, but she'd wanted to find some good news to share with the princess first. A happy ending instead of a heartless dead end...

A moan filled the dressing room, and wind ripped flames out of the firebird's wings. The imagining vanished into smoke, but a breeze kept blowing through the broken glass.

Sylvie realized what this meant: "There's something on the other side of the mirror!"

Shards fell to the dusty carpet as Honoré shoved the glass aside, revealing a passageway with a corkscrew staircase. There were no gilded cherubs on the walls, but the charcoal drawing of Mademoiselle Leroux kept on pointing down into darkness.

The heart hunters did not get much farther that night. The secret staircase ended in the deepest bowels of the opera house, at the edge of an underground lake. Marmalade had made quite a show of climbing onto Honoré's shoulders to keep away from the water. Sylvie didn't blame him. Even if she *could* swim to the tunnel on the other side, she didn't think it was wise to touch the water. The surface of the cistern was smooth, but she kept expecting to see scales. Or fins. Or worse.

"We could fly." Her voice dipped beneath the low arched ceilings. "Or conjure a boat."

Yet Anastasia didn't look up to imagining much of anything. She hadn't even managed another firebird—though that probably wouldn't have done much good, with how damp the air was here. The grand duchess was shivering. The fur on her coat grew an extra inch, but she didn't look any warmer.

"I want to go home," she said.

"Our treasure could be just around the corner," Sylvie protested.

That's not a corner. Marmalade gave a prickly growl. *It's an entrance to the catacombs. I smell death on the other side.*

Now it was Sylvie's turn to shiver.

Honoré frowned. "What's Marmalade saying?"

Lots and lots of death, the tomcat added.

Sylvie glanced back at the grand duchess and her chattering teeth. "He says he enjoys being your scarf."

Honoré's eyes narrowed, and Sylvie suddenly got the feeling that the other Enchantress knew more cat-speak than she let on. "I think the princess is right—we've gone far and it's late. Let's get her back to Russia before some maid finds an empty bed and her parents start a war."

So they made their way back to the pink door on rue de la Réunion. Anastasia looked a little less peaky as she stepped into the

Children's Palace and shrugged off her coat to hang in one of the many failed-portals-turned-closets. A miniature sloth crawled up to nest in one of the pockets. Rock-hard gumdrops littered the floor below; a naval frigate teetered on top of the growing mound. Sylvie was fairly sure the candy *would* crack a tooth at this point.

The door was locked shut, but not before a tin soldier tottered through.

Marmalade caught the toy gingerly between his teeth and dropped it at Honoré's feet. A much better friendship offering than a rotting mouse carcass, though one couldn't tell by the way the Enchantress stared at the metallic man.

"Listen, *ma rêveuse*, I know you like being friends with a princess, but I don't think it's a good idea to keep Anastasia Enlightened."

"It *is* a good idea!" Sylvie protested. "It's dozens of good ideas!"

Honoré kept turning the tin soldier, over and over, in her silver palm.

"Her magic helps mine! If we hadn't animated those statues together, we wouldn't have found that magical mirror—"

"Exactly," the other Enchantress cut in. "You're letting her see too much, Sylvie. Do you know what it's like watching your family be bound up with dark magic? To watch your brother held captive—" Her dragon fist closed over the tin soldier, too tight.

There was a crunching sound.

Tears stung Sylvie's eyes. She wasn't sure if it was from shame or because of the slap behind Honoré's question. *Do you know what it's like watching* your family*?*

She didn't.

And she did.

Sylvie didn't need an enchanted mirror to see that Céleste was in danger or that Honoré was afraid. "Erasing Anastasia's memory won't help Alexei either," she reasoned. "I know that magic can't fix everything, but *nothing* will get better if we're too scared to believe in it." She thought again of Île du Carnaval, with its overgrown tents. Of the wishing well gone dry. Of how many imaginings burned to dust under the morning sun. "We have to stay awake. We have to keep dreaming."

Into the Tunnels

Everything speaks if you know how to listen.

Even the dead.

Most people know this, even if they do not believe it. It's why they fall quiet when they walk past a churchyard. It is why they choose to hear the rush of their own blood in their ears or the tumble of leaves over a gravestone. It is why they read epitaphs with the same held-breath care as a Ouija board—why they take comfort in the distant dates. Yet, if you stop long enough and look at the numbers, you might feel your pocket watch ticking against your chest, urging you to hurry on to your next appointment: *Go, go, go, don't think too hard about what is to come!*

But perhaps you are not afraid.

Perhaps you are one of those people who pause at the smell of cool forgotten earth, who follow the call of the underworld down spiral staircases, where stones drip and skulls line the walls. Their epitaph is different from the rest: STOP! THIS IS THE EMPIRE OF DEATH.

You halt.

The lantern you lit with your many-colored matches sputters. You feel the breadth of these tunnels—their depth—as your own breath echoes. (Out. Out. The darkness sucks it back in.) You wonder why the bones are stacked just so: What was the mining engineer thinking when he shaped several heads into a heart? Was it a cruel joke? Some commentary on love outlasting death? Or could it mean something more?

If you stand in front of these skulls long enough, they might tell you.

You might hear about the rise and fall of Maximilien François Marie Isadore de Robespierre, who cut off many of the heads that now surround his own. *Vive la Révolution! Vive Monsieur Robespierre!* Neither of these lasted as long as the Sanct himself wanted. And, oh, how he wanted. Justice, at first. Power, next. Then more, then more, then more—the pull of blood as it sluiced from Madame Guillotine was too tempting. He went too far. He got too close. He lost everything. His heart, his jawbone, and even his teeth.

Or you might hear the story of the man who wrenched them out, one by one.

He dug the Sanct's secrets from his skull using a hair comb—of all things—even though the piece was purely decorative. There was an opal moon at the top, they say, much the same color as the flame in your lantern.

Chapter 27

Beware the Serpents

The mirror in Christine Leroux's dressing room was shattered.

But not beyond repair.

Honoré Côte stared into the cracks, surprised at the reflection they webbed. She hardly recognized herself. The short blonde hair and high cheekbones hadn't changed all that drastically since her visit two evenings ago. *It must be the lighting*... The soft golden glow of La Fée Verte's masque did wonders. Actual wonders. The Sanct had agreed to accompany Honoré to the opera house to resurrect the mirror's memory. There could be clues inside the glass, waiting to be pieced back together.

La Fée Verte stood in front of the secret passage, studying the tilted reflection next to it. "You say you punched the mirror?"

Honoré's eyes narrowed on a particularly jagged piece of glass. It sat at an angle that caught her ring arm—where silver ran up her wrist like streaks of sepsis. Yes, technically that hand had struck the mirror, but Honoré wasn't entirely sure that *she* had done it. She hadn't meant to shatter the glass—same as she hadn't intended to bite Céleste or crush the stray tin soldier. Her dragon ring had acted on a deeper instinct. A different memory. One where it was her mother's head shaking. Her father's shadow looming.

"My dragon hit the glass," she said finally. "I didn't want Sylvie and Anastasia to see Mademoiselle Leroux getting husked."

La Fée Verte did not look too thrilled at the prospect either. Her wings hugged her shoulders as she reached out and touched the mirror. There was a swelling glow. The cracks vanished, and the Sanct stepped back, close enough for her feathers to tickle Honoré's elbows. For one bright moment, she could see the two of them—side by side—and then the mirror's magic took hold.

An opera singer dressed in stars ran in to the room's reflection.

Darkness followed.

La Fée Verte flinched at the sight of him, leaning even closer to Honoré. She thought about wrapping her dragon arm around the other woman's shoulder—if only to keep herself from breaking the spell again. She had to watch Mademoiselle Leroux's fate to the end. It was not pretty. It wasn't quick. After the soprano's strike with the comb, the sorcerer's rage was like a swarm of locusts. His masque bled into her shadow, knotting and pulling. He made Christine Leroux drop the comb and fall on her knees. He tilted her face to his and opened his mouth—more of a snarl than a kiss. The dark clouds connecting them pulsed as he loomed over her.

As he *took* her.

She was his first husk... The difference between the opera singer's death and La Belle's made this painfully clear. Honoré had been horrified by that murder, but this was far worse. It was primal. The sorcerer even used his teeth. Every time he bit her bottom lip or the soft flesh of her neck, the surrounding shadows grew thicker. Christine—she must have been terrified, but there was no trace of it on her face. What glimpses Honoré got through the writhing black showed a blank expression. Then blanker. Then nothing at all. Even before her flesh began to wither, Mademoiselle Leroux was gone.

The sorcerer sat with the opera singer's body for a long while, cradling it in a way that made Honoré incredibly sick. His mouth and throat were a mess of red, but it was still possible to see the bleed of comb marks down his cheek. Patterned like tears.

Had he meant to kill her?

There was something about the scene that made Honoré wonder. She wondered if it was at all like the evening Maman died, when Lucien Durand had been a little too drunk, a little too loose with his hits, a little too close to the hearth. Or if it was more like the night he'd tried to beat his daughter instead, the night Fear's Bastard decided to bare her own teeth.

Not that any of that really mattered to Christine Leroux. The killer slung her desiccated body over his shoulder, then paused by the vanity to grab a wooden jewelry box before disappearing behind the mirror.

"I knew Christine." La Fée Verte sounded as broken as the glass she'd just fixed. "She came to my carnival quite often. She loved eating fairy floss. She dreamed of singing lullabies to her future children, but she told me she had terrible luck with suitors..."

No shit.

Honoré glanced back at the mirror. "How can you remember those things if he husked her?"

"My guess is that he hadn't learned how to gut a soul very thoroughly," La Fée Verte lamented. "He didn't touch Christine's memories. Nor did he know how to devour names. I taught him that nearly a year later."

So what did he do in the meantime? Honoré's eyes drifted toward the secret passage. She didn't exactly relish the thought of going back down to that underground lake and exploring the tunnels beyond, but there was no denying the possibility that the sorcerer had carved out his heart down there. Perhaps he'd even buried it with the rest of the catacombs' dead...

"If only I'd blinded him at the beginning." La Fée Verte was still watching the empty glass. The imprint of Christine's body marked the spot where the pair of them stood. Honoré couldn't see those marks on the carpet anymore. There weren't even bloodstains. Odd, considering how much the dark Sanct had spilled. "If I'd made him forget magic, then Christine would be singing songs to her *grand*children now. Instead, he stole her voice and butchered her beautiful anima and—"

"This isn't your fault, Verte." Honoré held up a hand. She meant to grab the Sanct's shoulder, but a green wing was there, so her fingers slid down to the delicate skin of La Fée Verte's inner elbow. It felt as soft as it looked. "Men like that... it's not magic that makes them awful."

"Men like that should stay men," La Fée Verte said. "I showed him how to become a god."

"You showed him beauty and art and hope," Honoré told her firmly. "You showed him how to grow wings, not cut out hearts."

The Sanct pinched her lips, her wings drawing even closer against her shoulders. "Perhaps, but... I'm afraid, Honoré." She kept watching the mirror, even as their reflections started rising back into it. The knight and the lady. There was a strange transitional moment—when Honoré thought she could see their devil again too, looming in the door behind them. "I've not felt fear like this in a very long time."

It took everything Honoré had not to look over her shoulder. She chose to focus on La Fée Verte's glowing face instead. "Can I tell you a secret?" She felt the Sanct's pulse pick up at the question, thrumming through her inner elbow. "Everyone is afraid, even the brave. Especially them." Honoré could feel her own heart beating madly. "I know it took a lot of courage for you to trust Céleste and Rafael, after what they did. I know that you did it for my sake. I know..."

La Fée Verte looked away from the mirror, her eyes meeting Honoré's. It was like staring straight into the sun—she knew because she'd done so several times at dawn, searching for that elusive flash of green that sometimes happened just before the orange orb rose over the Seine. *There's magic in that moment*, the other woman had told her.

Never mind that every moment with La Fée Verte felt magical.

Especially this one.

"What do you know, my dame?" she whispered.

I know that you are everything beautiful and I am everything sharp, and I never realized those two things could fit so well together, before I met you. I never thought I could hope for someone like this...

Honoré wanted to say these things, but she wasn't even sure *she* was that brave yet. So she broke the spell, letting her fingers fall from La Fée Verte's arm. "I know he won't win. Tonight I'll go down into the catacombs to search for more clues. I'm going to find that bastard's heart if it's the last thing I do."

La Fée Verte caught her hand, squeezing the fingers tightly. "Be careful, Honoré. The magical tunnels can be especially treacherous."

So can I.

Honoré was glad it wasn't her dragon hand the Sanct held. She could feel the whole warmth of her companion's hand. "I will, Verte. I promise."

When Honoré was a child, she'd heard whispers of the catacombs. Not just the stacks of bones that had been hauled from a failing cemetery nearly a century before and rearranged into pieces that would make a puzzle master envious, but the wider system of tunnels. The city under the city. It wound on for hundreds of miles, snaking under the Luxembourg gardens and reaching out under the Louvre, braiding all the way through the southern arrondissements. If you found one of its hidden entrances—at the bottom of a cistern or the roots of a church—an entire underworld opened up. Several old quarries that had been turned into mushroom farms and then into crypts. Passages that had once hidden Belleville's Communards. Fountains. Wells. Halls. Galleries. It was tempting to go deeper, ever deeper, but there was a reason Honoré's father had never let his Apaches follow the footsteps of their more rebellious ancestors.

It was too easy to get lost.

Honoré could see why—mostly thanks to a miniature moon Sylvie had conjured on her behalf, when she'd gone back to the salon to prepare for the underground excursion. The youngest Enchantress offered her a croissant as well.

"I should be back before breakfast," Honoré told her.

"It's not for eating!" That was a first, coming from Sylvie. "Well, not immediately. Have you ever heard the story of *Hänsel und Gretel*? It's about a brother and sister who get sent into the woods to starve. Hansel, the brother, takes a stale loaf of bread to mark their trail so they can find their path home." The girl took a giant bite of the pastry before handing it over. More flaky dough appeared, filling in the marks left by her teeth. "You can use this to do the same!

Marmalade wanted me to conjure you a ball of endless yarn instead, but this way you *will* have a snack on the way back."

"That's... smart," Honoré had said. "Good thinking, Sylvie."

"It was Anastasia's idea, actually."

Sylvie was still meeting the grand duchess at their door every evening. *We have to keep dreaming*, she'd said. How could Honoré argue with that, when she wore some of the girls' imaginings like knives?

She couldn't really argue with Marmalade either. The tomcat had followed her here on Sylvie's orders, down the secret passage's stairs, to the edge of the underground lake. Over it. Honoré folded her dragon's wings back into the ring as she studied the passage on the opposite side. The stolen jewelry box was not sitting just around the corner. Honoré hadn't been expecting it—at least not with the same unwavering optimism as Sylvie—but she found herself disappointed all the same. The tunnel was bare. No cryptic Latin marked its wall. There wasn't even a crude *X*. She had no way of knowing which path she should choose when she came across a fork in the Lutetian limestone. Both branches unspooled into a vaster network of paths.

The hunt for a heart? She dug a gold coin from her pocket. It landed on King Louis XIV's head after she flipped it. *More like a gamble.*

The Enchantresses' games had always been risky: To get caught impersonating government officials guaranteed prison time. But the stakes felt so much higher now that there were fairies and royals and heartless men in the mix.

They were wagering everything.

Céleste was trying her best, but she hadn't managed to get any solid leads on what Terreur's heart looked like, much less where he kept it. Until she did, all Honoré could do was guess. She chose the path to the right, dropping croissant crumbs as she went.

"The catacombs *would* be the obvious place to bury a heart." A full moon bobbed above Honoré's shoulder. Marmalade's head bobbed there as well, watching it. He'd hitched a ride across the lake and then decided he preferred to be carried. "But maybe it's too obvious?"

The tomcat stayed quiet. Quiet enough for Honoré to realize just how deep they were. There was no growl of Métropolitain trains, no clip-clop of carriages or shush of pneumatic tyres. Down here, the city La Fée Verte had built was a distant dream. Down here, Honoré could feel her old closet claustrophobia closing in. Muffled ears. Shapes in the darkness: squirming worms and glittering skulls...

Marmalade hissed.

The bones were real. Honoré paused in front of the ossuary. Its skulls had been stacked, yes, but they'd also been...decorated? The skeletons were gilded with precious metals. Silver. Gold. The light of her miniature moon shimmered against orbital ridges as she walked this shining path. It circled back in on itself, and by the time Honoré reached the exit (entrance?), she had the feeling the skulls were watching her.

"Excuse me." She thought of how Sylvie had gotten the statues to show them the way. It was worth a try... "Have you happened to see a small wooden box? I'm hunting for a heart that might—"

Hisses filled the chamber. All of them said the same thing:

"Beware..."

"Beware...

"Beware the serpents..."

A silver tongue slithered out of an unhinged jaw. No...not a tongue. A snake? It disappeared back into an eye socket before Honoré could get a better look. All around the depository, skulls' metal adornments started writhing. Seething. Reaching.

"Beware the serpents that eat their own tails."

Another snake snagged the edge of her tunic.

It tore as Honoré stumbled toward the ossuary door.

She didn't bother scattering any crumbs outside.

This was not a place she wanted to return to.

Honoré and Marmalade explored the left set of tunnels the following evening. She found they weren't the only ones. There were more skeletons in this section, yes, but the voices drifting down the passage belonged to the living. Cataphiles? Perhaps? She'd heard of people who held picnics down here. Some even listened to concerts by haunted candlelight. A man *was* humming, many meters away; his song kept getting interrupted by the *scrape*, *scrape* of shovels.

Someone was digging.

Digging and humming the song that accompanied La Danse Apache.

Honoré halted as soon as she recognized the notes, shoving Sylvie's moon into her pocket so the light would not give her away. Strange bones pressed into her spine as she peered around the corner.

Ten men filled the gallery ahead.

Ten Apaches.

Dirt streaked their striped shirts, stirred up by pickaxes and spades as they chipped away at the cavern wall. One gangster had untied his scarlet scarf and was using it to mop sweat from his brow. His tattoo—and the extra swirls of darkness around it—did not budge. Shadow strings slithered around his arms, stretching down the opposing tunnel.

Terreur must have sent them here.

They'd been digging for a good long while, carving out enough limestone to create a new passage. Honoré scanned the rubble for a jewelry box, but they hadn't unearthed the heart. Not yet. They were singing and swinging away. Oblivious to the young woman crouched around the corner, with an orange tomcat coiled around her heels, trying to decide their next move. There was nothing to steal. Nothing to stab. Perhaps it would be best to go back the way they came and—

Her breath caught as Gabriel emerged from the tunnel—the eleventh man. Her brother set down his pickaxe and started to fumble with his trouser buttons, moving toward Honoré's passageway. *Oh shit!*

Or piss, rather.

She pulled her jacket over her bandolier, covering the dreams there as she shrank back into darkness. It wasn't exactly as helpful as one of Sylvie's invisibility cloaks might have been—why hadn't the youngest Enchantress offered one of those?—but Gabriel didn't seem to see his sister. His eyes were surrounded by black markings now, just like all the others Terreur had under his sway. But Honoré could still see a spark of curiosity as he spied the pile of croissant crumbs.

She watched his interest grow as he spotted the second stack.

The closer her brother got, the more distinctly she could see the sorcerer's controlling shadow snaking from Gabriel's heels. It looked a little like the insides of a piano—pulsing and tugging. Her own heart staccatoed so hard that the dreams on her bandolier almost rattled. Honoré knew they were true this time—not like the sword that had shattered all over Caveau des Terreur's sandy floor.

She unsheathed an imagining.

Gabriel was so focused on the crumbs that he couldn't even manage a yell before his sister was behind him, severing shadows like tendons. *Snap! Snap! Snap!* Strings recoiled like the tentacles of a wounded sea beast. Gabriel shirked in the opposite direction. His shoulders clattered against a stack of skulls.

"A-Anne?"

Normally, the name made Honoré recoil. It belonged with these bones...

Her brother didn't though.

"Come on, *mon frère*—we have to go."

But Gabriel didn't move. She studied her brother again. There were no extra stripes on his sailor shirt. No more strings wrapped around his limbs, rooting him in place.

He should've been free to follow her.

He was staring at the dragon ring instead. His eyes glittered. His tattoo brambled along his cheekbones—swirls and thorns. "You think you can just come back, after all these years, and call me 'brother'? After you murdered my father?" Ink started sprouting from Gabriel's temple. His darkest memory. Honoré could see herself inside it. Their sire's body slouched over the bar. The red smeared across her brother's face—the sheer terror there.

"You shouldn't have had to see that," Honoré whispered. "I was trying to defend myself, Gabriel, I was trying to protect *you*—"

"Protect?" her brother spat. "How's that?"

This question hurt more than Honoré cared to admit. So did his other words. *My father*, he'd called the man, as if he and Honoré weren't cut from the same warped cloth. She supposed Lucien Durand had been a different person to his son. He'd actually tried to be a *papa*—letting

Gabriel wear his razor-edged cap or teaching him phrases in the gang's signature slang, *la langue verte*. The very same words he used when he swore at Maman on the other side of the closet door.

No, she shouldn't have covered Gabriel's ears.

She shouldn't have left him sleeping on the pile of coats, either, when she pulled one out to cover their mother's cold body.

"Rafael García wanted us to run away to Constantinople with him, but I figured you were too young for the journey, so I decided to wait another few years. But our father found the note Rafael had left for us, and he—he was going to kill me, Gabe."

Her brother tilted his head.

His eyes kept glittering.

He didn't believe her. Of course. Why would he if he had no memories of Rafael García or of his own father's true body count?

"You didn't protect me from nothing," he said in a low voice. "You cut and run, left me to fend for myself."

"I had Eleanor watching over you." Her reply felt watery, even more so when Gabriel frowned.

"Who?"

"Eleanor."

Her brother's frown grew, and Honoré knew then that his accusations weren't entirely false. She had cut and run—twice. And last time she'd left the barmaid to fend for herself too. As if an empty lemonade bottle could do shit against dark magic. *Oh, Eleanor...*

"Listen to me, Gabriel. This new Terreur is dangerous. Really fucking dangerous. He devours people and drinks up their souls. That's why you can't remember who Rafael and Eleanor are, and if you don't come with me now—"

"What?" her brother interrupted bitterly. "You'll stab me too?"

"You really think I'd do that?"

"Rémy says you're a ruthless bitch, and after what I saw you do to him..."

Gabriel's gaze slipped back to the lantern-lit part of the tunnel, and Honoré felt a flare of panic. Her dragon flared too. Silver bristled up and down her arm. There were no teeth when she reached for her brother's hand—of course. She didn't want to hurt him. She just wanted to pull Gabriel back to the salon or someplace where she could clear his head and keep him free from Terreur's shadow tethers.

Her fingers found Gabriel's.

Something strange happened with Honoré's dragon then. It wasn't all *hers*. The alchemy of silver meeting soul started to shift—parts of the metal pulling toward Gabriel. The ring began to drip down his hand. She could feel her brother's fears. His anger. His hurt. It mixed so well with Honoré's own, until it was impossible to tell their emotions apart. Gabriel hated her for the night she'd killed their father and left. She hated herself for it too.

"Durand!" Their once-shared surname was shouted from the gallery. "This tunnel isn't going to dig itself! What are you doing back there? Holding a séance?"

No.

Gabriel was holding her dragon.

Their father's ring bridged both his bastards' hands, but Honoré felt herself slipping—silver, soul, and bone.

"Durand!" The foreman's voice was closer now, and Honoré's ears prickled with eerie recognition.

As soon as a pair of yellow boots rounded the corner, Marmalade growled.

Rémy Lavigne halted.

The gangster was very much *not* dead. He wasn't wearing a shirt either, making it all too easy to see his newest scar: a dragon-shaped mark on his chest. Its jagged edges went from the top of his belly button to the base of his throat, where several more saint necklaces dangled. *Ah, shit.* His prayers had worked. Or rather, the icons had. If such charms could keep a Russian prince's soul from fleeing his body, then Honoré figured they could do the same for a sadistic cat-skinner. What a twisted world this was, that *he* got seven lives after what he'd done to that poor kitten...

"Oh, I've been waiting to see that look on your face," Rémy said with a split-scar smile. His gaze cut to Marmalade—who bristled and backed away. "Got me some promises to keep."

The gangster drew out a knife.

The tomcat vanished into the tunnels.

Honoré couldn't exactly blame him. It was the wisest course of action, especially since the rest of the Apaches had exchanged their shovels for sharper instruments. Pickaxes. Blades. She would've fled too, if she weren't bound to Gabriel. Their father's ring still twisted between them, twisted, twisted, and her brother refused to move. She couldn't pull him away. She couldn't separate her dragon from him either, couldn't control the silver enough to shield herself as the other gangsters moved in. Their silhouettes were all a step too eager. *This isn't how it was supposed to go...*

Honoré reached blindly for a knife, but her bandaged hand slipped, and then there was this horrible flame of a feeling sliding between her ribs.

All the air left her right lung.

The tunnel of bones stretched out around her. She wondered how many of these leering skulls had been killed by knives and if their deaths had felt like this: Such a simple punctuation. A period at the end of a wandering sentence.

Rémy Lavigne's blade was small. Its hilt jutted out of her ribcage, and she suspected, with a delirious laugh, that a corset might've stopped the knife from going so deep. Too late now. She felt the dragon rushing back—rage, oh, such rage—and she heard Gabriel screaming once more. She felt more metal than woman; silver spilled up Honoré's arm and down around her torso, fusing the knife in place. But the beast did not stop there. It grew and grew, shoving the rest of the Apaches into the skeletal walls, bones crushing into bones. Fear, oh, such fear. This was so much worse than shattering a mirror. But when Honoré tried to pull the ring back, she could see it had gone too far—cracks snaked along the cavern ceiling. Dust began raining down on the bodies.

Her brother's eyes locked with hers.

Too far, mon Dieu. She'd gone too far.

The cavern collapsed into darkness.

Chapter 28

The Seed of an Idea

Sylvie of a Single Name sat cross-legged on a futon, in a room she'd come to think of as the salon's library. There were plenty of books here, along with a fireplace that changed colors to match the mood of whatever passage you happened to be reading. Its smoke also changed scents. Right now, it smelled like sunshine and sand, which meant Rafe was either reading a story about pirates or doing more digging into the legends of pharaohs. His hair tangled down both sides of his face while he stared at the pages, as if the ink of the story were reaching up and pulling him in. Firelight glanced around his eyes—and it seemed as though every time the other thief glanced over at Céleste, her own hair began to light like a fuse.

Her cheeks went extra pink as well.

Sylvie didn't think this was the start of a masque. La Fée Verte's birds were too quick, when it came to keeping the oldest Enchantress's promise, snatching whatever dreams they could from her head.

Anastasia didn't have a masque either—just dark circles under her eyes. The grand duchess wasn't getting much sleep these nights, and this evening, when Sylvie had met the princess at rue de la Réunion, her face had looked extra puffy. Pink from tears instead of masque light. "Alexei fell today…" She pressed her lips together. "He was trying to sneak over to the Children's House, and he bruised himself climbing into the boat. Dyadka Andrei—his sailor nanny—found him drifting around the lake. Mama was beside herself. She telegrammed 'Our Friend,' and he arrived as soon as he could. The starets looks different now." Anastasia seemed to shrink inside herself when she said this. "He looks... awful."

You're letting her see too much, Sylvie. Honoré's warning lingered over the nearby cobblestones like stray fog.

"I tried not to stare," the princess went on, "but Mama couldn't tear her eyes off him. I think... I couldn't see her face very well. There's too much darkness around it. The papers are right... he's got her under some kind of spell."

"It's a curse," Sylvie managed to say.

"A curse?"

"Your 'Friend'... I don't think he's your friend. Not really," Sylvie said. "He works for the evil sorcerer from the mirror." She saw the implications of this flashing across the princess's face. "That's why it's important for us to make our own magic. If we can collect enough of our own dreams to become Sancts, then we can help La Fée Verte fight him. We can help your family too."

She'd figured then that it was a good time to introduce Anastasia to the salon. What better way to dry her tears than to take her wandering through a maze painted by Pablo Picasso? Or to help her lose herself in a good book? Literally. Some of the stories on this library's shelves opened like doors—Sylvie had already seen a few guests disappear between their gilded spines. She might have suggested following them, if she weren't so set on seeing her own story through.

The orphan who became a Sanct.

She was a good enough daydreamer now. She'd saved her imaginings. She'd Enlightened Anastasia; she'd even performed more spells with the grand duchess's help. But waking up some statues and creating a portal to Russia didn't make her a Sanct any more than her butterfly wings did.

She still felt... cocooned.

"What would you do?" Sylvie asked Rafe. "If you were trying to become a Sanct?"

The fire popped and snapped behind his shoulder as he thought this over. "Well, the main difference between a Sanct and a daydreamer lies in the volume of magic that's harvested. The power required to become a Sanct is more than one anima can manage. That's why not just anyone can cast spells. Most people who are Enlightened stay imaginers because they don't know any better. If you *do* know better and keep enough of your own creations to become a daydreamer, the next step is to start Enlightening others and saving their imaginings as well."

"That's why La Fée Verte opened this place," Céleste surmised.

"Exactly." Rafe nodded. "If I were free to do whatever I pleased? I'd start a magical artists' colony at La Ruche and spell its doors to open for anyone who needed room to dream. They could stay there and create for as long as they wanted."

"You'd have to address the roof's leaks," Céleste teased. "Maybe you could charm the water into diamonds so you could afford to keep the soup kitchen running..."

"Instead of having a soup kitchen, you should just serve ice cream," Sylvie said.

"Ice cream *does* turn to soup, when it melts," Anastasia pointed out.

"It sounds like I should put *you* two in charge of the menu." The shadow at Rafe's feet gave an excited leap in front of the fire. It always turned into a fox when he was happy, Sylvie had noticed. "Although, if you want to become a Sanct yourself, it might serve you better to open your own establishment. A pâtisserie, maybe?"

Céleste laughed. "Sylvie couldn't be a baker. She'd *eat* everything."

"Does every Sanct need a shop?" Anastasia wondered.

"Or a salon. Or a church. Or a cabaret. A place where people gather...a place where people can *be* gathered," Rafe explained. "Though my version of La Ruche would be a more Enlightened experiment. Artists could work on their landscapes for years instead of hours. Poets could make their stanzas as sharp as iron, and sculptors could shape fountains with them. We'd inspire each other. We'd become a—a league of imaginers."

"You'd need to feed them more than ice cream, in that case." A fresh voice entered the conversation.

The hearth fire shifted into greens and golds, overwhelming the room with the smells of spring leaves and gilded pages. La Fée Verte's feathers filled the doorway. No matter how many times Sylvie saw the Sanct's wings, they always woke something inside her. The part of her heart tied to a hot-air balloon...

"Contrary to popular belief, artists don't thrive when they starve." La Fée Verte laughed. "And if you wish to become a muse, you'll have to offer your dreamers more than food or drink. Imaginers need inspiration. Beauty. Wonder. Hope. They need ideas they can shape into something solid." Her honey-colored eyes stuck to Sylvie then. "I would suggest practicing that."

"You... want me to plant an idea in someone's head?"

"Like a flower?" Anastasia gasped.

"Flowers are far less finicky," La Fée Verte said. "All they need is water and sun and the correct kind of soil. Ideas need the right soul to root in. And even then, it takes time for such seeds to grow. If they do at all. They need exact conditions to thrive." Her eyes alighted on Rafe. "Your dream for La Ruche... if you tried to realize a magical artists' colony now, Terreur would destroy it." Other ideas sang along her wrist as she extended her hand, expectant. "Perhaps such a thought would be safer with me?"

Rafe looked hesitant.

Céleste looked fierce. "And what will you do? Turn Rafe's dream into a stalactite?"

La Fée Verte tilted her head. "I'll give it back when the time is right," she promised. "That's the difference between Terreur and me. There are far more brutal ways to gather anima. He chose one of the darkest. Becoming a muse or a baker is much more rewarding. That is the kind of Sanct you should strive to be."

Sylvie figured La Fée Verte was speaking to her, even though her golden eyes were locked with Céleste's gray stare. Even though she extended her hand again toward Rafe. He set down his book and pulled the dream from his head. It was long, too long to be a bracelet, so La Fée Verte twisted it into a necklace instead—a free-thinking La Ruche sitting over her breastbone like a pendant, close as a heart.

Becoming a muse was easier said than done.

Choosing a mind to inspire was a lot like selecting a mark. Sylvie sat on the bar top of the salon's front room, greeting guests as they retrieved their aperitif from the tower of flute glasses. Who seemed extra thirsty? Who paused to say more than just bonjour?

"Good midnight, mademoiselles!" Jean Cocteau swept through the door, exchanging his coat for a drink that turned bright blue when it hit his lips. "How fare we this fine evening?" His stare settled on Anastasia, who was skipping from one stool to the next. Céleste, seated at the end of the bar, was watching her as well. "I see we have a new imaginer in our midst! Sporting a nightgown nonetheless." He conjured up a dress made of dewdrops for the princess. There was, fittingly, a tiara to go with it. "Here you go, *ma chère*! An outfit worthy of... what did you say your name was again?"

"I didn't!" Anastasia answered cheerfully, as she splashed into the gown.

"This is Anastasia Nikolaevna." Sylvie scrunched her nose tighter with each syllable, hoping she got them right. "She's a grand duchess!"

"Always a pleasure to meet a fellow royal!" Jean laughed.

The dew on Anastasia's crown caught the light of the chandelier, shimmering as she paused. "I thought France didn't have a monarchy."

"My friends call me 'the Frivolous Prince,' but we do have a *true* duchess in our midst." Jean's smile turned sly—sly enough for Sylvie to realize he didn't believe Anastasia's pedigree. "Have you met

Manuela? That's her code name when she's mingling with creative commoners like us."

He pointed at a woman who was peeling off a set of gloves and shoving a pair of goggles up her forehead. There were wrinkles there, and the hair peeking from beneath her leather driving helmet was so threaded with silver that it was hard to know whether she was inspired. It hardly ever stayed that way, though. Sylvie *had* met the duchess. Many times over. Each interaction ended with the woman making the same wish—hair that matched Sylvie's in spirit, if not the exact shade. She often walked away with emerald curls or purple plaits...

It was a wind-whipped gray this evening, as she set her helmet on the bar.

Jean gave a bow. "I present to you Manuela! Sculptor, author, artist, chauffeuse—"

"What's a chauffeuse?" asked Anastasia.

"He means I prefer to drive myself places. Quickly," the older woman said with a wink.

"Duchess d'Uzès here was the first woman in France to get a speeding ticket," Jean told them. "But she receives francs for every sip of champagne someone else takes, so you shouldn't feel too poorly for her."

Sylvie didn't. She loved the idea of a duchess racing her own automobile through Paris's moonstruck streets, but there was no point in planting the thought if it was already true. She saw far more promise in the way Duchess d'Uzès smiled at her hair.

"Still pink, I see! I wish my colors wouldn't fade so easily." The older woman's goggles and gloves joined the pile on the bar. "This winter will be drab enough... I don't need to see more gray every time I meet a mirror. Would you mind passing me a glass, dear?"

You'll have to give dreamers more than food or drink. La Fée Verte's advice rang in Sylvie's own head as she plucked an aperitif from the top of the pyramid and handed it to the duchess. Was planting an idea just as straightforward? Or should that transaction be more like picking a pocket, sneaky and seamless? If so, it would be far easier with songbirds...

Céleste arched an eyebrow.

Back in the days when the Enchantresses had simply stolen coins, this served as a signal. *Stop!* A tap on the temple had meant *look!* Sylvie watched her friend lift the helmet from the bar.

"Would this really help you in a crash? Or is it meant more for keeping your coiffure contained?"

"Coiffure?" Anastasia asked.

"She means hairstyle," Sylvie said.

But what the oldest Enchantress really meant was that the Duchess d'Uzès would set this helmet back on her head again . . . probably at dawn, when she was walking back to her automobile, the rising sun stripping the older woman's memories, every imagining gone . . .

Except one.

"I do not crash," the duchess replied. "I cannot afford to, despite what Monsieur Cocteau infers. Men can make all the mangled wrecks they want, but the moment a woman collides with something—well, let's just say that I don't want to be the last French lady to receive a speeding ticket."

Sylvie didn't have to reach far to grab the helmet. She didn't have to reach too far inside herself for the inspiration either. She thought of all the wigs Céleste used to pin on before their cons. Then she pictured all the colors on the nearby artist's palette and started mixing them: Periwinkle and pink. Yellow sliding through blue, through green, into midnight.

She set the helmet on her head and threaded the thought of rainbow wigs through its lining. Would it slip into Duchess d'Uzès's waking mind once she put it on? Would it stick? Sylvie wished there were a better way to know, besides waiting for days or weeks or forever . . .

It takes time for such seeds to grow, La Fée Verte had explained. *If they do at all.*

Jean began to say something about deep-sea-diver helmets when the salon's door opened. Sylvie didn't take note at first—there were always guests following the fountain dragon here at this hour—but then a blur of fur appeared. All the glass flutes in the pyramid flashed orange before Marmalade plowed through them. Aperitif went everywhere, soaking Duchess d'Uzès's gloves and mixing with Anastasia's gown. Sylvie's stomach dropped at the sight of the tomcat. Marmalade's fur was standing on end. A growl grew over most of his words: *Bones! Brother! Below!*

Sylvie's insides kept falling, even though the flute tower had begun to rebuild itself.

"Where's Honoré?" she asked.

The prickly one found her brother digging through the bones down below, the ginger cat yowled. *She tried to slice his shadow, but—*

But the flute glasses were trembling again. Céleste had grabbed the bar, her knuckles nearly as pale as her hair, and at first Sylvie thought the oldest Enchantress was the one shaking things, but then she watched the chandelier swing wide, butterflies bursting everywhere. The salon's walls shuddered so hard that petals dropped from wallpaper flowers. Stained glass vines too lost their leaves. Songbirds squawked their dismay as they flew through shuddering curtains, and many imaginers had thrown themselves to the rug.

Out of all the people in the room, only Anastasia seemed unfazed. "That was my very first earthquake!" she announced, once the tremors stopped.

"I'm not sure it was an earthquake," said Duchess d'Uzès, as she retrieved her helmet. "Paris doesn't sit on any fault lines."

"No," Sylvie whispered. Marmalade's words were starting to sink in: *the bones down below*.

It wasn't an earthquake at all.

It was the catacombs.

Chapter 29

Flesh for Flesh

Céleste Artois did not understand what she was seeing. She'd followed the songbirds down to the Vault of Dreams and was now at the bottom of the corkscrew staircase. At least, it should have been the bottom. A large stretch of the cavern floor was gone—crumbled in on itself. Dreams shimmered over actual dust, and there was a different shine stirring out of the haze. Silver scales and wings...

"Is that a dragon?" Anastasia called out a few steps above.

"No." Sylvie appeared next to the princess, her orange wings fluttering. "That's Honoré!"

Only, Céleste had never seen her friend's ring grow so large before. It was nearly the size of a boat, rising from a sea of broken stones. Her mind scrambled, trying to make sense of the scene. What had happened? Why was the dragon writhing in the middle of the collapsed floor? Its tail thrashed across shards of stone. Its neck arched as it if were in pain.

Was Honoré hurt? Céleste searched the rubble for signs of the other Enchantress. Skulls started to appear. Fragments of bone had been scattered by a metallic tail, landing on a striped shirt. That pattern... it looked familiar...

"I thought Honoré was searching the catacombs," the princess kept saying.

"She was," Sylvie answered. "Marmalade told me she found her brother digging."

Céleste spied another striped shirt and a red scarf peeking out from the stones. A limp hand. A pickaxe handle. These were Terreur's men, she realized. *Were* being the operative word. Almost every one of them was dead, their faces plastered with the dust of even older bones. She hadn't known the catacombs snaked out this far, that there was something even deeper than dreams beneath La Fée Verte's salon.

Terreur must have though.

He'd sent these men.

To dig. To die.

"Honoré?" she croaked.

The dragon was still moving—that had to be a good sign, no? Only, the movements weren't silky silver, but clunky. Pained. The way a cart horse might limp along on three legs. Céleste looked past the last stair, trying to judge whether her own leg would break if she jumped.

"I wouldn't, *mon amour*." Rafe landed on the step beside her; his shadow wings fanned as he reached out and grabbed her hand. "That relic's agitated; best let La Fée Verte approach it first."

His palm was warm over hers, but it wasn't this that stopped Céleste. Rafe was holding the same hand that had taken the dragon's fang. Even though the wound was gone, she could still feel that sudden surge of silver. She still felt uneasy whenever she stood too close to Honoré's ring…

La Fée Verte had no such hesitations. The Sanct flew to the cavern's collapsed floor, surrounded by a cloud of songbirds. These swirled around the dragon's head too. It snapped at the first few before folding its own wings in.

In, in.

Metal began to pull back like a tide, revealing not a line of shells but a boy. *Gabriel*. That was the name Rafe had uttered, before *The*

Rite of Spring. It was easy to see why he'd mistaken Honoré for her brother. The effect of the siblings, side by side, was mirror-esque. In fact, Gabriel looked even more like his sister than she did. Honoré no longer resembled a knight so much as one of those effigy statues that lay over medieval tombs. When the dragon ring stopped moving, half the Enchantress stayed swallowed in metal—her entire right arm. Up the neck. Down the hip. Had she broken it? There seemed to be an extra bone jutting through...

No.

Not a bone.

After all this time playing with knives, Honoré Côte had finally gotten herself stabbed.

Céleste's breath sharpened when she saw the hilt.

Rafe squeezed her hand and swore softly.

La Fée Verte knelt over Honoré's chest, placing a hand over her breastbone.

It rose.

It fell.

"She's still alive."

Still. Céleste didn't like that word. It implied a ticking clock. She didn't like the location of the knife either, nor the way the dragon coiled around its hilt. *Agitated.* The silver even bared its fangs at Sylvie, when the youngest Enchantress flew down to join La Fée Verte.

"I can help you heal her." The girl didn't know what she was offering—obviously—as she held out her hand.

One person's flesh can only be mended with another's.

"No!" Céleste pulled her healed palm from Rafe's and jumped to the broken ground below, her ankle nearly twisting, her knees scraping against a larger piece of rubble. Time would tend to those wounds, but the knife in Honoré's torso was a different matter. "Use me," she said.

La Fée Verte looked up.

There was a gleam in her eyes that didn't belong to magic at all.

"She's dying," the Sanct said.

"So am I," Céleste argued. It was the only reason this mad scheme might work—her body was actively defying death thanks to Rasputin's magic. Surely that spell could handle a knife stab as well. "Give me Honoré's wound, and maybe we both have a chance at surviving…" She was all too aware of Anastasia Nikolaevna standing on the spiral staircase, all too aware that each breath she took belonged to the grand duchess's brother. It was his life Céleste was offering.

Since they'd been introduced, she'd hardly been able to look at the princess. But this truth was even harder to face: Honoré's lips were beginning to go blue, and Céleste could still taste horseshoes, and no one else in the Vault of Dreams could take her place. Certainly not Sylvie. The eleven-year-old somehow looked younger as she knelt over Honoré—and older too, when her eyes met Céleste's and she frowned.

La Fée Verte's own expression was unreadable.

A molten gold tear streaked her cheek as she studied Honoré.

"This is very noble of you and everything, but there's no guarantee this will work." Rafe landed next to Céleste, worry engraved on his face.

"I'll risk it," she said. "Better a bleeding heart than none at all."

"Well, *you* might bleed out before we reach rue des Ombres, and what the hell will I tell Terreur when I carry your corpse to his doorstep?" He raked a hand through his black, black hair. The worry on his face turned to agony. "I can't do this without you, Céleste."

And I can't do this without Honoré.

More rust fortified her tongue. "Tell him I got caught in the collapse." Céleste nodded at the Vault of Dreams. "We should have been forging dreams here, regardless." Instead, she'd been sitting at a bar, helping Sylvie seed silly ideas into a champagne heiress's head, while Honoré had been fighting for her life.

Their lives.

Céleste knelt beside her friend, pressing her own hand to La Fée Verte's, both over Honoré's chest. The Sanct's fingers trembled beneath hers. And beneath that? A faint heartbeat, growing fainter.

"I know you're afraid to perform this type of magic," she whispered to the Sanct, "but Honoré deserves more than your fear."

The corner of La Fée Verte's mouth twisted. "Even the brave..." she whispered to herself.

Her hand stilled.

Céleste reached for the offending knife. The dragon did not bite when her fist tightened around the hilt, but retreated to reveal a blood-stiffened tunic. Hot, torn skin.

"This wouldn't have happened with a cheese knife, *mon amie*." She knew the other Enchantress was past hearing, but it made what came next bearable.

Céleste pulled out the blade.

It felt as if she were stabbing herself—she was, in a way. La Fée Verte's masque flashed gold. The knife gleamed garnet. Céleste's right lung was on fire. She crumpled over it into Rafe's arms. He'd swept in to catch her, and there was such a sureness to the way he held her that she no longer felt like she was spinning to pieces. Burning, yes. The wound felt as if a hundred hornets had flown down her blouse, but when Rafe gently lifted the edges of the fabric, she found that she could breathe. Still breathe.

He stopped short of her corset, letting out a relieved breath of his own. "I don't see any blood, thank God..."

The Mad Monk's magic was working.

So was La Fée Verte's. It was like watching a daguerreotype come to life, as color returned to Honoré's face. Yet other parts of the Enchantress stayed silvered. Céleste kept waiting for the dragon to pull back from her newly healed wound, but it didn't, and it didn't.

Chapter 30

The Story Isn't Over Yet

Honoré Côte did not expect to wake up. She certainly didn't expect to wake up with a tomcat sitting on her chest. Marmalade had made himself at home, curled tight, his dry pink nose nearly level with hers. He didn't blink when she opened her eyes—simply stared at her with his endlessly judgmental orange ones. *I told you so.*

Told her what?

It all came crashing back then. Apaches digging through bone-riddled walls, croissant crumbs scattering the way to Honoré, Gabriel... oh, Gabriel... Where was her brother? Where was *she*? Back in the Quartier Secret, somehow, lying on a bed of leaves. Honoré could hear the steady *whir* of wings, an ebb and flow of voices in the hall beyond. They were grave tones, the way a physician might speak at the end of an ill-fated house call. *Was* it a doctor? Honoré remembered then that she'd been stabbed, stabbed by a resurrected Rémy Lavigne... Had she pulled off a similar miracle? There was no pain when she tried to sit up. Only heaviness.

Marmalade hopped off onto the leafy mattress, and Honoré could see that her limbs weren't just leaden but silver. Her neck was also stiff with it. As was the entire right side of her torso, from hip to jawline.

The metal wasn't impossible to move.

Just incredibly hard.

Her heart beat as fast as a smith's hammer when she bent herself upright. A curtain of vines hung around the bed, and through some breeze-swept leaves, she could see La Fée Verte conversing with Sylvie and the Fisherman of the Moon.

"I only just finished reading these accounts left by Robespierre's disciples." There was a thick stack of letters in the ragpicker's hands—he wasn't wearing fingerless gloves but fuller versions. His bronze masque glittered over a grim expression as he handed the papers to La Fée Verte. "I hope my revelations haven't come too late."

"Honoré's ring is *eating* her?" Sylvie exclaimed.

"That's not what I said—"

"It is!"

"You're putting words in my mouth. I said '*consuming*.'"

The youngest Enchantress crossed her arms. "I *consume* macarons all the time."

"Yes, but do the macarons swallow you?" the Fisherman asked. "I'm well equipped to handle feral antiques, but your friend's relic…" He tugged at his gloves. "I wouldn't dare touch it after what I discovered in those letters. Most of the rings they used to storm Versailles during the Revolution aren't rings anymore. They fused themselves to their wearer's bones. 'Beware the serpents that eat their own tails.'"

Echoes from that shining crypt. Hairs lit up all over Honoré's skin as she looked down at her dragon. Its head was draped over her shoulder—much the way Marmalade's had been in the tunnel—and its scales were too close to her jaw. Those skulls. They weren't gilded. They were the last gasps of men and women who'd suffocated in their own armor…

Her heart hammered even harder.

Her breath tightened.

She pushed herself then, managing to swing her legs off the bed.

"My dame!" La Fée Verte was there. "How are you feeling?"

"Like one of those damn tin soldiers." She tried to laugh, but the sound came out crumpled. "All I need is a cannon that shoots bonbons."

"They shoot gumdrops," Sylvie corrected. "And you need to take off that ring, Honoré. Right now!"

The youngest Enchantress made it sound so easy, as simple as a twist and a slip. Did she not see how deep the dragon went? How far? It wasn't just Honoré's second skin anymore. She'd have to saw off her right arm in order to do what the other girl asked—and more besides.

"I don't think I can," she whispered.

The girl's pink brows bent into a frown. "The Fisherman of the Moon says it's cursed!"

The ragpicker's coat lining clattered with keys as he peered through the vines. "Again, you put words in my mouth. That ring, and many others like it, were designed to deflect the magic of the Sancts who held court at Versailles—to absorb spells and protect their wearers. According to writings left by Robespierre's disciples, it was what gave his revolutionaries the upper hand and allowed them to establish their Republic of Virtue."

"That's an ambitious name." Honoré snorted.

"It was," the Fisherman agreed. "Almost as ambitious as its architect. Both failed miserably. I believe Robespierre began his Reign of Terror with good intentions, but he lost his way."

"I'm not sure I'd call guillotining seventeen thousand people a misstep," La Fée Verte said, with an edge that reminded Honoré that the Sanct's parents had numbered among them.

"No, but it's never just one step, is it?" The Fisherman pulled a handful of dice from his pocket. Only, their bottoms were strangely long, their black dots unevenly scattered. "Power is a path. It is one choice after another after another." He closed his fingers, and the dice rattled inside—like a gambler's fist. "Robespierre and his disciples chose to bathe themselves in blood, and their rings did what they'd been designed to do. They grew thirsty. They grew over their wearers. If I were you, Dame Honoré, I would choose not to use that ring."

Again, this sounded too easy.

"As for my choice..." The Fisherman of the Moon tipped the dice from his gloved hand into La Fée Verte's, and it was only after Sylvie made a face that Honoré realized why the pieces appeared so yellow.

"Are those *teeth*?" the youngest Enchantress asked.

"They're secrets," the Fisherman said. "Secrets I scraped from the ashes of Place de la Concorde all those years ago." His copper gaze beat against La Fée Verte's. "You were right that we cannot fight him as we are now. This . . . this may help."

The other Sanct stared at the loose teeth, then tucked them into her own gown's misty pockets. "Thank you, Fisherman."

She didn't sound thankful at all, but the other Sanct bowed. "You know where to find me, should you need my services for any more nefarious jewelry."

Honoré might have asked about the icon necklaces—how exactly was it they kept Rémy Lavigne in the land of the living? Had they somehow done the same for her? But Céleste appeared in the doorway then, brushing shoulders with the exiting Sanct. She leaned against the branched frame, her lashes fluttering like snow over storm-colored eyes, with her hands pressed to her side in such a precise spot that Honoré knew the exact reason she herself was still alive. It wasn't because of some damn saint.

This time, her heart didn't hammer, but burst.

"*Mon amie . . .*"

Céleste straightened, and La Fée Verte did too. There seemed to be a new tension between the women—something not even a knife could cut. But the knife *had* cut Honoré. She should be dead. Six feet under. Or however many meters below the catacombs sat. How had they found her down there?

"Céleste!" Sylvie waved at the other Enchantress. "Are you all right?"

A quick nod. "Rasputin renewed his healing spell."

"I know! Anastasia and I snuck over to Catherine Palace to watch through the windows."

The other Enchantress's lips tightened. She couldn't still be hurting. Could she?

"Honoré's fine too! Or she will be, after she removes her ring." Sylvie looked back at Honoré's silvered hand and stuck out her tongue. "If you really want a dragon to fight with, I can wake up the other statue at the Fontaine Saint-Michel. Or you could command some of Notre-Dame's gargoyles!"

"I can't fight with crustaceans," Honoré grumbled.

"What about a pelican?"

"That is sure to inspire fear in the hearts of my enemies." She paused, struck by what she'd just said. "Terreur's heart. I found it."

Céleste inhaled sharply, her eyes filling with shock, then joy. La Fée Verte's expression was similar, as she reached out to take Honoré's hand. The moment might have been more charged, if Sylvie hadn't bounced on the bed, her pink hair flaring. "You did? Without me?"

"Where?" Céleste asked.

"Terreur's men were digging for it in the catacombs. If we can go back to where you found me..." She paused again at the look on La Fée Verte's face.

Hope collapsed.

"You were in the Vault of Dreams," Céleste explained. "Terreur is getting impatient—he sent Apaches to tunnel into the salon so they could search for his lost memory too."

"They wouldn't have gotten so far without your dragon," La Fée Verte said. "It broke through my wards."

The ring had broken more than that, Honoré remembered. Her own bones felt dusty as she recalled the collapse, the feel of Gabriel's rage growing, growing, growing next to her. "My brother... he was in the tunnels too..."

"He's alive," Céleste said quickly.

And the other Apaches weren't. Honoré could hear as much in the other Enchantress's blunt punctuation. She saw it in the twist of Sylvie's face. The girl must have seen the bodies. Had she seen Rémy? Had any of the other workmen been wearing saint necklaces?

"Your brother looks a lot like you!" the youngest Enchantress said. "Except he had all these black squiggles around his eyes. We couldn't let him wake up and see that Céleste and Rafe were helping you, so we had to put him back in the catacombs before we re-established the wards."

Honoré lay back on the bed, staring at the fireflies that drifted through the overhead canopy. She hated the thought of her brother waking up in the dark, so far below, without a lantern. Not that he needed one... Instead of a trail of crumbs, he had his own fears, stringing him back to Terreur.

"I tried to free him, again—" Her voice felt tight. "I did."

La Fée Verte squeezed her hand.

"I cut through the fears Terreur was using to compel him, but he didn't want to come with me. I killed our father, you see, back when Gabriel was Sylvie's age, and I left him an orphan in one of Paris's worst neighborhoods, and he... he hates me."

She'd taken so much damage for her brother over the years—dragon bruises and broken bones—all with the thought that she was saving Gabriel. Shielding him. But in the end, none of her pain had mattered. *That* was what hurt so badly. Not the pinky that had gotten smashed to splinters along with the knight carvings.

"Well," Céleste said, after a moment, "if your father was anything like the other Terreur, I'm sure the bastard deserved it."

La Fée Verte gave a tiny nod and kept squeezing Honoré's hand.

"Your brother can't hate you," Sylvie said, ever the optimist.

"He does." That black loathing had been so much worse in her brother's clear gaze. "I could see it in his eyes. I could feel it in the ring. When I grabbed Gabriel, he tried to take my dragon."

"Maybe you should have let him." Sylvie had that same easy-enough tone she'd used along with Rémy's revolver, on that first excursion to Belleville. "Then you wouldn't have to worry about eating yourself—"

"What?" Céleste broke in.

"Honoré's ring is cursed," the youngest Enchantress explained. "If she keeps using it, her bones will turn silver. Or something."

Honoré shut her eyes, noting how the dragon half of her body felt none of the mossy sheets. She did seem cursed to go in circles. Fighting Terreur. Abandoning Gabriel. Again and again and again. Until what? She couldn't be crushed as thoroughly as her brother's wooden figurines, but even metal soldiers had their weaknesses. Like rusting shut.

"You can't save everyone, my dame," La Fée Verte said softly.

"I know," croaked Honoré. "But I wanted to save *him*."

"You will!" Again, the youngest Enchantress was using her golden-gun voice.

"Stop, Sylvie."

"Stop what?"

"Pretending that everything will have a happy ending. You're old enough to know better. Life isn't a fairy tale." Honoré knew her rage was mostly echoes. She knew she was acting like a ruthless bitch, but honestly, what else could she be, after understanding what had happened to Eleanor? After crushing nearly a dozen Apaches to death? "It's shit. Life is just people shitting on each other over and over until they die. That's it. Expect anything different, and you'll be in for years of pain."

La Fée Verte's hand stilled in hers. Honoré didn't want to open her eyes and see the Sanct's disappointment. Or anyone else's. Silence blanketed the canopy, almost as heavy as the weight of all those bones in the catacombs.

Sylvie's voice pierced it like a bullet.

"You're wrong," she said. "You're right too. Bad things happen. Awful things. Parents die, and food gets scarce, and you get so sad and so hungry. But I don't think that's ever *The End*. When the world feels ruined... well, that just means the story isn't over yet. You have to brace yourself and be more than the rot. You have to keep going!"

Well, damn. This was one fight Honoré didn't want to win. She cracked an eyelid to find the youngest Enchantress cross-legged at the end of the bed. Marmalade had curled up in Sylvie's lap, but he was still fixing Honoré with his *I told you so* stare.

"We'll keep searching for the evil sorcerer's heart," the girl continued. "And after we find it, we'll free everyone from his curses. Rafe and Céleste and Gabriel and the Romanovs. All of us will get our happily ever afters, but only if we don't give up hope."

Céleste put on a wry smile. "I think I have to agree with Sylvie, *mon amie*."

Honoré sighed. Her anger had ebbed, but the dragon didn't feel any softer. "I don't want to give up, though it might be a while before I start hunting again. I can't walk. And even if I could, I wouldn't know where to go..."

"I'll continue to dig for clues," Céleste said. "But I don't know how much more I can get out of Terreur without handing over the dream you took from him." She glanced over at La Fée Verte, who continued to stay still.

"We'll keep searching too," Sylvie offered.

"Do *not* go dragging that poor princess through the catacombs!" Honoré hadn't expected to enjoy the grand duchess's company so much. She hadn't expected to feel such a kinship with the young royal either, both their brothers doomed. "She's suffered enough."

"I didn't mean Anastasia." Sylvie nodded at the ginger tomcat curled up in her lap, scratching him between his torn ears. "Marmalade tells me he can enlist some of his feral friends to search the city. Cats can go lots of places that people can't, and they have good noses for magic."

"That would have been useful to know a week ago," Honoré said.

"Probably," Sylvie agreed, as Marmalade started to purr. "He says that herding cats usually takes a lot longer than that."

It was only after the other Enchantresses left—Sylvie to her hammock and Céleste to La Ruche—that Honoré understood exactly where she was. La Fée Verte's bed. There were no sheets but a plush coat of moss that served as a mattress. The surrounding leaves smelled evergreen and bright, and many weren't leaves at all but songbirds, which swirled through the clouds of fireflies that kept blinking over Honoré's pillow, drifting into starry shapes that reminded her of the constellations she used to make up with the other Enchantresses. Well, really it was Céleste and Sylvie doing most of the work connecting the dots. Without them, Honoré would have just drifted in the dark.

This felt even truer with La Fée Verte.

The Sanct glowed like an evening star as she sat at the edge of the mossy mattress; several of the vines started to bud from this golden magic, but most of it was aimed at the teeth in her palm. Incisors spun like compass needles, and Honoré felt her own molars grind together when she heard the rotten ones hiss. Their sounds were vaguely French, but many of the words seemed to disintegrate when Honoré tried to focus on them. She wondered if this was the dragon's fault—its silver did coat her right ear—though the metal didn't seem to muffle any other hearing.

"What are they saying?" she asked, when the teeth finally began to still.

"Nothing I want to hear." La Fée Verte closed her palm. "Terreur took them from Robespierre's skull many years ago, and they taught him how to remove his heart. They keep whispering the spell over and over..." Her wings shuddered, the ends of their feathers weeping into the mattress.

"That's good, isn't it?"

It was a clue, at least. Even if Céleste couldn't chase the information much further, the feral cats of Paris could step in. Honoré had more faith in Marmalade now. Sure, the ginger tom had left her tunic covered in fur, but compared to the dragon that was fused to the rest of the cloth, that felt as cozy as a knitted sweater.

La Fée Verte shivered again. So did the rest of the birds in the surrounding canopy. "The spell... it's just that tearing your heart from your chest would kill most people."

Well, sure. In her *défense dans la rue* lessons, Honoré had always pointed her students' blades to that part of the body. "It *is* a vital organ."

"That doesn't change much with magic."

Honoré thought back to the conversation she'd had in the opera house, filled with cupids and their rear ends. "I thought you could turn hearts into books or gold lockets or... was Sylvie just teasing me?"

"She spoke true."

"It's hard to tell, sometimes."

"Sylvie doesn't lie nearly as much as your other friend." There was no edge to La Fée Verte's voice when she said this. "But I see now why you trust them both so deeply. Your love binds you together—for better or worse—though Robespierre's spell would consider this the latter. Attachments are a weakness. Your heart cannot last long locked away unless it has withered into something not even your closest companion would recognize." Her fist curled even tighter over the teeth. "The spell doesn't just require you to cut into your own flesh. It asks you to sacrifice everyone your heart holds dear."

Lying there, half encased in metal that still hummed with her brother's hatred, Honoré could understand why. She didn't want to, of course. Life would be so much easier if everything were sunshine and roses—but no. There was rot. There was ruin. There was shit upon shit. And instead of battling such things, Terreur had chosen to embrace them. He'd turned himself into a dead man walking so he could live forever.

"I don't know what the Fisherman hoped to gain by giving me these." La Fée Verte summoned an empty aperitif flute and tipped the decayed molars inside. "He must know I could never perform such a spell."

"I suspect Picasso would make a poor sacrificial lamb, though I could see Jean playing up that role—he'd probably script out an entire play, complete with costumes." Honoré didn't know why she was going on so, or why she wanted the Sanct to laugh, or why her heart started to thunder when the other woman's amber gaze caught her.

"Oh, Honoré. It is not Picasso or Jean or any of the other imaginers who have my heart..."

No one had ever said her name like that before—as sacred as a psalm. Nor had she ever been touched quite like this. La Fée Verte had set the rotten teeth aside and leaned over the bed where Honoré lay so that her wings became a second canopy, the feathers sheltering both women. They were a secret shared only with each other. Skin whispering against skin. Just fingers joining, but somehow more, for when La Fée Verte reached for Honoré's palms, she touched not just flesh but the dragon part of her too. Fearless. La Fée Verte did not flinch back from the fangs, nor did she try to push into the scales' hardness. She simply held Honoré's hand and pressed it up to the warm skin of her breastbone. Her heart fluttered just below. Slowly, slowly, the ring began to move, shifting over the Sanct's chest much like it had clung to Gabriel, forming a bridge between them.

And, just as before, the metal flooded with feeling.

La Fée Verte's emotions felt nothing like her brother's. There was fear, yes, but that had been tempered, hammered out into something stronger, something that made Honoré sit up and stare deep into the other woman's gaze.

"Oh" was all she could whisper, before their lips met.

Honoré Cote had never kissed anyone before. Greeting pecks on the cheek did not count, nor did the unfortunate incident with Rémy—his tongue on her neck while her hand searched for a blade. It had been too dangerous to chase true kisses back at the Caveau, too risky to even imagine her lips meeting another's that way, so she'd stopped herself before she started.

But all this melted away at La Fée Verte's touch, and Honoré suddenly felt like one of those flowers by the windmill—color coaxed from burnt thorns. Light from the Sanct's masque glowed gently through her eyelids. There was a taste like nectar, a sweetness she couldn't quite put her finger on, lingering long after the kiss itself.

"When I saw the dragon curled up on the cavern floor, I thought I'd lost you," La Fée Verte murmured, her forehead touching Honoré's. "I never should have asked you to turn yourself into a weapon like that, my dame. You are more than a sword."

"I'm *your* sword."

La Fée Verte's smile glimmered, but Honoré could feel a surge of sorrow in the silver threads between them.

"Besides..." Honoré's words started to feel stumbly again. "I would've used the dragon whether you knighted me or not, so don't go blaming yourself if I end up swallowed." She hazarded a glance at the ring, barely able to contain her surprise when she saw that its edges had ebbed away from her leg and hip. Her neck was less stiff too. In fact, she could feel La Fée Verte's breath where scales had once sat. "Did you do that?"

"What?"

"The ring... it's... retreating. Did you enchant it?"

"I couldn't have." The Sanct pulled away, bathing Honoré with a golden stare. "You must have moved the silver."

"I needed a full-blown forge just to scratch my nose a few minutes ago."

La Fée Verte's brow furrowed. "Then, perhaps... perhaps the relic is doing what it was designed to do. There is power in a kiss. A *true* kiss," she amended. "It could be that the metal absorbed that magic and became more malleable. It yielded for my healing spell too, but if it hadn't surrendered then, you'd be dead..."

Honoré felt as if she'd taken a hearty swig of Chartreuse—head spinning, mouth still burning sweet. "Why does magic have to be so damn complicated?"

"Because people are, my dame." The Sanct's face flickered with soft laughter. Her wings folded back. "Magic is our fear and our love and our joy and our rage. It is what we choose to make of these things."

The flute full of rotten teeth stayed on the stump that served as a bedside table, still rattling. Honoré's heart stirred too while she stared. It was too easy to remember Sylvie's arguments, not just about happy endings, but sugar and tsars and the cost of cavities. *That's not how magic works*, Honoré had told the daydreamer. Then she'd joked that her heart was made of cheese. But the truth was so much more complicated...

It was a brother lost.

It was a future found.

It was a dragon cradled between two chests.

"Well, then," Honoré said, as she leaned back into La Fée Verte's arms, "let's choose to make something better."

The Whisper Network

Something strange is happening to Paris's cats.

They are not napping.

Normally, you would see them curled up in café chairs or lounging in windowsills, buttering their bellies with the afternoon sun. But lately the cane chairs sit empty. Sunbeams slant into nothing. Instead, you see streaks of fur in the corner of your eye—slipping into one alleyway and out the next. There are paw prints scattered all across the city's mansard roofs, patrolling forgotten attic eaves. Similar trails wind through cellars, circling around long-corked bottles of wine and passing holes fit for rats. None of the cats' steps seem to pause here, not the way they do in the cool crypts underneath Paris's chapels, where tabbies and tortoiseshells hop onto the stone likenesses of the bodies entombed beneath, their paws placed straight on the upper left part of the chest. Where the corpse's heart should have long since rotted…

It is this they are hunting for, you see.

They do not blink at the gray blur of a church mouse.

They do not bother the bats that roost in the bell towers.

They do not pause by the Seine to watch its fish or its even deeper eels.

Some cats do stop to exchange stories of the places they've searched. The gardens and the graves, the quais stacked with strangely stamped crates, the museum basements filled with much of the same. Treasures abound in such places. So do curses. A black cat by the name of Nix lost one of his seven lives sniffing around boxes stored in the bowels of the Louvre. If you've been studying your cat-speak, you might hear the hair-raising tale from the young animal himself—*I could taste the sands of time, but then they started to taste me.* His tail curls in an urgent tone. *Steer clear of the Sully Wing, oh hunters mine. Some things are meant to stay buried.*

Chapter 31

The Bones of Paris

Céleste Artois sat at the top of a fang-tipped mountain, sipping tea from a flask as snowflakes drifted around her. Each of these ice crystals was a tiny piece of art. Literally. They weren't cold though. Not nearly as freezing as the snow that had started to pile outside the windows at Catherine Palace. Autumn, as it turned out, was a short season in Russia. Even Paris was properly chilly, now that it was January. Céleste had started adding shed firebird feathers to her tea, which had the bonus of teaching her obscure Russian terms as well as keeping her warm. It helped her not to shiver in front of the Mad Monk. This task was getting more and more difficult, with the exchanges she was overhearing. There were stories about the tsarevitch, of course. How the young prince had tried—twice now—to sail off in a rowboat. Both times he'd nearly died on the lake...

"You should keep your icons closer to the boy, if they're the only thing keeping him alive. Instead of hanging them above his bed, why not a necklace? They've worked wonders for Monsieur Lavigne."

"Yes, your new lieutenant seems to go through lives faster than the cats he skins," the Mad Monk had said coolly. "There are only so many peasants in Saint Petersburg that I can canonize without stirring up stories of *upyr*."

Terreur's lip lifted then, revealing spotless incisors. "Let the stories stir," he'd said. "You, of all people, should know the power of rumors, Grigori Rasputin."

Often, during such exchanges, Céleste chose to focus on the charms hanging from the end of the Mad Monk's chains. The saints no longer looked so pious—no, the mouths she'd supposed to be singing hymns seemed to be screaming instead. She couldn't stare at them without wanting to do the same. Thank goodness for the fat flakes swirling outside the palace windows. Watching them, Céleste could let her thoughts go blank.

Here in the landscape room, however, that was the last thing she wanted. Every night she and Rafe stole away someplace different: a castle on a cliff that could be reached only by a staircase of sea-foam, a forest filled with leafy prehistoric beasts, a sky where whales swam through cloud islands. This evening, Rafe was piloting a zeppelin over the sharp-white mountain range, sketching each snowflake by hand, writing secret messages into the crystals that swirled past Céleste's face.

Are you quite done playing the hermit?

"I'm imagining!" she shouted back, her breath pluming into the shape of a tiger. The beast glittered through the air before landing on Rafe's zeppelin.

After a moment, another snowflake drifted past: **You're vexing the birds is what you're doing.**

Céleste sighed and watched a second tiger leap down the mountainside. It had become something of a game—seeing how many of her own dreams she could collect throughout the evening. She surrendered them at dawn, of course, but not before her cheeks were dewy with magic—the beginnings of a masque. This always evaporated as soon as the songbirds descended and La Fée Verte claimed the imaginings as her own.

"I'm just giving my ideas time to grow!" Céleste yelled, tugging at the *ushanka* covering her scalp. "La Fée Verte shouldn't be angry with that. The stronger they are, the stronger *she* becomes, no?"

Especially at the current exchange rate. The Sanct seemed to give one whim for every two of theirs she took, though the offerings had improved since the night of Honoré's stabbing. Good enough to tide over Terreur for another three months. Céleste wasn't sure how much longer they could keep this ruse up. Their hunt seemed to be at an impasse. Marmalade and the rest of Paris's cats claimed they'd found no trace of the bastard's heart in the city. Whenever Céleste tried to broach the subject, Terreur demanded his lost idea. He hadn't tried tunneling any more Apaches into the salon, but she had no doubt he was planning another attack soon.

Céleste did not believe her dreams alone could stop it.

She'd gotten better at conjuring, certainly. There was an entire headful of ideas glowing beneath the *ushanka*'s fur—which made her think of Duchess d'Uzès's driving helmet. Nothing much had come of the idea Sylvie had tucked inside its lining. The champagne heiress still attended the salon every few evenings and occasionally painted her hair festive colors, but Sylvie had moved on to other quests. Namely, cheering up the Romanov children.

Céleste shivered and took another swig of firebird-laced tea.

The zeppelin's anchor landed in the snow next to her. Rafe swung down from the ladder, his fob chains twinkling, his stubble glittering with frost as he leaned in to steal a kiss. It was not cold at all. His mouth melted against hers, and the rest of the mountain's snow began to feel pillowy. Céleste was just reaching up to grab the other artist's vest when he pulled back and eyed the flask in her hand.

"What's that I taste?" Rafe licked the edges of his own lips. "*Russkiy?*"

Céleste bit back the urge to pull him back down into the snow. The more time she spent in Rafe's arms, the worse it was returning with him to the Caveau des Terreurs.

Tell me... your arrangement with Monsieur García... Do you really love him?

The answer terrified Céleste.

She'd managed to hide it from Terreur for the past three months. But every time Rafe García dreamed at her side, every time he filled her with stars upon stars, it was harder to shake off the dust, that young lovers' glow... For Rafe's sake, though, she had to try.

"The tea helps with my Russian," she answered, extending the flask. "Would you like some?"

"I have no need. The grand duchess speaks fine enough French..." Rafe raised his scarred eyebrow. "Though I've never seen you talk to her."

"We don't have much in common." Aside from the princess's ill-fated brother, and even Céleste wasn't skilled enough to weave that subject into casual conversation. *Yes, do you know the real reason why Alexei can't conjure? It's because Rasputin has a hold on his soul. Oh, and your mother's too. Also, your brother's blood keeps me alive, so thank him for that...*

"That doesn't seem to stop Sylvie," Rafe said, with a twist of a smile.

"Nothing does," she lamented.

"You raised her well."

A third tiger iced the air as Céleste laughed. "I hardly think I can lay claim to that."

"No?"

"She only eats with utensils half the time—"

"Ah." He waved this off. "Trivial stuff. Besides, good manners make terrible stories. Our Magpie is meant for greater things. And the reason Sylvie is such a skilled daydreamer is because you and Honoré gave her enough freedom to explore. You offered her a safe place to return to at the end of her adventures. That's no small thing."

"The dead man's mausoleum surrounded by booby traps?"

A smirk scrawled across his rugged features. "A home. It's what I'd like La Ruche to become, when all this is over."

A sudden ache gripped Céleste's chest. She couldn't deny that she wanted this too—days where she could wake up beside *her* Rafe. Where their masques glittered in the afternoon sun and the halls of the artists' colony hummed with the magic of ideas.

"So you've said."

"Have I?"

"You told me you wanted to open its doors to a league of imaginers. Sylvie decided the soup kitchen should serve ice cream. La

Fée Verte decided to turn that dream into a necklace—pretty as you please."

It was curious to Céleste that a similar notion had started growing back in the missing dream's place. Though the more she considered this, the more it made sense. Jean Cocteau had conjured plenty of dresses embellished with flame, even after that first gown of dark stars was extinguished. Picasso kept trying to fill the landscape room with cubes. Guillaume had a poem about La Fée Verte that he'd only written in scraps and only in the daytime. Several drafts were drifting through La Ruche's shared halls. Its working title? "*In Somnis Veritas*."

"A League of Imaginers," Rafe murmured. "I like that."

"Me too."

As soon as Céleste pulled off her *ushanka*, the songbirds rushed in, coloring the sky emerald for almost an entire minute. She watched the flock with a melting gaze. Her masque went the color of frost, vanishing with the last of the birds.

Only...

Not quite.

A single bird remained perched on the zeppelin's anchor. There was a gray string in its beak, but the thought hadn't originated from Céleste. It didn't look like one of Rafe's silver imaginings either. There was no glow. Only a wormlike squirm as the songbird dropped the idea into the snow.

Céleste froze.

Rafe did too.

Both thieves stared at the strand, which looked as if it had been plucked from a corpse. Not as a hair, but as a very long, very wriggly maggot.

"Is that...?" She didn't dare finish her question.

Rafe nodded. For someone who'd spent over five years combing the salon for this lost thought, he didn't seem pleased to stumble across it. In fact, he stepped back when the string started to melt the surrounding snow. The mountain disappeared too, thawing into gray cobblestones. Buildings began to rise from the carpet of clouds, growing into familiar formations. Notre-Dame's bell towers unfurled in the distance. The Panthéon's dome. The layered designs of the Palais Garnier. Landmarks that were soon lost to closer structures.

The songbird stayed on the anchor.

A single splash of color in a dead landscape.

Céleste held her breath, studying the buildings. She and Rafe were standing on a nameless street with colorless doors and curtained windows. Nothing moved, yet there was a frantic flavor to the air. Undercurrents of desperation. It reminded her, somehow, of the sketches hanging from the walls of the attic loft in Montmartre. This was Terreur's handiwork. *His* city. So much so that she kept expecting to see him perched on a nearby rooftop.

It was La Fée Verte who flew down instead.

The Sanct landed next to her songbird. The worm-gray imagining wriggled at her bare feet, casting its vision across the landscape. Not even the light of her golden masque could soften its starkness.

"Welcome to the bones of Paris," La Fée Verte said, folding her wings.

"So this is what the city would look like without magic?" asked Céleste.

It was strange—all the architecture remained unchanged, but there was some essential *-ness* missing. Paris was not Paris. Statues sat blank-eyed. There wasn't even a sense that they might stir. It was the same with the curtains. Only the surrounding shadows flickered, the way they so often did in the corners of Catherine Palace or the edges of the Caveau.

"Without magic? No." La Fée Verte glanced at a nearby alley, where a withered leg stuck out between some crates. "This is Paris without hope."

There was a rumbling in the ash-colored sky, too sharp to be thunder. Céleste's tea tasted extra metallic as she swallowed. She couldn't help but wonder what kind of nightmare had sprouted in this one's place.

"I'm guessing you didn't keep this in the Vault of Dreams," Rafe said.

La Fée Verte shook her head. "It would've stunted the other imaginings."

"So we never would have found it." Rafe let out a rueful laugh. "I'll be damned. Well... double damned."

"What do you mean by bringing this to us now?" Céleste asked.

"You must both know my faith in you was thin, when we agreed to join forces and search for Terreur's heart... I supposed you were offering your services to save your own skins. And souls," she added. "I agreed to go along for Honoré's sake."

"So did I," Céleste said.

"I know that now—after what you did for her the night the catacombs collapsed." La Fée Verte swallowed. "The lengths you went to, to save her, they showed me that I needed to go even further myself." She knelt and picked up the idea, the way a fisherman might bait a hook. The gray city faded from sight. "Finding Terreur's heart may fix many things; but it will not heal you, Céleste Artois. He won't bow to blackmail. He'll drag you into a grave with him and scorch the rest of Rafe's soul along the way."

Again, Céleste shivered. She knew—deep down—that the Sanct spoke the truth.

"Honoré and I have been talking." La Fée Verte paused, long enough for Céleste to raise an eyebrow. Closed doors were an oddity in the salon, yet the vines around the Sanct's bedroom had grown much lusher as of late. Even stranger? Céleste sometimes heard Honoré's laughter through the leaves. "We believe there's a better way. She believes I can trust you with this."

The Sanct held the nightmare out on her flat palm.

Céleste felt more wriggling in her throat as she stared at Terreur's lost thought. She could see Rafe at the edge of her vision, shifting his weight from foot to foot. "Trust me to do what?"

"Once we find Terreur's heart, we'll keep it in its hiding place until you can present this dream to him. Hopefully, he'll then fulfill his end of the bargain. Heal you. Release Rafe from his service. Once these deeds are done, Dame Honoré will stab his heart. He'll have no chance to make this future come true."

The Rainbow Ball

You are cordially invited to the home of Duchess d'Uzès
for a colorful fête
to fight the bleak midwinter.

The invitation in your hand is gilded, but the party is not magical. At least not at first glance.

There is no starlight in the champagne—of course, you'd be served champagne, seeing as your hostess is the heir to the Veuve Clicquot fortune!—and the Mazarin paintings on the ceiling stay put no matter how long you stare. A doorman offers to take your coat, then gestures down the front hall at a long line of mannequins. They are not wearing gowns but wigs. The finest work Paris's perruquiers can manage—coiffed to perfection. Only someone of Duchess d'Uzès's standing could afford so many pieces. The dyes alone must have cost a fortune.

"The duchess requests you wear the color of your choosing."

The doorman himself is wearing a headpiece of the lightest violet—it is a subtle shade compared to the rest of the offerings. You drift down the hall, picturing yourself in different shades of blue: moonlight or steel or fairy pool. There are purples to rival the ripest of plums. Pinks that would make roses wilt for shame. A marquise has chosen an orange wig that makes her dark eyebrows look like tiger stripes. You do not know if you are that bold. Perhaps green is the color that's calling to you. Sea glass or spring leaves or the shine of a dragonfly's wing.

Yes, you think, when the piece settles over your head. *This fits.*

"Rainbow wigs!" another guest beside you exclaims, as she picks out a set of turquoise curls. "How on earth do you think the duchess comes up with such ideas?"

She isn't really expecting an answer, but one arrives anyway. The palace doors open for two girls the doorman does not seem to notice. He doesn't take their fur coats, nor does he point them toward the wigs. It looks as if one of the girls is already wearing one—pink that wouldn't just shame roses but Valentine's Day cards too. This doesn't stop her from snatching a sapphire piece for her friend.

"Look, Anastasia!" she exclaims. "We did it! The wigs are real!"

What else would they be?

You forget this question quickly, as you enter the party proper. A photographer stops you and asks to take your portrait for *L'Illustration*. The picture will be printed in color! It will be admired by ladies in London and New York and Melbourne... ladies who will then pay *their* wigmakers countless dollars and guineas to copy the idea. Of course they will! It's not just avant-garde. It's fun.

The camera's bulb flashes.

You smile, not just for posterity, but because you want to make the world a brighter place.

Chapter 32

Fairy Hair

Sylvie of a Single Name had never had her portrait taken before.

She wasn't sure if the photograph from Duchess d'Uzès's ball truly counted. The photographer didn't register her presence—he seemed much more focused on capturing Anastasia in her bright blue wig. The grand duchess obliged with a smile. "You've posed before!" the man behind the camera exclaimed, half a minute into the process. "Most children turn out a blur because they can't sit still." It was difficult, certainly. Sylvie was itching to explore the ballroom, which the champagne heiress had managed to decorate with flowers, even though there was a thick coat of snow blanketing the world outside. Potted orchids sat on stands, looking as delicate as a rich lady's slippers. Several of the guests had chosen hairpieces that matched the flowers. The dance floor was dizzy with color. Sylvie felt something even brighter bloom inside her chest as she watched the kaleidoscopic waltz.

All this had grown from a single inspired seed.

Her magic was no longer just make-believe.

The wigs were solid. Everyone in the room could see the fantastical colors they wore—and Duchess d'Uzès was already insisting they wear their hairpieces home. "Let us make it all the rage this new year! Everyone shall be clamoring for fairy hair in 1914!" She prodded her own oceanic curls, which covered her head like a swim cap, and waved to where the daydreamers were posing. "Especially after they see how well we wore it!"

It then occurred to Sylvie, as the photographer stepped back and pulled a glass plate from his camera, that their portrait was also very real. Anastasia's sapphire hair wasn't yet visible on the autochrome slide, but after a wash of chemicals, all that would change. No doubt one of *L'Illustration*'s readers would recognize the Russian princess...

It was a good reason to steal the exposure. Not that Sylvie needed a reason. She would have pocketed the picture anyway—a souvenir of her very first ball.

"Was it everything you dreamed it would be?" Anastasia asked, when the pair of them finally drifted back toward rue de la Réunion.

Sylvie considered. She had, after all, spent an unseemly number of hours imagining what it would be like to attend a ball where women sipped sparkling drinks and men wore mysterious velvet masks and at least one great love story unfolded during the waltzes. It seemed entirely possible that pieces of this fantasy had somehow woven into her idea for the rainbow wigs, before growing into the glorious party Duchess d'Uzès had just hosted.

"It wasn't as magical as the dances at Versailles." The ghost balls she'd witnessed in those mirrors had been dripping with enchantments, golden crowns growing on revelers' heads while they danced on the painted ceilings. "And this ball didn't have a prince."

"Nonsense! Wasn't your friend Jean there?"

The Frivolous Prince had made an appearance toward the evening's end, after the photographer had packed up his gear. There was no one to document his presence. Or the lavender wig he plucked from the doorman's head, after giving the man a peck on the cheek. It hadn't been quite a *bisou*. It had not been unwelcome either.

"I meant a real prince," Sylvie said, as they drew closer to their pink door. It looked especially inviting with the fresh snow—while most of the flakes that fell on rue de la Réunion's cobblestones had already melted, the ground that bordered Russia was powdery white. As if the presence of enchantment weren't obvious enough, icicles clung from the doorframe.

"Well, you can come and say hello to Alexei. He's been asking about you—" Anastasia tugged the wig from her head. Her smile also slipped when she opened the door. "He's been asking about 'Our Friend' too."

The chill that went through Sylvie's spine had nothing to do with the ice hanging from the doorframe. She'd given Grigori Rasputin a wide berth since the night Honoré had been stabbed, after Céleste discovered that Sylvie and Anastasia had watched the healing of that wound through Catherine Palace's windows.

"*Mon Dieu*, Sylvie!" the oldest Enchantress hissed. "It's bad enough that you steal the princess from her bed every night! If the Mad Monk catches you..." She fell silent, her eyes iced with fear.

It had been enough to make Sylvie stay quiet too. Céleste did not spook easily.

This was another reason Sylvie found her friend's behavior around the grand duchess strange. To say the least. Honoré had a soft spot for Anastasia—laughing at her jokes and even teaching her a bit of knifework. But Céleste never stayed in the same room as the princess long enough to watch.

This did not sit well with Sylvie.

Neither did the stories Anastasia brought back from Russia every evening. The dark cloud around Tsarina Alexandra's head was growing worse. Alexei's too. "I know the starets is evil. And I know we're not supposed to daydream on my side of the door anymore." The princess looked out over the floors of the Children's Palace. The tin soldier regiment had built a fort using gumdrops as building blocks. They were sturdy. Rock-hard, yes, but also enduring. In the four months since they'd been imagined, not a single candy had disappeared. This was the biggest reason Sylvie had decided not to enchant the tsarevitch's playroom anymore. "But...my brother needs our magic. It's all he talks about when we're alone. He keeps trying to sneak over here so he can play, and he keeps getting hurt, and Mama keeps asking for Rasputin..." Anastasia shuddered. Her fingers tightened around her wig. "I know we can't heal my brother's hemophilia until we've found the heart, but I'm afraid Alexei might break before then."

Sylvie looked from the cobalt strands of the hairpiece to Anastasia's long chestnut braid. They were too far from Paris's streetlamps for Sylvie to tell if there were any darker strings growing there. "You shouldn't be afraid."

"I know." The princess's voice trembled. "But I am."

Sylvie didn't know what to say. She figured she should probably take Anastasia's wig—that was another rule they'd established, that no items from Paris crossed over to Russia—but she slipped her hand into her pocket instead. The glass-plate exposure there felt as thin as the ice creeping over the outside lake. As fragile as the windows of Alexander Palace. The tsarevitch's room was glazed with moonlight.

A short flight.

"He'll be waiting up to hear about Duchess d'Uzès's ball," Anastasia said. "He's been waiting to hear about it ever since I told him about how you planted the idea in her head. He'll be so excited to see how close you are to becoming a Sanct." She held up the blue hairpiece. "But I know he'd be even more excited to see you."

"I guess a quick visit couldn't hurt," Sylvie answered, as she stepped into the Children's Palace.

Little did she know how wrong she was. Later, much later, Sylvie of a Single Name would spend hours studying the photograph in her pocket, wishing she'd known to stay still... all the autochrome plate had picked up of her presence was a glowing pink blur and the faintest outline of wings. Anastasia stood beside her. Hands folded. Hair stained the color of tears. Her smile seemed true, but Sylvie knew better now.

She wished she could turn back time and turn to her friend.

What would she say then?

Au revoir? Adieu? I'm so, so sorry.

Something about Catherine Palace felt different when Céleste Artois followed Terreur through the Door to Everywhere. It was cold. Damn cold. This was to be expected—Rasputin did not use the ceramic stoves made of delft tiles, and the snow was as blank as the days on a Parisian socialite's calendar. January 1914. Aside from the buzzed-about fête at Duchess d'Uzès's Champs-Élysées palace nearly a week ago, the City of Light had fallen into hibernation. It was hard to tell whether this was because of the weather or because more nameless bodies were surfacing—enough that street singers were starting to weave warnings into their songs: *The darkness shall eat you if you dare to tread, so heed your clocks and stay in bed.*

Céleste wasn't sure if Terreur had directly inspired the tune, but he didn't stop the musicians in Belleville from strumming it. He did halt at the center of the ballroom, however. His pale nostrils flared.

The Mad Monk's robes shifted with a nervous bow.

Other parts of the palace were shifting too. Gods on the ceiling hoisted spears and swords; the golden-bright angels over the doors looked ready to launch. Céleste tried not to let her own muscles coil as she paused beside Terreur.

"What's wrong?" her employer growled in Russian.

Rasputin's icy gaze flicked from Céleste to Terreur. "It could be nothing—"

"What?"

"I made a strange discovery when I went to collect some of the young tsarevitch earlier." The Mad Monk's spidery hand dipped into his robes, tangling the chains of his saint necklaces. "This was in his playroom."

The hairpiece was as blue as the walls of the palace and the winter sky beyond. Céleste trained her stare there, hoping neither of the Sancts would notice that extra pause in her pulse. *Sylvie. Oh, Sylvie.* She knew the girl had taken Anastasia to Duchess d'Uzès's party.

I was at a real ball with a real princess! It was a dream come true! So many dreams come true! You should've seen all the different wigs, Céleste!

Well, she was seeing one now.

"What am I staring at?" Terreur snarled. "A half-frozen rabbit?"

"I believe this is a wig."

"A . . . wig? The tsarevitch put that on his head?"

"He put it on his giant stuffed dog, but that's beside the point."

"And what *is* your point? That the prince of Russia plays dress-up?"

"I—" The Mad Monk faltered. "I don't know. But something isn't right. When I asked the boy how he acquired this, he refused to say."

"So pluck the answer from his head!" her employer snarled.

"The boy's anima is so thin, that might very well unravel him," Rasputin said. "The label says this wig was made in Paris, but the tsarina would not have ordered it. Alexandra isn't fanciful enough. She hardly lets her girls wear anything more than pearls—"

"Has it occurred to you that perhaps I have better things to do than listen to you wax poetic about dynastic wardrobes?"

"I am simply trying to be vigilant," the Mad Monk replied coolly. "You asked me to stand guard here, after all."

"It's a wig," Terreur told him. "It's nothing."

Yet Céleste could see the ballroom's murals stirring in the corners of her vision: wrecked ships and warring deities and a two-headed eagle flapping its restless wings. *Nothing can touch you*, she remembered her employer crowing, *because you have nothing to lose.* What a lie. If Terreur really believed this, why was the dark cloud of his mask still flaring? Why were all the gods bristling, their weapons pointed in the same direction? What had the Mad Monk been placed here to protect?

Only one answer made sense.

And it was not nothing.

"Terreur's heart is in Catherine Palace."

The salon also stirred, when Céleste delivered this news, but not with vengeful angels. La Fée Verte's birds rushed toward the settee she was sharing with Honoré. The chandelier's butterflies scattered as Sylvie spilled out of her vine hammock. Marmalade batted at them from the bar top. The blue elephant behind him made a trumpeting noise.

"How do you know?" the youngest Enchantress shouted over it. "Did you see it there? Did he tell you?"

"Not in so many words." Céleste raised her flask, which was down to the dregs with its language-learning tea. No matter. She repeated the exchange in French, sparing no details. Especially not the colorful wig.

Sylvie, at least, had the awareness to blush when she heard this, her cheeks matching her own bright hair. "Oh."

"Oh?" Honoré's voice was as piqued as her dragon. Despite the Fisherman's warnings, the other Enchantress claimed she'd found a way to manage the jewelry—and mostly that proved true. The silver seemed contained to her right arm, though at times like this, it started swallowing the skin past her shoulder. Molten metal crept alongside her neck veins. "You let Anastasia take a Parisian wig back to Alexander Palace, and all you have to say for yourself is '*oh*'?"

"It wasn't a *magical* wig," Sylvie protested. "I figured it would be fine. And it is! It's better than fine! Now we know where to send the cats!"

"She's right, my dame." La Fée Verte touched Honoré's knee.

Céleste did not miss how her friend suddenly softened, how the ring melted back from her throat as Honoré turned her gaze to the Sanct. "Cats are fine enough as scouts, but we can't send them to Catherine Palace. Not when we're this close. I'll go myself." Honoré looked to Céleste. "Did Terreur say anything about where the heart might be? Under a floorboard or something?"

"No," Céleste said. "But all the palace's paintings began pointing their weapons in the same direction when they believed there was a threat."

"Just like the statues in the Palais Garnier!"

"I'm not sure they'd be so helpful," Céleste told the youngest Enchantress.

"Perhaps not on purpose." Honoré grinned. "My guess is they're standing guard. If we go the opposite way of the weapons, maybe we'll find what they're so set on protecting. Could you tell which direction they were pointing?"

"Northeast, judging by the sunrise." The golden light had come too quickly for her to pass this news along to Rafe, who was asleep in La Ruche at this very moment. *We know where the heart is hidden. We'll find it soon. Our hour is almost here.* He would no doubt check his watch when she finally told him. They'd sit together on the dusk-washed mattress and pass their shared fate back and forth, until the golden chains were a-tangle between them.

Soon, very soon, they would both be free.

Chapter 33

Path of Swords

Catherine Palace was the saddest fancy building Honoré Cote had ever set eyes upon. Its emptiness was a mockery. So much space, and almost every square inch was covered in gold. It felt a lot like a mausoleum, but instead of an epitaph about christening stars, one of Céleste's favorite sayings echoed through her brain instead: *Corpses can be stripped, and kings can be beheaded, so it's best to be the taker.*

"I'm trying, *mon amie*," she whispered through gritted teeth, as she flew to the next window.

More emptiness.

More gold.

If Terreur's heart happened to be made of such metal, then their hunt was well and truly fucked. Honoré's search felt slow enough as it was—she'd spent most of the day circling the palace, holding her breath so it would not frost the glass as she peered through the panes. Her silver wings felt increasingly frozen between her shoulder blades. Her invisibility cloak itched. What she wouldn't give to toss it off and walk through the palace's front door. She *could*. Technically. But that would only result in an unwanted audience with the Mad Monk. The Sanct was wandering from room to room, his mouth moving as if in prayer, his masque flaring with icy light. Back and forth. Back and forth. Honoré watched his route, trying to determine if the Sanct paused in any particular place. The chapel perhaps? A ballroom? He did seem to spend more time in the southern portion of the palace—

"Have you found anything?"

Honoré's dagger was out of her sleeve before she recognized the voice as Sylvie. The youngest Enchantress's breath plumed from a nearby evergreen branch. Any nearer, and she might have gotten stabbed.

"You're not supposed to be here, *ma rêveuse*! I told you to wait for me at the Children's Palace."

"I got bored." Sylvie huffed. Some snow plopped onto the ground below as she settled on the bough.

"What? With all those toys?"

"I brought a few." There was a shimmer as Sylvie pushed aside her invisibility cloak—ostensibly to dig even deeper into her pocket. Her wrist-less hand appeared, holding two tin soldiers. The metal men themselves were holding trumpets, looking quite disgruntled to be out of their petrified gumdrop fort.

Honoré could relate. "Dare I ask why?"

"I figured we'd need some lookouts while we're searching the palace."

"What *I* need is for *you* to stay out of the way." Honoré could see the ghastly blue flash of the Mad Monk's masque drifting toward the gold-domed chapel. This was the palace's northernmost point, the logical place to start her search.

Sylvie must have been tracking the blue light too. "Looks like I'm not the one you have to get rid of," she said. "What's your contingency?"

One of the toy soldiers teetered off the branch, landing headfirst into the giant snowdrift below. Honoré watched the fruitless wiggle of its tiny legs. Again, she could relate. "I'm still working on the initial plan."

"Which is?"

"Rasputin's circuit through the palace takes thirty minutes. Give or take. If I time things carefully, I can search while he's at the opposite end—"

"That will take forever!" Sylvie snatched the second marching soldier before it could follow in its comrade's footsteps. "No. What you need is a decoy." Her breath swirled through the bare branches, toward where

Alexander Palace sat—its walls as pale and bright as this January sun. "Let me see if Anastasia and I can find a way to summon the Mad Monk so you'll have longer to search. There's a lot of cupid asses in there."

Honoré released a fraught sigh. "Don't swear, Sylvie."

"Don't treat me like a helpless child, Honoré."

"You're eleven."

"Maybe not," Sylvie's icy breath shot back. "I might be twelve by now, but that doesn't matter because the point is that I'm not powerless. Let me help. Please."

Honoré was struck by this last word—and the way the girl said it. Not with sticky chocolate fingers or a whining punctuation. Sylvie wasn't begging. She was right. She had power now. Purpose. And Honoré's hunt for the heart would go much more smoothly if Rasputin wasn't skulking around the place.

"Fine," she relented.

With a small shout of glee, Sylvie launched off her branch, shaking pine needles to the ground below.

The afternoon wore on; it seemed the sun itself was frozen in the sky. Honoré heard laughter weaving through the leafless trees. She could see the flash of blades on the canal—not knives, but skates. Russia's grand duchesses danced across the ice, their fur caps fluttering. Four became three, after Anastasia hurried inside.

Her sisters followed not ten minutes later, after a black cloud appeared over Alexander Palace's lawn. A person, Honoré realized, as this specter called to the older princesses. *I* have *seen strings like that before. They're all around my mother.* When Anastasia had said this, Honoré hadn't quite grasped the severity of Tsarina Alexandra's situation. She'd pictured wild black hairs or an extra stretch of shadow…There *was* a ribbon of darkness spooling out from the empress's feet. Or, rather, where her feet should be. The woman was so entirely shrouded that Honoré couldn't see her at all.

Instead, she watched thousands of strands pull taut across the snow, creating a dim path through the park. At the end? The Mad Monk halted. A look of annoyance flashed across his face. Then magic. He rushed out of Catherine Palace—following the queen's shadowy call. The drifts looked whiter once his robes dragged over them, erasing his way to Alexander Palace.

Honoré swooped in, wondering if she should pause to shake snow off her invisibility cloak before climbing the entryway's stairs. She wasn't sure how much time she had—though surely it would be enough for the flakes that fell from her shoulders to melt into the crimson carpet.

She did a cursory scan of the chambers leading into the palace's left wing. Sylvie was right. There were plenty of gilded cupids' asses here. Céleste had been on to something too—every painting wielding a weapon aimed it in the same direction. Tridents. Scythes. Arrows. Pointing, all pointing. Honoré held her breath as she followed away from the tips of these blades, tiptoeing across parquet floors. No booby traps, so far. That, or the dragon ring was shielding her from such curses.

The fifth room was different, not just for the amber covering the walls, but because the cherub painted in the ceiling had aimed its arrow down toward the floor. A step into the adjoining room only confirmed Honoré's suspicions; Mercury pointed his snake-entwined staff toward the southwest.

Terreur's heart had to be here.

Somewhere.

Honoré stepped back into the amber room, studying the precious stones that covered the walls—thousands of pieces in hundreds of shades. The colors should have reminded her of La Fée Verte's eyes, but they seemed a little too stagnant. Several pieces had bubbles trapped inside, unbreathed air left there for thousands of years. They'd since been carved into shapes: Crowns and cornucopias filled with fruit and chariot battles. Women with bare breasts and warriors holding their enemies' heads and walled-off citadels. Seashells and garlands. A vast array of weaponry.

Again, Honoré followed the arrows to a corner table. She could see the shape of a box beneath its white sheet. Dare she look beneath? The surrounding mirrored panels showed nothing special in their reflections, though she supposed that if Terreur had really hidden his heart here, he would take care to keep it under wraps.

Or a dust cover.

Honoré lifted the cloth slowly, gently, so that not even a mote stirred. Her heart did though, at the thought that one of the cherubs perched above the mirrors had moved. Were they watching? Really watching? She waited a moment, then lifted the cloth another inch, revealing a pair of engraved letters:

CL

The initials of one Christine Leroux.

This was the opera singer's jewelry box. The one her murderer had stolen away with the night she'd died. The one Honoré had been so sure had been buried in Paris's catacombs. How had it ended up in a palace outside Saint Petersburg, Russia? And more importantly, what did it hold within?

There was a keyhole between the letters. Locked, surely. Not that Honoré would have been fool enough to try. Their plan—to hand over Terreur's dream so that he might heal Céleste—would only work if he had no inkling his heart had been discovered. She'd already pushed her luck by shifting the sheet. She stole a glance through the keyhole instead. Her own heart thrashed like a bat's broken wing. Yes, yes. That was him. Without a doubt. She could end Terreur. Right here. Right now. Forever.

Kill the bastard.

The dragon on Honoré's arm went stiff.

The ring did not back down when she turned her thoughts to Céleste, how stabbing this heart now would seal her friend's fate, so she shut her eyes and focused on La Fée Verte instead—her emerald laughter, her glowing touch, the better path they'd chosen for each other. *You are more than a sword.*

The heirloom's metal softened then, just enough for Honoré to drop the sheet.

Soon, she whispered to the silver beast in her head. *We'll circle back soon.*

Chapter 34

A Less Morbid Cheers

Sylvie of a Single Name sat by the fireplace of the salon's library. Her cup of smoky cocoa steamed beside her, untouched, as Honoré recounted her expedition through Catherine Palace. Sylvie didn't even lift it in a toast alongside the other Enchantresses and La Fée Verte: "To destroying the evil sorcerer's heart!" Céleste's purple aperitif clinked with Honoré's silver drink and La Fée Verte's glowing gold flute—their motions so exuberant that the glasses nearly chipped.

"What's wrong, *ma rêveuse*?" Céleste paused before her drink could reach her lips. "Should we have a less morbid cheers? 'To our happily ever afters,' perhaps?"

Sylvie shook her head.

Honoré set her glass down too. "What, Sylvie?"

"It's . . . I just don't have much of an appetite."

She could tell the other Enchantress didn't believe her. "Here." Honoré handed over her aperitif—the colors of the liquid inside started to shift. "As you said earlier, you're older now. You should at least have a celebratory sip."

Sylvie watched the silver tarnish into maroon. It would lighten into pink soon—the way it always did when she snuck tastes of the welcoming drink from the flute pyramid. Those had always made her think of her first proper picnic with the Enchantresses. A full plate of food with her newfound family. But as she gripped Honoré's glass, a darker memory bubbled up. It didn't have far to rise—for it was only one hour old.

Anastasia Nikolaevna with her skates slung over her shoulder.

Alexei on the edge of his camp bed, eyeing the blades.

"Too sharp," his sister had said. "All we need is a distraction, Alyosha, not your death."

Sylvie hadn't known what to expect when the tsarevitch grabbed a book from his bedside table. Alexei was already as pale as the page he used to slice his finger—the tsarevitch put on a brave face as he ran his thumb across the gilded paper. Quick. Crimson. There was only a bead at first, as if the prince were holding a tiny ruby. Then it began to braid down his forefinger, lacing Alexei's wrist. The amount of blood was unbelievable for the size of the cut. Sylvie shirked back to a corner of the bedroom, almost too stunned to wrap herself back in her invisibility cloak. By the time Anastasia screamed for their mother, the boy's shirt was soaked with red, and the camp bed's sheets were spattered. The tsarevitch lay down in them, and while it was the same color as roses, he looked like the worst possible ending of a fairy tale. A corpse no kiss could stir.

The bleeding was awful, yes.

But the "healing" was worse. Grigori Rasputin paused at the prince's threshold, his grim nostrils flaring. For a moment, Sylvie feared he'd smelled her, but the scent of iron was too thick. Every breath of hers drowned with it. Alexei's breathing sounded damp too. He gasped as his mother shadowed the foot of his bed. The Mad Monk leaned down toward the tsarevitch's pillow and...

Drank.

The Sanct wasn't swallowing with his throat, but Sylvie couldn't come up with a better word to describe the scene. Prayers were whispered. Blood vanished. The ragged sounds from the bed stopped, and Alexei Nikolaevich still looked dead. His chest was not moving. Not moving. Sylvie too forgot to breathe. Anastasia let out a sob.

Just then, one of the luminescent icons on the wall above the bed fell, landing straight on the tsarevitch's chest.

He sat up with a gasp.

His mother gasped as well, something that sounded like an *alleluia*. The Mad Monk made the sign of the cross again, knotting more dark strings between himself and the tsarina. Anastasia stopped sobbing, but her face stayed crumpled as she retrieved the icon from the carpet. She glanced in Sylvie's direction, and when the grand duchess lifted the frame higher, Sylvie saw that it sat empty. No saint stood against the shining background...

The sight would've been enough to spoil anyone's appetite. Sylvie wasn't sure she could even toast to a happily ever after, not after she'd left the Romanovs like that, so she stared at her drink's bubbles as they rose to the top. Popped.

"Rafe and I will take Terreur's dream to him at dawn," Céleste said. "Honoré can return to Russia and hide near Catherine Palace—once I'm healed, she can grab the heart and start stabbing."

"I very much look forward to that." Honoré grabbed another aperitif glass and raised it in a second cheers. The silver looked like molten metal sliding down her throat.

Sylvie swallowed. Her own drink was unsipped.

"What about Rasputin?" she asked.

"He can't hurt me." Honoré nodded at the dragon relic coiling up her arm. "Not with magic anyway."

No, but Sylvie couldn't get the scene from the tsarevitch's bedroom out of her head. Alexei's paper cut had nearly killed him, and the Mad Monk's "miracle" had made things far worse before the prince became better.

"Rasputin will be distracted," Céleste said. "It's quite possible I'll be in a ballroom in the opposite wing of the palace."

"You shouldn't underestimate him," La Fée Verte told them. "He may serve as Terreur's guard, but the Mad Monk is a fearsome Sanct in his own right. An entire empire believes the stories of Rasputin's sorcery. That alone gives him immense power, but his hold over the royal family is... well, it doesn't bode well."

Sylvie kept watching the bubbles of her drink. Pop, pop, popping. It was the color of bougainvillea now. Rather darker than the aperitif she'd grabbed on her very first night here. It smelled different as well—no more *pain au chocolat* at a graveyard picnic. Instead she caught scents of orchids and waltzes and snow. Blue moonlight. A bluer wig. A princess's hand in hers.

"I saw the tsarina this afternoon." Honoré hesitated. "You're right, La Fée Verte. It's better for us not to tangle with Rasputin. While he's healing Céleste, I'll sneak into the Amber Room and steal the jewelry box. Once Terreur closes the Door to Everywhere—" Honoré drew a line across her throat. The dragon on her arm grinned.

"What do you want me to do?" Sylvie wondered.

"Just... don't go peeking through the Catherine Palace windows with Anastasia," Céleste told her. "Make sure the grand duchess knows to stay away. Take her to Stohrer or something."

Just this morning, Sylvie might have argued differently. She *had*. But a magical bakery sounded like a much better distraction than the bloodbath she'd witnessed. Nay, inspired. Her aperitif shuddered in her hand, creating even more fuchsia fizz. She took a small sip, determined not to dwell on gore anymore. She pictured cakes in her future—Alexei's too. After Terreur's heart was stabbed, she and Anastasia could bring back a box of magical macarons to share with the tsarevitch. He deserved a sugary thank-you. He deserved far more than that, and when Sylvie of a Single Name became a Sanct, she'd find a way to make his blood thicker. His future brighter. As bright as La Fée Verte's masque, or the smile that slid across Honoré's face when she stared there, or the twinkle in Céleste's eyes as the Enchantress entertained dreams of her own.

Sylvie raised her glass then, determined.

"To all our happily ever afters!" she said.

"We found it."

The scene was just as Céleste had envisioned. La Ruche was awash in evening light—amber gasps of sun gave way to more velvety violets. Shadows sat softly on Rafe's face as he perched on the edge of the mattress. His fox materialized on the pillow as he raked a hand through his wild black hair. His other hand fished for the watch.

"Really?" His whisper glimmered almost as brightly as the chains he pulled from his pocket. "When? Where? What does his heart look like? I always figured it would be something like a musket ball or a dried-out housefly—"

"Honoré didn't say." Céleste settled onto the bed beside him. "But we figured out Terreur has been hiding his heart in Catherine Palace. Sylvie left a blue wig in the royals' nursery, and that led Rasputin to let slip he was guarding something. Honoré confirmed the heart's location this afternoon—she's going to return at dawn to stab it."

"Dawn," Rafe repeated, as he opened the watch. "What time does the sun rise these days?"

Céleste didn't have to speak the answer, not when it was so clearly marked by the timepiece's hands—*8:45*. The gears didn't move when Rafe passed his relic to her. How many times had they traded their fateful hour back and forth, wondering when it would finally arrive?

"We've got the fucker." The fire of it all crackled in Rafe's eyes. His voice dipped precariously low. "I've spent so many moments imagining this one—where I'd stumble out of a sandy tomb with a scarab beetle in my fist or come across some book in Terreur's study with the pages carved out. But no matter how many scenarios I pictured, there was always a part of me that feared I'd be trapped in his shadows forever."

Céleste could hear this fear, still. She watched as his fox curled on top of the pillow, its nose tucked protectively under its tail. "You won't, Rafe. At eight forty-five tomorrow morning, our deal with Terreur will be done. You and I, we'll both be free."

"I know..." Rafe kept looking at the watch in her hand. Even though the artist was seated, he somehow looked as if he were standing at the edge of a cliff. "It's just, now that our hour is actually here, I can't quite bring myself to believe it."

Céleste understood. Hope was dangerous. It was the best and

worst kind of feeling, coming so close to a far-fetched dream. She'd seen such things shattered too many times before. She herself had done the breaking, reeling men in, only to cut their purse strings loose.

But this hope between them?

It was different.

It was two golden chains pulled tight.

"You don't have to believe in fate," Céleste whispered, as she drew Rafe to her. "Just believe *me*."

Most of their studio had fallen into darkness by then, but that didn't matter. They could make their own light—kissing until sparks caught into something brighter. They didn't need the landscape room to conjure anymore, Céleste realized, when she saw Rafe's old horizons beside her salon scenes, both bathed in silver rays on this moonless night. They had each other. Wholly. Dreaming new futures for themselves until La Ruche itself shone like a star—and every constellation in the City of Light shifted.

They shimmered.

On and on and on, awaiting the dawn.

Chapter 35

Pretty Little Saint

Anastasia Nikolaevna was not waiting at rue de la Réunion, come midnight. She wasn't pacing the street's cobblestones or retrieving her key from the pink door, as was her custom. Nor was the grand duchess waiting on the other side.

Her magical fur coat hung limp in the makeshift closet of the Children's Palace. Sylvie paused beside it, struck by the rest of the room's stillness. There were no jungle creatures bathing in teacups. No sentinels stood watch on the ramparts of the candy fort. No battleships shot more gumdrops into its sweetened walls.

The toys were gone.

It wasn't hard to guess where. When Sylvie stepped outside, she could see light flickering through falling snow. A fire. From Alexei's playroom window. And more shining things besides. *Mon Dieu!* Anastasia was so busy conjuring imaginings that she hadn't thought to close the curtain. Sylvie had a crystal-clear view as she flew up to the window. Not only had the grand duchess brought up most of the enchanted toys from the Children's Palace, but she'd created several new ones. A tiny model of the Orient Express looped around the nursery, pouring real smoke from its small stack. There was smoke from the double-headed firebird nesting in the fireplace, as well.

Several miniature monkeys scaled the open drapes, startling to the carpet when Sylvie rapped on the glass.

Anastasia jumped too.

Her firebird spilled sparks all over the carpet, and the grand duchess had to rush to stamp them out before she went to open the window. "Oh, hello! I was hoping you'd show up—"

"What do you think you're doing?" It struck Sylvie how much she sounded like Honoré in that moment. Her voice was a silver knife, slicing the wintry air. She looked back over her shoulder toward the park. There were too many flakes falling to see Catherine Palace through the trees, but that didn't mean Rasputin wouldn't see the winged firelight. The Mad Monk might come to investigate.

Or worse.

Anastasia picked up one of the fallen monkeys and glanced toward the open door to Alexei's room. Dark, but for the icons over his bed. Thanks to the firebird's glow, Sylvie could see dozens of eyes screaming back from the frames. She could see the tsarevitch lying beneath them. Somehow Alexei seemed even stiller than the paintings…

"He asked for the toys," the grand duchess said, with a shaky voice. "I couldn't say no, after what he did for us today."

Sylvie shut the window and closed the curtains, but the nursery still felt like winter and knives. The same smells she'd come to associate with a hospital.

Or a morgue.

"Alexei?" She stepped over several regiments of tin soldiers and paused in his doorway. "How are you feeling?"

The heir to Russia's crown turned his head then. It looked as if the Mad Monk had missed a spot of blood, there on the pillow, but as he reached for Sylvie, she could see it was something else oozing from the boy's skull.

"Scared," he said. "Scared and cold."

Anastasia appeared beside her. The firebird soared over the girls' heads, through the door, its flames catching the room's gold decor just as they had in the opera house. Saint icons burned bright. The blade-edged pages did too. *Anything can be a weapon.* Even a fairy book. For that's what it was. Sylvie had been too fraught earlier to notice its author, but now Andrew Lang's name shivered to life. The rest of the cover was the missing color of her rainbow... only it was no longer purely lilac. The star-dancing fae was spattered with blood that the Mad Monk had missed.

This didn't stop the woman from shining, though, as the firebird perched beside the book. Jewels of sweat started to sprout on Alexei's brow—a phantom crown. It shimmered as the prince tried to push himself up.

"I'll get better soon, right? Aren't you close to finding the evil sorcerer's heart?"

"Yes," Sylvie answered, her own heart in her throat. It no longer felt as if it might be made of books. "But..."

"But what?"

Alexei had asked the question, but it was Anastasia who narrowed her eyes. Her firebird burned a few degrees brighter. Sylvie was starting to sweat now too. Words felt slick in her throat. "We can't conjure here. I'm sorry, Alexei, but we have to take the imaginings away—"

"*No.*" There was something powerful in Anastasia's voice. Imperial and ancient. The firebird perched at the end of her brother's bed twisted both its heads, its feathers flaring. "No," the princess said again. "Alyosha needs our magic!"

Sylvie glanced toward the curtains, wondering if they were thick enough. She looked back at the toy soldiers she'd animated, all those months ago, and wished their limbs would still. Instantly, the army froze, back to their factory-cast formations. A mechanical expression fell over the tsarevitch's face too, almost bleak enough for Sylvie to stop, but too many other happy endings depended on this. She snuffed the sparks inside the battleships next. Their cannons went quiet.

"No!" Anastasia's firebird swelled even brighter as the grand duchess knelt to the floor and gathered up the soldiers. "Stop this, Sylvie!"

"It's too dangerous to have these toys here now," Sylvie managed. "Let's go back to Paris and wait—"

"I'm not leaving Alyosha."

"We'll come back. We can bring him some macarons."

"He doesn't need cookies! He needs..." Anastasia faltered then. She stepped out of Alexei's bedroom, her whisper as dark as the nursery shadows. "Please, Sylvie. I can't stand by and watch my brother... *die.* I can't stay in this palace and watch my parents unravel. I can't even *see* Mama anymore. I have to save my family. What's the point of our magic if we can't use it?"

Sylvie watched the model train loop around and around.

The imagining was Anastasia's, which meant Sylvie would not be able to stop it.

Nor could she control the firebird that was growing far too large for the tsarevitch's bedroom. Flames licked every which way. Normally, Anastasia's signature imagining did not scorch its surroundings, but the princess was angry this evening. Angry enough that the edges of the bloody fairy book were beginning to turn brown. Alexei's nightshirt was wet with sweat as the prince stumbled toward his window, coughing from the smoke.

"Nastya! It's too hot!"

"Don't!" Sylvie called, when the tsarevitch reached for his curtains. "Anastasia, you have to put your firebird out!"

"I can't!" A look of panic flashed across the princess's face.

The flaming bird flashed too, small fires spattering everywhere. The edges of the curtains singed as Alexei threw them open. He opened the window next. Fiery wings rushed into the howling night. Sylvie hoped the snow and wind would be enough to extinguish it; but this firebird was no longer like the imagining that had flown over them in the opera house. It was stronger than the storm. It was furious.

It was a midnight sun, burning bright enough to be seen from miles away.

The fires in the bedroom were spreading too. The air ribboned with heat as Sylvie looked over at the grand duchess. She understood then why the tents of the Carnaval des Merveilles sat empty, as empty as the imaginers' eyes outside the Quartier Secret every dawn.

Anastasia's were as blue as water, shimmering at the edges.

Sylvie could feel the bond between them.

She felt the exact moment she broke it, taking back the Enlightenment she'd wished on the princess all those months ago. Every single moment they'd experienced together evaporated from Anastasia's mind. The fires went out too. The model train fell still, and a giant cloud of sparks drifted slowly down over Alexander Park. They left no marks on the thick blanket of snow. The grounds remained as blank as the grand duchess's face. She was no longer a daydreamer, nor even a midnight waker, but a sleepwalker, turning back toward her bedroom without so much as a goodbye.

"What happened?" Alexei was still standing by the open window, carved thin by the wind.

"I—I had to take away her memories of magic so the starets wouldn't see her firebird." Sylvie herself couldn't see anything beyond the first few meters of flurries, which danced against the light of her pink masque. "I'm sorry, Alexei."

"I know." Russia's crown prince kept staring out into the snow.

He looked so damn lonely.

Sylvie reached out and touched Alexei on the arm. "I'll Enlighten Nastya again after we steal the evil sorcerer's heart," she said. "I'll come back tomorrow evening."

The tsarevitch laid his hand on top of hers. His fingers felt like ice. Not just cold, but hard, digging into Sylvie's wrist. She yelped and looked down, realizing too late that there was an extra shadow there, twining around his arm and coiling up hers, until she was too tangled to move. Someone else was controlling Alexei's grip. Someone strong enough to use the tsarevitch to pull her to the open window, where the snow was now an eerie swirl of blue.

"Tak, chto u nas zdes?"

The Mad Monk called up to Sylvie from where the firebird's ashes had fallen. His eyes were tunnels of ice with no light at the end; his robes lay ragged against the snow. When Sylvie tried to spread her own wings and launch herself from the window, the tsarevitch lashed out with another shadow-wrapped arm and *tore.*

Rasputin said something in cold, cold Russian. He tugged at the shadow strings that tied Alexei Nikolaevich to him, forcing a translation from the tsarevitch's throat. "I think not, daydreamer."

The Mad Monk kept pulling at the prince like a puppet. Alexei kept pulling at Sylvie's wings. Red-hot pain ripped through her shoulder blades. And . . . orange. Orange dust flew everywhere as the butterfly wings were crushed to a pulp beneath the tsarevitch's feet. It was almost like a ballroom dance, the way the Mad Monk moved him, the way Alexei's arm stayed locked with Sylvie's. Only the prince's eyes seemed to stay his, clinging to echoes of her apology. *I'm sorry. I'm sorry. I'm sorry.*

The Mad Monk flew to their window.

Sylvie shuddered as Rasputin reached for her—only to stroke some hair. He didn't even pull a strand, but the motion felt sinister. Even more so, when Rasputin's spidery hand moved to the golden chains draped around his neck. He spoke in a crawling sort of voice—more words she could not understand, until Alexei translated once more.

"Pink is most unexpected." The sentence seemed wrenched from the tsarevitch's mouth. "But you will make a very pretty little saint."

Chapter 36

Play the Hand You're Dealt

Céleste Artois held the fate of Paris in her hands.

The sky above Place de la Concorde looked much like the stones below—lumpy and gray. It wouldn't make a paint-worthy sunrise. This was what Céleste chose to focus on, as she and Rafe approached the Hotel Crillon, for it was too easy to let her thoughts stray, otherwise. To stare down the rue des Ombres and see its black walls for what they were: deaths. She remembered the Mapmaker burning away in La Fée Verte's memory. And the rest of the Sancts gathered behind her—their masques burning and burning and burning. All to stop the future that now wriggled in her fist. The idea was as restless as a worm cut in two with a garden spade, searching desperately for its head.

She wondered if the nightmare would move the same way in Terreur's palm, when she handed it to him. Thank God he wouldn't have much time to hold his hopeless Paris, much less make that city's shadowy streets come true.

She squeezed her own fingers tighter and glanced over at Rafe.

Her thief was smiling.

Oh, how Céleste wanted to sketch his tousled dark hair. The pop of his collar. The scars beneath. Rafe should have looked undone, but for the way his eyes twinkled. Brighter even than the fob chains that swung from his pocket.

"You're going to have to wipe that grin off your face," she said through her own half-smile.

"Not really," Rafe answered. "Even without our subtle sabotage, I'd be happy. He knows I've hoped for this day."

"It's not here yet," Céleste reminded him, looking back at the sky.

They had ten minutes until the sun broke. Tsarskoe Selo would sit in darkness a few minutes more, but that wouldn't stop Honoré from flying through the snow-sugared pines. Céleste would have to try not to stare too hard at the trees, during Rasputin's final "prayer," though she wasn't sure she could stomach staring at the Mad Monk's necklaces either. Well, she *could*. It just made her insides heavy, heavier than horseshoes...

But what was her alternative?

Be the taker or be taken.

Céleste held on to this thought, even as her fist tightened around the other. No more searching for the sun. Her eyes bored straight ahead into the tunnel, finding the keyhole. One way or another—dead or not—this was the end.

Their final meeting with Terreur.

The Caveau was more crowded than Céleste had expected. Usually, at this hour, most of the gangsters who frequented the bar were passed out in their beds. Or in their cups. But there were still cards being played. Four Apaches and Terreur sat around a table piled high with coins and a bright yellow boot. Items worth betting. Céleste very much doubted the game was fair, seeing as most of the players were covered in compulsive black marks, Honoré's brother included. The scar-faced fellow next to him was yanking a second boot off his foot, though he paused at the sight of Céleste and Rafe.

"Ah, my tender-hearted artists!" Terreur appeared flush—cards in his hands and flesh on his cheeks. "Join us!"

More of a command than a request, judging by the tug on her own shadow.

Rafe strolled to the table and pulled up two more chairs.

He'd managed to stop grinning, at least.

Céleste settled across from their employer. Her palm squirmed as the rest of the players folded their hands. The spoils went to Terreur, of course. A fresh round of cards was dealt. *Shnick. Shnick.* Céleste didn't bother looking at hers. She knew the idea in her fist trumped everything. This game would be over as soon as she played it.

But the scar-faced fellow snarled when Céleste began to move. "Ain't your turn, doll. Goes left of the dealer!"

Gabriel tossed a few francs into the pot.

Rafe was next.

Céleste felt the hair on the back of her neck rise when the other thief pulled out his pocket watch. They went even stiffer as he undid both fob chains before tossing the timepiece into the middle of the table. She couldn't see from this angle if his shadow had been twisted or not, but she doubted he'd bet the relic on his own.

A smile flickered beneath the darkness on Terreur's face. "A fateful hour! You must be confident, Monsieur García! And what of you, Monsieur Lavigne? Will you see his call or raise it?"

The man with the scar glanced at his cards, then fished inside his shirt. More gold chains glittered as he dropped a necklace onto the table. It looked a great deal like the adornments Grigori Rasputin so proudly wore.

It also looked a great deal like Sylvie.

The youngest Enchantress's hair was undeniably bright. Her eyes were sky wide. Her mouth gaped with a soundless scream, and as Céleste stared, she could hear it in the deepest chords of her soul. *Oh God, oh God, oh God, Sylvie has gotten herself turned into a saint, which means—*

"Would you like to fold, Mademoiselle Artois?" Terreur's teeth were still bared, the ghost of his smile. "Or do you have something to wager?"

Céleste understood then. The trap they'd walked into. The *test*. She could see the horror of it all playing out in Rafe's eyes as well. He stared at Sylvie overlapping the engraved hourglass of his pocket watch. They could not stop this. They could not win. If Céleste folded now, Terreur would call her bluff. She could try to destroy the nightmare, but then she would die drowning in her own blood, with no fucking lily pads or Shakespearean soliloquies.

But if she gave the Sanct what he wanted and made him the shadow king of Paris...

Céleste did not finish this thought.

She tried not to think at all as she placed Terreur's dream on the table. Every shadow in the room went a shade darker when their employer saw what she'd set down. His nostrils flared. His pupils too. He looked almost hesitant to reach out and touch what had been so long lost.

Rafe, however, lunged at the pile.

Céleste wasn't sure what the other thief was aiming for—his pocket watch or Sylvie or the nightmare or all three. A scream sprouted in her throat, but it had no time to grow, not like the shadows that rose around Rafe's waist and lashed him back into his chair. He growled and spat, until the jaws of his fox sank in around his own throat, until there was silent foam around his lips. A horrific match to Sylvie's cries. Céleste's fingernails dug four crimson moons into her life line. She wished she could not feel a thing, but she was only flesh and blood. She was scared. She was full of shit. Shit upon shit upon shit.

She was *surviving*.

"Thank you, Monsieur García, for showing your hand," Terreur said. "As for you, Mademoiselle Artois, I was curious what your true colors might be..." The Sanct reached out and plucked his dreadful dream from the pile. It writhed in his fingers, up, up, over his straw-gold hair, before slithering into his skull when he dropped it there. "Ah, yes. At last."

Céleste clenched her hand even tighter, until it was covered in blood. La Fée Verte did not stand a chance now. None of the rest of them did...

A foaming gargle came from Rafe's chair.

"Don't play the victim, Monsieur García. I did warn you what would happen if you tried to deceive me again. Yet you still sent this fairy child to steal my heart!" Terreur nodded at the necklace, his eyes glittering as he looked back to Céleste. "And *you*. You will get what you deserve too."

"We had a deal," she said tightly.

"We did," their employer replied. "I intend to honor it. You wanted more than days, so I shall give you a lifetime." Another glance at Sylvie's saint charm. Another snarl from Rafe's chair. "His, I think."

The shadow fox's jaws tightened even more; its tail split and slithered across the table, winding around Céleste's throat, pouring new hours, weeks, months, years down her windpipe, clearing out her lungs. On the opposite side of the table, Rafe began to cough. Clots of red landed on his cards, so thick that you could no longer read their suit. No hearts. No diamonds. Only blood.

Their game was over.

"No," Céleste gasped. Too freely.

"No?" Terreur tilted his head, and the dark cord fell slack. Rafe slumped over the table as well, his lips dribbling, red pooling into that once-perfect chin divot. "I thought you wished to be like me. No weakness. No pain. No death."

"I—" She couldn't help but sob then.

Rafe responded with a low moan. He wasn't dead yet, but it was only a matter of time.

"I warned you too, Mademoiselle Artois. My path to immortality is not easy to tread; few are willing to go this far." His voice was worse than winter, his face just as cold, when he dropped Rafe's shadow completely, gesturing to it. "Will you take the next step and seize the last remnants of your lover? Or should I let Monsieur Lavigne here have a chance to drain Monsieur García's anima?"

The scar-faced gangster unsheathed a dagger from his belt.

"No!" Céleste threw herself over the table, crawling toward Rafe. Francs spilled everywhere. Chains got caught in her skirts—she dragged these tangled fates as close as she could to Rafe García's limp hand. Their eyes met. His were full of hurt—worse than hurt. The light there was dimming, and no apologies or magic kisses could bring that flame back.

All she could do was press that damn watch to his palm.

Would it work? Did Rafe have enough strength to wind the timepiece? Could he stop time and escape while his shadow was still his? Should she pretend to seize it or—

Between one breath and the next, Rafe García was gone.

Céleste sat trembling over the blood-spattered cards and coins. Never had she felt so alone—not even the night she'd grabbed the gates of the old Artois château, locked out of everything she once was, traumatized so deeply that every single one of her hairs had turned white. Some of the strands spilling over her shoulders had blackened once more. She let this darkness fall over her face as she climbed into the empty chair. Set herself down in that still-warm seat.

The rest of the Apaches were blinking, searching the sandy dance floor with confused expressions.

"Where the hell did he go?" Gabriel asked.

The scar-faced man stabbed the table. "That bastard stole my necklace!"

"Pity," Terreur said flatly. "Though I doubt Monsieur García will get very far—even with that magical watch. His time has run out, and he's too soft to use that saint." His eyes cut over to Céleste. "You though . . . you have a good deal further to go."

Chapter 37

Infernos

A storm had struck sometime between Honoré Côte's first visit to Russia and her last.

It's too damn cold here, she thought, as she flew over the white grounds of Tsarskoe Selo. *Pretty though.* Catherine Palace looked like a snow globe before the shaking. The golden domes of its chapel were dusted with fresh flakes; blue lights illuminated the windows below. The Mad Monk was likely keeping vigil there, waiting for Terreur's summons to the nearby ballroom.

Honoré waited too.

She spent several minutes perched in a tree, until she started shivering so hard that snow began shaking from the boughs. If Grigori Rasputin glanced out the window, he'd be sure to notice, but he was far enough away from the palace entrance to let Honoré slip inside undetected. It wasn't much warmer here—but at least the wind no longer had teeth. Only the paintings. Honoré glanced twice at some of the pieces she crept past. Had the old powder-wigged empresses always been smiling so ferally? Had there always been a portrait of a dead stag in the dining room? It was a bizarre choice of decor. Or perhaps a little too on point? Those forked horns must have reminded diners of their own utensils as they sawed into choice cuts of meat bleeding on their fine china.

Honoré patted her own blade-laced outfit as she passed the blanket-covered table. She'd brought as many weapons as she could—daggers and dreams. There was even a cheese knife, slipped into her bandolier by Céleste.

"You never know," the other Enchantress had said, with a cheeky grin.

"I did get a peek through the jewelry box's lock," Honoré informed her. "That heart sure as shit isn't made of camembert."

Hers wasn't either, it seemed.

Honoré's chest fluttered when La Fée Verte handed her the final weapon—much like that first sword, but shorter. And stronger. The blade had been forged with imaginings from all the salon's regular guests. Picasso's cubes. Jean Cocteau's costumes. A speeding automobile—compliments of Duchess d'Uzès. Holding all these together? The dream of a magical artists' colony. Rafael's, no doubt. It held the same flavor of hope as all his childhood fantasies of Constantinople.

It even shimmered gold.

So did La Fée Verte's masque as she leaned in to kiss Honoré. "Remember, you are more than my sword. Take care, my dame. Come back to me."

"I will," Honoré had breathed, before kissing her back. "I promise."

But first, she had a devil to kill.

The anticipation of it prickled her every step. Her dragon ring stirred too. *Soon, soon.* All Honoré had to do was grab the jewelry box, choose a blade, and wait. In a few more minutes, sunrise would strike Paris. She'd no doubt see its light through the open portal in the ballroom…

The Amber Room was dark when Honoré entered; none of its candelabras lit. You almost couldn't tell there was gold foil backing the fragments on the wall. The white sheet covering the corner table looked like a ghost as she reached for it with her dragon hand.

Soon, soon.

The sheet fell away.

Again, it was too dim to see the box's details, but as soon as

Honoré lifted it from the table, she knew something was off. Nothing rattled inside. And when she pulled out a dream knife to pry apart the lock, she saw no engraved letters buttressing the keyhole, which meant only one thing: This was not Christine Leroux's jewelry box.

It had been swapped.

And Terreur's heart with it.

"Oh, shit."

This was the same oath Honoré had used back in the Montmartre alley, when the ink of the Tournée du Chat Noir pulled itself out of the poster. She should've spat it another hundred times, just to match what she was seeing now. Catherine Palace had started *crawling*. Bare-bosomed women and war-thirsty gods twisted themselves out of the ceiling paint and skittered like spiders down the walls, joined by cherub statues whose gold-leafed wings hummed like a kicked hornet's nest.

The wall statues struck first. Fuck, they were fast. And *heavy*. Maybe they weren't as gilded as they looked... Honoré beat the first two back with her blade, but there were twenty more just after, a number not even the fastest swordswoman could strike down. One smashed into her left shoulder. Another had fashioned a piece of gold garland as a whip and might have taken off Honoré's head with it, but the jagged leaves did not hit a soft jugular.

They met the dragon ring instead.

She'd been so careful these past months to keep the silver asleep, lest it creep closer, ever closer, to her skull. But Honoré had no heads to spare, so she let her relic grow, smashing the remaining cherubs to dust. These remains glittered over the paintings, which had reached the parquet floor, moving across it more like insects than not, bent into impossible shapes. When Honoré's dragon lashed out at the paintings, they simply splashed apart into colored droplets. Each strike soaked up the magic that moved them, coursing through her ring instead. The beast grew. It roared. It cut down kings' likenesses and archangels and maybe even Zeus himself, but paintings kept pouring through the Amber Room's doors. The dead stag stumbled in, its horns twisting. Behind that was a slavering three-headed dog, and if they kept coming like this, she'd be cornered. Stuck—not just in this hellish palace—but inside herself. The dragon was already up to Honoré's chin. Too much more fighting, and she wouldn't be able to breathe.

This thought propelled Honoré toward the window.

Through it.

Glass rained over snow. Silver wings cut through fading night—she had to get back to La Fée Verte, before it was too late. *Mon Dieu.* She prayed it was not too late. Maybe Céleste hadn't made the trade yet. Maybe there was some other miracle they could count on.

But as Honoré flew back toward the Children's Island, over the chapel domes, there was a thunderous flash of blue. The crosses began to bend. They turned into claws and plucked her out of the sky, flinging her back into the gardens. The force should have shattered Honoré's spine, but her dragon absorbed most of the impact. It had absorbed whatever spell had moved the steeples too. They slanted like wind-stunted trees.

They stayed this way as Honoré sat up, catching her breath with gasps.

Then she spotted the Mad Monk.

He stood only a few yards away, at the center of a swirling hedge pattern. He could have been out for a meditative stroll—if it weren't for all the snow and the even colder magic flaring from his masque. Another curse. She could feel Rasputin's power, the *immensity* of it, folding around her. Squeezing. Trying to make Honoré small enough to match the flashing saints around his neck.

He might have managed it, if she weren't already wearing a ring.

Her dragon refused to bend.

The curse rolled right off its scales as Honoré pulled herself upright. The Mad Monk shifted in the snow, his palms moving in the sign of another cross. She felt her hair stand on end; fears started surfacing too. What was happening back in Paris? Had Céleste surrendered the dream? Was Terreur attacking La Fée Verte's salon? Was Sylvie safe? *Oh, Sylvie.* Honoré blanched then, remembering that the door at rue de la Réunion had been cracked. She'd figured the youngest Enchantress had left it unlocked, but it seemed more likely that the daydreamer had never left Russia at all…

"What did you do to Sylvie?" Biting words. Frost-filled. Her dragon snapped through the air too. "I swear to God, if you've harmed a single fuchsia hair on her head, I'll give you a real fucking reason to pray."

She didn't know if the Mad Monk spoke French, but his smile told her he understood. He reached into his robes and pulled out a tattered kerchief, before tossing it onto the snow the way an ancient warlord might offer terms of surrender. Only, it wasn't a white rag. It wasn't a rag at all, Honoré realized.

She was staring at a pair of crumpled butterfly wings.

The rage that filled her then wasn't red but silver. It was cake crumbs everywhere and cat fur too. It was the promise of a happy ending ripped out at the roots. It was Honoré's own roots, rising, up, up, into snarling metal fangs. Fear's Bastard threw herself at Grigori Rasputin, and together they plowed through the snow. His masque flickered. Her heirloom sparked. Honoré screamed. The dragon sank its teeth into the Mad Monk's throat and tore, until the flesh there was as tattered as Sylvie's old wings, until they turned scarlet with the rest of the snow.

It was enough blood to end a man.

Honoré knew this because Lucien Durand had lost far less, despite it spreading everywhere. He'd died midswear. Rasputin was gagging, no words bubbling from his holey throat. His hand wandered up, pausing just beneath the wound. Pressing. One of the chains around his neck began to glow. Miraculously, no blood had spattered on its charm, but the saint's throat reddened, as if some invisible hand were painting an injury there. Honoré's skin crawled. The skin around the Mad Monk's wound crept back into place too…

She hadn't killed him.

But she had the sick revelation that she had killed *someone*. It was hard to tell whom. They were already disappearing, their outline growing fainter, their features erased. All that remained was the blood on the snow, on her ring, on Rasputin's own teeth as he smiled again and spoke in Russian.

Honoré had no translation, but she understood. The Mad Monk had over a dozen people strung around his neck. She had her dragon, yes, but if she kept battling the Sanct, the dragon might have *her.*

Robespierre and his disciples chose to bathe themselves in blood, and their rings did what they'd been designed to do. They grew thirsty. They grew over their wearers. Beware the serpents that eat their own tails. The Fisherman's warning echoed in Honoré's head as she forced herself back from the bloody snow. Her ring's silver already felt stiffer.

She had to be better than her rage.

She had to get back to Paris before Terreur gutted the place.

She pulled a dream knife from her bandolier and threw it at Grigori Rasputin's chest—not waiting around to see what kind of wound it left. The chapel's crosses stayed bent as Honoré soared back over the domes, off and away.

Her prayer had gone unanswered. La Fée Verte's defenses had failed. Honoré knew this as soon as she flew above rue de la Réunion, into a skyline slashed with smoke. Ashes danced over a Montmartre cabaret. Flaming pages turned above the ninth arrondissement—where Libris's bookstore had once stood. The dome of the Palais Garnier was darkened by a scorched café. The Fisherman's flea market booth burned beyond that.

Sylvie's magical map would be useless now, charred beyond recognition.

Honoré felt that way too when she looked toward the Quartier Secret. A pillar of ruin rose beside Notre-Dame de Paris, as tall and thick as a third bell tower.

And above that?

If any of the cathedral's priests had paused their morning prayers and peered beyond the church windows, they might have seen a scene that belonged in stained glass. An emerald-winged angel. A devil rising on the updraft of ashes. A knight in shining armor trying her best to reach them...

Honoré often had a nightmare, over and over, where she would try to run. Destinations varied—sometimes she was fleeing to Gare de l'Est to catch Rafael's train. Sometimes she was trying to get to Maman at the fireplace mantel, before that final skull-splitting hit. It didn't matter. It never did. That was the horror of the dream. Air porridged around her limbs and no matter how hard she pushed, she wasn't fast enough. She always woke up sweating bullets. Honoré wished, very much, that she could do so now—as she struggled through the smoke-slurred sky—but this dream didn't belong to her.

This nightmare had come straight from Terreur.

Céleste must have handed over his idea, not knowing the Sanct's heart was beyond stabbing. He was still invincible. Not only that—he was strong. Far stronger than La Fée Verte. Her golden masque flickered much like the inferno below. She couldn't fight Terreur's fires. He'd burned too much of the salon and the imaginings inside. Too much of *her*. Flames blackened the ends of La Fée Verte's hair and caught her feathers too. Songbirds started to scream, flying wherever they could to escape the heat. One slammed straight into Honoré's breastplate. She caught it in both palms, horrified to see the bird was no longer green but pink. Raw flesh oozed beneath the remains of its plumage.

More birds fell past her, their bodies breaking on the street below.

Over the muddy waters of the Seine, Terreur grabbed La Fée Verte by the throat. Honoré's scream was sulphuric. Her wings weren't fast enough. She was stuck in a burning sky, trapped in such heavy, heavy armor, while her love's feathers fell. One after the other after the other, until the only songbird left was the burnt thing shuddering in Honoré's cupped palms.

La Fée Verte's masque went dark.

Terreur's masque did too. When he finally released the muse, his smile was the color of her wing bones. That's all they were anymore. White and hollow as flutes, whistling as the woman fell, down, down. A splash. A bubbling gasp. The river took her quickly.

The Final Pages of *The Unbreakable Curse of Raf[redacted]e[redacted] García*

Raf[redacted]e[redacted] García was dying.

Dying without living.

He stumbled out of the Caveau des Terreurs, clutching a stolen moment in one hand. A pink-haired icon swung from the other. Tick, tock, tick. The sands were trickling too fast. His strength had ebbed. He couldn't hold on to an entire hour. It was all he could manage to drag himself out of Belleville. Finally. By the time the automobiles began moving again, Rafe was bracing himself against the outer wall of Père Lachaise, wondering if there was a point in pushing much farther. His chin stubble was stiff with blood. That would only grow worse as the day went on, along with so many other things…

The watch's hourglass had trickled out, matching the gravestone engravings just past the gate. Rafe slumped by the wall to catch his breath and then laughed at the thought—ha!

What a shit fate.

That had always been Raf[redacted]e[redacted] García's curse. His fatal flaw. Not the knifing nor the stealing nor the lies, but the fact his eyes always wandered to the sky, hoping for something better. Today it was as gray as Céleste Artois's gaze. As heavy as his own lids. Growing heavier. Darker. Would there be a light at the end of the tunnel? *he wondered. Did he even have enough soul left to reach it?*

An orange blur.

Whiskers.

These brushed against his bloody face, and Rafe's vision cleared enough to see the tailless tom in his lap. Several other cats perched on top of Père Lachaise's walls. There had to be almost twenty of them.

"Oh." Rafe cleared his rusty throat. "Hello, Marmalade."

"Rowr?"

"Well, it all went to hell." He glanced back up at the sky. "Terreur's still got a heart. He's got his goddamn dream too." Again, Rafe thought of Céleste's eyes and what a fool he'd been, hoping for the best. "I expect he'll be attacking the salon soon—"

Marmalade let out a yowl, and several strays leapt off the cemetery walls. They flashed across the boulevard, fanning out in all directions. To sound the alarm, *Rafe realized. He wasn't sure how much good the Whisper Network would do at this point, but he supposed it was better than sitting beside a bunch of graves, waiting to die.*

Raf[redacted]*e*[redacted] *García was better than that too.*

Marmalade spilled out of Rafe's lap as he pushed himself to his feet and edged to the curb to catch a taxi.

The first hint of smoke drifted through the cab's windows by the Bastille. The fortress itself was over one hundred years gone, only a commemorative pillar standing in its place, and when Rafe looked above this, he could see the clouds souring. No rain. Only that horrible choking black that brought back memories of his windmill. I will be worse. I will be so much worse. *Terreur was many terrible things, but he'd never been much of a liar.*

This burning was so much worse than that morning in Montmartre.

Rafe's taxi was just turning down Boulevard du Palais when he caught his first glimpse of flames. A giant ball of fire barreled past the cab. The driver did not flinch. Rafe did, when he realized what he was seeing: a blue elephant screaming its last.

The animal wasn't real, he knew, but this didn't stop his hand from tightening over Sylvie's charm as he watched the creature crumble through the cab's rear window. The charred remains of mannequins followed, no longer dressed in designers' dreams. By the time the taxi stopped at the Pont Saint-Michel, there were so many torched imaginings swarming the bridge that Rafe didn't bother crossing. What good did he think he could do? Not even God was lending a hand. The cathedral's statues did not come to La Fée Verte's defense when Terreur caught the muse over the river.

Rafe watched their battle from below, until the smoke became too thick, as thick as the center of a fortune teller's crystal ball. He didn't need to see the end. He wouldn't have seen any of this at all, if he weren't dying... He'd be on the other side of this bridge, admiring the sunrise with Jean Cocteau and all the other imaginers, blissfully unaware of what they'd just lost.

No more midnights filled with magic.

No more fairies, no more tales, no more paintings come to life.

Nothing more for his soul to soar for.

There was a set of slimy stone steps by Rafe's feet. He sank onto the first one and clutched Sylvie's likeness tightly, letting the pocket watch dangle from the opposite hand. He thought of Céleste then. His heart went to ashes. Rafe couldn't exactly fault her for handing over that nightmare and damning everything. He knew what it felt like to see your life so instantly unraveled. All those nameless sketches fluttering past Saint Stephen's Basilica... He understood the lengths a person would go to, to take their future back. He'd been to Venice's wandering canals and Siberia's howling forests and the Vatican's cryptic library. He'd combed the golden grasses of savannas and the New World's blooming prairies. He'd learned languages long lost to desert sands. He'd come so fucking far, only to end up right here once more.

Yet what hurt the most was how much Raf[redacted]*e*[redacted] *García wanted to stay.*

With her.

Still.

"Come to trade your fortune, dizzy fox?"

Rafe started at the voice. Slick as eels. Closer than the water. When he lifted his gaze, he saw the Seer of the Seine standing at the bottom of the lichen-laced staircase—pupilless eyes, no boat in sight. The Sanct's bare feet stood on Parisian soil. There was a net in her hands, as always, but she had yet to catch anything. The woven fibers shimmered strangely. The fingers looped through them weren't gnarled, and Rafe was startled to see that the rest of the Seer's skin was just as smooth. She looked centuries younger without those wrinkles.

She looked...familiar.

Rafe could've sworn he'd seen that face before; but for the life of him, he couldn't place it. For the life of me. Ha. *"It'd be a shit deal for you, I'm afraid."*

"You don't know shit, Rafe García. Not like I do." The woman cast her net into the hazy waters. "I've waded in it for a long, long time, but I've been patient. Weaving fates and tasting rust. Waiting for the white hand to flip the cards. Waiting for this day—oh yes." She gazed back out into the smoke, swaying. The lines of her net went taut. "I've found my way back to land again."

Because La Fée Verte's wards were finally broken.

There was a break in the smoke too, and Rafe could see Terreur rising above the cathedral's bell towers. The heartless bastard had won.

"You were right about Céleste," he told the Seer.

"The turner?"

"She cheated death, just like you said she would." Rafe glanced at the pillar where they'd stood that first evening. The Seine parted quickly around this stone, sweeping the broken bodies of birds in its currents.

"That was not Mademoiselle Artois's fortune I told." The Sanct began pulling her net in. Something heavy had gotten tangled there—judging by the way her biceps bulged. "You can cheat death, Rafe García. You hold such a power in your very hand."

He stared down at his trembling palms. Sylvie of a Single Name stared back. Rafe wasn't sure if she could see him or not, if she could hear what the Seer of the Seine was proposing. A terrible choice, a chance to stay... He hated himself for even considering such a trade...

"I can't," he croaked.

"I've seen differently," the Sanct by the water said. "Don't be a fool, Monsieur García."

PART V

WHAT DREAMS MAY WAKE

Once upon a time, there was a fortune teller who saw a terrible future.

She also saw a way to change it.

Death, the Devil,** and **the Fool.

Madame Arcana placed these cards facedown on her table and then walked out of her tent. When she reached the edge of Île du Carnaval's shore, she did not stop. She walked on into the water, and she has been in the Seine ever since, weaving and waiting and waiting and waiting.

For even stars will end if you are patient enough.

Devils too.

AIII 118

June 28, 1914

There are no seers in Sarajevo.

The city's river—the Miljacka—has no houseboat anchored against its currents. Its waters aren't deep enough for that sort of thing. If you jumped in to escape the crowds gathered along the parade route, you'd only get splashed a bit about the shins. No eels would slide across your ankles. There would be no smoky voice to lure you beneath the darkened arches of the Latin Bridge . . . to warn you about the destruction that shall soon unfold.

To the casual observer, the 28th of June is a perfect day. The sky is a baby-blue blanket over a cradle of hills. Sarajevo's red-tiled roofs fill the valley, yielding only to spires, steeples, and roads—which are themselves filled with horses, handcarts, and vendors who have grain sacks slung over their shoulders. Appel Quay is the busiest thoroughfare of all, glutted with people gathered to watch a passing car. More specifically, a Gräf & Stift automobile carrying Archduke Franz Ferdinand of the House of Habsburg. Storefronts and houses sport the black-and-yellow flag of the monarchy, fluttering almost as much as the crowd beneath: men wearing traditional fezzes, women dressed in too many damn petticoats for this sort of weather, children clutching flowers, assassins with FN Model 1910 pistols tucked into their waistbands.

Ah, yes.

That.

That is the first portent. There are seven men walking through the crowd whose shadows tilt all wrong against the morning sun. Three of these assassins have tuberculosis. All of them have nothing to lose—they've been chosen by the Black Hand to save Serbia.

The second sign is much harder to miss.

The bomb glances off Franz Ferdinand's elbow, detonating in the road and scattering harsh fragments. The crowd is shaken. A haze settles across the river. The flags of the Austrian-Hungarian empire are edged with this same smoke, but they keep flying. So do the green feathers of the archduke's helmet—rippling as the car continues forward to city hall. He must believe, feeling the wind thread past his head this way, that he is invincible. He decides that the worst has already happened.

He decides to keep driving on that day.

A fortune teller might have warned him otherwise, for they would have read the third omen—not in tea leaves or river shit, but on the Gräf & Stift's front license plate: AIII 118.

These numbers hold no real meaning to anyone in the crowd at Appel Quay. Their significance will not be noted for many years more, after the smoke has finally cleared and the bomb-scarred metal is carried off to a museum. *This is the car that drove the entire world into war. Millions upon millions of lives might have been spared, if only the driver had turned left instead of right. If only Gavrilo Princip had not been standing in line for a sandwich. If only the Gräf & Stift hadn't stalled in front of the nineteen-year-old assassin. If only he hadn't shot the archduke and his wife. If only Europe's peace treaties hadn't collapsed into dust. If only the kings had swallowed their pride and stopped their armies. This whole bloody affair might have ended before the armistice. November 11, 1918. Oh, yes, isn't that spooky? Quite the coincidence, no?*

But that—that is flipping too far ahead—past the final page.

There is no one to read the future in Sarajevo.

And so, the chauffeur turns right.

Chapter 38

The Last Enchantress of Paris

Paris had gone to shit, and the world had gone to hell.

But Céleste Artois was still alive.

Even eight months after trading Terreur's nightmare in exchange for her life, it was hard for her to be glad of this fact. Au contraire. She was quite unsettled as she wandered the streets of her once-sparkling city, past cafés stacked high with chairs. Most storefronts were shuttered—partly because a portion of the population had been shipped off to the Western Front to fight and mostly because those soldiers were losing. Germany was marching for the City of Light. Parisians were scared. They spoke of what might happen if the kaiser's army crossed the Seine. If you *could* find an open pâtisserie, you wouldn't be able to buy bread without some stale scraps of rumors. *I heard that Germans are raping women and murdering babies in Belgium! What would those beasts do if they reached Paris?*

Well, they wouldn't drink absinthe. Certainly.

The café in the Latin Quarter where she'd enjoyed *une correspondance* after *The Rite of Spring*—well over a year ago—was closed. When Céleste peered through the windows, she saw the miraculous sparkling water advertisement had been papered over with a mobilization poster, calling all its young customers to war. To add insult to injury, absinthe itself had been banned by the minister of the interior. *To protect the soldiers' will to fight.* Never mind that the tafia they served in the trenches—a rum so combustible, it could serve as artillery—was more likely to send men to an asylum. That and the endless onslaught of bullets.

But yes, outlaw the elegant sugar spoons, instead. The thought was bitter in Céleste's mouth. Far more bitter than the anise had been—or even the blood. *There's no longer a green fairy to summon anyhow.*

Her shadow shuddered over cobblestones as she kept walking through the Latin Quarter, past the glass flowers of the MÉTROPOLITAIN sign's lamps, past the statues of the Fontaine Saint-Michel. She sometimes stopped here, staring into the dragon's unseeing eyes. This wasn't a confession, but it was close.

Penance, perhaps?

Céleste didn't have any other reason to keep coming back to this arrondissement. The alley across the boulevard was choked with dead vines, and even if you managed to get past that tangle, there was nothing on the other side. Terreur had made sure of this. He'd burned almost all the other Sancts' holdings, but the destruction of the salon? Well, that had been personal. Rue des Ombres was a shining wonderland compared to what was left of the Quartier Secret.

Nowadays the nights stayed dark, the city's curtains drawn. There was no whir of wings, no cinnamon-cigarette zeppelins—only the fear of real airships and their bombs. If imaginers were smoking anything, it was tar. It was orange ember stars dotting the trenches, some hundreds of miles away. The whole world was burning, one way or another. Bodies piling. Borders broken. Ashes spread across the entire continent so that it looked as dark from the skies as it did on Terreur's globe.

The war, at least, was not Céleste's fault. She could see this from the way Russia's armies moved—by order of Tsar Nicholas II. By suggestion of Tsarina Alexandra. By the will of Grigori Rasputin.

She could see this in the way that Terreur was always feasting, guzzling goblets of blood. Enough had spilled on Europe's battlefields to last him... well, forever. He need not wither when thousands of young men were mown down in muddy fields, their uniform pants as bright as poppies. Or damn roses. There'd been plenty of flowers at their send-off too, when they'd marched through Paris's streets to the tune of "La Marseillaise," lilies and carnations wedged into their bayonets. Not the best place for planting, Céleste had thought, as she watched the parade. Seeds needed soil and sun and time to grow…

Terreur must have been dreaming of this war for a long while, long before he'd met Céleste, but she couldn't help but be sorry. Sorry that she'd failed to stop him. Sorry that she was alive when so many others were not.

She turned from the sightless dragon and walked on.

Survivor's guilt wouldn't do Céleste any good. She was due back at the Palais Garnier soon, and even though she now had enough power to fly or summon a portal to the opera house, she chose to wander the streets instead. She crossed the Seine and strolled into the second arrondissement. Some shops had stayed open here: A *fromagerie* filled with white wheels of cheese. A perruquier trying to sell patriotic wigs in the colors of France's flag. A few doors down from that was a butcher—busy as ever. The Parisians who'd decided to stay and face the opposing forces had to fill their bellies, after all. The same held true with cake. Céleste could feel her own stomach growl as she walked down rue Montorgueil.

She could hear the street singer from several blocks away, plucking at his instrument as he sang choruses about the war. It was how many preferred to hear terrible news—set to the tune of F major. *"GERMANY SUPPORTS AUSTRIA-HUNGARY. FRANCE AND RUSSIA STRENGTHEN THEIR ALLIANCE WITH SERBIA. CLOUDS OF WAR GATHER OVER EUROPE."*

Except this song.

It was not terrible.

She rounded the corner to find a crowd gathered at the Place des Victories, beneath a statue of the Sun King and his horse. The minstrel was standing by the monument. At first, Céleste thought his hair might be gold, but then she saw an even brighter shimmer around the man's head. Like a halo.

It made sense, she realized, for he was singing about an angel.

The song's lilting verses did not come from a Psalm or any other biblical story. No, they'd been plucked straight from the battlefield. They told of a woman whose silver wings turned back bullets, who wielded a flaming sword and brought hope to men drowning in mud. She saved soldiers and made them sing. She would save Paris too—of course.

Hope had started to spark through the crowd, filling the heads of balding men and erasing the gray-haired worry of young wives. Their children looked on in wonder. One of them was clutching a Stohrer bag to his chest, his face a mess of powdered sugar, his eyes lit like a tree on Christmas Eve.

"Is the angel real, Maman?" he asked after the final chorus.

His mother didn't answer, but a crown of dreams flickered around her brow.

"Could be a saint," answered an elderly man next to them. "Could be Joan of Arc herself, come down from heaven to fight for France!"

Let the stories stir, Terreur had once said. For there was power in a rumor. There was even more power in a legend, so Honoré, clever Honoré—named after the patron saint of pastries—had decided to become one. A story every man and woman and child in Paris was desperate to believe.

Céleste included.

She let her lips slip into the smallest of smiles.

"Quite real," she told the mesmerized child, as she plucked a single bright thought from her head and handed it over to him, before continuing to the opera house.

War was far worse than Honoré Côte had ever imagined. She'd expected gore, certainly. As a girl she'd heard plenty of tales from the old soldiers of Belleville, men who'd fought in the Franco-Prussian war and then as Communards—red-blooded revolutionaries. To hear them talk, she'd figured battlefields were places where heroes were forged. Where bravery was tested and the person loading a gun at your side became your brother. And even if you died, there was a reason for it: *liberté*, *égalité*, *fraternité*.

There was nothing heroic about this.

Mud. Shit. Horses screaming, their intestines tangling in their hooves as they tried to gallop away from their own awful deaths. Forests bombed to splinters. Bones too. There was hardly a chance to learn the name of the soldier next to you before his head got blown off and the rest of his corpse was left to feed the rats—rats as big as goddamn cats. A few of those vermin *did* get christened by men who needed something to cling to. Gallows humor at its finest—in the form of a flesh-eating rodent who went by the name of Machiavelli. He'd become something of a mascot for Honoré's unit.

So had she.

She'd enlisted under the dead man's name and marched off to Gare de l'Est along with many of La Fée Verte's old imaginers. And more besides: Bakers and booksellers, painters and poets. Farm boys with deep tans and even deeper provincial accents. Street kids who looked itchy in their fresh blue uniforms.

Young fathers kissed their infants' bubble cheeks. Oldest sons hugged their mothers one last time. Honoré Côte had no goodbyes to say, and when the men in her unit started telling stories of their loved ones, she simply stared down at her dragon ring.

"Who've you got back home?" asked a young man with pianist's fingers. Long and delicate. They tapped some unheard song on the butt of his 1907/15 Berthier rifle. "Anyone special you're fighting for?"

The silver around her throat went tight, and the fields through the train windows became a green, green blur. Paris fell away. Something deep inside Honoré kept falling too.

"I'm not here to fight," she answered in her huskiest voice.

The farm boy seated across from them laughed. "Careful. That kind of talk will get you a white feather. Or a bullet between the eyes for cowardice."

Honoré simply smiled. Bullets wouldn't touch her, thanks to the dragon ring. And while she did have some feathers tucked away in her uniform, they were not white. Not like the lily wedged into the barrel of the pianist's gun, as if he were off to shoot petals instead of lead.

"Why are you here, then?" His fingers kept tapping the butt of the rifle. His flower kept quivering. Just above this, Honoré could see the gleam of the song he was composing. Far different from the tunes he'd played in La Fée Verte's salon, last winter.

"Because you are."

A songbird peered out of Honoré's sky-blue uniform. It hopped across her shoulders—even eight months after the fact, its emerald feathers had not filled in enough for it to fly. It fluttered to the pianist's scalp the way a hen might hop to a fence-post. The imaginer did not see the creature, same as he couldn't see the silver scales coating Honoré's skin or the shining sword sheathed at her side. But when the bird plucked the inspiration from the musician's head, his fingers stopped tapping.

"You some kind of chaplain or something?" the farm boy asked.

"Or something," Honoré replied, as the songbird slipped back into the safety of her breastplate.

She was more than a sword.

She was a shield now.

She was two hearts in a single chest, beating as one. Her other half was back home, lying in a glass casket, under glass stars, guarded by cats and stray dreams, though they weren't enough to wake La Fée Verte from her enchanted sleep. The Sanct's eyes hadn't opened since Honoré found her at the edge of the Seine, tangled in a net made of fates. Powerless. Only the last songbird trembled in Honoré's hands like a faint pulse, and when she laid the creature between the woman's breasts, it simply let out a distressed squawk.

"La Fée Verte needs imaginings," the Fisherman of the Moon told her, after examining the other Sanct's lightless masque. "Strong ones. Gather enough of them, and she'll rise again."

"You make it sound like she's dead." Honoré's voice echoed around her namesake's mausoleum. Her own heart shuddered as she scooped the songbird back into her palms. She hated how cold the Sanct's chest felt beneath her fingers. How still.

La Fée Verte couldn't be dead.

She couldn't.

She and Honoré had found a better way together, after the magic of their first kiss. They'd gone even deeper. Delving into the idea that Robespierre's spell was not the sole path to invincibility. What if you didn't have to cut all ties to remove your heart from your chest? What if your love wasn't a weakness but the greatest possible strength? What if you turned your heart into a green bird and sent it soaring across the burning sky, into your love's arms, so that you might escape death?

What then?

"La Fée Verte's not dead. No more than this one is." The Fisherman held up Sylvie's saint necklace, and Honoré struggled not to scream, the way she had when Rafael handed the relic over to the ragpicker. "Your heart spell worked, but La Fée Verte doesn't have enough magic to return to herself. We just have to find the right powers to break these curses, is all."

"But Terreur burned everything," she replied bitterly.

It was why they stood in a grave instead of the salon, why the Fisherman's handcart was parked over the paint-spattered picnic blanket. His stall had gone up in smoke, most of his trash and treasures lost. The Sanct couldn't even go gather more, not without risking a battle with one of Terreur's disciples.

The heartless bastard had set himself up at the Palais Garnier, watching operas from his old hidden box and sending Apaches to hunt down blood on his behalf. Honoré had figured that was the worst of it, until the assassination. Until Europe's kings had decided to act more like dominoes than chess pieces.

"Terreur burned buildings," the Fisherman corrected her. "The salon was only ever a place. You carry La Fée Verte's spirit with you, so go to the dreamers."

It hadn't been simple at first, but she'd managed.

Visits to La Ruche, to Twenty-Seven rue de Fleurus, to a candlelit catacomb concert, to Temple de l'Amitié, where writers gathered in a garden to eat chocolate cake and discuss the poetry of Sappho.

Honoré ghosted through these gatherings. She let the songbird hop from head to head. She watched its feathers slowly bud with the arrival of spring, with the rest of Paris's flowers.

And then, the war.

Honoré had not marched off to Gare de l'Est to fight. She was following the dreamers. The men who took brass shells and turned them into vases, who carved sculptures out of enemy rifle butts, who scribbled poetry by the light of artillery, who looked out across no-man's-land and still saw something worth sketching: a sunrise, a butterfly, an angel.

Many did see her, once they reached the battlefield. When the farm boy tried to be a hero and got a belly full of lead for his trouble, he gasped up at Honoré's wings. He begged for last rites, for a miracle, for his mother, his mother, who was a sodden photograph in his pocket, whose face shimmered in the dark puddle that gathered by Honoré's boots. What a waste... eighteen years and so many more lost. She shirked back from the blood, watching the boy's anima swirl and his eyes fade. There was already a rat slinking through the muck, its yellow teeth chattering. There were worse carrion eaters too, she knew, flying in the skies above the crows and slipping through the doorways of burnt Belgian houses, making long shadows longer.

Honoré could not stop them from feasting.

So, instead, she tried her best to focus on the imaginings. They did not grow easily here, but the dreams that did take root were strong. The pianist took the *dadera-dadera* tempo of machine guns and hummed even louder. There was a poet in their unit too—the one who'd christened Machiavelli—who turned the shrapnel into stanzas. Honoré took these ideas and slipped them beneath her armor, where La Fée Verte's heart fluttered. She watched the imaginers frown and readjust their helmets. She hated leaving them so bereft. It was far easier in Paris, where torches flickered in the gardens and beautiful sculptures melted under moonbeams. Bombshells and clouds of bone didn't have quite the same effect.

But Honoré stayed true to her oath.

She found a better way.

She defended the dreamers.

It didn't take long for other soldiers in her unit to notice that bullets never landed on them when Honoré Côte was nearby. *Damn lucky*, they called her at first, but mere luck couldn't account for the sparks they sometimes saw bouncing off her chest, the cartridges that dropped harmlessly to her hobnailed boots. It didn't explain why an artillery shell exploded around her company and fire parted around them in the shape of *wings*. After that incident, Honoré got herself a new nickname. *Battlefield Angel! A guardian as good as Gabriel himself!* Men toasted her with sips of tafia and talk started to spread, the way talk does when it's fueled by such strong rum and the constant presence of death. *You need divine intervention? Fight by Honoré Côte's side. He'll keep hell at bay!*

"It's a little too late for that, don't you think?" Honoré said, as she looked down the line. Cigarettes winked against spent bullet casings, and the farm boy's rat-gnawed body was still halfway there in the mud. Her wings could only stretch so far...

But the songbird in her armor felt stronger.

Almost ready to fly.

She wondered if this had anything to do with the way the company was staring back at her. It wasn't just cigarettes flickering from the soldier's faces. It was faith. They really believed what they were telling themselves.

As a child, Honoré had hated her given name. *Anne* wasn't strong. It didn't make men quake in their boots or piss their pants, the way her father's title did. She'd always known him as Fear, and she knew that if she was Fear's Bastard, she might stand a chance of surviving. There was power in a name, yes, but the real power lay in the myth behind the man. The reputation. Terreur—who'd yank your teeth out with pliers if you told a lie, who'd steal your house out from under you with a dirty deed, who'd pull up your wife's skirts whether or not she fancied it, who'd take whatever he wanted without an ounce of remorse.

Honoré had survived a long time in her father's shadow.

But she could feel her own myth taking shape beneath Lucien Durand's old ring. Feathers growing so that the silver spreading from her back no longer looked like dragon's scales but like the wings of the archangel these soldiers believed her to be. Their faith *was* making a difference, and Honoré hoped that she could too, so during the next skirmish, when a hail of bullets rained down on their unit, she let these wings be seen. Her blade too. She let the pianist compose a tune. She let the poet write some accompanying verses. She let them sing the song to the rest of the company, with only one complaint.

"*He* is a *she*." This revelation made the soldiers' jaws drop even more than the supernatural armor. *Figures.* "Men shouldn't have all the glory."

But the story of Honoré Côte—*Battlefield Angel*—spread quickly after that. Trench to trench. Unit to unit. Fast as a fuse, trailing all the way back to the City of Light.

As far as curses went, being a necklace was fairly boring.

The worst part—aside from the initial spell cast by Rasputin to squish Sylvie of a Single Name down to the size of a thumbnail—was the fact her nose itched yet she couldn't lift a finger to scratch it. She was so thoroughly trapped in the charm that she could not even blink. She'd been forced to watch the fluttering cobwebs on the ceiling of the Caveau, then a tumble over the table, then Rafe's blood-crusted face staring down at her in agony. This went shaky when the thief's hand trembled, turning him into a blur of red. She heard voices but not words; it was all an underwater gargle. And then she was in a pocket.

The next face that leaned in to hers belonged to a Sanct.

The Fisherman of the Moon!

Of course, I'm nefarious jewelry now. Sylvie wanted to laugh. She couldn't, of course. She couldn't stick her tongue out either while the ragpicker examined her with his jeweler's loupe, same as he'd done with Honoré's dragon ring. His frown was just as grim as it had been then. His bronze masque glittered, but nothing happened.

Sylvie stayed stuck.

Her nose itched for a long, long while. She had no idea *how* long, only that the Fisherman of the Moon's winter coat got shed, and his eyes became more weathered each time they looked through the loupe, each time his shine could not break Rasputin's curse.

And then, one evening, it did.

A lightning crack broke through the charm, and Sylvie spilled out, arms, legs, earth on her knees. Orange fur appeared there too, as Marmalade rushed to greet her with a wild *yowl*. An entire chorus of *meows* followed, and she looked up to see a throng of lamplit eyes—orange and green and blue. The latter belonged to Fable, who was perched protectively on a stack of Sylvie's fairy books, and for a dizzy moment, she wondered why the cat was sitting in a mausoleum instead of her bookstore. Why was the Fisherman of the Moon's handcart parked outside the scrolling doors? Why was the Sanct himself sitting by the edge of Honoré's mattress with a smile on his beaten bronze face?

"Welcome back, daydreamer," he said, brushing his gloved hands.

"I didn't exactly *go* anywhere," Sylvie muttered, scratching her nose just short of bloody. Then she began scratching Marmalade between the ears. The tom had clambered in her lap, his claws pricking through the fur coat that was *far* too warm for the air that now swelled through the tomb. It smelled like summer's end—when drying dahlias were laid on the tops of graves.

"You've been to Russia, I'd wager. Was that not the Mad Monk's curse I just cracked?"

Sylvie shuddered. Marmalade curled even closer to her chest, over her butterfly heart. It was still palpitating at the sight of Grigori Rasputin perched in the tsarevitch's window, at the pain of her uprooted wings, at the growing understanding that their plan to steal the evil sorcerer's heart had failed.

"What happened here?" She looked around the Enchantresses' tomb again. "Where are Céleste and Honoré? Where's Rafe?"

The Fisherman of the Moon cleared his throat, the way adults sometimes did when they had news they did not want to share. "Monsieur García brought you to me on the day we lost Paris." He glanced toward the central stone, and that's when Sylvie realized what most of the feral cats were sitting on: a glass casket. Inside lay La Fée Verte. Her masque was extinguished. Her wings were even more ruined than Sylvie's.

When she saw them, she let out a small sob—sharp as those bones.

"It's not what it looks like," the Fisherman said quickly. "Her body is in stasis, same as you were, stuck just as she was when she was fished out of the Seine. I built this box after studying your charm for a while. Rasputin's spell was easier to replicate than break."

"So La Fée Verte's just... sleeping?"

"She's not here," the Sanct explained. "She's with your friend Honoré, gathering enough dreams to get back to her old self."

Sylvie looked up at the rose-colored imaginings that shimmered over the mausoleum roof—a pale imitation of the Vault of Dreams. "Are they in the Quartier Secret?"

Marmalade huddled even closer to Sylvie's chest.

"The salon's gone," the Fisherman whispered. "Terreur torched it. Same as my stall and Cabaret d'Ailes and Libris's shop."

Fable let out an ashen *meow* from the fairy book stack, and Sylvie paled at the translation. *No. No!* This wasn't how their story was supposed to go... but she'd never know for sure now, would she? The book behind the glass case was no more. The store had burned fast—all its pages the perfect kindling—and Libris had gone back in to grab Lore, into a building full of flaming endings.

Neither of them had ever come out again.

Sylvie let out another sob. She thought of the lost look on Anastasia's face—the withering betrayal as the grand duchess's Enlightened memories faded. All that had been for nothing. The firebird's flames had spread too far... and now the rest of Paris's magic was lost too. The bookstore. The cabaret. The salon. She didn't want to believe it, but belief didn't matter so much now that Terreur had won.

"What—what about Céleste?" she asked in a wobbly voice. "Is she alive?"

The Fisherman of the Moon nodded. "She surrendered the dream to Terreur, according to Monsieur García. I hear she's living with that devil at the Palais Garnier now."

Several of the strays started meowing then, but Sylvie's ears were ringing too much to translate. She looked over at Céleste's old corner, where beaded opera gowns hung next to a spare set of moth wings.

"No..." Sylvie rasped. "Céleste wouldn't."

Would she?

"Even the best people can make the worst choices, when it comes to surviving," the Fisherman said. "She's not the only Sanct who joined Terreur. Plume did too— Wait, where are you going?"

Sylvie's insides were roaring as she pulled the wings from the easel and rushed out of the mausoleum. It was late afternoon—nearly golden hour—but as she flew out over the streets, she felt a pall over the city. This grayness only got worse when she crossed the Seine. When she landed on the rooftops where La Fée Verte's salon used to be...

It looked as if a bomb had been dropped. It felt that way too, when Sylvie fluttered into the crater. There were few things she recognized—a mannequin that looked too much like a body, a smashed aperitif flute, the skeleton of the spiral staircase that once had led to the Vault of Dreams. Nothing more glittered here. Leaves, it seemed, burned just as fast as pages. Just as hot as Anastasia's double-headed firebird.

A third sob bubbled up in Sylvie's throat.

She knelt in the ruins, cursing herself for being so careless. Honoré had been right; she'd let the princess see too much. It was Sylvie's fault they'd gotten caught. Her fault Céleste had been forced to make such a horrible choice. Her fault everything here was ashes...

Well, perhaps not everything.

Something was squirming through the long-cooled cinders by Sylvie's knees. She kept thinking of firebirds, as she reached for it, those phoenixes who were born again after burning. That legend had been one of Céleste's favorites—her eyes always twinkled with the telling as she'd tucked the youngest Enchantress into bed.

But the thing Sylvie pulled from the ashes wasn't shining at all.

It twisted on her palm.

Terrible.

Wonderful.

She wasn't sure. It looked identical to the idea she'd seen in La Fée Verte's memory. Exactly like the vision that had been ripped from the evil sorcerer's head. But... that didn't make sense... unless...

Oh!

"Always have a backup plan." Sylvie laughed, thinking of the lesson Céleste had recited to her over and over before every single one of their cons. Of course, the oldest Enchantress hadn't walked into the Caveau des Terreurs without a contingency. Or a forgery. That was what she must have handed the heartless sorcerer...

A damn good forgery.

Sylvie's laugh faded as she looked back over the wreckage. It vanished altogether when she saw a figure perched on one of the nearby rooftops, shadow stretching around his shoulders, gold glimmering from his neck. *No!* Sylvie scrambled, kicking up a cloud of black ash. She couldn't get caught again. She was sick at the thought of getting turned back into jewelry and taken to Terreur—much less holding his real idea. Sylvie didn't exactly know what Céleste had planned, what kind of game the other Enchantress was playing over in the haunted halls of the Palais Garnier, but she wasn't about to sabotage those efforts a second time.

Her masque flashed—furious and fuchsia.

Shadows dropped from the rooftops.

The man's wings twisted back into a four-legged beast. His lips were drawn in not quite a smile. "Don't get too shiny on me, Magpie! It's dangerous to be so bright in Paris nowadays!"

The chains around Rafe García's neck winked when he said this. Not a saint necklace, Sylvie realized. The rogue artist had taken the double chains of his pocket watch and fused them together so that the winged hourglass lay against his bare skin. This looked a touch paler than usual. Not quite as porcelain as Céleste's complexion had been last summer, but there was a similar fragility. Sylvie figured she shouldn't hug him too hard, but she did run to his side, her arms and wings flapping.

"Rafe!"

His full smile surfaced then. His fox did a small spin. "It's good to see you too, Sylvie. Outside that necklace, especially."

"What are you doing here?"

"The Whisper Network warned me you'd bolted for the Quartier Secret, so I've come to take you where it's safe. Or…do you mean here on this earthly plane?" He paused, his fingers tracing the relic that hung from his neck. "That's a tale we don't have time for, at the moment. We're too exposed."

"Can't you *stop* time?" Sylvie pointed out.

"Cheeky as ever, I see." Rafe's shadow stilled when he caught sight of the gray thread writhing in her palm. "I see you've managed to dig up a secret too."

"Céleste is tricking Terreur, isn't she? She's planted something else in his head!"

A curt nod. "I'll explain everything when we reach the bakery."

"The bakery?"

Another nod. The fox shadow swirled around the pair, cloaking them, as Rafe jerked his chin at the unsettled ash. "I'd leave that nightmare here, if I were you."

Chapter 39

Pièce de Résistance

Stohrer was still the oldest pâtisserie in Paris. Terreur had tried to burn it along with everything else, but his flames had simply sputtered against the baker Sanct's wards. The magic of cake was far older, far harder to break than that of the city's other enchanted establishments, and just as Nicolas had served sweets throughout the bloody years of the Revolution, so he would keep his macaron towers full now too.

Sylvie breathed deeply when she and Rafe walked through the door, overwhelmed by the smell of sugar, the warm hug of dough. There was a sense of safety here that she hadn't realized she'd been missing until she stepped across the threshold.

Rafe looked relieved too, once they were inside. "There are few spots in the city that Terreur can't reach—this is one of them. And Honoré Côte's tomb, of course, but we didn't have enough room there."

"Room for what?"

"You'll see."

His fox slid away, trotting beneath the glass chandelier into a back room, where sacks of flour and sugar guarded an even deeper door, down into the cellars. Only, Sylvie had never seen a cellar quite like this. It was large—large in the way that made her suspect magic was involved. Light shone through walls of colored glass, illuminating bookshelves and velvet settees and steaming pots of tea to go with pastries fresh from the oven upstairs. *Artists don't thrive when they starve*, after all, and Sylvie smiled when she saw a sculptor in the corner, nibbling the edges of a gold-foiled macaron as she stepped back to examine her work. The statue looked like Joan of Arc, only, this Joan had wings. Engraved on her armor was a most familiar dragon…

"Welcome to the resistance!" Rafe's shadow gave a small bow as he stepped into the room.

"You've started the League of Imaginers?"

Sylvie could see other artists scattered through the subterranean landscape, working with charcoal and fiddles and typewriters. Bright red birds flew around sparkling limestone stalactites, some of which had been carved into delightful shapes: Bunches of grapes. Coiled serpents. Swords.

"'Started' is a generous word," Rafe said, as he waved Sylvie past a velvet chaise where Désirée—formerly of the Cabaret d'Ailes—was sharing a cup of tea with a swan-limbed ballerina. Swan-winged too. "So is 'league,' but yes, Honoré helped recruit some imaginers to our cause before she marched off to that bloody war."

"War? What war?" Sylvie realized then that most of the artists in this underground were women. That, or their hair was silvered with age instead of dreams.

"They're calling it the war to end all wars!" said the ballerina.

"If it did, that'd mean everyone in the world was dead," Rafe replied.

"Everyone but you." Désirée lifted her teacup, her eyes cutting to the thief's watch.

"And Terreur. And the Mad Monk. And all his other disciples." Rafe sighed. "Though that heartless bastard would probably turn on them then. He's always wanted more. After he seized Paris, he—" Rafe paused, catching the look on Sylvie's face. "Well, I suppose I should start from the beginning. What's the last thing you remember?"

A firebird in the furious snow.

Sylvie was still wearing her old friend's fur coat. And beneath that? She felt a sharp edge of glass—the exposure from Duchess d'Uzès's party remained in her pocket. At least *that* wasn't broken. "I—I was going to get Anastasia so that we'd be out of the way when Honoré snuck back to stab the heart, but the grand duchess was upset about Alexei, and she lost control of her imagining. It burned too bright."

Rafe said nothing.

"Is Russia fighting in this war too?" she asked, suddenly thinking about how Rasputin's shadow had fallen over all those tin soldiers in Alexei's playroom. "Have you heard anything about the royal family?"

"Everyone is fighting," the ballerina said. "All the kings of Europe seem to have gone mad."

"I haven't heard any news about your princess friend," Rafe told Sylvie gently, "but the front lines aren't anywhere near her palace. She should be safe."

Sylvie wasn't so sure. "I—I had to take Anastasia's memories of magic." This thought still burned. "But Rasputin discovered me anyway. He turned me into a necklace. I couldn't hear anything after that. I saw—well, I saw you. Coughing blood. And then I was with the Fisherman of the Moon."

Rafe nodded. "I took you to him, after I met Madame Arcana—"

"Who?"

"The Seer of the Seine. That's her true name."

"She worked at the Carnaval des Merveilles." Sylvie remembered. "She was the fortune teller who disappeared the night La Fée Verte first met Terreur, right?"

"That's right." Désirée nodded and poured two more cups of tea. "We thought she'd chosen to become his disciple, especially when she started collecting fates from people who visited her under the bridge, but she was just keeping her cards close to her chest, much like your silver-tongued friend."

"The Seer was the one who first recommended Céleste to Terreur," Rafe added. "It's why he trusts her. That and the other thought

Céleste managed to plant in his head . . . I wasn't in on it. I couldn't be. Terreur needed to believe she'd chosen him, and *damn* if she wasn't convincing—I'm not half the liar Céleste Artois is. She didn't even crack when Terreur used my flesh to heal hers."

"I didn't know about her plan either," Sylvie said, slightly put out.

"The only person she told was Honoré," Rafe said. "And Honoré had her own contingency in place—she and La Fée Verte discovered how to share their hearts without performing Robespierre's spell. To use their love as an amplifier, instead of seeing it as weakness. She'd made plans to take La Fée Verte's heart and guard it, should the worst happen."

"And it did."

"It did," Rafe echoed. "Though the Seer says this was the best path forward. She saw it in her crystal ball thirty-odd years ago . . ."

"That's a very long con," Sylvie said, taking a sip of her lavender tea.

"*Oui*," Rafe answered. "Though it's taken her all those years to weave the net she used to pull La Fée Verte from the river. 'To shift the currents,' she told me."

"What does that mean?" the ballerina wondered.

Rafe shrugged.

"Madame Arcana always was a cryptic creature," Désirée added. "Though I suppose seeing so many possible futures all at once would make anyone speak in riddles."

"Yes, well, I would've appreciated a bit more clarity regarding my relic," Rafe grumbled. "She led me to believe that sacrificing Sylvie was the only way to survive this consumption. If I hadn't gone to the Fisherman of the Moon and learned otherwise, I'd be six feet under right about now."

"We're more than that, I figure." Sylvie glanced up at the sparkling ceilings, then back at Rafe's pocket watch. "So why aren't you, you know, dead?"

"Because time cannot touch me as long as this watch does." He tapped the gold engraving against his skin. "It belonged to Nicolas Flamel."

"Oh!" Sylvie remembered this name as well. "The Fisherman mentioned him when he was teaching me and Honoré about relics during our first visit to his booth. He told us old magical objects have layers."

Rafe nodded. "He told *me* that this watch predicted a person's fateful hour. After I purchased the relic, I discovered its second function: It could stop time for its wearer. But there was a third level to the pocket watch—one Monsieur Flamel himself used for many centuries. It can protect its wearer from the passage of time. Céleste's consumption is in my lungs, but as long as I'm wearing this watch, the disease can't progress. I'm cheating death."

Sylvie looked at the thief more closely. There was no more blood on his chin, true, but its scruff had stayed the same length. "Well, that sure seems fairer than the way Terreur does it." Rasputin too. A shiver ran through Sylvie as she recalled the frame that had fallen on Alexei's unmoving chest. That saint could have been her. It would have been, if Rafe García had chosen differently. "Thanks for not killing me."

He raised his scarred eyebrow. "Even if I had stolen your life, I would've been short-lived. Marmalade would have stalked me to death. Do you know he's followed the Fisherman everywhere for the past eight months? Along with every other feral stray in Père Lachaise? It was quite the sight to see: a ragpicker and an army of cats wandering the cemetery."

As if on cue, the tailless tom appeared, hopping onto the settee and settling back into Sylvie's lap with a grunt. *We must stay close, oh hunter mine. We must take care until the tiger changes her stripes and the prickly one returns.*

"Tiger?" Sylvie wondered.

Rafe tilted his head. "What's he saying? We've had trouble understanding the Whisper Network after we lost you and Libris."

They would have lost more, if we had not warned all the magic ones. Marmalade rattled. *Now we watch. Now we wait.*

"He tells me the cats are waiting for Honoré to come back to Paris," Sylvie said, scratching the tom's back. He'd grown skinnier since last winter.

"It's not just the cats." Rafe waved back over the settee toward the first sculptor, and now that they were closer, Sylvie realized she knew the woman. Duchess d'Uzès, wearing a periwinkle wig under her driving helmet. She knew the statue too. That dagger-pointed smile. "Honoré has made quite the name for herself on the battlefield. Half of Paris believes she's Saint Geneviève, summoned by their prayers to save the city."

Sylvie snorted at this.

"It's not all that untrue," Rafe said. "She's stronger now than she's ever been."

The Duchess d'Uzès set down her hammer and chisel and gave the daydreamer a wave. "Sylvie, my dear! Thank goodness you're here! They told me what happened to you just after my midwinter fête—or should I say, *your* fête." She slipped off her driving helmet, and Sylvie realized the lavender wig underneath wasn't a wig at all. Some of the older woman's strands were shining. There was the smallest twinkle around her eyes as well. "It's a shame Rasputin took the wig and didn't even try it on... The man could really use one. If I ever run across him, I'd like to give him a piece of my mind for turning you into a locket like that!"

Sylvie wasn't sure if the champagne heiress meant this literally or not.

"Don't worry," the duchess replied, seeing the look on her face. "I won't go seeking the Mad Monk out. I know my strengths." She glanced back over her shoulder at the half-finished statue of Honoré. "Smashing rocks and driving fast." Her eyes widened. "Do you know, I just thought of something... an ambulance service! We could reach hopelessly wounded soldiers and take them back to my château at Bonnelles to convalesce. Not just physically, you see, but *here*." The woman tapped her head, and the idea flared brighter, so Sylvie could catch glimpses of a green-lawned estate, where more shining hairs poked through soldiers' gauze-wrapped heads. "I should think it's equally important that they have a place for their souls to heal after so much ruin. We could even recruit the more creative patients to our cause! This war is so massive—I don't think a single angel can win it."

"I'm not sure anyone can," Rafe murmured. "It's a good idea, Manuela, but we aren't here to end the war."

The duchess pinched her lips together. "Certainly! I wasn't suggesting we conquer Europe, but we're here to fight fear, are we not? Why should we bury our brightest ideas down here while Honoré is out risking life and limb on the battlefield? What's the point of our power if we hide it?"

Sylvie flinched at this, so close to the last question Anastasia had asked her. She understood why the princess voiced it and Duchess d'Uzès too, but Sylvie also knew why Rafe answered the way he did.

"The point is patience," he said. "We can't strike Terreur until we're certain we can deliver a fatal blow."

"Not all of us have all the time in the world, Monsieur García. I am an aging woman, and I wish to leave this earth a better place than I found it—so far, that prospect does not look promising." Duchess d'Uzès sighed and touched the edges of her purple hair. "How much longer, do you think?"

Rafe glanced down at the pocket watch on his chest. "However long it takes that bastard to surrender his heart."

To Céleste, Sylvie realized. That was the twist. That must be why the oldest Enchantress had settled with Terreur at the Palais Garnier—she'd seeded this idea inside her forgery. She must be waiting, waiting in those dark and thorny halls, for something to bloom.

Chapter 40

Safe and Sound

Céleste Artois sat atop of one of the tallest palaces in Paris. Up here, she couldn't help but think of her father and wonder what the man might think of her now—with all the world's wealth at her fingertips. And wings too. There was no danger in falling from the Palais Garnier's famous wedding cake dome. For her, at least.

It doesn't matter if you're six feet under or on top of the goddamn world. Corpses can be stripped, and kings can be beheaded. There is always more to be taken, so it's best to be the taker.

The prayer looped through her head. It was getting harder to believe lately. Harder to keep up the mask... and her masque. Terreur had taught her to knot shadows and blot the sun—only a few days ago, she'd plunged the daytime sky into absolute black. He'd also taught Céleste how to wring enough power out of dying men so she could do such deeds. She didn't kill them—the bullets did that—but she did stand over their broken bodies and watch their eyes go as dark as her eclipse. She leaned in close as a kiss and let her own gaze darken.

Céleste hated what she saw in the dressing room mirrors these days.

Her opera gowns were often covered in mud and blood after she returned from the battlefield, and the costumes she found to replace them were... well, costumes. She dressed like Egyptian queens and tragic Italian lovers and whatever else had been left inside Mademoiselle Leroux's wardrobe. She sat in front of the mirror, hoping for glimpses of the other Enchantresses hunting for Terreur's elusive heart, but often all she saw was the undoing of the prima donna. That, or the swirl of her own black masque. It looked as if someone had taken a tattoo needle to her cheekbones—piercing the skin with ink again and again and again.

It fit a bit too well.

This was one reason why Céleste had chosen to raid the dead soprano's closet. If she dressed theatrically, she could remind herself that she was playing a part, without Terreur getting suspicious. He rarely read her thoughts these days, but every once in a while, Céleste would catch the Sanct looking. Watching her from his opera box or regarding her through a battalion of bleeding men or appearing behind the mirror like some unholy apparition, as if trying to scare her. She did not flinch. An Egyptian queen would simply smile instead.

Terreur was starting to smile back.

It wasn't *love* behind his gaze; Céleste understood the Sanct was not capable of that. But admiration?

Perhaps.

She'd have to wait and see.

Eight months in and no end in sight. It wasn't ideal, but desperate times called for desperate measures. They also called for a forger. Céleste had taken great care to copy what she'd found in Terreur's original vision: the shuttered shops and bleak streets. It was only after she'd imagined these things that she slipped her own thought in. The tiniest seed of a suggestion: *I will give Céleste Artois my heart.*

She'd buried it deep in the dreary dream.

Too deep, perhaps.

Sylvie's wigs hadn't taken this long to manifest. Pants for women hadn't become fashionable at all, despite Honoré's best efforts, and *damn*, Céleste missed her friends more than she could say, more than she could even think—

"Hey!" One of the Apaches was clambering up to her perch, the wind licking his red scarf around his straining neck. It ruffled Gabriel's blond hair too as he scaled the roof. "The boss is looking for you!" Céleste didn't move when the young man settled next to her. "Damn!" He huffed and took in the view—one could see all the way across the Seine on a good evening. "I always wondered why you sat up here so much."

She tried not to stiffen at this.

Tried not to notice how much the boy resembled Honoré. Gabriel even sat the same way—hunched like a gargoyle, his hands never still. He didn't fidget for knives though. Céleste sometimes saw him tinkering at the grand piano in the studio where the ballerinas rehearsed, but he'd stopped playing bar tunes. He'd stopped playing much of anything when Terreur was around. Up here, though, at the top of the opera house dome, Gabriel Durand started to hum.

Céleste raised her eyebrows. "What song is that?"

"Oh." The gangster pressed his knees to his chest, his fingers going still. "Nothing."

A lie.

Interesting.

Céleste tilted her head, for she knew the tune. It was his sister's hymn. The ballad of the Battlefield Angel. Judging by the way Gabriel was watching her now, he knew this too.

"You should take more care, Monsieur Durand," she said, nodding at the patinaed zinc slope he'd just scaled. "It would be a nasty fall."

The young man shrugged. "I might not have wings, but I got a second chance. And a third." The necklaces, he meant. Gabriel wore saints, same as the rest of Terreur's disciples, but he didn't seem to go through them at quite the same rate as someone like Rémy. He hadn't harvested much power from Belgium's battlefields either. Céleste figured the only reason the boy wasn't a husk himself was because Terreur knew his value to Honoré, knew she would die for her younger brother.

"It would still hurt a hell of a lot," she told him.

"Not if I had my father's ring." Gabriel's mouth twisted to the side, the way Honoré's did whenever Sylvie said something terrible yet funny. "Hard to believe there was magic under my nose all along... Pa always said his dragon was lucky, but there was something about it. Something..." He paused, his eyes hardening. "Well, you never did know when it would turn on you."

"Everything has a cost. Especially magic." Céleste thought of the dragon climbing up Honoré's neck, the way her friend had sobbed about leaving her brother behind in the catacombs with the rest of the dead. "I'm not sure the pain is always such a bad thing. We'd get too careless without it."

"Like your friend Monsieur García?"

Céleste bit her lip; she couldn't tell if the boy was baiting her or not. "He wasn't a friend."

"He was plotting with my sister though, no? And you were close with her?" Gabriel wrung his hands together. "When Anne's dragon ring tried to swallow me in the catacombs, I saw things. I *felt* them... I always figured she was a liar. She lied all the time when we were little, see, telling me she bruised her ankle falling down the stairs or that Maman's closet was a door to a secret world where no monsters could go or that my knights had ridden away on our black kitten's back to have an adventure..."

That *did* sound awfully whimsical for Honoré.

"I thought she was lying about Rafael too, but after I got back to the Caveau, I started seeing things... things that had always been there. The fox carving on the bar. That train poster in the supply closet. Stuff that matched my new memories..." He shook his head, hard as a dog trying to get dry. The shadows on his face flickered.

Céleste wondered if he'd stumbled across Eleanor as well, wondered if he understood the risk he was taking just speaking to her now.

"You saw what happened to Rafe García too," she said, her voice low. "There's no second chance with Terreur—doesn't matter how many saints you're wearing."

Gabriel fell quiet, his hand going up to his charms.

"You said he's looking for me?"

"*Oui*," the young man said. "He's waiting in the main theatre. He seems... on edge."

"I'd better see to him, then." Céleste's wings stretched as she stood. She didn't dare wear feathers—but she'd copied the color of crows under sun. The same oil-spill shade of that first gown Jean Cocteau had dressed her in. When they were folded against her back, they looked like an iridescent cape.

Gabriel eyed them with a mixture of awe and envy.

"Do you need help getting down?" she asked the boy.

"I think I'll stay up here," he said, shaking his head. His fingers had gone back to playing unseen keys. His gaze strayed toward the horizon, flanked by the Palais Garnier's angelic statues. "Enjoy the view a while longer."

The Palais Garnier was strangely empty as Céleste flew over the grand staircase. At this hour, there were often performers about, or stagehands at the very least, but tonight the theatre's curtains would not rise. Ballets and operas had dwindled since the start of the war—there was the matter of a smaller audience, yes, but Céleste had also overheard the workers complain that they thought the opera house might be haunted.

That phantom has returned...

What? The one from thirty-four years ago?

Oui! *Haven't you felt those strange drafts? Wind from nowhere? Smells like shit. And then there are the screams from empty rooms and the mud marks they got us scrubbing from the carpets.*

It ain't the old phantom. Ghosts don't take holidays like that. My guess is it's Jean-Luc's restless soul. You know, that understudy? I heard he got himself killed in Belgium a few weeks back.

Both custodians were correct. Neither of them could see Céleste stepping out of the battlefield portal onto their freshly mopped floor, but they would have to wash the tiles again. And again. And again.

Rémy was the worst offender, slapping dirt off his yellow boots at all hours of the day and night, drunk on blood. He was a hungry one too. Céleste sometimes caught him looking at the seams of her dress and the skin beneath—wanting to rip. The gangster wasn't in the main theatre now, thankfully. None of the Apaches were. Terreur sat alone in the vast room, taking in the empty stage from his private box. It was one of the hidden corners of the Palais Garnier that never got dusted. The angel carvings that guarded the ornate balustrade wept with cobwebs. Some fell as Céleste flew up to them, drifting to the sea of crimson seats below. More work for the custodians, she supposed.

Terreur's box had a spectacular view: just close enough to the curtains to see the beautiful details of the set—hieroglyphs on temple pillars and jewels at the soprano's trembling throat—without seeing the ugly mechanics of it all. Only Céleste, landing at the very edge of the balcony, could glimpse a tangle of pulleys and counterweights. She could see strings around Terreur too. He was always pulling someone's shadow these days. There was plenty of fear to play with.

Céleste felt her own edges tug.

Terreur was seated in an ebony armchair, his decanter within easy reach. He wanted Céleste to sit too. It was a fine balance—knowing when to move at his whim or when the Sanct really wanted her to push back. She could have stood her ground, what little she had, on the narrow ledge by the weeping angel, but one look at Terreur warned her not to. He seemed agitated. His cheeks were red, redder than they normally were after a glass or two of some poor poilu.

Céleste folded her wings and slipped to the adjoining seat. "The Durant boy said you wished to see me?"

"Where have you been?"

"Getting some fresh air."

"You seem to be doing that a lot."

"Yes, well, it's a requirement for those of us who still need to breathe," she told him. "I'm not sure if you've noticed, but it smells like hell where the portals are open. Even the un-Enlightened theatre staff are catching whiffs."

"I have taught you to extinguish the sun. Surely you can use your powers to mask those scents."

"What? Make death smell like roses?"

"Why not?"

Céleste closed her eyes and crafted the spell. It wasn't difficult, not if she didn't think about the dying soldier who'd powered it.

"There," Terreur said, followed by the slithering sound of his inhale. "Much better. You've come a long way, Mademoiselle Artois. I'm curious: Have you seen any strange happenings in your walks around Paris?"

"I've hardly seen anything," Céleste answered as she opened her eyes. "Half the city has fled because of the Germans. Almost all the shops are closed."

"Not all." Another inhale. She wondered if he was searching for a different scent—sugar maybe.

"Are you worried about that Stohrer baker? He's simply selling cakes—"

"I'm not worried about Nicolas, no." Terreur reached over to the side table and grabbed something from behind the decanter. "I'm more concerned about La Fée Verte's knight. You've heard the tune about her, I assume?"

"Once or twice," Céleste said.

"It's quite catchy."

"It's just a song."

The Sanct's hands tightened over whatever it was he was holding. "She seems to be drawing strength from its verses. She's drawing closer to Paris as well, matching the movements of the troops. The French soldiers are retreating, but I don't think that's the case with the knight." Terreur paused, and Céleste caught a glimpse of wood between his fingers. "She is coming for us."

"You fear her?" she asked, after a moment.

"I didn't at first. But that relic makes her a formidable opponent. As long as she's wearing it, she's untouchable." Terreur's own grip shifted to show it was a box he was holding. A jewelry box. "The knight came too close to killing me in Russia. I cannot risk her hunting down my heart again. I must guard my life more carefully. Keep it where Honoré Côte would not dare place a blade..."

Céleste measured her breaths. Roses, roses, and more roses.

Terreur opened the lid.

There was no diamond nor gold bar nestled inside. What Céleste saw instead was a dark lump. Coal, maybe? Or iron ore? It didn't look like a heart. It didn't look like much of anything.

"I considered using her brother for this purpose, but his loyalty seems to be wavering lately. Yours has proven true." Terreur picked up the dark stone and held it between his fingers. He leaned closer to Céleste's chair and swept her hair back from her shoulder. "I had my doubts, certainly. There were concerning strands... enough connection between you and La Fée Verte's knight to make me wary. But you've shown me that you value your life above all else. Even some enchanted sisterhood."

Roses and more roses.

Terreur's hand wandered down to Céleste's chest.

His masque flared.

Her flesh gave way, and for a horrifying moment, she glimpsed her own pulpy insides—so soft against the stone he set there. *I will give Céleste Artois my heart.* She'd feared she'd buried this seed too deep, but, no, the notion had grown, and now Terreur was burying himself in *her*. His heart sat just over Céleste's, and she knew there would be no stabbing one without the other. They were too close. Close enough that she could feel an extra weight with every breath. Her chest felt so heavy. Like an anchor dropping to the ocean floor, pinning Céleste to the bottom, water smothering her...

Bone closed back over the wound.

Then skin.

"There," Terreur said, with a smile. "Safe and sound."

The Tiger's Stripes

There are not many tigers left in Paris. The flaming ones have all been extinguished, and the animals of the Jardin des Plantes menagerie have been safely locked away, their keepers recalling stories from the last great siege of the city, in 1870, when citizens ate zoo animals to stave off starvation. Elephant soup and fried camel nuggets and kangaroo stew. The perfect Christmas feast!

You hope it does not come to that.

They promised the war would be won by Christmas, but with the German army closing in like a noose, you are beginning to have your doubts. You've once more started walking your beloved city at night—not to stumble upon some new enchantment but to say goodbye. Adieu, even. After hearing about the atrocities in Belgium, you find it hard not to wonder how much the kaiser's soldiers might destroy. Will they set torches to the Jardin des Tuileries? Will they smash the statues lining the garden's gravel paths?

They might have a difficult time of it with the tigress.

The bronze beast stands with her cubs in a long stretch of emerald grass. She has always called to you in a way—for you've come back again and again. Often enough to memorize every detail. Auguste-Nicolas Cain spent three years of his life casting this tiger's stripes, her proud stance as she brings a limp peacock to her young. Her strength... it's more than feral. More than the claws and jaws of her male counterpart on the other side of the garden. He wrestles a crocodile to death, yes, but *she*, she hunts for something better. She has mouths to feed.

You aren't this statue's only admirer. There is a white-haired woman standing by the tigress, her palm placed on its flank. You cannot see her face, but the way her shoulders move suggests she might be weeping. Her dark cape does not smear the dew as she walks to the other side of the statue. Out of sight. Vanished completely.

She leaves no footprints either.

You notice this as you walk to the spot where she stood. Another thing you notice? While the dewdrops stayed in perfect jeweled spheres, the statue's bronze shifted at the woman's touch. The deep grooves Monsieur Cain carved over four decades ago are all rearranged.

The tigress's stripes have changed.

A much smaller orange cat emerges from some nearby hedges and picks his way across the lawn. He pauses by your ankles long enough for you to swear that he is studying the altered sculpture too. His ragged ears flatten. His tail stub twitches. He fixes his orange eyes on you, and you get the sudden feeling that you've seen a secret. A signal. A promise. A hope that has nothing to do with the war...

You decide, as you walk away, that you shall not say goodbye.

You will keep wandering.

You will keep wondering.

Chapter 41

What Was Lost Has Been Found

She has the heart. This message traveled fast, as fast as Marmalade could dash from the Jardin des Tuileries, past the Louvre and down rue Saint-Honoré. The street was not named after the prickly one, but it did lead back to the bakery, and once the tom reached Stohrer and signaled the Whisper Network, word would be well on its way to her. Fable would take it to Nix, who would pass it on to the rest of the Père Lachaise strays, who would go to the outskirts of the city and talk to the farm cats. Then this news would prowl through France's fields. It would slip through barns where retreating soldiers lay their heads on bales of hay. It would search through orchards thick with apples—still a sickly, unripe green. It would find Honoré Côte in the form of a young black kitten, who did not quite understand why the knight started tearing up when she saw him, or why she cried even more when he mewled his missive: *What was lost has been found.*

Come home now.

Chapter 42

The Kiss at the Glass Casket

Sylvie of a Single Name sat outside the Enchantresses' mausoleum, rummaging through the handcart that belonged to the Fisherman of the Moon. Waiting for Honoré to return was far easier if she had something to keep her hands busy. She'd hardly sat still since the Sanct had freed her from the necklace. She couldn't. There was too much to do, so much lost time to make up for—

"Careful!" the ragpicker called out from the mausoleum step. Sylvie paused, her hand hovering over a gold-leafed tiara set on the head of a bust. "You put that crown on, and you might never take it off again!"

Sylvie shuddered. She had no desire to get tangled up inside another piece of jewelry, so she set the unhappy-looking statue aside and kept digging through the Fisherman's loot. He'd managed to save a number of things from Terreur's fire—thanks to the warning of the Whisper Network. He'd packed only the essentials: thimbles and spools of stray ribbon and old posters.

She chose to pluck out one of these, unrolling it to find a beautiful advertisement for the Carnaval des Merveilles. The tents looked almost like lilies, the way they sprouted from the carnival grounds. If Sylvie stared for long enough, she could see their edges flapping, open and inviting. She glimpsed Madame Arcana too, peering into the twisting fog of her crystal ball. The fortune teller hadn't been much help since she'd netted La Fée Verte's body from the river. The few times Sylvie had tried to sneak out to the Sanct's houseboat, she found the door locked tight. Even though she heard sounds on the other side, she hadn't tried to pick it open the way she'd once broken into Libris's fancy display case...

The bookseller had been right to keep Sylvie from spoiling her own story.

She certainly would've skipped the chapter with the necklace.

And erasing Anastasia's memory.

But if Sylvie of a Single Name had not lived through those things, she figured she wouldn't be sitting here now, staring at this reminder of what had risen from the Revolution's ashes.

"Do you have any more of these?" She held the poster up for the Fisherman to see.

"There should be an absinthe advertisement in there—"

"No, I mean for the carnival."

"That's my only copy. Though there may be more on Île du Carnaval." The Fisherman of the Moon tilted his head, his masque gleaming the same color as the brass telescope he'd been peering through. Not searching for stars but Honoré. "Why do you ask?"

Sylvie wasn't sure she wanted to say. She glanced back at the poster's flowery script. Surely Rafe could copy it onto fresh pieces of paper... They would need to change the dates blooming at the bottom anyway. "No reason."

Yet.

"That reminds me, you know what I do have?" The Fisherman let go of the telescope to start rifling through his coat. "The photograph from that plate you asked me to have developed."

Sylvie's breath suddenly felt as sharp as the glass she'd handed the ragpicker several days ago. She'd wanted something less fragile to carry around in her pocket, alongside the key to the door at rue de la Réunion, but the paper the Fisherman handed over didn't feel much sturdier. Neither did Sylvie, when she caught her first sight of the portrait. Blue and pink. A princess and a phantasm.

Grand Duchess Anastasia Nikolaevna was smiling.

Sylvie—next to her—was a blur.

Just as much a ghost in the picture as she was in the grand duchess's memory.

Sylvie folded her hand over the photograph, instantly regretting the motion as the paper bent and warped Anastasia's face. Had their friendship been worth it? Truly? Or was this just something she told herself to sleep better at night? Never mind how many evenings she spent standing in front of the pink door, staring through its keyhole, trying to catch glimpses of the grand duchess. She didn't dare try to unlock the portal. Not while the Mad Monk still lurked on the other side. According to the cats of Saint Petersburg—well, Petrograd, it was Petrograd now—the sorcerer kept himself quite busy with the royal family. The tsarina and her two eldest daughters had even taken an interest in healing people, training to become *sestry miloserdiya*. Sisters of mercy, dedicated to the Red Cross.

As for Alexei?

The prince lives on borrowed time. All the Romanovs are unraveling. They are too tangled up in Rasputin's shadow to last much longer…

And there was no way for Sylvie to save them.

She'd known this when she finally caught sight of Anastasia, not through the keyhole, but a mirror in the grand duchess's bedroom. It was just a glimpse—her spell couldn't last long against Rasputin's wards—but she knew the room belonged to Nastya, thanks to the butterflies stenciled around the pink walls. Sylvie felt immediately at home, as if *she* were the one who shared the room with Anastasia, instead of the grand duchess's older sister. Both girls were in their beds. Maria seemed to be sleeping. Anastasia looked awake, though it was difficult to know for sure. Shadows stained her pillow. They shaded the princess's eyes as well, but a candle flickered on her bedside table. Its light danced across the story Anastasia was reading.

The lilac fairy book.

It was no longer truly lilac. The blood on the cover had dried enough to match the singe marks—rusted brown. Sylvie found she could see the gilded fae on the front better for it. Stars at her feet. Moon through her hair.

Anastasia's own hair was a tangle of black. *She's so afraid*... Sylvie ached at the thought, and she knew that even if she could somehow step through the mirror and use a dream to cut the grand duchess free from Rasputin's grasp, the princess would not leave.

I don't know what I would do without my family. They're my heart...

Sylvie's own heart felt just as crumpled as the photograph. She wanted it to be smooth again. She wanted hide-and-seek games in Libris's bookstore. She wanted to laugh in a ballroom full of colorful wigs. She wanted tea parties lit with firebirds. She wanted her friend back.

"Here." The Fisherman of the Moon pulled more prints from his pocket and handed them to her. "I had several copies developed, just in case."

"In case what?" Sylvie asked.

The ragpicker shrugged. "You never know when you'll find yourself needing a reminder of how to hope. That ball was your first real muse magic. If you ever struggle to make more, you can look back at these photographs and see proof of your power. You bring joy to those around you, Sylvie of a Single Name. You brought joy to Russia's youngest grand duchess too. That is never wrong. And it's never wasted."

Sylvie bit her lip as she looked down at Anastasia's smiling face.

It went blurry with tears.

She tucked the fresh photographs into her own pocket before she could ruin those too. She wiped the moisture from her eyes and looked back down at the Carnaval des Merveilles poster. *No*, Sylvie decided, *it will not be wasted.* She wondered if she could ask Rafe to add a firebird to the carnival's next iteration.

She was rolling the advertisement back up when Marmalade appeared by the handcart's wheel, his paws moving in a quick dance.

The prickly one! She comes!

Sylvie craned her neck to look at the sky. In the song, Honoré was compared to a comet—but there was no new light above them, only the cemetery wall the Enchantress had lined with broken glass well over a year ago. A bird flew down and landed between the pieces. With how dark it was outside, it took Sylvie an extra moment to realize the feathers were green. The beak, gold.

"Oh!"

The leaves of the nearby tree whispered as a cloaked figure stepped beneath their branches.

"Honoré!"

The newcomer halted by the mausoleum steps. "*Ma rêveuse!* Back to stealing necklaces instead of being them, I see! Oof!"

Sylvie threw her arms around Honoré's waist and hugged tight enough for the cloak to fall away. "You're . . . shiny!"

She looked more like the song than Sylvie had first believed. The glowing sword of dreams hung at her hip, yes, but there was a shimmer around her eyes as well. Silver beams. The color of a knife sharpened by moonlight. This shine caught the edges of her wings, which had somehow grown feathers . . . No wonder the soldiers thought Honoré was an angel!

"*Oui*," the other Enchantress sighed. "I feel like a walking torch."

"At least you're feeling something," the Fisherman of the Moon said from the steps. He was scanning Honoré's armor with his telescope. "I wasn't sure you'd be able to keep your relic under control, especially in a place so bloody as war."

"I managed," Honoré answered.

"You've done more than that!" Sylvie told her. "Everyone is talking about you, Honoré! Duchess d'Uzès even carved a statue. She wants to display it at the château hospital, but I think we should unveil it at the carnival."

Honoré's eyebrows rose. "Carnival?"

"Yes!" Sylvie waved the poster she was holding. "We'll need something to distract Terreur while we stab his heart, and I figure La Fée Verte will want a new place to gather dreams anyway once she wakes up—" She glanced through the mausoleum's iron doors, where the songbird sat on the edge of the glass casket. It seemed to be waiting for Honoré. Of course it was. Sylvie cleared her throat and tucked the advertisement behind her back. "I suppose you should go do that."

Honoré Côte stepped into the tomb that held her name. Her name and her love. This was a sacred moment, too private to allow for an audience, so she shut the iron doors behind her and stared into the box crafted by the Fisherman of the Moon. She knew it wasn't a coffin. Not really. She knew it wasn't glass she pushed away from La Fée Verte's form but a spell that had held the Sanct still since the moment Honoré left her here.

Her body anyway.

Her heart—the songbird Honoré had caught in the ash-choked sky—hopped onto the Sanct's unmoving chest. Its wings spread out over her breasts. Trembling. Its dark eyes looked back up at Honoré. Again, it seemed to be waiting.

Honoré took a deep breath, trying not to tremble as well. In all her time in the trenches, she hadn't dared doubt, but now that the moment was finally here, now that she was staring at La Fée Verte's waxen form, she couldn't help but question herself.

What if Honoré touched those cold lips and nothing happened?

What if she wasn't enough?

What if—

What if she kissed the woman she loved and it all worked out splendidly well?

What if La Fée Verte rose up from the grave and kissed her back?

Honoré had only one way to find out which ending was true. She leaned down into the glass casket—her hope as sharp as hurt—and pressed her lips to La Fée Verte's.

The dreams gathered over the past eight months swirled up all at once, pouring into La Fée Verte's masque like molten metal, swallowing both women in light. Life. Power. Honoré felt feathers quiver around her head, felt the chest beneath hers rise and fall, felt the bird vanish.

"My dame…"

The shine faded as Honoré pulled away just enough for her to see La Fée Verte's wings were no longer stripped down to bone. Her feathers had filled back in, and her cheeks were rosy, and her smile was everything good in this world…Honoré wanted to fall back into it, but the Sanct was already sitting up, her hair spilling off her shoulders as she rose from the casket. As she reached out and cupped Honoré's face in her hand.

Honoré mirrored the other woman's motion, tracing the beautiful whorls of her masque. Lit once more. They sat this way for a small eternity, saying nothing. They might have sat longer, if there weren't a not-so-shy knock on the door.

"Did it work? I saw a flash!" Sylvie's head poked through. "Oh, good! Have you told her about Stohrer's secret basement and that the Seer of the Seine was really on our side and Céleste is too, of course—"

"She didn't have to," La Fée Verte said, as she stretched her wings wide so wide that they brushed Honoré's own. "I've been with her this entire time."

Strange but true.

She'd never known such closeness, letting someone in even nearer than skin. For the past eight months, La Fée Verte had been under Honoré's every breath. She'd colored every thought. She'd kept every secret. She'd shared every dream. They'd both become bigger than themselves. And while Honoré had long yearned for this moment, a small part of her had begun to dread it too…Would there be new gaps in her armor, now that the songbird no longer nested there?

Her ring's wings were still shaped like feathers, however.

And when Honoré glanced at the open coffin, she could see her silver masque reflected in the glass. The song of the soldiers kept humming through her—it felt even louder here in the city. If Honoré focused, she could hear thousands of voices, thousands of *hopes*, lighting up the night. She felt the mothers tucking their babes into bed. She felt the priests in their cathedrals, clasping their hands, offering up prayers like incense. She felt the radio operator at the top of the Eiffel Tower, sending even more messages. She felt the cataphiles and the boulevardiers, the taxi drivers and the moonlight sinners, the belly dancers inside Moulin Rouge's elephant, the rich youths who'd once watched them, another young man sitting on the roof of an opera house...

She felt La Fée Verte too.

The other Sanct watched her with a smile. "Their hope suits you, Honoré."

"I—" Honoré wasn't quite sure what to say. "I didn't mean to become a Sanct. I figured all the power would pass to you." But it hadn't. And now that Honoré studied La Fée Verte more closely, she saw the woman's masque was flickering. Not with a spell, but more like a candle in the wind. "You need more, don't you?"

"Here!" There were still dozens of rose-colored dreams hanging from the ceiling, but Sylvie pulled one from her head instead. Honoré glimpsed a carousel inside, as it passed to La Fée Verte. "Use this!"

"The Carnaval des Merveilles..." Wooden horses kept spinning around and around between La Fée Verte's fingers.

"I know why you closed it now," Sylvie said, her voice strangely soft. "I know why you were so afraid to let me into the salon after you invited Honoré...but you did it anyway, and now you have two more Sancts to help you fight Terreur. If you open the carnival again and invite every imaginer in Paris to join you...well, I don't think he'd stand much of a chance."

Certainly not, if Céleste had gotten ahold of his heart—though Honoré knew the youngest Enchantress was right. They'd need a distraction. Something sparkly to divert Terreur's attention so he wouldn't stop them from stabbing it.

"One night is all we need," she said.

La Fée Verte's masque sputtered as she shook her head. "I don't have enough magic to open the carnival."

"We do!" Sylvie chirped. "The League of Imaginers, I mean. Rafe and Duchess d'Uzès and Jean Cocteau and Guillaume Apollinaire and . . . well, everyone who's been gathering dreams under Stohrer. There's a lot. And once we move to Île du Carnaval, there will be even more! We can inspire other imaginers. We can share enough power to rebuild everything Terreur destroyed. The cafés and cabarets and your salon . . ."

"Perhaps." La Fée Verte stared back at the dream she was holding.

Honoré could feel her want.

She could feel the other woman's fear too: that history might repeat itself, that their dreams might not be enough.

"Would anyone even venture out when war is so close to the city?"

"They might if you gave them a reason." The Fisherman of the Moon had appeared in the doorway. There was a roll of **ADMIT ONE** tickets in in his hands. They looked far fresher than the stub he'd offered La Fée Verte last time. "Let them see more than the rot, Verte. Let them *be* more."

Chapter 43

The Beginning of the End

Who knows what dreams may wake at the Carnaval des Merveilles?

Come and See:

- **Shadow Puppets**
- **A Menagerie of Imaginings**
- **The Double-Headed Firebird**
- **La Fée Verte**
- **The Battlefield Angel**

One Night Only

Admission Is Anything You Can Think Of

The posters went up overnight. They were bright and quite noticeable—even in the city's shadowier corners—making people pause in the ivy-lined Passage de Dantzig or in the stairwells of Métropolitain stations. Even Rémy Lavigne stopped to study the scene, with his one good eye, before ripping it from the wall and returning to the opera house.

"What are they playing at?" he spat as he laid the paper at Terreur's feet. "Circus?"

Céleste sat close, close enough to recognize the art of the advertisement. It was much like the poster she'd seen on the drifting island, with the same blooming letters and swirling birds, but there were new additions too. Instead of a trapeze artist, it was a pink-haired fairy girl walking on a razor-thin tightrope. A two-headed firebird soared above her. And at the bottom left of the poster?

Rafe's signature. Not *Raf*, but a shadow.

The fox chasing his own tail.

Her heart squeezed when she saw this. Not too noticeably, since it already felt so crushed against Terreur's.

The other Sanct leaned forward in his seat. Céleste saw the recognition flicker behind his face as he studied the flourishing fairgrounds. His lips curled with disgusted amusement.

"It is a carnival," he told Rémy.

"Same difference," the gangster said, his yellow boots kicking the poster's edge. "Looks like they're trying to attract a crowd. Idiots! It's like eating cake while the world burns."

"I think the saying is about playing fiddles," Céleste told him.

Terreur's own gaze flickered as he picked the advertisement off the floor—the piece where Sylvie balanced on the tightrope tore beneath Rémy's boot. The Sanct stared very hard at the list of attractions, his eyes boring into La Fée Verte's name.

"The bitch found a way to survive then," he seethed. *La Fée Verte* started smoking. *The Battlefield Angel* did too. A ragged line of embers began to eat through the rest. "I'll have to be more thorough this time around. Bring me the brother," he told Rémy.

"Gabriel?"

Again, Céleste's heart squeezed.

"He can strip the knight's armor, can he not?" Terreur asked. "Or were you lying about what happened in the catacombs?"

Rémy shook his head. "Gabriel did grab that dragon. I swear it on all my saints! The ring really belongs to him, you know—"

Terreur's hand made a jerking movement, and Rémy's jaw snapped shut.

"It will be mine by the night's end. Bring me the brother and prepare the rest of the Apaches." The Sanct looked down at the burning carnival in his hands. His eyes cut back to Céleste. "You should get yourself ready for the Carnaval des Merveilles too," he told her. "I want you close."

One final costume.

The dress Céleste picked from Christine Leroux's armoire was red as sin. It must have been designed for a demon, for there was a pair of bat-like wings sewn to the back, but Céleste paid them no mind. She was more focused on the front of the gown. How low-cut the neckline was. How exposed her cleavage would be. She wore no corset to cover the view. She wore no necklaces either. There would only be a small window of opportunity... She couldn't risk a chain falling in the way.

She swept her hair from her shoulders as well, studying the prima donna's collection of decorative combs. Beautiful but sharp. Céleste paid more attention to the teeth than the designs, and it was only after she slid the hairpiece in place that she realized which symbol she'd picked.

An ouroboros.

The circular serpent didn't match her gown. It must have been meant to go with one of the Egyptian costumes, but when Céleste stared at her reflection, she found it fitting. *Poor snake, bit off more than it could chew, and now it's right back where it started.*

At the beginning of the end.

Chapter 44

Full Circle

For the first time in thirty-four years, Île du Carnaval had stopped drifting. The island stayed still on Sylvie's map too—right past the bend in the Seine, where Gustav Eiffel's tower rose over the water, flying France's tricolor flag from its radio antenna. She'd found herself staring at the monument at odd moments throughout that afternoon, pausing her preparations just long enough to remember Céleste's scheme to sell the structure for scrap metal. Or the time Sylvie had flown to the top to show Anastasia the secrets of her city…when she'd tried to explain the carnival's empty tents.

They were no longer so empty.

The League of Imaginers had been hard at work getting ready for the evening, taming the island's wild vines and its animals too. Sylvie had harvested an entire basket of silver apples to lure the wooden creatures back to their carousel, and now the carnival's crowning jewel had returned to its former glory, turning to the calliope's version of "The Battlefield Angel." Pegasi spun at the center of the tents, though not all of them stayed there, much to their riders' delight. They trotted off their stands and wandered through the festivities. Past the tent of the Frivolous Prince, where you might walk out with a blooming flower crown or a foxtail. Around the miniature racetrack game where Duchess d'Uzès handed out brightly colored wigs to the winning cars' drivers. Through a menagerie of rainbow-scaled boas and leopards made of snow and a blue elephant, of course. There were parrots too—reciting lines of Guillaume Apollinaire's poetry. If you stopped and listened long enough, a saying might stick to you, like a tattoo.

If your carousel horse kept going, you might find yourself riding through the wilds of some famous painter's mind. Or you might decide to try out life as an acrobat, with the wings Désirée was exchanging for wishes. The skies were busy though. Green songbirds swirled just as they did in the poster. Sylvie's butterflies were there too. Some even fluttered as high as the monument on the opposite shore. No one who'd seen Rafe's advertisement and made up their mind to go would get lost...

La Fée Verte had helped Sylvie weave Enlightenment spells into the ink so that anyone who stopped long enough and read the poster all the way to the end would see where to go.

They'll probably smell it too. Nicolas Stohrer's booth sat close to the entrance, offering cloud crème éclairs and bonbons with a firework filling. There were macarons too. Sylvie's favorite. Yet she hadn't so much as touched them. Her stomach was too fluttery. Her eyes kept drifting back to the Eiffel Tower, its scrap metal now lit a glowing pink.

What's the point of our power if we hide it?

They certainly weren't hiding anymore.

"Good turnout, no?" Rafe appeared by her ticket seller's stand, nodding at the roll of **ADMIT ONE** tickets Sylvie was holding. It was significantly shorter than it had been at the start of the evening. Beside it lay a large pile of imaginings. Silver, brass, gold, gold, gold...

There were even more stuffed inside Sylvie's pockets.

"Aren't you supposed to be putting on a shadow-puppet show?" she asked.

"I took a break." He shrugged. "Not many people were coming to see it anyway. I can't blame them: Paris has had enough of shadows."

Rafe stared over the lily pad bridge that connected Île du Carnaval to the opposite shore. His eyes widened.

Sylvie looked out over the water too.

Céleste! Oh, what a terrible and beautiful sight she was, dressed in red. She looked ready to attend a masquerade ball, with her hair swept back and her masque whispering across her face. She didn't seem to be carrying a heart though... Her hands clenched the sides of her carmine gown as she crossed the river, marching straight past Sylvie's ticket booth, over Rafe's shadow, all the way to the carousel.

She was not alone.

The rest of Terreur's disciples had arrived with her, their dark wings slashing over the Eiffel Tower. Sylvie's insides twisted even more as they ripped through her butterflies. She felt the insects fade and fall. Gray as ash. Gray as Céleste's eyes when Terreur landed at her side. The wooden pegasi spooked at the sorcerer's nearness, tearing off into the neon jungles of the painters' tent. Much of the crowd followed, leaving wigs and éclair wrappers in their wake. The calliope music came to a stop with the merry-go-round, and an eerie silence fell over the carnival.

The hungry man looked around the littered grounds.

"Is this all?" His voice slithered along the tent flaps, his eyes narrowing at the songbirds perched on the big top. "I believe I was promised a show. A chance to see La Fée Verte and her Battlefield Angel one last time? No?"

Sylvie crept out of the ticket booth, quiet as a cat. She didn't even dare to breathe. It was difficult to see Céleste—the oldest Enchantress was surrounded by Apaches. Sylvie recognized a few. Yellow Boots was there, only now he didn't have his pretty gold gun. He wore far more saints around his neck than the young man next to him. Honoré's brother... the boy looked uneasy. He kept clenching and unclenching his fists, balling them up even tighter when the Battlefield Angel stepped out of the largest tent.

Sylvie released a single breath.

Céleste let go of her gown.

Even Terreur hesitated.

Honoré was fully armed, the dragon sheathing her from neck to toe. She held her sword of dreams aloft, and as its light met her silver masque, her very pupils seemed to glow. Even brighter, when La Fée Verte came out to stand beside her.

"You'll have to pay first." As Honoré's voice rang out, the rest of the surrounding tents started to open.

Frost-clawed leopards sat next to alley cats. Jean Cocteau was dressed in an airy kimono—paired with a strand of pearls and his sharpest horns. The Fisherman of the Moon held a rusted tin can. Duchess d'Uzès stood by her finished statue, a hammer and chisel in hand. There was an entire company of artists from La Ruche guarding the painters' tent with dripping brushes. Rafe García, in turn, guarded them. His fox was now as large as a horse. Nicolas Stohrer had stepped in front of the drawbridge, and Désirée winged her way to the top of the carousel.

And on the tightrope?

Fire.

Fire that belonged to the largest double-headed bird Sylvie could conjure.

It did not burn with rage, the way Anastasia's had. No. It flickered with the immense love Sylvie felt as she looked out over this gathering. With the jagged pieces of loss—shaped like parents and a princess and a bookseller. With the way her heart kept beating around these things, making room for more. For *hope*.

The story isn't over yet.

She kept skirting the tents, trying to get closer to Céleste, trying to see where the oldest Enchantress was hiding Terreur's heart. Did that dress have pockets? Was it tucked up her sleeve? No, Céleste seemed to be reaching past this. Her hand wandered upward...

"Pay?" Terreur's laughter rang across the grounds. Sylvie's firebird flickered. "What? Do you really believe you can take a thought and banish me again?" A shadow uncoiled from him, thick as a kraken's tentacle, and whipped toward La Fée Verte. Honoré's wings spread out to stop it with a burst of sparks. When she swung her sword down, the shadow was severed. It writhed for a moment before melting back into the ground. Two more shadow tentacles sprang out from Terreur's masque in its place. "Do you think one pathetic song can give you enough power to fight my war? I am blood upon blood. I am endless. You are clowns. Fools." Both the dark ropes twisted back and grabbed Gabriel by the ankles. They twined up the young man's legs and sent him marching forward. They coiled down his arms and forced his fists to reach for Honoré. "Your dreams will die with you. Your lives will mean nothing."

Honoré tried to sidestep her brother, but another black shadow tentacle was unspooling toward La Fée Verte. When her armored wing went to block it, Gabriel grabbed the silver feathers, pulling them into a molten mess up his own arm.

Sylvie was close enough to stab the tentacle that reached for La Fée Verte with one of her own dreams. Terreur snarled as the shadow dissolved, and when his gaze landed on Sylvie, she felt his strength. His endlessness. She saw the teeth that broke stars and souls and knew he'd eat the rest of her name—given the chance.

Sylvie chose to look past this.

Her eyes found Céleste's.

The oldest Enchantress wore a strange expression. She was smiling as she pulled the comb from her hair, but it wasn't the grin she used when she told the twist in her bedtime stories. It was not a happily ever after.

She gripped the comb in her right hand.

With her left, she signaled. A small wave. A flutter of the fingers. The sign the Enchantresses used to send Sylvie off to bed, if a con went on too long or too late. *Goodnight, ma rêveuse*, it meant. *Sweet dreams.*

Sylvie understood then.

It was too much love, too much loss. Her firebird roared as Céleste turned the sterling teeth inward...The comb wasn't Terreur's heart after all. It was a weapon. A weapon sinking deep into the oldest Enchantress's chest.

Céleste Artois did not want to die. This was the reason she'd made her deal with the devil in the first place and why she'd lasted so long by his side—it was all Terreur saw when he looked at her. The liar. The taker. The woman who'd do anything in her power to survive.

She was this, certainly. She'd tried her best to think of loopholes, a way to kill Terreur without sharing his fate, but there was no getting around the fact she had to stab herself to defeat him. If Céleste tried to remove the heart from her chest beforehand, he might get suspicious. He might take it back.

There were no saints to save her either.

She couldn't risk Terreur's heart healing. Her cut needed to be as clean as possible. Deep too, though she still wasn't sure she'd have the strength to plunge the comb far enough into her chest. It was sharper than a cheese knife, yes, but it wasn't as neat as the blades Honoré had taught her to stab old flour sacks with. Nor was Céleste full of straw, the way those had been.

She was flesh.

She was bone.

She was hearts.

And Céleste would only have one chance to pierce through these things. There could be no hesitation, or Terreur would turn her into a husk... He would take everything that made her *her*. Tiger clouds and hours bent over canvases and kisses stolen between dusk-covered sheets, and, oh, if she could only go back to that last night with Rafe, if she could only pause by the ticket booth and tell him the truth: How much she loved him. How much this hurt. How she was damned, but the rest of the carnival wouldn't be, if she steeled herself.

She hoped the show would go on after tonight. The Carnaval des Merveilles was even more vivid than its posters—with so many swan boats and that wondrous merry-go-round and all the tents folding open.

She wanted so badly to step inside.

To stay.

But the sight of Honoré—holding that sword and looking so

goddamn glorious—helped Céleste reach for her own blade. Every *défense dans la rue* lesson they'd ever had together came rushing back. Every watchword. Every shared wheel of Camembert. Every ounce of gold they'd stolen and buried.

You'll have to pay.

Terreur was laughing. Distracted. He'd seized control of Gabriel, and soon he would try to take Honoré's armor. His prize was in sight, and Céleste was not, so she grabbed the ouroboros with shaking fingers.

More moments came rushing back as she locked eyes with Sylvie. Croissants under pillows and making up myths to match constellations. *Oh, just one more story? Please? Please?* But Céleste could see Sylvie's last birthday candle stuck in that *tarte au chocolat*, the memory itself twisting from the girl's head, floating between her and Terreur like a strand of smoke before vanishing into his masque.

He was starting to devour the youngest Enchantress.

That.

That was the all the strength Céleste Artois needed.

Flames in her chest. Fire from the skies. Everything went molten as the comb sank in. Her knees buckled too. She spilled to the ground, into its long, long shadows, and waited for death to take her...

...

...

Darkness swept around Céleste, and she could still feel heat pressing down on the crown of her head. *Hell really is full of fire and brimstone!* She must not have spent enough time confessing her sins to Père Lachaise's cemetery statues...

A laugh escaped her.

A hand landed on her shoulder.

"What is it you find so funny, *mon amour*? I, for one, am not amused at this wanton waste of my lifetime."

She lifted her eyes to see Rafe. Oh, Rafe. Once upon a time, she'd thought he looked like Orpheus, standing at the edge of rue des Ombres, but she'd never imagined he actually *would* follow her down into hell. *No*, Céleste realized, as she took in the whole of him.

The other thief knelt at her side, clutching his pocket watch, stealing one last moment for her. The rest of the carnival remained frozen. Sylvie's firebird had exploded overhead, and if not for Rafe's shadow wrapped around them, Céleste might have been too blinded to see Honoré trying to twist away from her brother or the menagerie animals leaping at the Apaches or the look of devastation on Terreur's face. The bastard had clearly realized she'd stabbed his heart, but Rafe had stopped time before death could truly take hold.

"Is that what you think this is?" she echoed the other thief's ice palace words, shivering a little, despite her burning breast. The wound there was agony. It made her words tremble even more. "A waste?"

All the blood drained from Rafe's own face when he saw her chest, making his teardrop tattoo that much starker. His hand tightened on her shoulder. "Céleste, *mon amour*, what have you done?"

"You have to let me go, Rafe," she managed. "Let me die."

"After all this?" His pocket watch dangled like a portent between them. His eyes flashed gold. His fingers tensed. "No. *No*."

"I don't want to—" Céleste choked. It was everything she could do not to look down at the comb in her chest, but she sure as shit could feel the prongs. The pain wasn't quite as intense as she'd expected. She could still speak, for one thing. She could still tell Rafe all the things she'd kept locked so deeply inside over these past eight months. "I never wanted to. If it weren't for you, I'd be buried already, but you took my bloody hand after *The Rite of Spring* and showed me all the dreams Paris had to offer. All the dreams I thought I'd lost. Because of you I finally did something worth a damn..." She took another shuddering breath. "I love you, Rafe García. Every sliver of stardust. Every last shadow. Never forget that."

His face looked so beautiful, even crumpled. "I can't. I— You're my life, Céleste."

"And I'm Terreur's death," she said, with such a heavy, blistering chest. "He hid his heart over mine. I had to stab both."

Rafe looked back down at her wound. "Oh shit," he whispered.

"I know—"

Again, his fingers tightened. "No, Céleste, look at the comb!"

It was difficult to tell the difference between her blood and her dress, though Céleste supposed this was a good thing. It made the ugliness easier to look at. The comb though . . . she had trouble wrapping her mind around it. The circular serpent symbol jutted too far out. The prongs beneath were crooked and warped, bent by the sheer force of her blow.

"That bastard's heart is too hard," Rafe hissed. "It didn't go through."

He was right, she realized, as she pulled the comb free. Its teeth hadn't been sharp enough. They'd made a mess of her flesh, but they hadn't scratched the black stone below. Nor had they bitten into her own heart . . .

Céleste wanted to laugh again, but it was hard to be happy about her miracle.

She was not dying.

And neither was Terreur.

The Sanct's stare was abysmal. His darkness was coming for her. Céleste realized, with a sick lurch in her gut, that it wasn't Rafe's fox surrounding the pair, but every other shadow from the carnival, whipped into submission by Terreur's masque. Even her own silhouette was beginning to bend back, like a fingernail caught in a doorjamb. Once the flying hourglass on Rafe's pocket watch ran out of sand, they were well and truly fucked.

"Shit," she said, gripping the comb in her red, red hand. "What do we do?"

"I can't hold on to the moment much longer." Rafe coughed. His lips matched her dress—and she began to realize what this spell was costing him. "Try to reach Honoré's sword. That might work—shit! It's slipping!"

The shadows around them shuddered. Céleste stood and tried to push toward Honoré. The other Enchantress was only a few meters away, but with each new step, more of the scene started to move. Different dreams danced across the broadsword. The silver of the dragon ring crept up Gabriel's arm. Sylvie's firebird flickered at the edges, and the flaps of the open tents began to flutter.

Céleste felt her true heart do the same as she reached for Honoré's blade.

The pocket watch's spell snapped.

Terreur's magic stormed through the carnival. Céleste's own shadow caught her by the ankles and clawed up her dress, then threw her into the carousel with such force that one of its mirrors smashed. Shards pierced her wings. Kept piercing them. She was spread-eagled against the broken glass, her arms splayed as wide as that crucifix that had once hung in her childhood bedroom.

The devil was coming for her.

"You..." His voice was charred. Even his footprints were black, his steps singeing the grass as he approached the carousel. "You backstabbing bitch."

Front, really, Céleste thought grimly.

She'd never dropped the comb. Terreur's rage bent around her fingers, around the ouroboros, so hard that fresh blood braided down her wrist.

"You thought you had me, didn't you?" Terreur looked from the weapon to Céleste's raw chest wound. "It seems I'm too far gone—"

A frost leopard lunged at the Sanct, but its claws melted into a puddle, along with the rest of the imagining. Other animals from the menagerie tangled with the Apaches. Several imaginers did too. Jean Cocteau had removed his pearls and was using them to beat back a group of Terreur's disciples from the painters' tent. Duchess d'Uzès, with her hammer and chisel, had joined him.

The other Sancts were rallying against Terreur. Masque rays shot through the night like spotlights—copper, ruby, silver, gold, pink, pink, pink. Sylvie's magic shone the brightest. Dreams of every size and shade spilled to the ground as the girl turned out her pockets. She stepped into their light and joined hands with La Fée Verte, who then found the Fisherman's gloved hand, who linked arms with Désirée, who grabbed the café Sanct and Nicolas Stohrer.

Terreur did not seem bothered by this.

His boots steamed through the mud, past a horrified Honoré, who had locked arms with Gabriel, too trapped in her armor to join the other Sancts, much less protect Céleste.

"Robespierre's spell has worked even better than I hoped... Nothing can touch me. Not a comb. Not the Battlefield Angel. Not even a liar as twisted as you." He halted by the empty carousel poles and spat. "My heart will never bleed again. But yours, Mademoiselle Artois... shall we see how well it fares outside your chest?"

The shadows squeezed around her fist, turning the comb inward.

Céleste tried to fight.

Her muscles were no match for Terreur's will. Her masque wasn't much better.

"You think a few weeks playing vulture on the battlefield can stop me?" He laughed.

No. Céleste understood how powerful he was. She'd seen how many lives he'd destroyed and knew that was only a fraction of what Terreur was capable of, but she could also see Sylvie gathering the other Sancts' magic and feeding it straight into her firebird so that its wings grew and grew and became the whole sky.

The imagining might have grown even bigger, if not for Rémy Lavigne.

The gangster threw himself at Sylvie.

The youngest Enchantress landed on her back, her arms flailing as her wings beat against the ground. Her firebird dove off the high wire—not at Rémy, but Terreur. Flames engulfed the evil sorcerer. They were nothing like the fires he'd used to destroy the windmill and the salon and the bookstore. They reminded Céleste more of the opal lamps that had once lit the way to the Quartier Secret. They were burning desires and long-stoked hopes and chocolate melting on the tongue and golden spires on the horizon and all the beauty that made life worth living.

They seemed to hurt Terreur.

He let out a scream, and his shadow tethers dropped. Céleste fell too, gasping with pain as she landed on the floor of the carousel. She tossed the comb as far from herself as she could and started digging through her wound with her fingers. Terreur was bullshitting about his heart. He had to be. If she could just rip the goddamn thing out of her chest and get back to Honoré's sword—

The carnival grounds were chaos. Spells shot across tents, and an army of cats had rushed to Sylvie's defense, Marmalade leading the charge. Rafe was trying to punch his way toward the carousel, seizing Apaches by their scarves and wings, then tossing them to the ground. There was more blood on his face and a look just as red—as red as love and loss—when his stare found Céleste's. She stumbled off the merry-go-round, her fingers slipping. She could feel the cold hardness of Terreur's heart, just behind her ribcage. She could see the sorcerer—still standing—between her and everyone she held dear.

Their firebird had done its best.

Most of the flames had faded, though a few pale tongues continued to dance up Terreur's sleeves. His clothes had not been singed by the enchanted fire, but his skin no longer looked like gypsum. There was an ashen quality to it, a flakiness usually exclusive to overcooked fish. His cheeks had gone gray, the color of those awful trench bodies that had been eaten by rats. His flesh too was coming off in tatters. Sloughing from Terreur's jaw, until she could see all thirty-two of his teeth. Peeling from his chest, until Céleste could see his hollowed-out ribs.

His stare held the same terrible emptiness.

She wasn't sure if Terreur's eyes were still there—his masque had grown too thick to tell—but she knew all that power, all his fury, was now focused on her. She knew there was no stopping him. Terreur used no shadows this time when he seized her, merely his own skeletal hand. Bones locked around Céleste's wrist and pulled her blood-soaked fist from her chest. Kept pulling. Blood began wicking off her fingers, onto his. It vanished from Christine Leroux's costume too, and she wondered if this was how the opera singer had felt in her final moments.

Not enough.

Never enough.

"I did promise that fantasies would not save you." Terreur's flesh grew back over his teeth, but she could still see them bared in a snarl of a smile. "You should have listened."

Honoré Côte had been here too many times before.

At the mouth of an alleyway, a spoiled bowl of milk by her feet.

At the edge of a fireplace, next to Maman's ice-cold fingers.

At the center of the Caveau, clutching her father's bloody ring.

At the rock bottom of Paris, fighting her brother for the same damn thing.

She'd hoped it would be different this evening. Simpler. Stab the bad guy, save the day.

She should have known better.

Gabriel held fast to their father's ring, and the dragon, in turn, held her. Not because the metal had stiffened but because it was slipping, slipping away, and if Honoré did not use her entire heart and soul to stop the silver, she knew Lucien Durand's heirloom would swallow them all. If she let go now, everyone she'd ever loved would be lost. Including Gabriel. Terreur would use her brother to kill until the entire carnival was dead. Or the dragon ring entombed him.

So the Battlefield Angel stood helpless, despite all her power, watching their plan fall to pieces. Céleste, stabbing herself, appearing suddenly at Honoré's side, then just as suddenly getting smashed into the carousel. The speech. The struggle for the comb. The firebird.

She'd felt another flicker of hope when the imagining attacked Terreur.

She felt a flicker through the dragon too, as the sorcerer's shadow strings around Gabriel dissolved. Her brother was in control of himself again, staring across the ring at Honoré. It wasn't hatred she saw there. She recognized her little brother's fear well enough, felt a surge of it herself as she watched Rémy Lavigne struggling with Sylvie. She knew what it was like, to be pinned beneath him, to smell his rotten breath, to thank heaven for your knife. Only, Sylvie didn't have a blade—

Come, oh hunters mine! We must save Sylvie's skin from the carver! She recognized Marmalade's yowl. The orange tomcat launched at Rémy with a lionlike boldness, just as he had in Belleville, only this time there was an army of felines with him. Hissing and spitting and scratching.

Perhaps there's some poetic justice in this shitty world after all, Honoré thought, as she watched Rémy's yellow boots disappear beneath a mountain of fur. Sylvie had managed to slip away, holding a fistful of the butcher's saint necklaces.

"That's what happened to our kitten?" Gabriel's question wavered across the silver. Through it. He must have picked up on her memory the same way. "Rémy? I spent all these years believing his lies about you, while he... Shit. Why didn't you tell me?"

"You were too young, Gabriel."

"So were you," he said.

A sob surged in her throat at that, and her brother's face crumpled. Dozens of other memories flickered through the dragon's scales: All their father's rage. All the hurt Honoré had tried so hard to hold inside herself and how it had spilled out anyway...

"I understand now, Honoré," her brother whispered.

The dragon coiled up Gabriel's arm, and she felt flashes from his life: How alone he'd felt after she'd fled, so alone that he'd kept sleeping in the coat closet. Rémy had taken the boy under his wing—there had been darkness there, yes, but safety too, safety in knowing *you* were the worst thing that could happen.

Honoré knew this feeling well.

She knew too, the horror that followed it.

The Terreur.

"You were right, *ma sœur*," Gabriel muttered. "He's fucking dangerous."

"Glad you've finally come around," Honoré replied.

But it was too little, too late. The imaginers' firebird had faded. The sorcerer was skeletal—he might have fit into the catacomb walls but for the fact he was lurching forward. Grabbing Céleste. A heavy numbness settled over Honoré as she watched her friend's blood disappear into Terreur's body.

He was using the Enchantress's flesh to restore his.

I am blood upon blood.

I am endless.

A few feet away, Honoré could see the hair comb in the mud, broken by the sorcerer's heart. He was right. Robespierre's spell *had* worked too well. Terreur had cut out every piece of his humanity so he might live forever—he was too far gone, and now he would keep going and going and going until there was nothing left.

The teeth of the comb were so twisted, so awful, that Honoré almost didn't see their ornament. Even when she did, it took her a moment to recognize the shape. A circle? Yes, but also more. The silver had been hammered into the shape of a snake...

Beware the serpents that eat their own tails.

Honoré sucked in a sharp breath.

A crypt of gilded skulls—each stacked over the other—shuddered through the dragon. Gabriel straightened at this memory. More followed. The Fisherman of the Moon standing at her bedside, diagnosing her relic: *Power is a path. It is one choice after another after another. Robespierre and his disciples chose to bathe themselves in blood, and their rings did what they'd been designed to do. They grew thirsty. They grew over their wearers.* Said as rotten teeth rattled like dice in the ragpicker's fist.

"Are you sure?" her brother whispered.

"No," she answered.

It was a gamble, certainly. Honoré had no way of knowing if this choice was the right one, but what else could they do? Nothing? She and Gabriel could encase themselves in the relic, true, but then they'd be stuck at the center of Île du Carnaval forever, Fear's Bastards displayed next to the duchess's armored angel...

Gabriel's hold on the dragon started to slip. "I don't want that," he said.

Honoré understood. Her side of the heirloom was shrinking too—down to her middle finger with its misshapen bone. So much of her life had been marked by Lucien Durand, even after he was gone, and she couldn't stand the thought of her death belonging to him too.

No.

She wanted a brighter future.

A better legacy.

So Honoré turned toward the newest Terreur. Gabriel did too. Her brother's hand rose alongside hers, and they threw the heirloom together. They let go of their father's power and watched the dragon soar. It was a mesmerizing sight—the silver unspooled like an aurora through the night sky. The ring arced over the mud puddles and the bent comb, shining in Céleste's eyes, brighter and brighter, until it spilled onto Terreur's head. The relic shimmered on his skull, bending into the shape of a crown. The sorcerer released Céleste, his hands touching the metal, his gaze finding the shattered carousel mirror, where his image was cast back hundreds upon hundreds of times. Almost infinitely...

Honoré felt unshelled.

She felt everything. The mud at her feet. An ash-flecked breeze on her feathered wings. She felt La Fée Verte's songbird land on her shoulder, then felt Gabriel's hand slipping into hers, holding tight. She squeezed back even harder and fixed her grip on her sword.

There would be no running this time.

Terreur turned. He had an eerie smile on his face. Rictus, considering the shape of his skull. Silver began to drip down the jagged sutures, over his triumphant expression. The dragon gathered its head at the bridge of the sorcerer's nose, bristling at the carnivalgoers. "You fools! Now I am—"

The dragon never let him finish this sentence.

Honoré's crooked fingers locked with Gabriel's as the silver slid into Terreur's mouth. Over his lips, his teeth, his tongue, washing down his throat as fine as any wine. There was plenty of room for the relic to settle—Honoré caught flashes of fangs between the sorcerer's ribcage, exactly where his heart should be. It had been so long gone that he did not need to breathe, true, but this didn't stop the Sanct from flailing. He grasped at his face, his skeletal fingers coming back with beads of molten silver. It didn't stay molten. Once the metal crawled up his arms and over his chest and down his legs, the relic did what it was designed to do. For all his power, Terreur couldn't stop the ring from swallowing him whole. It *was* his power. His thirst for blood upon blood. His endless hunger.

All turned back upon himself.

Silver encased the sorcerer. Arms, legs, everything froze, except for the scales that kept sliding, sliding into his mouth.

Honoré had escaped by the skin of her teeth.

She stood there in disbelief, waiting, waiting. But Terreur did not move, not even when La Fée Verte flew to Honoré's side and cupped her face in her hands. Honoré marvelled at how warm their flesh was, at how incredibly alive she felt.

"Are you all right, my dame?" the Sanct asked breathlessly.

Honoré felt breathless too.

Not for fear.

He was gone. Truly, gone. Terreur was no longer able to touch the woman she loved, but Honoré could. Her hands felt so light as she lifted them to La Fée Verte's beaming face. What if, what if, what if it all worked out splendidly well?

What then?

"I've never been better," she said with a laugh.

Sylvie let out a short laugh too as she marched over to the carnival's newest statue and gave it a kick. Terreur's gilded form fell face-first into the mud.

"There!" the youngest Enchantress exclaimed.

Most of the Apaches scattered at this. It seemed their loyalty to the sorcerer was mostly shadows—and the ring had severed all the strings holding the gangsters in place. Rémy had fled too, pursued by half the feral cats in Paris. Marmalade had chosen to stay at Sylvie's side, trailing the girl as she kept walking through the mud toward Céleste.

Céleste... oh, it hurt Honoré's chest to see hers. That meaty mess, looking even rawer for lack of blood. Past strips of torn flesh, she saw the heart they'd so long hunted. It looked just as black as it had through the keyhole of Christine Leroux's jewelry box, only now it was locked behind her friend's ribs. Honoré wanted to rush over and comfort the oldest Enchantress, but Rafael had already beaten her there. He held Céleste in his arms, to his own chest, so close that the watch around his neck touched hers as well.

His eyes met Honoré's.

She recognized that look all too well. The look of a drowning man hanging on to driftwood. She knew the pocket watch was buoying them both with its magic—otherwise Céleste would be going into shock from that ghastly wound. Had they been in the trenches, she would've been placed on a stretcher and left there.

As it was, the oldest Enchantress looked dazed, her gray eyes going in and out of focus as she stared toward the mud-spattered statue. "I'll be damned."

"Not if I can help it," Rafael growled tenderly into her ear. "I'm not letting you go, Céleste Artois. I'll stay here in the mud with you forever, if that's what it takes."

Honoré knelt next to them as well. The ouroboros glimmered by her filthy knee. As much damage as the comb had done to Céleste's chest, they wouldn't have won the battle without it. Honoré never would have surrendered her ring if she hadn't seen that snake choking itself down.

"We'll get you patched up, *mon amie*." The injury was awful, but if it was halved, Honoré figured they both might be able to heal naturally. "First we've got to get that rock out of your chest."

"You mean the evil sorcerer's heart?" Sylvie leaned in to examine the open wound. In the girl's lap, Marmalade growled. "You're right!" she replied to the tomcat. "He must have loved nothing... it's so small. In fact, I think it's just small enough..." A pink butterfly left Sylvie's masque and slipped through Céleste's ribs. It came back out with a dark pebble curled in its proboscis. The stone must have been far heavier than it looked, because the insect dropped it straight into the mud only a foot or so from the Enchantresses.

The Fisherman of the Moon scooped up the heart with a rusted tea tin, pulling out his monocle and eyeing the bottom of the container warily while Sylvie's butterfly settled back into her masque.

"There!" the youngest Enchantress declared. "Now we can heal

Céleste! Wait—how *do* you heal someone without killing a person trapped in a painting?"

"I'll take as much of her wound as I can," Honoré said, though she was aware there was no more dragon silver to cover her chest. It was just as exposed as everyone else's. "If enough of my flesh fills hers, she won't get sepsis as soon as Rafael releases her back into time."

The man in question fixed her with his lost-at-sea stare. "Honoré, you and I both know that's not the kind of injury you patch up with a sewing kit. It's a fucking hole in her chest! If you ended up taking half of it, I'd be stuck holding both of you for the rest of our lives. Three gets a bit crowded... no offense."

Honoré wasn't offended, just desperate, as she looked into Céleste's glassy eyes. Her hand trembled when she placed it just above the raw comb marks on her friend's skin.

"But what if it's three people sharing the wound?" Sylvie piped up. "Or even more? That way everyone would have only a little bit of pain. You don't have to take all the hurt, Honoré."

"Sylvie's right," La Fée Verte said over Honoré's shoulder. Her hand settled there, softly. "Let me help you with this, my dame."

"Me too!" Sylvie declared, as she handed her fistful of Rémy's icons to the Fisherman of the Moon.

"No." The word left Honoré automatically. "You can't be the fourth person. You're—"

Too young.

She would have said this, if not for Gabriel. Her brother had come to stand behind Sylvie. He stared down at Céleste and Rafael, his hands wandering to his neck. Honoré swallowed her words. No. None of them were so young anymore, but they all still had room to grow. Especially if Honoré was brave enough to take a step back.

"I'd offer to take Sylvie's place," Rafael said. "But my body won't naturally heal unless I remove Flamel's watch."

The dried bloodstains around his lips made it clear what would happen in that instance. Rafael García had already given Céleste more than his fair share of life. "That's all right," Honoré told him. "Just... keep holding her."

Céleste was watching them with all the fervor of a fever dream. Her white hair splayed over Rafael's tunic—which he'd half ripped open to expose the watch. Her skin looked a little less chalky wherever it touched his, especially around the timepiece.

Honoré felt her own pulse *tick-tocking* at her throat.

She prayed their plan would work.

Meanwhile, Gabriel was removing his own chains. The three saint necklaces. He offered these to the Fisherman of the Moon. Honoré said nothing as Sylvie grabbed her brother's hand and pulled him into their inner circle.

Your love binds you together, La Fée Verte had once said, *for better or worse.*

Honoré's masque pulsed with these words. Their truth. She felt the coal of it over her own chest—warm, but not unbearable. She saw a pink stain bloom through Sylvie's tunic. Gabriel's striped shirt. La Fée Verte's gown. It was much the same color as the new flesh that had come to cover Céleste's wound. As well as the color that crept back into the oldest Enchantress's cheeks.

She blinked, and the glassy sheen in her eyes fell away.

The circle broke, each one of them stepping back to look at their chests. It hurt, certainly, but Honoré's new wound wasn't deadly. She could cover it with gauze and forget about it. Well, perhaps not completely. All five of them would heal, but they would also scar, sharing this moment on their skin forever.

Céleste's scar looked a little bit like a cupid's ass…a heart over a heart. She patted the tender skin once, twice, with a look of disbelief. She scanned the circle, pausing not on Honoré or Rafael, but past them, where the Fisherman of the Moon stood. Saint necklaces dangled from one of the ragpicker's hands, while he stared hard into that rusted tea tin.

"Can you destroy the heart?" she called to him.

The Fisherman shook his head. "It's too mummified. A sword wouldn't scratch this any more than that comb did," he declared, before looking back at the mud-spattered dragon—a strange but fitting sarcophagus. "We should thank our lucky stars Honoré had her relic on hand."

"Our stars, yes." La Fée Verte looked up from her tender chest; her gaze wandered past the carousel, to where the fortune teller's tent sat. Honoré could see a figure inside. "Though I'm beginning to believe luck had little to do with it..."

Madame Arcana emerged from the tent, holding three cards. The first and last time Honoré had seen the Sanct, she was dredging La Fée Verte's fallen form from the river with a net of fates. *To shift the currents.* It sounded like a load of bullshit at the time—what good would a few snipped lifelines do? Honoré hadn't had much patience for the woman's riddles when La Fée Verte was splayed so limply against the quai.

She studied the Seer more carefully now.

The woman's gown was still soaked with river water, dripping over her bare feet. The skin of her face remained dewy, her masque silver. There was no more fog over her eyes, however. They were blue. Blue as an ocean and just as deep. It was clear they'd seen many things.

"A tea tin? Ha!" she said, as she drew close to the Fisherman. "The last Terreur never did want me to read his leaves, but they were all shit..." Madame Arcana tossed her cards into the air. They fluttered over Terreur's entombed body before landing faceup. *Death* rode a pale horse. *The Fool* traveled on foot—looking quite a lot happier than the *Devil* at his back. "They were shit upon shit," the Seer repeated, with a piercing glance at Honoré. "There was only one way to break the cycle and start anew."

"You didn't think to tell us?" Honoré grunted.

"Some futures cannot be told, or they would cease to be," the Seer said. "Had I warned La Fée Verte of this man's hunger thirty years ago, she would have sent him away, and he would have stumbled across even deeper shadows..." A sigh left her. "There are many black mirrors out there, full of worlds where nothing is left to see. Our existence is so very fragile. We are tightropes and tapestries—the threads must be arranged carefully so they do not tangle."

Honoré was having a hard enough time following what Madame Arcana was saying. She wasn't the only one. Céleste and Rafael wore matching frowns. The Fisherman's brow was wrinkled, and La Fée Verte's birds looked more restless than normal.

"But we did it, right?" Sylvie asked. "We won?"

"I should say so," the Seer answered.

"Good!" the girl chirped. "Then... what do we do now? Or are you not supposed to say?"

The fortune teller knelt over Terreur's twisted form. "He shall hold himself prisoner, untouchable until the end of time. Toss his heart in a trash heap. Carry on this carnival." She picked up the card that depicted the traveler. "To be a Fool is not such a bad thing... It represents fresh horizons." Madame Arcana handed the card to Céleste. "There's a new castle waiting for you, Mademoiselle Artois. You and your dizzy fox."

"What about me?" Sylvie wondered. "Do I get a castle?"

The Seer simply smiled. Fresh lines creased her face.

Céleste had a few of those as well, as she considered the card in her hands. Her smile only grew as she turned toward Rafael. They were so close—his arms still around her—that their foreheads touched, and though they were not kissing, there was an intimacy to the moment that made Honoré focus intently on the shadow around them. A fox, again. Chasing his own tail in the slow-moving lights of the carousel. The calliope had started playing music once more, and wooden horses answered its call, stepping from the painters' tent to take their place back on the carousel. Colors streaked their hoofprints, covering up the muddy marks of battle. A few of the guests who followed them stopped to see Terreur's display—but in the way someone might examine a museum piece. He was art now. *Ha!* Honoré grinned at this. She smiled even more at the sight of a talking parrot perched on Jean Cocteau's horn as he refastened his pearls and sashayed toward their group.

He paused by Céleste, offering a smattering of solo applause. "Well done, *ma chère*! Such drama! Such flair! I couldn't have scripted it better myself. Though the outfit is..." The parrot on his horns squawked an obscenity. "Yes, well, I was going to say 'dated.' Never mind that crimson is *not* your color."

"I don't think she looks that terrible," Rafael said.

"That's because you are in love," Jean replied. "Not to mention you took several blows to the head fighting off those gangsters. Anyone without a concussion can see that the red is washing out this poor young woman's complexion. Come!" The Frivolous Prince plucked Céleste to her feet and guided the oldest Enchantress to his tent. "Let's get you changed!"

Chapter 45

Last of His Name

Père Lachaise was home to some very unusual ghosts.

And now, a phantom.

The new tomb sat in the cemetery's most overgrown corner, not far from the original Honoré Côte's resting place. It was much less grand. There were no glass stars or scrolled iron doors. There almost hadn't even been a name chiseled into the black stone. Paris's memorial masons were swamped with epitaphs, especially since the German armies had been driven away from the city. France had won the Battle of the Marne—with a fleet of taxis, nonetheless—but the cost was high. Eighty-five thousand new gravestones. And counting.

It was tempting for Honoré to leave the sorcerer's resting place anonymous: bury him, brush the dirt off her hands, and be done with it.

She chose to carve the truth instead.

Here Lies Terreur, Last of His Name

There was power in these words, not just because of the binding spell she infused into each letter, but for their very existence. What they marked.

He ended here.

No one would disturb this patch of earth. Certainly not the junior groundskeepers, who'd sworn off this section of the cemetery altogether. Honoré had rearranged some of her old booby traps to keep any lost mourners on their toes. There were other safeguards against those who might have darker intentions. Duchess d'Uzès's *Battlefield Angel* stood over the grave, her sword planted in the ground, waiting. There were a good number of cats keeping an eye on the plot as well. If anyone started digging—above *or* below—Honoré would be the first to know.

She doubted this would happen.

The Apaches were no longer such a threat. Few of them wanted to go to war—magical or otherwise—so they returned to Belleville. Lying low with card games and a cobwebbed piano. Now that Gabriel was no longer there to play it, the instrument's keys were dustier than ever. A sorry sight. But what had struck Honoré even more, on her last visit to the Caveau, was that there was neither hide nor hair of Rémy Lavigne. She supposed it was possible the gangster had left Paris and joined forces with the Mad Monk. Grigori Rasputin had more power than ever, now that Terreur was imprisoned. By all reports, his grip on Russia was as unyielding as its winter. The peasants the Fisherman of the Moon had freed from the icon necklaces had tales of the "holy man" that would send ice down anyone's spine. Every single one had refused to go back to Petrograd. Why would they, when they found themselves sipping steaming cups of French tea beside a tent full of fire-breathing bears? When La Fée Verte herself had extended an invitation for them to stay and help build the carnival into something even brighter?

Rémy though…

His boots had been more mud than yellow leather when he'd fled. Most of the gleam had been in the eyes of the hunters tailing him. Their claws. Their teeth. Their tiger souls. It didn't matter how small the cats were. Not when there were so damn many of them…

No, Honoré decided, as she glanced back at the tom sitting by her string of rusted bells, batting one with his paw. *The grave is quite safe.*

"This really is the perfect purgatory," Rafael said, as a calico marched over to the freshly churned dirt and proceeded to desecrate it.

Shit upon shit.

The group around the grave watched with various levels of epicaricacy. They were a strange collection of mourners: no kerchiefs, no veils, no black whatsoever. Céleste's masque had changed almost as fast as her gown—it now shone like the insides of a broken-open seashell. Gabriel's temple had turned almost as silver as his sister's after he'd sat down at the calliope and tried his hand at some new tunes. La Fée Verte and Sylvie were both brighter than ever, thanks to the growing popularity of the Carnaval des Merveilles. The decision to keep the carnival open had not been made lightly. Honoré knew how her other half worried about history repeating itself. She could see it in the way Verte kept reading the gravestone's inscription.

"I can think of no better way for that bastard to spend all eternity," Céleste agreed. "Endless tolling bells and cat piss."

Gabriel kicked some of the soil. Honoré stared at the scuffed dirt—out of all the people gathered around this grave, her brother was the hardest to read. He felt like a native language she'd stopped speaking years ago. Like *la langue verte*. Faded, but never truly forgotten. She was just thankful she had a chance to talk to him again. Their conversations weren't easy—how could they be, with all those missing years and what had come before?—but *mon Dieu*, it was better than fighting. Better to share their wounds than create more.

"What's wrong, *mon frère*?" Honoré asked, hoping *she* was not the answer.

"Are we sure that fortune teller was telling the truth?" he ventured.

"She was right about Céleste getting a whole new castle," Sylvie pointed out.

"Technically, Château de Bonnelles belongs to Duchess d'Uzès," the oldest Enchantress reminded her. "Rafe and I will be more like artists-in-residence."

A strange twist. Honoré knew things hadn't exactly panned out the way Rafael García had once dreamed they would. She could still remember that boy, even after surrendering the dragon. But outside of Honoré and Gabriel, a part of him would always be lost. Not the fun kind of lost—not painting his way around Europe, like his younger self had planned. The Orient Express had suspended its services to make way for trains filled with wounded soldiers. A fraction of these would find their way to an estate in the north of France, where the grandiose halls of Duchess d'Uzès's hunting lodge had been converted into a hospital.

The château would undergo an even deeper transformation, if everything went according to plan. The house would hold hidden halls. The grounds would harbor secret gardens. More than just flowers would bloom there…

Honoré knew all this not because she'd seen the future but because she'd handed a piece of it to Rafael. His idea of a magical artists' colony had transformed during the time it spent serving as her sword. She was not sorry to break the blade apart. Not for this. Besides, she'd barely used the blade anyway. The look on the timeless man's face when she offered him his dream was enough. Céleste stood grinning beside him. Even his teardrop tattoo shimmered.

"You know," he said, after examining the idea, "on second thought, I'm not sure La Ruche is the right venue…so many of its artists are off getting shot to pieces anyway."

Honoré remembered the men her armor's wings had not reached: That farm boy with his belly full of lead. The bodies that Machiavelli had so cheerfully gnawed on. She couldn't help but wonder how the rest of the unit was faring without her.

"What did you have in mind?" she asked him.

"Well, it's not from my mind," Rafael said. "Manuela mentioned putting together an ambulance service to take wounded souls back to her castle—" He paused at this word and grinned toward Céleste. "We could start something there, *mon amour*."

"An artists' colony?" Honoré posited.

"More than that," Rafael said. "War is living hell, so there should be some alternative, no? A sanctuary. A space safe enough to help their souls grow back."

A year ago, Honoré Côte might have snorted.

Now though, she found herself recalling the sweet scent of wood shavings curled beneath Rafael's old drafting table. Proof enough that such things were possible. "Ever the savior, aren't you, Rafael García?"

He'd smirked. "Fine words, coming from a knight in shining armor."

"I've been upgraded to *angel*, thank you very much."

There were moments where Honoré found herself missing the armor—how could she not?—but standing around this grave wasn't one of them. She knew just how close she'd come to being buried alive. She couldn't forget how strongly the silver had gripped her, after the catacombs and during her snowy battle with Rasputin. It would have taken her altogether, if not for La Fée Verte...

She reached out and grabbed the other woman's hand. "Terreur is gone," Honoré declared, her voice striking stone. "He's gone, and he is never coming back."

Sylvie gave a cheer, while Céleste rested her head on Rafael's shoulder.

Gabriel exhaled.

La Fée Verte's fingers tightened in Honoré's. The woman's golden gaze rose from the grave, holding hers the same way it had after the Sanct's waking from her own glass casket. Radiating with hope. So much hope. Honoré had figured, at the time, that all their powers had been saved for the sake of defeating Terreur, but now he was deep in the ground, and they were still shining. They were an island of light—not just because of Île du Carnaval—but for the rest of Europe. Paris was fast becoming a refuge. A place where soldiers on leave could return from the front and find a few days of normalcy. A few nights of wonder. More, perhaps, if La Fée Verte and Honoré kept up with the carnival. Magic grew faster than the old vines, spreading its tendrils throughout the arrondissements. There was enough for the Fisherman of the Moon to build an antique shop in Les Puces. Désirée's cabaret had opened its doors again too.

Was history merely repeating itself? At first Enlightened glance, perhaps. La Fée Verte still took care, considering which carnival-goers should be able to remember the enchanted parts of their evening, but there were new daydreamers too. The Frivolous Prince. Manuela. Men and women who wanted wings. Who—even in the midst of a continent torn apart by war—believed they could leave the world a better place than they'd found it.

They were pretty damn inspiring.

As for Honoré…well, she missed her dragon ring, true, but the Fisherman of the Moon had helped her find new ones. A matching set of gold bands—magical only for the fact that Honoré smiled every time she saw them together. When La Fée Verte's hand joined hers.

She smiled a lot these days.

Even here. At Terreur's graveside. The others had begun to drift away—Céleste and Rafael walked back to the Enchantresses' old campsite, and Sylvie grabbed Gabriel's hand and pulled him along. She could hear the girl promising her brother a treasure hunt. "There's gold all around here if you know where to look! And if you don't, just ask Marmalade!"

"I don't think that cat likes me," Gabriel replied.

"But he brought you a rotten rat carcass!" Sylvie said, as if this explained everything.

"He keeps calling me a small prick."

The youngest Enchantress giggled as they hopped over the alarm bells. "No, you're the small prickly one. Because 'prickly one' is their honorific for Honoré, and you're her brother."

"But I'm *taller* than her!" Gabriel protested.

"Your body is, sure, but cats have different categorizations than we do…"

Their voices faded into the underbrush, and Honoré squeezed her true love's hand. "Shall we?"

La Fée Verte nodded.

Honoré Côte did not glance over her shoulder as they walked away. Not once.

There was too much to look forward to.

Chapter 46

Heart of Gold

Céleste Artois was quite a bit wealthier than she'd realized.

She and Rafe had both gotten roped into collecting the Enchantresses' deposits from La Banque d'Ossements, retrieving francs from all sorts of mossy corners. *A treasure hunt*, Sylvie had called the chore. It was—though it wasn't the glimpses of gold that made Céleste keep digging.

It was the stories.

She felt like an archaeologist of her own past, brushing the dirt from coin pouches and unearthing memory after memory. Countless cafés where she'd left her counterfeit canvases. Delacroixes and van Goghs and Monets. Lily pads and drowning women and wars. Or, rather, what the romantic artists had believed war to be... Céleste didn't think she could copy the style now even if she'd wanted to, thanks to her time with Terreur.

"This was a hefty haul." Rafe whistled as he plucked a heavy purse from the sepulchre of Susan Durant. He weighed the take in his hand for a moment before tossing it toward Céleste. "What did you sell? The Sistine Chapel?"

"Not quite." Her lips quirked as she opened the pouch. "But I like the way you think."

Rafe smiled back. His fox shadow crept through the ivy and brushed around Céleste's ankles. He was even more of a wonder to her, now that she realized just how much he had survived. Over five years in Terreur's service. Céleste had only managed a fraction of that, and it felt like a miracle that she was standing here.

It *was*, Céleste reminded herself.

She remembered this every time she saw her scar—not just on her own chest, but on Honoré and Sylvie and Gabriel and La Fée Verte. She remembered the miracle too, every time she traced Rafe's old wounds. There was none over his heart, just a pocket watch that never ticked, yet when both their breasts were pressed against its golden surface, Céleste could feel the beat: *I love you, I love you, I love you.*

There was no more fear in this.

Only a lifetime of stardust. Possibly longer.

Nicolas Flamel and his wife, Perenelle, had lived for several centuries—though this couldn't have been entirely due to the pocket watch. According to the Fisherman of the Moon, the timepiece's technology was too modern. The alchemist had crafted the relic toward the end of his very long life. Why? Well, why did anyone make anything? Céleste figured that even men who'd learned how to conquer time would want to leave their signature upon it.

This was the reason Rafe had started adding *e*'s to all his canvases.

She'd interrupted after the first few flourishes with an offer to fill in his name—after all *Cé*[redacted]*este* [redacted]*rtois* had an *a* and an *l* to spare.

The other artist shook his head and kept signing paintings.

"Why not? It would be a fair trade for the days you gave me," she said.

His brush then paused. His eyebrows rose. "Since when have you cared about such things?"

"I care about you," she said fiercely. "I know the letters won't bring back the memories Terreur swallowed, but—"

Rafe had stopped her with a kiss. "All is fair in love and war, *mon amour*. You've already helped me find myself, and to be entirely truthful, I think I should prefer Rafe García to the boy who made it to Constantinople."

Céleste understood.

She'd gotten better at signing her name too.

"This was one of my first attempts at a van Gogh—" Céleste said now, as she opened the coin pouch. "I painted a starry night, only I used the glass constellations in the mausoleum and placed them over a lavender field...He painted the original at a monastery in Provence, you know, so it's the view he would have had from his window." Lullabies of soft purple, washing in from the horizon. She'd remembered it well enough from her own turret. "Honoré came up with this whole spiel about how she could tell it was a lost masterpiece because of the flowers, but it was so sweltering outside that day that her moustache started sliding off. She barely made it out of the café with a straight face."

Rafe laughed.

He had hardly changed, physically, since the morning she'd asked him to *believe*. Stubble forever shaded his face, and the rest of his hair had stopped growing. Crow's feet would not deepen, nor would smile lines. His muscles would not waste. Neither would the rest of him. His body might as well have been stuck in amber, for how well the pocket watch's magic preserved it.

But something fundamental had shifted, once Honoré trapped Terreur inside the dragon ring. Rafe moved differently. *Freely*, Céleste noted with a smile. He walked as if a one-hundred-kilogram weight had been lifted from his shoulders. His laughter was light too. It made her think of doves' startled wings and steam rising out of a fresh broken croissant and the way the sun first danced across the river, come morning. *The most terribly beautiful view in all the world*, the Frivolous Prince had once called it.

No more.

Dawn was no longer something to dread. Sunlight did not reduce everyone's imaginings to sparks—Céleste and Rafe could perch together on the Pont Saint-Michel and watch Île du Carnaval's glow grow twofold.

"You must have made a hell of an impression, to get your mark to miss that. Honoré Côte and the melting moustache..." Dimples grew across the other thief's face, and Céleste wondered how she'd never noticed them before. How well they matched his chin divot. His roguish grin.

She loved that there were still new things to discover.

They kept on digging, with Céleste recounting the Enchantresses' escapades. More fiddle games, of course. Blackmailing the cemetery's senior groundskeeper. Picking pockets and sweet-talking businessmen and a whole number of things that would land a person in handcuffs. Guilty as charged—these were the very same moments Terreur had used to judge her. *I don't have to pull your strings to get you to steal. It's already in your nature.*

But if he *had* pulled the strings of Céleste's memory just a bit further, he might have realized his mistake. He would have seen more. Melting moustaches, duels with baguettes as sabers, forgotten watchwords, and picnic blankets full of smelly cheese.

These were her true treasures.

Still, when the withdrawals from the La Banque d'Ossements were counted and divided three ways on the paint-spattered tarp outside the mausoleum, Céleste found herself with a not-small pile of gold. And a few diamond necklaces, to boot.

"We're rich!" Sylvie declared, doing a magpie dance.

Honoré watched with a knowing gleam in her eye. "Don't go spending it all on pastries, *ma rêveuse*."

"I won't! Besides, I don't need francs for that. Nicolas Stohrer gives me all the cake I want for the joy of it." Despite this, Céleste had noticed a change in the youngest Enchantress's diet. There was plenty of sugar, still, but there was more balance to her meals than before. She snacked on silver-skinned apples and regularly split cans of pâté with Marmalade. "I think I'd like to use this money to start my own establishment."

Céleste was both surprised and not. Sylvie was turning into a powerful Sanct, certainly, but she'd figured the girl was happy floating along with the Carnaval des Merveilles. "What sort of establishment?" she wondered. "A café?"

"No," Sylvie answered. She glanced at her stack of fairy books just past the mausoleum doors. "I miss Libris. And Lore. And... well, I should think Paris needs another magical bookshop."

"You're right," La Fée Verte told her. "There's nothing quite like the power of a good story."

"What about you, *mon amour*? What will you use your cut for?" Rafe picked up one of the diamond necklaces as he said this, examining the piece with a practiced eye.

It wasn't hard to see the irony—Céleste no longer needed the francs. Duchess d'Uzès had become her official patroness and was providing more than enough gold to outfit the League of Imaginers' new ambulance service. And the castle, besides. There would be room and board and plenty of space to help them inspire injured soldiers. Céleste figured it was the least she could do, with the powers she'd collected during her time on the front. She couldn't put the anima back into husked corpses, but what of the men next to them? The ones who'd survived?

She watched as the diamond caught the late-afternoon light, spraying a rainbow across Rafe's face. It looked almost like a dream.

"I think I'll donate my profits to La Ruche's soup kitchen." Sure, most of the men at the commune had gone off to war, but Céleste could only imagine how she might have felt if she'd found the studio when she'd first arrived in Paris. Penniless. There were plenty of other young women out there—with ink in their veins and hunger that was more than just a metaphor. "Artists have got to eat, right?"

Gabriel gaped at her from across the blanket. "You're going to give all this away?"

Honoré also looked surprised. "Truly, *mon amie*?"

Sylvie looked gleeful. "You're like... like Robin Hood!"

"Who?" Céleste asked.

"Robin Hood!" The girl waved at her stack of fairy books. She'd started reading their tales in earnest lately—with the help of English tea that she sipped in order to talk to the British soldiers who stumbled across the carnival on leave. "He's a robber from England who stole from the rich and gave to the poor. An outlaw with a heart of gold!"

Céleste knew for a fact hers was much bloodier.

"It's a smart investment," La Fée Verte said from her place on the blanket beside Honoré. "Keep La Ruche running. When the war is over, you can come back to Paris and become their muse."

That was the long game. Though Céleste found she preferred the way La Fée Verte had phrased the plan. *Investment.* Not something to be played, like a fiddle or a board of chess, but built.

Like a family.

Like a future.

Her heart swelled as she looked around the blanket. La Fée Verte's green wings blended beside Honoré's silver ones. Gabriel sat on the other side of his sister, mirroring her crouch. He copied Rafe too—picking up the sapphire necklace Sylvie had purloined after *The Rite of Spring*. The youngest Enchantress didn't try to snatch it back. She was too busy scratching Marmalade's belly. The tailless tomcat was laid out like a loaf, purring loudly.

Why would that thief name himself after such a tasty bird? he rattled in a drowsy, nearly drunk way. *Perhaps this Robin was once a Sanct too? I will have to ask my London brethren...*

They stayed this way until the sun slipped below the far wall. Clouds swept past steeples—setting themselves up for a magnificent sunset. The carnival would soon be rousing itself too. Some of La Fée Verte's birds had already started flying toward the Seine as the Sanct stood.

"We should get back to Île du Carnaval," she told Honoré. "The Frivolous Prince wanted to meet before dusk. He says he has suggestions for the league's ambulance service uniform."

"Uniform?" Honoré glanced down at her own outfit: Clothes fit for running. Boots too. The fanciest piece was her dream-filled bandolier. "What more does he want?"

"Knowing Jean?" Céleste snorted. "Who knows."

Her oldest friend sighed. "I hope it involves pants."

"You *can* hope that, you know." Rafe laughed.

"The world has bigger problems than women's lack of trousers—"

"Yes. Corsets," Céleste teased. "Just think of what an entire half of

Earth's population might accomplish if they were allowed to breathe. How much more if they could dress themselves comfortably?"

"You're not wrong." La Fée Verte had quite the shining smile on her face. One of her birds landed on her head and pulled out a thought—and as the creature came to land on Honoré's shoulder, Céleste saw a familiar sight. A painted pantsuit. Her first true dream. "I clung to this idea, even when Terreur tore everything else away, because I believed we could defeat him together. Now I know we can do even more than just fight..." The songbird slipped the imagining into Honoré's bandolier. "We can imagine a better world. We can make it so."

Chapter 47

And So She Lived

Sylvie of a Single Name had read her fair share of happy endings.

It seemed to her, as she sat outside the magnificent mausoleum of Honoré Côte, that this had the makings of a perfect one: an empty glass casket, lost siblings who'd followed a trail of enchanted breadcrumbs back to each other, and *two* true love stories. There was even a striking sunset for her friends to fly off into—and as Sylvie watched them winging away, to their castle and their carnival, she found herself thinking about the phrase *ever after.* It seemed so simple in books, but standing by her colorful stack of fairy tales in the almost-empty tomb, she understood that real life didn't just *end.* (Until it did.) The sun would rise again tomorrow. And the day after that. And the day after that.

And so they lived...

A lot could happen in those four short words.

Sylvie decided not to fly into the stained glass sky with the rest of the Enchantresses. She walked out of the cemetery instead, through the southernmost entrance, where stairs and a battered blue door led down to the cobbled stones of rue de la Réunion. Though most of the city's bakeries had started flipping their signs to OUVERT after the German army's retreat, the one she'd once plundered for a breakfast croissant remained closed. The door to Tsarskoe Selo was locked too. Sylvie paused by its fuchsia wood and shoved her hands into her pockets. She carried the key everywhere with her, running her fingers over the teeth so often, she figured that even if she lost it in the barrel of keys the Fisherman kept in the corner of his shop, she'd be able to fish it out again.

The photographs were still there too.

Just in case.

She'd thought a lot about what the Fisherman of the Moon had told her—about the magic of joy and hope. These were important things to consider, now that she was gathering more than just her own imaginings. If Sylvie was going to become a Sanct, she'd better be like La Fée Verte or Nicolas Stohrer. The alternative was too terrible...

Sylvie stared at the keyhole and tried not to think about Rasputin. She tried not to imagine his unholy blue eyes staring back.

The Mad Monk did not know about this door. It was too obscure. Too *childish* for him to stumble across. Besides he was too busy harvesting the anima of dying Russian infantry to sit in the Children's Palace waiting for Sylvie... if she was quick and careful, she might be able to reach Anastasia's bedroom...

Marmalade leaned on her, rubbing his ragged ear against her calf. *What is wrong, oh hunter mine?*

Sylvie pulled out the key, along with one of the smoother photographs. "I promised I would Enlighten Nastya again, but then I never came back. I left her there in the dark."

That is understandable, the tomcat purred. *You were trapped inside a necklace.*

Sylvie could feel the beginnings of another firebird flickering through her mind, defiantly bright. "I'm not trapped anymore."

Marmalade narrowed his orange eyes. *Not inside jewelry, no. But if you awaken the princess, the Mad Monk will know. He will use Anastasia to hurt you. You are not strong enough to fight him yet, oh hunter mine.*

Sylvie's fist wrapped harder around the key. She knew the tomcat was right. The grand duchess had too many fears tying her to the palace. Opening Anastasia's eyes to them would be cruel at best. Even worse? The princess might be puppeteered the same way Alexei had been when he'd torn Sylvie's wings from her back. The same way the rest of the Romanovs were when it came to waging this war.

Some curses could not be broken.

Some futures could not be told.

But maybe, just maybe, the tangled threads coming out of the grand duchess's head could be rewoven. Sylvie remembered what Madame Arcana had said—about tightropes and tapestries. She also remembered the things she herself had told Honoré, when the other Enchantress despaired about the shadow strings wrapping around Gabriel.

"Anastasia's story isn't over yet," she told Marmalade firmly, as she slid the key into the lock. "I might not be able to Enlighten the princess, but I don't have to abandon her either."

The door to Russia creaked open. The other side was empty. Too empty. Sylvie shivered as she stepped over the threshold. The walls of the Children's Palace seemed to be pressing in, in, with the same suffocating smallness she'd known inside the necklace. It helped, some, when Marmalade padded into the room after her. He lifted his nose to the air and sniffed.

The Mad Monk is not here, oh hunter mine, but you must take care. His spells are strung everywhere—like a spider's web.

All Sylvie could smell was drying foliage and cold smoke. The same stage of autumn it had been when she'd first arrived here. "What about Nastya?"

You'll find the princess in her room, the tom answered. *If you must go to her, then I will go with you. I will keep watch. I will guard you with the rest of my lives.*

She scooped the cat up into her arms, feeling his deep purr against her freshly healed scar. Beneath that was the heat of Sylvie's firebird, growing with all the glowing memories she'd made here with the princess. That first thermos of smoky cocoa on the fur coat.

Their two days spent imagining doors. The ice bridge they'd imagined over the lake, long since melted.

Sylvie had to fly over the water this time. It was an amethyst evening, too dark for her to see the turning leaves as she soared toward Anastasia's window. Even though it was early—too early, even, for Anastasia's older sister to be in the room—it seemed that the youngest grand duchess had fallen asleep reading in her camp bed. A candle sputtered on the bedside table, lighting the lilac fairy book splayed across her chest. The gilded fairy on the cover shimmered as the princess snored.

When Sylvie approached the bed, these sounds softened.

"Marie?" Anastasia mumbled her sister's name, then cracked an eyelid. "You're so . . . pink."

Sylvie halted, watching the grand duchess warily. Her hair was jet-black against her pillow, but when Anastasia's eyes opened, she could see a sliver of blue fighting through their dimness. But how could the princess see Sylvie? Had she walked straight into a trap set by Rasputin?

Sylvie glanced over her shoulder, but the window she'd entered through was empty.

Marmalade squirmed against her chest and hopped down to the floor. *The princess is almost asleep. She sees you on the edge of dreams . . . You might be able to talk with her, quietly.*

"Oh," Sylvie whispered. She wasn't entirely sure what else to say. How could any words compare to the magic she felt inside? To everything Anastasia Nikolaevna did not remember?

"Hello, Nastya."

The princess gave a sleepy groan and twisted under her covers. The lilac fairy book went tumbling to the floor by Sylvie's feet. It was the same copy Libris had saved in order to complete her rainbow. The volume had never joined the rest of her Andrew Lang books though. As soon as they'd left the shop that evening, Sylvie had lent it to Anastasia, which meant she'd never had a chance to read the final stories of her favorite author.

It was just as well.

Anastasia needed them more. Sylvie could tell by the way the book's spine was cracked that the princess had read through the volume multiple times. That was a good sign. It meant there was still room for fairy tales in the dark and fearful forest of her mind. There were still places where Sylvie might be able to plant a seed.

"My name is Sylvie. Just Sylvie. You and I, we went on some amazing adventures together." She swallowed, thinking of the memories she'd stolen: Exploring the haunted opera house. Making the city's statues dance the tango—an especially amusing spectacle with Emperor Charlemagne and his horse. Lying on the floor of Saint Chapelle and watching the stained glass windows swirl. All of it felt like a lifetime ago. "When we first met, I thought I was the luckiest orphan alive. Never in my wildest dreams did I think I'd ever get to become best friends with a real princess. But I did. And then I got to show you other dreams, and it was so, so wonderful..." *Until it wasn't.* Until Alexei's hand had felt as cold as death around her wrist. "We used magic to create beautiful things, but there's a darker side to it too. There are men who use their powers to unmake other people...I didn't realize that was what Rasputin was doing to your family. I didn't see how selfish it was to make you see those things too..."

She thought of Alexei's frigid hand again. So cold, in spite of the heat of his sister's firebird. It made sense. The tsarevitch was a dead child walking, beyond saving even before Sylvie had brought his tin soldiers to life.

Anastasia's fingers were warm, though, when Sylvie knelt by the princess's bed and grabbed them. "I want to stop the Mad Monk, but I'm not strong enough. Yet," she added. "We've established the League of Imaginers, and I'm finding more daydreamers to help me grow, but none of them fit as well as you did. I miss you, Nastya. I miss you so very, very much."

The grand duchess gave another groan. Less sleepy.

Sylvie let her friend's hand fall back on the bed. She picked up the book, leafing through its blood-flecked golden pages all the way past *The End*. From her pocket, she pulled out the smoothest photograph of the two of them, slipping it between the novel's endpapers the same way Libris used to preserve imaginings. It was only a picture, simply paper and ink, but if Anastasia found the photograph, she would begin to wonder where it had been taken.

Wonder. That was the first step.

Sylvie could imagine the second. The fiery feeling in her chest should not come out as a bird, not here. Instead, she took their joined memories and created copies—much like the photographs in her pocket. Or the way a locksmith might match a key. *Her* key. That's what the spell looked like, when Sylvie pulled it from her mind. She'd shaped the thoughts using a technique La Fée Verte had taught her. *I've used this to forge swords, but there are many reasons you might want to fuse ideas together…*

The shining key was a contingency, really. Meant to sit in the back of Anastasia's mind, until Sylvie was strong enough to break Rasputin's curses. If the princess needed to escape before that happened? Well, the spell would unlock all sorts of things: the grand duchess's memories, her magic, even the door to rue de la Réunion.

They would be together again, one day.

Sylvie believed this with all her flaming heart.

"I promise I'll keep dreaming for you," she whispered, slipping the glowing key beneath the princess's pillow. Then she placed the fairy-tale book on the bedside table and blew out the candle there. "Go back to sleep now, Nastya. You'll wake up and find me when you're ready."

The Next Chapter

The lamps are going out all over Europe, and we shall not see them lit again in our lifetime."

The sentence reads like a prophecy, though you are not so sure. It's printed in a book that has not yet been written. The memoir of Sir Edward Grey remains ten years from press, but it has still somehow found its way to the bouquiniste booth you are currently perusing. The quote itself was uttered last August, in a London office. Clearly London, for no one who's set foot in Paris since then could say such things.

The City of Light has changed, certainly. Women no longer waltz about in gowns as big as circus tents. Fabric, like so many other items, has been rationed. A few resourceful souls have taken to using flare parachutes to make up the difference, but you find you quite prefer the Egyptian style tunics that have replaced traditional dresses. They have more flow. More freedom. Indeed, more mademoiselles are exploring the city than ever before, out after sunset without chaperones, stretching their wings.

Your own are shaped like a dragonfly's, for you've already been to Montmartre this evening. You've stopped in the Fisherman of the Moon's shop too, admiring a display of jewelry made of the shell casings of .75s. Beauty brought out of bullets. Such rings and bracelets are all the rage, these days, though it may take some time to understand their true magic.

The whole of Paris feels this way. It has changed, yes, but it is not darker. War's shadow has done the opposite—the constant threat of death brings a new urgency to the city's glittering corners. Joie de vivre is a precious commodity, but when you look up from the page, it is everywhere: Soldiers' faces flicker orange at a café table across the lane, off-duty officers having a glass of good spirits. A singer strums his instrument nearby, his hair shining almost gold beneath the streetlamp. The butterfly that lands on your shoulder shines too—a phosphorescent pink.

"Find anything interesting?" the bookseller asks.

She is as distinct as her shop. Most of the vendors who sell stories on the Seine are old men. Too old to get sent off to war, so they sit by the river instead, selling postcards and antique books from their sage-green booths. Most of them go home at night, locking up their wares and disappearing with the last glow of the sun, but this booth keeps odd hours. It's a strange color too. Not the herbal hue of the other booths, but a shade that matches the shopkeeper's hair.

You hold up the memoir you've found. "A book from the future, I believe."

"Really?" the bookseller asks, though she doesn't seem at all surprised. "What year?"

"1925."

She exchanges a look with the orange tomcat draped on the top of her booth. "That *is* interesting. And it's written in English, I presume?"

Is it? You hadn't noticed. Then again, you've had every sip of tea you can from Café des Langues. Russian, English, Italian, even Esperanto . . . it helps to be a polyglot in a city so filled with foreign fighters.

"These have been popping up every few days. I'll open the booth come dusk and find books that shouldn't exist yet. I must've missed this one," the bookseller explains, as she takes the volume and flips to the end pages, where a bookplate is pasted to the marbled paper. "Ah, *Ex Libris Ezra Bright*," she reads. "Same as all the others. What do you make of it, Marmalade? Are we the victims of a time-traveling thief?"

The tom yowls. You recognize him, now, as the same cat you saw by the base of Monsieur Cain's tiger statue.

"You're right. A thief wouldn't *leave* items..." The girl frowns and flips through the pages once more.

"Maybe it's a message," you say, still thinking of the sculpture and its slightly changed stripes. "A secret code or something."

The bookseller's pink eyebrows furrow.

"Perhaps," she says.

Down the river, by the east end of Île de la Cité, you can see the lights of the carnival, drifting. It is your next stop, but it will certainly not be your last.

Author's Note

I initially set out to write this novel because I wanted to learn more about World War I—a conflict that changed the course of history, yet is neglected in the American schooling system. I certainly didn't know much about that war. This was partly due to my high school US History teacher, who skipped all of the wars in her curriculum because they were—in her own words—"icky." World War I certainly fit that description. Around forty million people died over four grueling years. Young men were systematically fed to machine-gun fire. Their bodies became entangled in barbed wire. Or swamped in the endless mud. Or eaten by rats.

During the span of my research, I wasn't shocked by the war's hellishness. What did end up surprising me was the art that flourished in Europe's trenches. Soldiers penned poetry and fashioned jewelry out of bullet casings. They carved sculptures out of the butts of enemy rifles. The resilience of these artists moved me deeply. I wondered at how such a terrible war could trigger one of the largest outpourings of art in modern history. At how humanity could have such a simultaneous capacity for creation and destruction.

It was this question that led me to discover the story you just read: a book about the inherent magic of imagination and the power of art. In 2017, when I first began drafting *The Enchanted Lies of Céleste Artois*, I had no idea these things would be threatened by the rise of artificial intelligence. I didn't know that AI models would start robbing artists of their work and livelihoods—yet that is the world we now find ourselves in. Fears abound in the artistic community. I can't help but wonder what my own future as an author looks like. How will I manage to compete with an AI that spits out novel-length works instantaneously?

Through all these misgivings, I keep thinking back to the poets who wrote in the mud of World War I's trenches. How they composed the rhythm of their poetry against the *dadera-dadera* tempo of machine guns. Many of these men must have thought that their world was ending. They must have believed that grass would never grow back where they sat hunched over their blood-spattered notebooks.

And yet, they kept creating.

I have never fought in a war, but I have seen death. I have kissed my mother's cold cheek. I have sobbed into my dog's stiff body. I have bled out a child who never took their first breath. I have seen birth too. I have hugged two healthy young baby girls to my chest. I have held their hands as they learned to walk. I have delighted at their first words. I have marvelled at the miracle of life.

An AI system could never do those things. And therein lies its limits. I firmly believe that artificial intelligence will never be able to create true art. Why? Because art has never been paint streaks or pen strokes. Art is an inherently human act. Our novels and paintings and poetry matter because *we* matter. Our joy and our pain and our rage and our hope. All of it matters.

So let's keep creating.

In this spirit, I've created an Instagram handle for the League of Imaginers, where I intend to share any art that readers may share with me. If you feel at all inspired by *The Enchanted Lies of Céleste Artois*, I would love to see the results! Please visit @leagueofimaginers for more details and to revel in the creative imaginations of your fellow readers.

In Somnis Veritas

Acknowledgments

Once upon a time, there was an author who dreamed of writing a magical book. She thought she might pluck words from her head like silver strings, setting them down to paper inside the span of a year, as she had with her previous novels.

This particular story had other ideas.

Here I am, on a brisk January morning, sitting at my desk typing out the acknowledgments for *The Enchanted Lies of Céleste Artois*. This is a moment I've yearned for. A moment I wasn't always sure would come to pass, for although this is my tenth published novel, it was by far the most impossible to write. *Warbook* was my nickname for the project when I first sat down to draft it in 2017. Little did I know how apt that term would become, how grueling it would be to reach *The End*.

This book took seven years, five full rewrites, four editors, two publishers, and over five hundred thousand words to become what you are now holding in your hands. It was written through births and deaths, hurricanes, a global pandemic, and the DIY renovation of a crumbling Victorian house that my husband and I decided to tackle while raising two small humans. (Many well-meaning people have asked me how I juggle all of this. I inform them that I no longer have a stomach lining.)

But here we are, finally. My house is still standing. My daughters are laughing in the adjoining room. This book is finished. Thus, the first person I will thank in these acknowledgments is myself. I am so very proud of that author who, when she heard the words *not quite good enough*, turned around and kept chasing that fiery tiger's tail of a story.

Of course, this author had quite a bit of help along the way. This book literally wouldn't exist without Roshani Chokshi—who, from the earliest reads, understood my vision. Thank you, Rosh, for your many words of encouragement and for leading me to the perfect editor.

Priyanka Krishnan has not only been my editor extraordinaire, but my muse. There was no flock of birds involved (at least to my knowledge), yet she still pulled the story out of me and allowed plenty of time for those ideas to grow into a coherent book.

My agent, Tracey Adams, has also been incredibly patient with me, handling phone calls both celebratory and panicked, telling me *It's all going to work out.* I would be lost without Tracey, Josh, Anna Munger, Stephen Moore, and all of Adams Literary's subsidiary rights agents.

Tim Holman and the team at Orbit/Redhook have made the absolute perfect home for *Enchanted Lies*. My thanks to Alyea Canada for swooping in with a final round of edits, as well as to Tiana Coven and Nick Burnham for their editorial support. Bryn A. McDonald also worked so hard to get this book into shape! Lauren Panepinto, Lisa Marie Pompilio, and Alexia Mazis made *Enchanted Lies* so very beautiful—seriously, look at that cover! Alex Lencicki, Kayleigh Webb, Natassja Haught, Rachel Hairston and the rest of the HBG sales team, Zoe Morgan-Weinman, and Ellen Wright were all so very instrumental in getting this story into readers' hands.

All my thanks to my cheerleaders and early readers: Kate J. Armstrong, Megan Shepherd, Roshani Chokshi, Corrie Wang, Pam Gruber, Alvina Ling, Amie Kaufman, and Lyra Selene. A special shoutout to Amy Plum for making sure that my French was accurate. I also have to thank Daniel Kraus for pointing me toward World War I research sources. On the home front, I must thank the ladies at the wonderful bookstore Itinerant Literate, whose open mic night provided the perfect opportunity to test out the opening scene of this book. To Elizabeth Hiott and Margaret Wright, thank you for the evening walks and the margaritas. To Laura Cannon, thank you for childcare and your ever-listening ear. To my support groups: ClubSup, Rad Moms, and the Overworked Writer Moms. To my family: Dad, Jacob, Hannah, Adam, Meredith, Marcia, Cara, Mache, Ariana, Zoe, Mark, Amy, Stephen, Anna Beth, and the rest of the Graudins and the Strausses. To the readers who've followed along ever since I first posted hints about Warbook.

To David—*phew*. We did it. We're doing it! Thank you for being such a constant source of encouragement and unconditional love. My heart is so very safe with you. I can't imagine building houses, creating worlds, and raising children with anyone else.

To Sabriel and Gemma, my loves: I hope that when you're both grown, you'll understand the power of dreams. That the two of you will imagine a better world and make it so.

Soli Deo Gloria